I'M TRAVELING ALONE

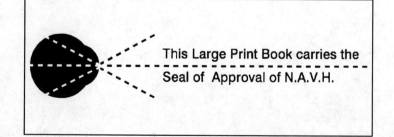

This Large Print Book carries the
Seal of Approval of N.A.V.H.

I'm Traveling Alone

Samuel Bjørk

Translated from the Norwegian by Charlotte Barslund

WHEELER PUBLISHING
A part of Gale, Cengage Learning

GALE
CENGAGE Learning·

Farmington Hills, Mich • San Francisco • New York • Waterville, Maine
Meriden, Conn • Mason, Ohio • Chicago

LIBRARY OF CONGRESS CATALOGING-IN-PUBLICATION DATA

Names: Bjørk, Samuel, author. | Barslund, Charlotte, translator.
Title: I'm traveling alone / by Samuel Bjørk ; translated from the Norwegian by Charlotte Barslund.
Other titles: Der henger en engel alene i skogen. English | I am traveling alone
Description: Large print edition. | Waterville, Maine : Wheeler Publishing, 2016. | © 2015 | Series: Wheeler Publishing large print hardcover
Identifiers: LCCN 2016013321 | ISBN 9781410491336 (hardcover) | ISBN 1410491331 (hardcover)
Subjects: LCSH: Murder—Investigation—Norway—Fiction. | Police—Norway—Oslo—Fiction. | Large type books. | GSAFD: Suspense fiction.
Classification: LCC PT8952.12.J66 H4613 2016b | DDC 839.823/8—dc23
LC record available at http://lccn.loc.gov/2016013321

Published in 2016 by arrangement with Viking, an imprint of Penguin Publishing Group, a division of Penguin Random House LLC

Printed in Mexico
1 2 3 4 5 6 7 20 19 18 17 16

On August 28, 2006, a girl was born in the maternity unit of Ringerike Hospital in Høne-foss. The baby's mother, a twenty-five-year-old nursery-school teacher named Katarina Olsen, was a hemophiliac and died during the birth. The midwife and some of the nurses who had been present later described the little girl as exceptionally beautiful. She was quiet and remarkably alert, with a gaze that caused everyone who worked in the ward to develop a very special bond with her. On her admission to the hospital, Katarina Olsen had registered the father as "Unknown." In the days that followed, the management of Ringerike Hospital, working in collaboration with Ringerike Social Services, tried to track down the child's maternal grandmother, who lived in Bergen. Unaware that her daughter had been pregnant, she arrived at the hospital only to discover that the newborn baby had disappeared from the maternity ward. Ringerike Police Department immediately initiated a major hunt for the child, but without result. Two months later a Swedish nurse named Joachim Wicklund was found dead in his studio apartment in the center of Hønefoss. He had hanged himself. A typed note was found on the floor below Wicklund's body, reading only "I'm sorry."

The baby girl was never found.

Ladybird, ladybird, fly away home.
Your house is on fire and your children
are gone.

I

1

Walter Henriksen took a seat at the kitchen table and made a desperate attempt to force down a little of the breakfast his wife had prepared for him. Bacon and eggs. Herring, salami, and freshly baked bread. A cup of tea brewed with herbs from their very own garden, the one she had always dreamed of having and which was the reason they had bought this house so far from the center of Oslo, with a forest as their nearest neighbor. Here they could pursue healthy interests. Go for walks in the woods. Grow their own vegetables. Pick wild berries and mushrooms and, not least, offer more freedom to their dog, a cocker spaniel that Walter Henriksen could not stand the sight of, but he loved his wife, which explained why he had agreed to all of the above.

He swallowed a bit of bread with herring and fought to keep the food down. He took a large swig of orange juice and tried to look happy, even though his head was throbbing as if someone had clobbered him with a hammer. Last night's office party had not gone according to plan; yet again he had failed to stay off the booze.

The news droned along in the background while Walter tried to read his wife's face. Her mood. If she had secretly been awake when he'd collapsed into bed in the early hours. What time that was he did not know, but it had been late, far too late; he did remember taking off his clothes, a vague memory of his wife being asleep — *Thank Christ,* he'd thought before he passed out on the too-hard mattress she had insisted they buy because she'd started having back problems.

Walter coughed lightly, wiped his mouth with the napkin, and patted his stomach to pretend he had enjoyed the meal and was now full.

"I thought I might take Lady for a walk," he said with what he hoped resembled a smile.

"Oh, all right, then." His wife nodded, somewhat surprised at his offer, because although they rarely discussed it, she was perfectly aware that he cared little for the three-year-old bitch. "Perhaps you could go a bit farther than just walk her around the house this time?"

He searched for the subtly passive-aggressive tone she often adopted when she was displeased with him. But she seemed content, unaware that anything was amiss. Phew, he'd gotten away with it again. And he promised himself that it was the last time. Healthy living for him from now on. No more office parties.

"I was thinking of taking her up to Maridalen, perhaps follow the path down to Lake Dau."

"That sounds perfect," his wife agreed.

She stroked the dog's head, kissed its forehead, and scratched it behind the ear.

"You and your daddy are going to have a lovely time, yes you are, aren't you, Lady, my lovely little doggy."

On the walk up to Maridalen, he followed his usual route on the rare occasion he took the dog out. Walter Henriksen had never liked dogs, knew nothing about dogs; had it been up to him, the world could do without them. He sensed a growing irritation toward the stupid bitch that was straining on the leash, wanting him to walk more quickly. Or stop. Or go in any other direction than the one Walter wanted to.

At last he reached the path that took them

13

down to Lake Dau, where he could finally let the dog off the leash. He squatted on his haunches and attempted to pat the dog's head, show it some kindness as he undid the leash.

"There, have yourself a bit of a run."

The dog stared at him with dumb eyes and stuck out its tongue. Walter lit a cigarette and briefly felt something almost resembling love toward the little bitch. After all, it wasn't the dog's fault. She was all right. His headache was starting to lift; the fresh air did him good. He was going to like the dog from now on. Nice doggy. And strolling around the forest . . . well, life could be worse. They were almost friends, he and the dog, and would you just look how well behaved she was now, good doggy. She was no longer on the leash and yet she walked nicely by his side.

And it was at that very moment that the cocker spaniel decided to take off, abandon the path, and run wild through the forest. Damn!

"Lady!"

Walter Henriksen stayed on the path and spent some time calling the dog, but to no avail. Then, muttering curses under his breath, he threw down his cigarette and started scrambling up the hill. Soon he stopped in his tracks. The dog was lying very calmly in a small clearing. And that was when he saw the little girl hanging from the tree. Dangling above the ground. With a satchel on her back. And a note around her neck:

I'm traveling alone.

Walter Henriksen fell to his knees and did something he had wanted to do since the moment he first woke up.

He threw up all over himself and burst into tears.

2

The screeching seagulls woke Mia Krüger.

By now she really should have grown used to them; after all, it had been four months since she'd bought this house near the mouth of the fjord, but Oslo refused to release its hold on her. Back in her apartment in Vogtsgate, there had always been noise, buses, trams, police sirens, ambulances, and none of them had ever disturbed her — if anything, they had calmed her down — but she was unable to ignore this cacophony of seagulls. Perhaps it was because everything else around here was so quiet.

She reached out for the alarm clock on the bedside table but could not read the time. The hands appeared to be missing; lost in a fog somewhere, a quarter past two or twenty-five minutes to nothing. The pills she had taken last night were still working. Calming, sedating, sensory-depriving. *"Do not take with alcohol"* — yeah, right. After all, she was going to be dead in twelve days. She had ticked off the days on the calendar in the kitchen, twelve blank squares left.

Twelve days. April 18.

She sat up in bed, pulled on her Icelandic sweater, and shuffled downstairs to the living room.

A colleague had prescribed her the pills. A mandatory "friend," someone whose job it was to help her forget, process events, move on. A police psychologist, or was he a psychiatrist? She guessed he had to be the latter, so he could issue prescriptions. Whatever, she had access to anything she wanted. Even in this far-flung corner of the world and even though it required considerable effort. She had to get dressed. Start the outboard motor on the boat. Freeze for the fifteen minutes it took her to sail to Hitra, the main island. Start the car. Stay on the road for forty minutes until she reached Fillan, the nearest town around here — not that it was much of a town, but there the pharmacy could be found, and then a visit to the liquor store. The prescriptions would be ready and waiting for her, as they had been telephoned through from Oslo. Xanax, Valium, Lamictal, Celexa. Some from the psychiatrist along with some from her GP.

They were all so helpful, so kind — *Now, don't take too many, please be careful* — but Mia Krüger had absolutely no intention of being careful. She had not moved out here to get better. She had come here to seek oblivion.

Twelve days left. April 18.

Mia Krüger took a bottle of mineral water from the fridge, got dressed, and walked down to the sea. She sat on a rock, pulled her jacket more tightly around her, and got ready to take the first of today's pills. She shoved a hand into her pants pocket. A spectrum of colors. Her head still felt groggy, and she could not remember which ones she was supposed to be taking today, but it didn't matter. She washed them down with a gulp from the bottle and dangled her feet over the water. She stared at her boots. It made no sense; it was as if they were not her feet but someone else's, and they seemed far, far away. She shifted her gaze to the sea instead. That made no sense either, but she forced herself to stick with it and looked across the sea, toward the distant horizon, at the small island out there, a place whose name she did not know.

She had chosen this location at random. Hitra. A little island in Trøndelag, off the west-central coast of Norway. It could have been anywhere as long as she was left alone. She had let the real-estate agent decide. *Sell my apartment and find me something else.* He had looked at her and cocked his head as if she were a lunatic or simpleminded, but he wanted his commission, so what did he care? The friendly white smile that had said yes, of course he could, did she want a quick sale? Did she have something specific in mind? Professional courtesy, but she had seen his true nature. She felt nauseous just thinking about it. Fake, revolting eyes. She had always been able to see straight through anyone she came near. On that occasion it had been the agent, a slippery eel in a suit and tie, and she had not liked what she saw.

You have to use this talent you have been given. Don't you see? You need to use it for something. And this is what you're meant to use it for.

No, she bloody wouldn't. Not anymore. Never again. The thought made her feel strangely calm.

Mia Krüger got up from the rock and followed the path back to the house. It was time for the first drink of the day. She did not know what time it was, but it was definitely due now. She had bought expensive alcohol, ordered it especially. It was possibly a contradiction in terms, but why

19

not enjoy something luxurious, given how little time she had left? Why this? Why that? She had stopped sweating the small stuff long ago. She opened a bottle of Armagnac Domaine de Pantagnan 1965 Labeyrie and filled the teacup, which was sitting unwashed on the kitchen counter, three-quarters full. An eight-hundred-kroner Armagnac in a filthy teacup. *Look how little it bothers me. Do you think I care?* She smiled faintly to herself, found some more pills in her pocket, and walked back down to the rocks.

If she had to live somewhere, it might as well be here. Fresh air, a sea view, the tranquillity beneath the white clouds. She had no links to Trøndelag, but she had liked this island from the moment she first saw it. They had deer here. Countless herds of them, and it had intrigued her — deer belonged elsewhere, in Alaska, in the movies. These beautiful animals that people insisted on hunting. Mia Krüger had learned to shoot at the police academy, but she had never liked guns. Guns were not for fun; guns were something you used only when you had no other choice, and not even then. The deer season on Hitra lasted from September to November. One day on her way to the pharmacy, she had passed a group of young people busy tying a dead deer to the bed of their truck. It had been February, outside the hunting season, and for a moment she had contemplated pulling over, taking down their names, and reporting them to ensure they got their well-deserved punishment, but she'd choked it back and let it go.

Once a police officer, always a police officer?

Not anymore. No way.

Twelve days to go. April 18.

She drank the last of her Armagnac, rested her head against the rock, and closed her eyes.

3

Holger Munch was sweating as he waited in the arrivals terminal at Værnes Airport to pick up a rental car. As usual, the plane had been late due to fog at Gardermoen Airport, and once again Holger was reminded of Jan Fredrik Wiborg, the civil engineer who had supposedly killed himself in Copenhagen after criticizing the expansion plans for Oslo's main airport, citing unfavorable weather conditions. Even now, eighteen years later, Munch was unable to forget that the body of a fully grown man had been found beneath a hotel-room window too small for him to have gotten through, just before the Airport Bill was due to be debated in Stortinget, the Norwegian parliament. And why had the Danish and the Norwegian police been reluctant to investigate his death properly?

Holger Munch abandoned his train of thought as a blond girl behind the Europcar counter cleared her throat to let him know it was his turn to be served.

"Munch," he said curtly. "I believe a car has been booked for me."

"Right, so you're the guy who is getting a new museum in Oslo?" The girl in the green uniform winked at him.

Munch did not get the joke immediately.

"Or maybe you're *not* the artist?" The girl smiled as she cheerfully bashed the keyboard in front of her.

"Eh? No, not the artist, no," Munch said drily. "Not even related."

Or I wouldn't be standing here, not if I had that *inheritance,* Munch thought as the girl handed him a form to sign.

Holger Munch hated flying, which explained his bad mood. Not because he feared that the plane might crash. Holger Munch was an amateur mathematician and knew that the risk of a crash was less than that of being struck by lightning twice in the same day. No, Holger Munch hated planes because he could barely fit into the seat.

"There you are." The girl in the green uniform smiled kindly and handed him the keys. "A nice big Volvo V70, all paid for, open-ended rental period and mileage. You can return it when and where you like. Have a nice trip."

Big? Was this another one of her jokes, or was she merely trying to reassure him? Here's a nice big car for you, because you have grown so fat that you can barely see your own feet?

On his way to the garage, Holger Munch caught a glimpse of his reflection in the large windows outside the arrivals terminal. Perhaps it was about time. Start exercising. Eat a slightly healthier diet. Lose a bit of weight. Lately he had begun to think along those lines. He no longer had to run down the streets chasing criminals — he had people working for him who could do that, so that was not the reason. No, in the last few weeks, Holger Munch had become rather vain.

Wow, Holger, new sweater? Wow, Holger, new jacket? Wow, Holger, have you trimmed your beard?

He unlocked the Volvo, placed his cell phone in the cradle, and turned it on. He fastened his seat belt and was heading toward the center of Trondheim when his messages began coming through. He heaved a sigh. One hour with his phone turned off and now it was starting again. No respite from the world. It was not entirely fair to say that it was the flight alone that had put him in a bad mood. There'd been a lot happening recently, both at work and at home. Holger swiped his finger across the smartphone screen, a model they'd told him to buy — it was all about high-tech these days, the twenty-first-century police force, even in Hønefoss, where he had worked for the last eighteen months for Ringerike Police. This was where he'd started his career, and now he'd come back. Because of the Tryvann incident.

Seven calls from Oslo Police Headquarters at Grønland. Two from his ex-wife. One from his daughter. Two from the nursing home. Plus countless text messages.

Holger Munch decided to ignore the world for a little longer and turned on the radio. He found the classical station, opened the window, and lit a cigarette. Cigarettes were his only vice — apart from food, obviously, but they were in a different league in terms of attraction. Holger Munch had no intention of ever quitting smoking no matter how many laws the politicians came up with and how many No Smoking signs they put up all over Norway, including on the dashboard of his rental car.

He could not think without a cigarette, and there was nothing Holger Munch loved more than thinking. Using his brain. Never mind about the body as long as his brain worked. They were playing Handel's *Messiah* on the radio, not Munch's favorite, but he was okay with it. He was more of a Bach man himself. He liked the mathematics of the music, not all those emotional composers: Wagner's bellicose tempo, Ravel's impressionistic emotional landscape. Munch listened to classical music precisely to escape these human feelings. If people were mathematical equations, life would be much simpler. He quickly touched his wedding ring and thought about Marianne, his ex-wife. It had been ten years now, and still he could not make himself take it off. She had phoned him. Perhaps she was . . .

No. It would be about the wedding, obviously. She wanted to talk about the wedding. They had a daughter together, Miriam, who was getting married shortly. There were practicalities to discuss. That was all. Holger Munch flicked the cigarette out the window and lit another one.

I don't drink coffee, I don't touch alcohol. Surely I'm allowed a stupid cigarette.

Holger Munch had been drunk only once, at the age of fourteen on his father's cherry brandy at their vacation cottage, and he had never touched a drop of alcohol since.

The desire was just not there. He didn't

26

want it. It would never cross his mind to do anything that might impair his brain cells. Not in a million years. Now, smoking, on the other hand, and the occasional burger — that was something else again.

He pulled over at a Shell station and ordered a bacon-burger meal deal, which he ate sitting on a bench overlooking Trondheim Fjord. If his colleagues had been asked to describe Holger Munch in three words, two of them were likely to be "nerd." "Clever" would possibly be the third, or "too clever for his own good" if they were permitted more than a single word. But a nerd definitely. A fat, amiable nerd who never touched alcohol, loved mathematics, classical music, crossword puzzles, and chess. A little dull perhaps, but an extremely talented investigator. And a fair boss. So what if he never joined his colleagues for a beer after work or had not been on a date since his wife left him for a teacher with eight weeks of annual vacation who never had to get up in the middle of the night without telling her where he was going? There was no one whose clear-up rate was as high as Holger Munch's, everyone knew that. Everyone liked Holger Munch. And even so he had ended up back in Hønefoss.

I'm not demoting you, I'm reassigning you.

The way I see it, you should count yourself lucky that you still have a job.

He had almost quit on the spot that day outside Mikkelson's office, but he'd bitten his tongue. What else would he do? Work as a security guard?

Holger Munch got back into the car and took the E6 toward Trondheim. He lit a fresh cigarette and followed the ring road around the city, heading south. The rental car was equipped with GPS, but he did not turn it on. He knew where he was going.

Mia Krüger.

He thought warmly about his former colleague just as his cell phone rang again.

"Munch speaking."

"Where the hell are you?"

It was an agitated Mikkelson, on the verge of a heart attack as usual; how that man had survived ten years in the boss's chair down at Grønland was a mystery.

"I'm in the car. Where the hell are *you*?" Munch snapped back.

"In the car where? Haven't you gotten there yet?"

"No, I haven't gotten there yet, I've only just landed — I thought you knew that. What do you want?"

"I wanted to check that you're sticking with the plan."

"I have the file here, and I intend to deliver it in person, if that's what you mean." Munch sighed. "Was it really necessary to send me all the way up here just for this? How about a courier? Or we could have used the local police."

"You know exactly why you're there," Mikkelson replied. "And this time I want you to do as you've been told."

"One," Munch said as he flicked the cigarette butt out of the window, "I owe you nothing. Two, I owe you nothing. Three, it's your own fault you're no longer using my brain for its intended purpose, so I suggest you shut up. Do you want to know the cases I'm working these days? Do you, Mikkelson? Want to know what I'm working on?"

A brief silence followed at the other end. Munch chuckled contentedly to himself.

Mikkelson hated nothing more than having to ask for a favor. Munch knew that Mikkelson was fuming now, and he savored how his former boss was having to control himself rather than speak his mind.

"Just do it."

"Aye, aye, sir." Munch grinned as he saluted in the car.

"Drop the irony, Munch, and call me when you've got something."

"Will do. Oh, by the way, there was one

thing . . ."

"What?" Mikkelson grunted.

"If she's in, then so am I. No more Høne-foss for me. And I want our old offices in Mariboesgate. We work away from police headquarters. And I want the same team as before."

There was total silence before the reply came.

"That's completely out of the question. It's never going to happen, Munch. It's —"

Munch smiled and pressed the red button to end the call before Mikkelson had time to say anything else. He lit another cigarette, turned the radio on again, and took the road leading to Orkanger.

4

Mia Krüger had been dozing on the sofa under a blanket near the fireplace. She'd been dreaming about Sigrid and had woken up feeling as if her twin sister were still there. With her. Alive. That they were together again like they always used to be. Sigrid and Mia. Mia and Sigrid. Two peas in a pod, born two minutes apart, one blond, the other dark, so different and yet so alike.

All Mia wanted to do was return to her dream, join Sigrid, but she made herself get up and go to the kitchen. Eat some breakfast. To keep the alcohol down. If she carried on like this, she would die prematurely, and that was completely out of the question.

April 18.

Ten days left.

She had to hold out, last another ten days. Mia forced down two pieces of crispbread and considered drinking a glass of milk but opted for water instead. Two glasses of water and two pills. From her pants pocket. Didn't matter which ones. One white and one pale blue today.

Sigrid Krüger
Sister, friend, and daughter
Born November 11, 1979.
Died April 18, 2002.
Much loved. Deeply missed.

Mia Krüger returned to the sofa and stayed there until she felt the pills starting to kick in. Numb her. Form a membrane between her and the world. She needed one now. It was almost three weeks since she had last looked at herself, and she could put it off no longer. Time for a shower. The bathroom was on the first floor. She had avoided it for as long as possible, didn't want to look at herself in the large mirror that the previous owner had put up right inside the door. She'd been meaning to find a screwdriver. Remove the damn thing. She felt bad enough as it was and did not need it confirmed, but she hadn't had the energy. No energy for anything. Just for the pills. And the alcohol. Liquid Valium in her veins, little smiles in her bloodstream, lovely protection against all the barbs that had been swimming around inside her for so long. She steeled herself and walked up the stairs. She opened the door to the bathroom and almost had a shock when she saw the figure in the mirror. It was not her. It was someone else. Mia Krüger had always been slim, but now she looked emaciated. She had always been healthy. Always strong. Now there was practically nothing left of her. She pulled off her sweater and her jeans and stood in only her underwear in front of the mirror. Her underpants were sagging. The flesh on her stomach and hips was all gone. Carefully she ran a hand over her protruding ribs — she could feel them clearly, count them all. She made herself walk right up close to the mirror, caught a glimpse of her own eyes in the rusty silver surface. People had always remarked on her blue eyes. *No one has eyes as Norwegian as yours, Mia,* someone had said to her once, and she still remembered how proud she'd been, *Norwegian eyes.* It had sounded so fine. At a time when she wanted to fit in, not be different. Sigrid had always been the prettier one. Perhaps that explained why it had felt so good? Sparkling blue eyes. Not much of that left now. They looked dead already.

My little Indian, her grandmother used to call her. And she could have been — apart from the blue eyes. An American Indian. Kiowa or Sioux or Apache. Mia had always been fascinated by Indians when she was a child; there had never been any doubt whose side she was on. The cowboys were the bad guys. The Indians the good guys. *How are you today, Mia Moonbeam?* Mia touched her face in the mirror and remembered her grandmother with love. She looked at her long hair. Raven black hair flowing down her delicate shoulders. She had not had hair as long as this for ages. She'd started to wear it short when she started at the police academy. She hadn't gone to a hairdresser's but cut it herself at home, just grabbed a pair of scissors and snipped it off. To show that she didn't care about looking pretty. About showing off. She didn't wear makeup either. *You're naturally beautiful, my little Indian,* her grandmother had said one evening when she braided Mia's hair in front of the fireplace back home in Åsgårdstrand.

Sigrid had always been the favorite. Sigrid with her long blond hair. Who was good at school. Who played the flute, who played handball and was everyone's friend. Mia had not resented the attention Sigrid got.

Sigrid was never one to exploit it to her advantage, never said a bad word about anyone. Sigrid was quite simply fantastic, but whenever their grandmother had pulled Mia to one side and told her that she was special, she'd felt great.

You're very special, did you know that? The other children are fine, but you know things, Mia, don't you? You see the things that other people tend to overlook.

A grandmother who had taken notice of her, seen who she was, told her she was special.

Fly like the ladybird, Mia, never forget that.

Her grandmother's last words on her deathbed, spoken with a wink to her very special friend.

Ten days left.

April 18.

She was not particularly interested in what it would be like. Her final moment. If it would hurt. If it would be difficult to let go. She did not believe the stories about how your life flashed in front of your eyes as you died. Or perhaps it was true? It didn't really matter. The story of Mia Krüger's life was imprinted on her body. She could see her life in the mirror. An Indian with Norwegian eyes. Long black hair that she used to cut short but was now cascading down her thin white shoulders. She tugged her hair behind one ear and studied the scar near her left eye. An inch-long cut, a scar that would never fade away completely. She'd been interrogating a murder suspect after a young girl from Latvia had been found floating in the river Aker. Mia had failed to pay attention, hadn't seen the knife; luckily, she'd managed to swerve so that it did not blind her. She'd worn a patch over her eye for several months afterward; thanks to the doctors, she still had sight in both eyes. She held up her left hand in front of the mirror and looked at the missing fingertip. Another suspect, a farm outside Moss, *mind the dog*. The rottweiler had gone for her throat, but she raised her hand just in time. She could still feel its teeth around her fingers, how the panic had spread inside her in the few seconds it took before she got the pistol out of her holster and blew the head off the manic dog. She shifted her eyes down to the small butterfly she'd had tattooed on her hip. She had been a nineteen-year-old girl in Prague, thinking herself a woman of the world. She met a Spanish guy, a summer fling, they'd drunk far too much Becherovka and both woken up with a tattoo. Hers was a small purple, yellow, and green butterfly. Mia was tempted to smile.

She had considered having it removed several times, embarrassed by the idiocy of her youth, but had never gotten around to it, and now it no longer mattered. She stroked the slender silver bracelet on her right wrist. They'd been given one each as confirmation presents, Sigrid and she. A charm bracelet with a heart and an anchor and an initial. An *M* on hers. An *S* on Sigrid's. That night, when the party was over and the guests had gone home, they'd sat in their shared bedroom at home in Åsgårdstrand when Sigrid had suddenly suggested they swap.

You take mine and I'll have yours?

From that day Mia had never taken the silver bracelet off.

The tablets were making her feel even dopier — she could barely see herself in the mirror. Her body was like a ghost's; it seemed far away. She stumbled into the shower cubicle and stood underneath the warm water for so long that it finally turned icy.

She avoided the mirror as she stepped out. Walked naked down to the living room and dried herself in front of the unlit fireplace. Went into the kitchen and poured herself another drink. Found more pills in a drawer. Chewed them while she got dressed. Even more spaced out now. Clean on the outside and soon also on the inside.

Mia put on her knitted cap and jacket and left the house.

April 18.

It had suddenly come to her one day, like a kind of vision, and from then on, everything slotted into place. Sigrid was found dead on April 18, 2002. In a basement in Tøyen in Oslo, on a rotting mattress, still with the needle in her arm. She'd not even had time to undo the strap. The overdose had killed her instantly. In ten days it would be exactly ten years ago. Lovely little sweet, beautiful Sigrid had died from an overdose of heroin in a filthy basement. Just one week after Mia had picked her up from the rehab clinic in Valdres.

Oh, but she'd looked wonderful, Sigrid, after four weeks at the facility. Her cheeks glowing, her smile back. In the car heading home to Oslo, it had been almost like the old days, the two of them laughing and joking the way they used to in the garden at home in Åsgårdstrand.

"You're Snow White and I'm Sleeping Beauty."

"But I want to be Sleeping Beauty! Why do I always have to be Snow White?"

"Because you have dark hair, Mia."

Sigrid's prince, unfortunately, had been an idiot from Horten. He thought of himself as a musician, even played in some kind of band that never gave concerts. All they ever did was hang out in the park, where they smoked joints or took speed. He was just another skinny, opinionated loser. Mia Krüger could not bear even to say his name. The mere thought of him made her feel sick. She followed the path along the rocks, past the boathouse, and sat down on the jetty. On the distant shore, she could see activity. People doing people things. She took a swig from the bottle she'd brought with her as she felt the pills starting to take effect, strip her of her senses, make her indifferent. She dangled her feet over the edge of the jetty and turned her face to the sun.

Markus Skog.

Sigrid had been eighteen, the scrawny idiot twenty-two. He'd moved to Oslo. A few months later, Sigrid had joined him.

Four weeks in rehab. It was not the first time Mia had picked up her sister from a rehab center, but this time had been different. Sigrid's motivation had been completely different. Not the usual junkie smile after such a stay, lies and more lies, just itching to get out and shoot up again — no,

39

there'd been something in her eyes. She'd seemed more determined, almost back to her old self.

Mia had thought so much about her sister over the years that it had almost driven her insane. Why Sigrid? Was it boredom? Because their parents had died? Or just because of some skinny, scrawny idiot? Was it love?

Their mother could be strict, but she was never particularly harsh. Their father had spoiled them, but surely that could do no harm? Eva and Kyrre Krüger had adopted the twins right after their birth. They had made arrangements with the biological mother in advance; she was young, single, desperate. Did not want to and could not cope with looking after two children. For a childless couple, the girls were a gift from heaven, exactly what they had always wanted. Their happiness was complete.

Their mother, Eva, taught at Åsgården Primary School. Their father, Kyrre, sold paint and owned a shop called Ole Krüger in the center of Horten.

Mia had searched high and low for an explanation, anything that could tell her why Sigrid ended up a junkie, but she never found one.

Markus Skog.

It was his fault.

It was just one week after leaving rehab. They had gotten along so well in her apartment in Vogtsgate. Sigrid and Mia. Mia and Sigrid. Snow White and Sleeping Beauty. The two peas were back in their pod. Mia had even taken a couple of days off work, for the first time in God knows how long. Then one evening she found a note on the kitchen table:

Have to talk to M.
Back soon. S.

Mia Krüger got up from the edge of the jetty. She was already starting to sway. The pills from her pocket made her groggy. Mia Krüger took a few more and leaned back against the rock.

You're very special, did you know that?

Perhaps that explained why she had chosen to go to the police academy? To do something different? She'd thought about this as well these last few days — why had she applied? She could no longer make the pieces fit together. Time kept shifting. Her brain was out of kilter. Sigrid was no longer little blond Sigrid. She was junkie Sigrid now, the nightmare. Their parents had been devastated, withdrawn from the world, from each other, from Mia. She had moved to Oslo, started with absolutely no enthusiasm to study at the university in Blindern. She hadn't even been able to summon the energy to turn up for her exams. Perhaps the police academy had chosen her? So that she might rid the world of people like Markus Skog.

She had shot him.

Markus Skog.

Twice. In the chest.

It was a chance encounter; they'd been out on another assignment. A girl had disappeared, and the special unit had been called in — just sniff around and take a peek at things, as Holger had put it. *We don't have a lot on right now, Mia. I think we should check this one out.*

Holger Munch. Mia Krüger thought fondly of her old colleague as she dangled her boots over the edge of the jetty. The whole incident was bizarre. She'd killed another human being, but she didn't feel bad about it. She felt worse about the consequences. The media outrage and the uproar down at Grønland. Holger Munch, who had led the unit, who had cherry-picked her from the police academy, had been reassigned, the special unit closed down. This hurt her deeply, and it had cut her to the core that Holger had paid the price for her actions, but the actual killing, strangely enough, no. They'd been following a lead that took them to Tryvann. Some junkies or hippies — the public always had difficulty telling the two apart when they called to complain — anyway, someone had parked a camper in Tryvann and was partying and making a racket. Holger thought the missing girl might be there. And indeed they did come across a young girl, not the girl who was missing, but another one, glazed eyes, a needle in her arm, inside the filthy camper and with her, unexpectedly, Markus Skog. And Mia had, as the internal affairs unit's report quite accurately stated:

Acted carelessly, with unnecessary use of force.

Mia shook her head at her own immorality. Holger Munch had stood by her, said that Skog had attacked her first — after all, a knife and an ax were found at the crime scene — but Mia should have known better. She was trained to defend herself without backup against a frenzied junkie brandishing a knife or wielding an ax. She could have shot him in the foot. Or in his arm. But she hadn't. She had killed him. A moment of hatred when the rest of the world had simply disappeared. Two shots to the center of his chest.

She would have gone to prison if it had not been for Holger Munch. She took the empty bottle from her pocket, licked the last few drops, and raised it toward the clouds once more. It didn't matter now. It would all be over soon.

She lay down, rested her cheek against the coarse wooden planks of the jetty, and closed her eyes.

5

Holger Munch was fed up with driving and decided to take a break. He pulled over and got out to stretch his legs. He did not have much farther to go. The man who would be taking him to the island in his boat could not take him there until after two o'clock for some reason — Munch hadn't had the energy to ask why. He had spoken to the local police officer, who didn't seem particularly bright. He wasn't prejudiced against regional police officers, but Holger had been used to another pace in Oslo. Not these days, for obvious reasons. You would be hard-pressed to claim that the pace at Ringerike Police was fast-moving. Munch swore softly under his breath and cursed Mikkelson but regretted it immediately. It was not Mikkelson's fault. There had been an investigation afterward and there had to be some repercussions — he knew that only too well — but surely there were limits.

Munch took a seat on a bench and lit another cigarette. Spring had come early to Trøndelag this year. There were green leaves on the trees in several places, and the snow had almost melted away. Not that he knew very much about when spring usually came to Trøndelag, but he had heard them talk about it on the local radio when he'd taken a break from the music to listen to the news. He wondered if they'd managed to keep it out of the media or if some idiot down at police headquarters had leaked the discovery to a news-hungry journalist with deep pockets, but fortunately there was nothing. Nothing about the little girl who'd been found hanging from a tree in Maridalen.

His cell had been ringing and beeping all the time he was in the car, but Holger had ignored it. He did not want to make calls or send text messages while driving. He'd attended too many accidents caused by just one second of distraction. Besides, none of it was urgent. And he savored this brief moment of freedom. He hated to admit it to himself, but at times it got to him. The work. And family life. He did not mind visiting his mother in the nursing home. He did not mind helping his daughter with the preparations for her wedding. And he certainly never minded hours spent with Marion, his granddaughter, who had just turned six, but even so, yes, at times it all got to be too much for him.

He and Marianne. He had never imagined anything else. Even now, ten years after the divorce, he still had the feeling that something inside him was so broken that it could never be fixed.

He shuddered and checked his cell. Another two unanswered calls from Mikkelson; he knew what they would be about. There was no reason to call back. Another message from Miriam, his daughter, brief and impersonal as usual. Some calls from Marianne, his ex-wife. Shit, he had forgotten to call the nursing home. After all, today was a Wednesday. He really should have done it before he started driving. He found the number, got up, and straightened his legs.

"Høvikveien Nursing Home, Karen speaking."

"Yes, hello, Karen, it's Holger Munch."

"Hi, Holger, how are you?" The soft voice at the other end almost made Munch blush. He had expected one of the older caregivers to answer the phone, as they usually did.

Wow, Holger, new sweater? Wow, Holger, new jacket? Wow, Holger, have you trimmed your beard?

"Oh, I'm all right," Munch replied. "But I'm afraid I'm about to ask you to do me yet another favor."

"Go on, then, ask away, Holger." The woman on the telephone laughed.

They had been nodding acquaintances for some years. Karen was one of the aides at the home where his mother initially had refused to live but where she now appeared to have settled in.

"It's Wednesday again." Munch heaved a sigh.

"And you won't be able to make it?"

"No, sadly not," Munch replied. "I'm out of town."

"I understand," Karen said, chuckling softly. "I'll see if somebody here can give her a lift. If not, I'll order her a cab."

"I'll pay for it, of course," Munch quickly interjected.

"No problem."

"Thank you, Karen."

"Don't mention it, Holger. You'll manage next Wednesday, I expect?"

"Oh, I will."

"Great. Perhaps we'll see each other then?"

"That's very likely." Munch coughed. "Thank you so much, and . . . well, give her my best."

"Will do."

Munch ended the call and returned to the bench.

Why don't you ask her out? Where's the harm? A cup of coffee? A trip to the movies?

He dismissed the idea just as an email pinged to announce its arrival on his cell. He'd been dead set against it, these newfangled phones where everything was gathered in one place. How would he ever get a moment's peace? Still, right now it suited him just fine. He smiled as he opened the email and read another challenge from Yuri, a man from Belarus he'd met on the Net some years ago. Nerds the world over gathered on Math2.org's message board. Yuri was a sixty-something-year-old professor from Minsk. Munch would not go as far as calling him a friend — after all, they had never met in real life, but they had exchanged email addresses and were in contact from time to time. They discussed chess, and every now and then they would challenge each other with brain teasers, as was the case now.

Water flows into a tank. The volume of water doubles every minute. The tank is full in one hour. How long does it take for the tank to be half full? Y.

Munch lit another cigarette and pondered the question for a while before he found the answer. Ha, ha. He liked Yuri. He had actually considered going to visit him one day, and why not? He'd never been to Belarus, so why not meet up with people you had gotten to know on the Internet? He had made several acquaintances in this way: mrmichigan40 from the United States, Margrete_08 from Sweden, Birrrdman from South Africa. Chess and mathematics nerds but, more important, people like him, so yes, why not? Organize a trip, make new friends, surely that would be all right? He wasn't that old, was he? And when was the last time he traveled anywhere? He caught a glimpse of his own reflection in the screen of his cell phone and put it down on the bench next to him.

Fifty-four. He didn't think that number could be quite right. He felt much older. He had aged ten years on the day Marianne had told him about the teacher from Hurum. He had tried to stay calm. He should have seen it coming. His long days at work and his general absentmindedness. Ultimately there would be a price to pay, but now, and like this? She had been completely relaxed, as if she'd rehearsed her speech several times. They had met in a class.

Stayed in touch ever since. They had developed feelings for each other. They had gotten together a few times, in secret, but she no longer wanted to live a dishonest life. In the end Munch had failed to keep his cool. He who had never raised a hand to anyone. He had howled and hurled his dinner plate at the wall. Shouted and chased her around the house. He was still ashamed of his behavior. Miriam had come running down from her room, crying. Fifteen years old then, now twenty-five and about to get married. Fifteen years and taking her mother's side. Not surprising, really. How much time had he ever spent at home and been available to them during all those years?

He felt reluctant to reply to Miriam's message. It was so short and cold, symbolic of how their relationship was and had been. It only piled on the pressure, as if the folder lying in the rented car were not enough.

Could you add a few thousand extra? We have decided to invite cousins. M.

The wedding. Of course, he texted, adding a smiley face and then deleting it. He saw the message go out while he thought about his granddaughter, Marion. Miriam had told him to his face soon after Marion's birth that she was not at all certain that he deserved to have any contact with the baby. Fortunately, she had changed her mind. Now these were his most treasured moments. His hours with lovely, totally straightforward Marion, a bright light in his daily life, which, to be completely honest, had been fairly dark after his transfer back to Hønefoss.

He had let Marianne keep the house after the divorce. It seemed like the right thing to do. Otherwise Miriam would have had to move away from her friends and her school and her handball. He'd bought a small apartment in Bislett, suitably near to them and suitably far from his work. He had kept the place after his transfer and was now renting a studio apartment on Ringveien, not far from Hønefoss Police Station. His belongings were still in cardboard boxes. He had not taken very much, had expected a quick return to the capital once the public outcry had died down, but now, almost two years later, he was still there and had yet to unpack, as neither place felt like home.

Stop feeling sorry for yourself. There are people much worse off than you.

Munch stubbed out the cigarette and thought about the file in his car. A six-year-

52

old girl had been found hanging from a tree in Maridalen by a random dog walker. He had not seen a case like this for a long time. No wonder they were sweating down at Grønland.

He picked up his cell and replied to Yuri's email.

59 minutes;) hm

Munch was loath to admit it to himself, but the file on the passenger seat sent shivers down his spine. He started the car, pulled out onto the main road, and continued his journey east to Hitra.

6

The man with the eagle tattoo on his neck had put on a turtleneck for the occasion. He used to really like Oslo Central Station — the crowds had made it the perfect place for a man of his profession — but these days there were so many cameras that practically nowhere was safe. He had long ago started arranging his meetings and transactions at other venues, movie theaters and kebab shops, places where you were less likely to be identified should your business lead to a major investigation, though it rarely did; he did not operate on such a large scale anymore, but still, better safe than sorry.

The man with the eagle tattoo pulled the cap deep down over his head and entered the station concourse. He had not chosen the venue, but the amount offered was so high that he was happy to obey orders. He had no idea how the client had found him, but one day he had received an MMS with a photo, an assignment, and a sum of money. And he had done what he always did, replied "OK" without asking any questions. It was a strange assignment, no doubt about it, and he had never done anything like it, but over the years he had learned not to probe, to just do the job and collect the money. It was what you needed to do in order to survive and retain your credibility out there in the shadowy world. Though the number of assignments was falling, as were the amounts, every now and again something big would fall into his lap. Like this one. A bizarre request, yes — quite extraordinary, in fact — but well paid, and that was exactly what he was about to do now, pick up his check.

Suit jacket, smart trousers, shiny shoes, business briefcase, turtleneck. Even a pair of fake eyeglasses. The man with the eagle tattoo looked like the complete opposite of what he was, and that was precisely the intention. In his profession you never knew when the police might order a complete review of all CCTV recordings, so it was best to blend in. He looked like an accountant or any other kind of businessman, and though you might not think so, the man with the eagle tattoo was rather vain. You would never mistake him for a well-groomed, privileged member of the elite; he liked his rough appearance, his tattoos, and the leather jacket. These revolting trousers rubbed his groin, and he felt like a jerk in the tight jacket and the stupid shiny brown shoes. Never mind, just grin and bear it. The money waiting for him in one of the safe-deposit boxes was worth it. Totally worth it. He needed the cash. He was going to party now. He smiled faintly under the unfamiliar glasses and walked calmly but vigilantly through the station building.

The first message had arrived about a year ago, and more had followed. An MMS with a photograph and an amount. That first time the request had been so unusual and bizarre that he had taken it to be some kind of joke, but he carried it out nevertheless. And been paid. As he was the next time. And the time after that. Then he had ceased caring what it was about.

He stopped at a kiosk and bought a newspaper and a pack of cigarettes. A completely ordinary man commuting home after a day at the office. Nothing unusual about this accountant. He tucked the newspaper under his arm and continued down toward the safe-deposit boxes. Stopped outside the entrance to the boxes and sent the text message.

I'm here.

He waited only a short while for the reply. As usual it came promptly. The number of the safe-deposit box and the code to open it beeped as it whizzed into his cell phone. He glanced around a few times before he walked along the boxes to find the right one. He would have to grant Oslo Central Station at least one thing: the days of keys changing hands in back streets and alleyways were over. Now all you needed was a code. The man with the eagle tattoo entered the digits on the keypad and heard a click as the box opened. As usual, the familiar brown envelope was lying within. He removed the envelope from the box and tried not to look around, drawing as little attention to himself as possible in view of all the cameras present before he opened the briefcase and deftly slipped the envelope inside it. There was a smile at one corner of his mouth as he gauged that the envelope was much fatter this time. His final assignment. Time to settle his accounts. He left the safe-deposit boxes, walked up the steps, continued through the station, entered a Burger King, and locked himself in a cubicle in the men's room. He opened the briefcase and took out the envelope. He could hardly contain himself. He grinned from ear to ear when he saw the contents. There was more than just the agreed sum of money, in two-hundred-kroner notes as he always requested; there was also a small bag of white powder. The man with the eagle tattoo opened the transparent plastic bag, carefully tasted the contents, and the smile on his face broadened even further. He had no idea who his client was, but there was clearly nothing wrong with his contacts or information. Those who knew him well were also aware of his great love for this substance.

He took out his cell and sent his usual reply.

ok. thanks.

He did not normally say thank you — this was pure business, nothing personal — but he couldn't help it this time, what with the bonus and all. It took a few seconds before the reply came.

have fun.

The man with the eagle tattoo smiled as he returned the envelope and the bag to the briefcase and made his way back to the station concourse.

7

Tobias Iversen covered his younger brother's ears so that he wouldn't hear the row coming from downstairs. They tended to kick off at this time, when their mother came home from work and discovered that their stepfather had not done what he was supposed to do. Cook dinner for the boys. Tidy the house a bit. Find himself a job. Tobias did not want his brother to hear them, so he'd invented a game.

I'll cover your ears, and you tell me what you can see inside your head, yeah?

"A red truck with flames on it." Torben smiled, and Tobias nodded and smiled back at him. What else?

"A knight fighting a dragon." His brother grinned, and Tobias nodded again.

The noise level below increased. Angry voices crept up between the walls and slipped under his skin. Tobias could not handle what would happen next — things being thrown at the walls, the screaming getting louder, perhaps worse — so he decided to take his brother outside. He whispered between his hand and his younger brother's ear.

"Why don't we go outside and hunt some bison?"

His brother smiled and nodded eagerly.

Hunt bison. Run around the forest pretending to be Indians. He would love that. Not many other children lived out here, so Tobias and his brother usually played together even though Tobias was thirteen and Torben only seven. It was not a good idea to be inside most of the time. Outside was better.

Tobias helped his brother put on his jacket and sneakers, and then he hummed, sang, and stomped hard on the back stairs as they made their way out. As usual, his brother gazed at him with admiration — his big brother always entertained him, making these loud, strange noises. Torben thought it was funny; he loved his big brother very much, loved joining him on all the exciting, strange adventures his brother came up with.

Tobias went to the woodshed, found some string and a knife, and told Torben to run ahead without him. They had a secret place in the forest that was perfectly safe, where his brother was free to roam; farther in, there was a clearing between the spruces where the two of them had built a hut, a little home away from home.

When they reached the hut, Torben was already settled on the old mattress, had found a comic book, and was absorbed by the pictures and all these exciting new letters and words that he finally, after a huge effort, both at school and with some help from his big brother, was beginning to grasp.

Tobias took out the knife and chose a suitable willow branch, cut it off at the base, and stripped away the bark in the middle, the section that was going to form the handle of the bow. The grip improved when the bark was removed and the wood had had time to dry slightly. He bent the willow over his knees, tied the thin rope to each end, and presto, a new bow. He placed the bow on the ground and went off to find suitable material for arrows. They did not have to be willow; most types of wood would do, except for spruce, since the branches were too limp. He returned with straight, narrow branches and started stripping off the bark. Soon four new arrows were lying near the tree stump he was sitting on.

"Tobias, what does it say here?"

His brother came padding out from the hut with the comic in his hand.

"Kryptonite," Tobias told him.

"Superman doesn't like that," his younger brother said.

"You're right," Tobias replied, wiping a bit of snot from his brother's nose with the sleeve of his sweater.

"Do you think it'll be a good one?"

Tobias got up and put an arrow against the string, then pulled the bow string as far as he could and let the arrow fly in between the trees.

"Awesome!" his brother cried out. "Would you make one for me, too, please?"

"This one is for you," Tobias said with a wink.

His brother's cheeks flushed, his gaze happy. The young boy tightened the bow as hard as he could and managed to get the arrow to go a few meters. He looked to Tobias, who nodded affirmatively, good shot, and then went to fetch the arrow.

"Why don't we shoot the Christian girls?" Torben said when he came back.

"What do you mean?" Tobias said, somewhat startled.

"The Christian girls who live in the forest? Why don't we shoot them?"

"We don't shoot people," Tobias said, taking his brother by the arm quite firmly. "And how come you know about the Christian girls?"

"I heard it at school," his brother said. "That Christian girls live in the forest now and that they eat people."

Tobias chuckled to himself. "It's true there are new people living in the forest." He smiled. "But they're not dangerous, and they definitely don't eat people."

"So why don't they go to our school?" his wide-eyed brother demanded to know. "If they live here?"

"I'm not sure," Tobias replied. "I think they have their own school."

His brother's face turned very serious. "I bet it's really good. And that's why they don't want to go to ours."

"Probably," Tobias agreed. "So where do you want to hunt bison today?" he asked, ruffling his brother's hair. "Up by Rundvann?"

"Probably," said the younger boy, who wanted to be just like his brother. "I think so."

"Rundvann it is. Please, would you go get the first arrow I shot? That is, if you think you can find it?"

His brother nodded. "I guess I can," he

said with a sly smile, and raced off into the
trees.

8

Holger Munch was not feeling entirely comfortable as he sat in the small motorboat going from Hitra to an even smaller island just beyond it. Not that he was seasick, no, Holger Munch loved being at sea, but he had just spoken to Mikkelson on the phone. Mikkelson had sounded very strange, not his usual brusque self at all. He'd been almost humble, wishing Munch the best of luck, hoping that he would do his best. Said it was important that the police work together as a team now, lots of morale boosting, very uncharacteristic of Mikkelson, and Munch did not like it one bit. Something had quite clearly happened. Something Mikkelson did not want to tell Munch about.

Munch pulled his jacket tighter against the wind and tried to light a cigarette as the boat chugged steadily toward the mouth of the fjord. He did not think that the young man with the disheveled hair steering the boat was a police officer, rather some sort of local volunteer, and the reason he hadn't been able to take Munch to the island earlier was still unclear. He had met him on the quay, asked him if he knew where the island was, and the young man with the unruly hair had nodded and pointed. Only fifteen minutes by boat. It was Rigmor's old place. She had lived there with her son, but then her son had moved to Australia, probably because of a woman, and Rigmor had had no choice but to move to Hitra. Her place had been sold, apparently to some girl from East Norway — no one knew much about her; he had seen her heading to town a couple of times, a pretty girl, about thirty, long black hair, always wore sunglasses. Was that where he was going? Was it important?

The young man shouted the latter over the noise from the engine, but Holger Munch, who had not said a word since greeting him at the quay, stayed silent. He just let the lad talk while for the third time he shielded his lighter against the wind with his hand and tried to light the cigarette, again without success.

As they approached the island, the faint nausea he had felt after talking to Mikkelson began to dissipate. He realized he would be seeing her soon. He had missed her. He had last seen her a year ago. At the convalescent home. Or the madhouse, or whatever they called it these days. She had not been herself, and he had barely been able to make contact with her. He had tried reaching her a couple of times, by phone and email, but there had been no reply, and when he saw the pretty little island in front of him, he understood why. She did not want to be reached. She wanted to be alone.

The motorboat docked at a small jetty, and Munch climbed ashore, not as nimbly as he would have done ten years ago, but his fitness level was nowhere near as poor as people's comments tended to suggest.

"Do you want me to wait, or will you give me a call when you want to go back?" said the young man with the messy hair, clearly hoping he would be asked to wait, join in the excitement; Munch had a hunch that not a lot happened out here.

"I'll call you," Munch said tersely, and raised his hand to his forehead in a salute by way of good-bye.

He turned and looked up toward the house. He waited while he listened to the sound of the engine disappear across the sea behind him. It was a pretty place. She had taste, Mia, no doubt about it. She had picked the perfect place to hide. Her own little island close to the mouth of the fjord. From the jetty a narrow path led up to an idyllic small white house. Munch was no expert, but it looked as if the place might have been built in the 1950s, perhaps originally as a summer cabin that had later been turned into a year-round accommodation. Mia Krüger. It would be good to see her again.

He remembered the first time he met her. Shortly after the special investigation unit had been set up, he'd had a call from Magnar Yttre, an old colleague and now dean of the police academy. Although he had not spoken to Yttre for years, his old colleague did not waste one second on small talk. *I think I've found one for you,* he had announced, sounding almost as proud as a little kid showing his parents a drawing.

"Hi, Magnar, it's been a long time. What have you got?"

"I've found one for you. You have to meet her."

Yttre had spoken so fast that Munch had missed some of the details, but the short version went as follows: During their second year, police academy students underwent a test developed by scientists from the psychology department at UCLA. The test, which had a technical name that Munch missed, consisted of showing the students a photograph of a murder victim along with several pictures from the crime scene. The students' task was to free-associate based on the photographs, give their observations and responses to them; the test was presented as quite relaxed, almost a game, so that the students would not feel pressured or realize that they were participating in something significant.

"I have lost count of the number of times we've run this test, but we've never seen a result like this. This girl is unique," Yttre had declared, still brimming with enthusiasm.

Holger Munch had met her at a café, a casual meeting outside police headquarters. Mia Krüger. In her early twenties, wearing a white sweater and tight black trousers, with dark hair, not very well cut, and the clearest blue eyes he had ever seen. He'd taken to her immediately. It was something about the way she moved and talked. How her eyes reacted to his questions. As if she knew that he was testing her, but she replied politely all the same, with a twinkle in her eye as if to say, *What do you think I am? Dumb or something?*

A few weeks later, he picked her up from

the police academy with Yttre's blessing, as Yttre had been happy to sort out all the paperwork. There was no need for her to stay in school any longer. This girl was already fully qualified.

Munch smiled to himself and started walking toward the house. The front door was ajar, but there were no signs of her anywhere.

"Hello? Mia?"

He knocked on the door and took a couple of cautious steps inside the hallway. It suddenly struck him that even though they had worked together for many years and were close friends, he had never been to her home. He began to feel like an intruder and lingered in the hall before he took a few more reluctant steps inside. He knocked on another half-open door and entered the living room. The room was sparsely furnished — a table, an old sofa, some spindle-back chairs, a fireplace in one corner. The overall effect was rather odd, as if it were not a home, merely a place to stay, no photographs, no personal effects anywhere.

Perhaps he'd been mistaken? What if she was not here? Perhaps she had just stayed here for a brief period before moving on, hiding somewhere else?

"Hello? Mia?"

Munch continued into the kitchen and heaved a sigh of relief. On the kitchen counter below one of the windows, there was a coffee machine, one of those big, complicated ones you saw in coffee bars, rather than the kind in people's homes. He smiled to himself. Now he was sure that he was in the right place. Mia Krüger had few vices, but the one thing she could not do without was good coffee. He'd lost count of the number of times she'd drunk his coffee at work and scrunched up her nose. *How do you drink this dishwater? Doesn't it make you sick?*

Munch walked over to the counter and touched the shiny machine. It was cold. It had not been used for a while. That didn't necessarily mean anything. She could still be nearby. But something felt very wrong. He could not quite put his finger on it, but it was there. He couldn't resist the temptation and started opening cupboards and drawers.

"Hello? Mia? Where are you?"

9

Mia Krüger awoke with a jolt and sat upright in her bed.

Someone was in her house.

She had no idea how she'd ended up upstairs, she did not remember getting undressed or going to bed, but that was irrelevant right now. *There was someone in the house.* She could hear noises coming from the kitchen. Bottles being taken out of a cupboard and put on the floor. She slipped out of bed, pulled on her jeans and a T-shirt, stuck her hand inside her underwear drawer, and pulled out her gun, a small Glock 17. Mia Krüger did not like guns, but she was not an idiot either. She tiptoed barefoot from the bedroom, opened the window in the passage, and crept onto the small roof. Shaking the remnants of sleep from her body, Mia tucked the gun into her waistband, leaped off the roof, and landed as soft as a cat in the grass.

Who the hell could it be? Out here? In her house? About as far from civilization as it was possible to get? She edged around the corner and glanced quickly through the living-room window. No one there. She continued steadily toward the back door, which also had a small window — no one inside. Carefully she pushed open the door and waited in the doorway for a few seconds before she tiptoed into the hall. She positioned herself by the entrance to the living room with her back against the wall and took a deep breath before she went in, still with her pistol held out in front of her.

"Is that any way to greet an old friend?"

Holger Munch was sitting on the sofa with his feet on the table, smiling at her.

"You idiot." Mia sighed. "I could have shot you."

"Oh, I don't think so." Munch grinned and got up. "I'm not much of a target."

He patted his stomach and laughed briefly. Mia placed the gun on the windowsill and went over to give her old colleague a hug. It was not until then that she realized that she was cold, that she was not wearing any shoes and wasn't properly dressed, and that the pills from last night had yet to leave her system. Her instinct had taken over. Provided her with strength she did not have.

She collapsed on the sofa and wrapped herself in a throw.

"Are you okay?"

Mia nodded.

"I didn't mean to scare you. Did I scare you?"

"A little," Mia conceded.

"Sorry," Munch apologized. "I've made some tea, do you want some? I would have made coffee, but I have no idea how to work that spaceship of yours."

Mia smiled. She had not seen her colleague for a long time, but their banter was the same. "Tea would be good."

"Two seconds." Munch returned her smile and disappeared into the kitchen.

Mia glanced sideways at the thick file lying on the table. She did not have a telephone, Internet, or access to newspapers, but it wasn't difficult to work out that something had happened in the outside world. Something important. So important that Holger Munch had gotten onto a plane, into a car, and then onto a boat to talk to her.

"Do we go straight to business, or do you want to do small talk first?" Munch set the teacup on the table in front of her.

"No more cases for me, Holger." Mia shook her head and sipped her tea.

74

"No, I know, I know." Munch heaved a sigh as he slumped down on one of the spindle-back chairs. "That's why you're hiding out here, I get it. Not even a cell phone? You're difficult to track down."

"That's kind of the point," Mia said drily.

"I get it, I get it." Munch heaved another sigh. "Do you want me to leave right now?"

"No, you can stay for a while."

Suddenly Mia felt uncertain. Of two minds. Up until now she had felt resolved and determined. She rummaged around her pocket but could find no more pills. Not that she wanted some, not with Holger Munch there, but a drink would have been welcome.

"So what do you think?" Munch asked, and tilted his head a little.

"What do I think about what?"

"Are you going to take a peek at it?" He nodded toward the file on the table between them.

"I think I'll pass," Mia said, tightening the throw around her.

"Okay," Munch said, and took out his phone. He entered the number of the young man with the messy hair. "Munch speaking, can you pick me up, please? I'm done out here."

Mia Krüger shook her head. He had not

changed. He knew exactly how to get his way. "You're an idiot."

Munch covered the microphone with his hand. "What did you say?"

"All right, all right. I'll take a quick look at it, but that's it. Okay?"

"Forget about picking me up. I'll call you later." Munch ended the call and edged his chair nearer the table. "So how do we play it?" he asked, placing his hand on the file.

"I want a pair of socks and a thick sweater. You'll find everything in my bedroom. And then I want a drink. There's a bottle of cognac in the cupboard below the kitchen counter."

"Have you started drinking?" Munch said as he got up. "That's unlike you."

"And if you can keep quiet, that would be great," Mia said, and opened the file on the table in front of her.

It contained about twenty-five photographs and a crime-scene report. Mia Krüger spread the photographs across the table.

"What do you think? First impression?" Munch called out from the kitchen.

"I can see why you've come," Mia said quietly.

Munch returned, put the drink on the floor beside her, and disappeared again.

"Take as long as you need. I'll fetch anything you want, and then I'll go down and look at the sea, all right?"

Mia did not hear what he said. She had already shut out the world. She took a large gulp of her drink, exhaled deeply, and began studying the photographs.

10

Munch sat on a rock watching the sun go down in the horizon. He had always thought of Hønefoss as quiet; when he lay in his room at night, there was barely a sound, but it was nothing compared to this. This was true silence. And beauty. Munch could not remember when he'd last seen a view like this. He could understand why she had chosen this place. Such calm. And what clean air. He inhaled deeply through his nose. It really was unique. He looked at the clock on his phone. Two hours had passed. It was a long time, but she could have all the time in the world. After all, he wasn't going anywhere. Perhaps he should just stay out here? Follow her example, throw away his cell phone? Ignore the world? Let go completely? No, there was Marion to think about; he could never abandon her. He didn't care much about anyone else. But then he started to feel guilty. An image of his mother in her wheelchair on her way to her prayer meeting flashed in his mind. He hoped that it had gone well. That was supposed to be his job. Taking her to the chapel every Wednesday. He had no idea why she insisted on going. She had never been very religious in the past, not that it made any difference. The situation made Munch feel uncomfortable, but his mother was old enough to know her own mind.

"Holger?"

Munch's train of thought was interrupted by Mia's voice calling out from the house.

"Are you done?"

"I think so."

Munch got up quickly, stretched to combat the stiffness, and walked briskly back toward the house.

"So what do you think?" he asked her.

"I think we need food," Mia said. "I've heated some soup."

Munch entered the living room and sat down on the spindle-back chair again. The photographs were no longer scattered across the table but were back inside the folder.

Mia appeared, said nothing, put a bowl of steaming-hot soup on the table in front of him. It was clear that she was distracted, he recognized that look of hers: she was lost in thought and did not want to be disturbed.

He ate his soup without saying a word and let her finish hers before he coughed softly to rouse her.

"Pauline Olsen. That's an old-fashioned name for a six-year-old girl," Mia said.

"She was known as Line," Munch said.

"Eh?"

"She was named after her maternal grandmother, but she was only ever called Line."

Mia Krüger looked at him with an expression he could not quite fathom. She was still somewhere deep inside herself.

"Line Olsen," Munch continued. "Aged six, due to start school this autumn. Found hanging from a tree in Maridalen by a random passerby. No signs of sexual assault. Killed with an overdose of methohexital. Backpack on her back. It was stuffed full of schoolbooks, not hers — as I said, she had yet to start school. Pencil case, ruler, all the books were wrapped with paper covers, no fingerprints. Every book is labeled with the name Toni J. W. Smith rather than the victim's own, for some reason. Her clothes are clean, freshly ironed, none of them her own, according to her mother. Everything is new."

"It's a doll," Mia said.

"Pardon?" Munch said.

A glassy-eyed Mia slowly poured herself a

refill; she had fetched the cognac bottle from the kitchen while he'd been outside, and it was almost empty.

"The clothes belong to a doll," Mia continued. "The whole outfit does. Where are they from?"

Munch shrugged apologetically. "Sorry, I only know what it says in the report. I'm not investigating the case."

"Mikkelson sent you?"

Munch nodded.

"There will be others," Mia said quietly.

"What do you mean?"

"There will be others. She's just the first."

"Are you sure?"

Mia gave him a look.

"Sorry," Munch said.

"She has a number on the nail of her little finger," Mia said.

Mia took a photograph from the folder. A close-up of the girl's left hand. She placed it in front of Munch and pointed.

"Do you see? A number has been scraped into the nail of her little finger. It might look like just a scratch, but it isn't. It's the number one. There will be others."

Munch stroked his beard. To him it looked like just a scratch, and it had been noted in the report as such, but he said nothing. "How many?" he said to prompt her.

"As many as the number of fingers perhaps."

"Ten?"

"It's hard to say. Could be."

"So you're sure? That there will be others, I mean?"

Mia rolled her eyes at him again and took another swig of her drink. "This is clinical. The killer took his time. Incidentally, I'm not sure that it is a man, or it could be a man, but he isn't . . . well . . ."

"What?"

"I don't know. Normal. If it is a man, then he's not normal."

"You mean in terms of sexual inclination?"

"It doesn't quite add up, and yet it does, if you know what I mean. Yes, it adds up, but not exactly, something doesn't add up, and yet it does somehow."

She had left him behind now. She was no longer in the room but back inside her own head. Munch let her continue without interrupting her.

"What is methohexital?"

Munch opened the folder and flicked through the crime-scene report before he found the answer. She had not read it, of course. Only looked at the photographs like she used to.

"It's marketed under the brand name Brevital. A barbiturate derivative. It's used by anesthesiologists."

"An anesthetic," Mia said, and disappeared back inside herself.

Munch was desperate for a cigarette, but he stayed put. He wouldn't light up inside, nor would he leave her, not now.

"He didn't want to hurt her," she suddenly said.

"What do you mean?"

"The killer didn't want to hurt her. He dressed her up, he washed her. Gave her an anesthetic. He didn't want her to suffer. He liked her."

"He liked her?"

Mia Krüger nodded softly.

"Then why did he hang her with a jump rope?"

"She was about to start school."

"Why the backpack and the books?"

She looked at him as if he were a complete idiot. "Same reason."

"Why does it say Toni J. W. Smith rather than Pauline Olsen on the books?"

"I don't know." Mia sighed. "That's the bit that doesn't add up. Everything else does, except for that, wouldn't you agree?"

Munch made no reply.

"The embroidered label at the back of her

dress. 'M10:14.' That adds up," she continued.

"Mark 10:14. From the Bible? 'Suffer the little children to come unto me'?"

Munch had remembered this detail from the report, which was actually quite thorough, but they had overlooked the significance of the line on the nail.

Mia nodded. "But that's not important. M10:14. He's just messing with us. There's something else that matters more."

"More than the name on the books?"

"I don't know," Mia said.

"Mikkelson wants you back."

"To work this case?"

"Just back."

"No way. I'm not coming back."

"Are you sure?"

"I'm not coming back!" she exploded. "Didn't you hear me? I'm not going back."

Munch had never seen her like this before. She was trembling; she seemed on the verge of tears. He got up and walked over to the sofa. Sat down next to her and put his arm around her shoulders. He drew her head toward his chest and stroked her hair.

"There, there, Mia. Let's call it a day. Thank you so much."

Mia made no reply; Holger could feel her skinny body quiver against him. She really was unwell. This was something new. He pulled her to standing and helped her up the stairs. Ushered her into the room, to the bed, and covered her with the duvet.

"You want me to stay the night? Sit here with you? Sleep downstairs on the sofa? Make you some breakfast? I could try to get that spaceship to work. Wake you with a cup of coffee?"

Mia Krüger said nothing. The pretty girl he was so fond of was lying almost lifeless under the duvet, unmoving. Holger Munch sat down on a chair next to the bed, and a few minutes later he heard her deep breathing enter a calmer tempo. She was asleep.

Mia? In this state?

He had seen her exhausted and run-down in the past, but never like this. This was completely different. He gazed at her tenderly, made sure that she would not be cold, and walked downstairs. He found the path leading to the jetty and took his phone from the pocket of his jacket.

"Mikkelson speaking?"

"It's Munch."

"Yes?"

"She's not coming."

There was silence on the other end.

"Damn," he heard at length. "Did she say anything useful? Something we have missed?"

"There will be others."

"What do you mean?"

"What I just said. There will be others. The girl has a number scratched into the nail of her little finger. Your people missed that."

"Damn," Mikkelson swore, then fell silent again.

"Is there something you're not telling me?" Munch said eventually.

"You had better come back," Mikkelson said.

"I'm staying here until tomorrow. She needs me."

"That's not what I meant. I want you to come back."

"We're reopening the unit?"

"Yes, you'll report directly to me. I'll make some phone calls tomorrow."

"Okay, I'll see you tomorrow evening," Munch replied.

"Good," Mikkelson said, and another silence followed.

"And no, Mia won't be coming," Munch said in answer to the question that was hanging in the air.

"Are you sure?"

"I guarantee you," Munch said flatly. "Mariboesgate, the same offices?"

"It has already been taken care of," Mikkelson told him. "The unit has been reopened unofficially. You can pick your crew when you return to Oslo."

"Okay," Munch said, and quickly hung up.

He could feel the joy rise in him, but he did not want Mikkelson to know it. He was going back where he belonged. To Oslo. The unit was up and running again. He'd gotten his old job back, and yet his joy was not complete. He had never seen Mia Krüger like this, so far gone, and he would not be bringing her back with him. And the thought of the little girl hanging from the tree continued to send shivers down the spine of the otherwise levelheaded investigator.

Munch looked up at the sky. The horizon was darkening now. The stars bathed the silence in a cold light. He tossed his cigarette into the sea and walked slowly back to the house.

11

Tobias Iversen found another branch and began making yet another arrow while he waited for his brother to come back. He liked using the knife. Liked the way the blade sliced its way through the wood, liked how steadily he had to angle the knife between bark and wood in order not to dent the arrow. Tobias Iversen was good with his hands — it was in art and woodworking lessons where he received the most praise. He was only average in the other subjects, especially in math, but when it came to his hands, there he was gifted. And in Norwegian. Tobias Iversen loved reading. Up until now he had preferred fantasy and sci-fi, but last autumn they had gotten a cool, new Norwegian teacher, Emilie Isaksen, who laughed out loud and had lots of freckles; it was almost as if she were not a teacher but a really nice, grown-up girl whose lessons were incredible fun, so different from their last teacher, who had just — Come to think of it, Tobias couldn't remember anything they had done during those lessons. Emilie had given him a long list of books she thought he ought to read. He had almost finished *Lord of the Flies,* one of her suggestions, and realized how much he was looking forward to going home so he could carry on reading in bed. Or at least the reading-in-bed part. He wasn't very keen on being at home. On paper, Tobias Iversen was only thirteen years old, but he was much older inside, and he had experienced things that should never happen to children. He often thought of running away, packing what little he owned into his knapsack and heading out into the world, away from the dark house, but it was a pipe dream. Where would he go? He had saved up some money from birthdays and Christmas, but not enough to travel anywhere, and besides, he could not abandon his younger brother. Who would look after Torben, if not Tobias? He tried to think about something else, sliding the blade of the knife smoothly under the bark, and smiled contentedly to himself when he managed to slice off a long strip without breaking it.

Torben was keeping him waiting. Tobias glanced into the forest but didn't worry unduly. His younger brother was an inquisitive little boy; he had probably just stumbled across an interesting mushroom or an anthill.

Why don't we shoot the Christian girls?

Tobias had to laugh. Kids, so innocent, they knew nothing, they would say just about anything that came into their heads. It was the opposite in Tobias's class or the school playground, where you had to watch every word or thought in case it didn't fall in line with the majority. Tobias had seen it happen so many times. It was just like in *Lord of the Flies.* If you showed weakness, you were marked out as a victim instantly. Right now he was worried about PE; he was athletic, fortunately, could run quickly, jump long and high, and his soccer skills were good. The trouble was his gym clothes. A couple of new boys who had moved out here from Oslo had brought with them other ways, more money. It was all Adidas or Nike or Puma or Reebok now, and Tobias had had a few snide comments recently about his crappy shoes and shorts, his jogging pants, and the old T-shirts that didn't have the right logo on them. Luckily, there was one thing that mattered more, and that was if girls liked you. If girls liked you, then no one cared about your gym clothes or how clever you were or what music you listened to, and girls liked Tobias Iversen. Not just because he was fit but because he was a really nice guy. Then it didn't matter that his soccer boots had only one stripe and the soles had holes in them.

The Christian girls. The rumors had started the moment new people had moved into the old farm near Litjønna, which had been empty for a long time. They had done up the place, it looked completely different now, and everyone thought that was highly suspicious. Some of the locals believed that the newcomers belonged to Brunstad Christian Church, but that turned out to be wrong. Apparently they *used* to belong to Brunstad Christian Church but had decided that they didn't agree with its doctrines, so they'd started their own religion, or whatever you would call it. All the locals thought they knew something, but no one really knew the full story, only that the children who lived there did not go to school and that it was very Christian and all about God and stuff. Tobias was pleased they'd come. He had figured out quite early on that whenever people made comments about his clothes or about poverty in general, all he had to do was turn the conversation to the Christian girls and presto, everyone forgot about designer labels. Once after PE he had even lied about having seen them, just to shut up the two new boys from Oslo, and it had worked. He made up a story about the girls wearing strange clothes and having almost-dead eyes and how they had chased him away when they spotted him. It was a dumb thing to do, obviously, because he didn't know the Christian girls personally and had no opinion about them, but what else could he do?

Tobias put down the knife and looked at his watch. His brother had been gone for quite a while now, and he started to worry. Not that they had to get home — they had no curfew, no one noticed whether they were in or out. Tobias could only hope that there would be something in the fridge so that he could give his brother some dinner. He had taught himself most household tasks. He could change the sheets, use the washing machine, pack his brother's school bag. He could manage most things, really, except buy food; he didn't want to spend his own money on food, he didn't think that was fair, but most of the time there was something in the kitchen cupboards, instant soup or a bit of bread and jam. They usually managed.

He stuck the arrow into the ground next

to the tree stump and got up. If they were to have time to hunt bison up near Rund-vann, they would have to get a move on. He liked having his brother in bed by nine o'clock, at least on school days. Both for his brother's benefit and for his own, they shared the attic room, and he enjoyed the few hours he had to himself by the reading lamp once his brother had fallen asleep.

"Torben?" he called out.

Tobias started walking through the forest in the direction where the arrow and his brother had disappeared. The wind had increased slightly, and the leaves rustled around him. He wasn't scared. He'd been out here alone many times and in stronger winds and worse weather; he loved how nature took over and shook everything around him, but his brother scared easily.

"Torben? Where are you?"

Once more he felt bad for the things he'd said about the Christian girls. He had lied, invented stories in the boys' locker room. He decided to go on an expedition soon, like the boys in *Lord of the Flies,* who had no adults around. Sneak out, pack some provisions and his flashlight, make a trip up there. He knew the way. See for himself if it was true what they said about the new farm and the fence and everything else. Exciting and educational. *Now* he remembered the phrase his former Norwegian teacher had been so fond of: everything they were going to do was always exciting and educational, so they had to sit still and listen, but then it never was. It was never exciting, and it could not have been all that educational either, because he couldn't recall anything from those lessons. Then he remembered something his grandfather had said once when they were out for a drive in the old red Volvo: that not everyone is suited to have children, that some people should never have become parents. It had struck a chord with Tobias. Perhaps it was the same with teachers. That some were not suited to it, and that explained their sad faces every time they entered the classroom.

His train of thought was interrupted by a rustling in the bushes in front of him. Suddenly his brother appeared out of nowhere with a strange look on his face and a large wet stain on his trousers.

"Torben? What's wrong?"

His brother looked at him with empty eyes. "There's an angel hanging all alone in the forest."

"What are you talking about?"

"There's an angel hanging all alone in the forest."

Tobias put his arms around his brother and could feel how the little boy continued to tremble.

"Are you making this up, Torben?"

"No. She's in there."

"Please, would you show me?"

His brother looked up at him. "She doesn't have any wings, but she's definitely an angel."

"Show me," Tobias said gravely, and nudged his brother in front of him through the spruces.

12

Mia Krüger sat on the rock watching the sun set over Hitra for the last time.

April 17. One day to go. Tomorrow she would rejoin Sigrid.

She felt tired. Not tired in the sense that she needed sleep but tired of everything. Of life. Of humanity. Of everything that had happened. She had found a kind of peace before Holger showed her the photographs in the folder, but once he left, it had crept over her again. This vile feeling.

Evil.

She took a swig from the bottle she'd brought with her and pulled the knitted cap farther over her ears. It had grown colder now; spring had not come early after all. It had only tricked everyone into thinking it was coming. Mia was pleased that she had the bottle to warm her up. This wasn't how she'd imagined her last day. She had actually planned to cram as much as she could into her final twenty-four hours of life. The birds, the trees, the sea, the light. Have a day off from self-medicating so that she could feel things, be aware of herself, one last time. It had not worked out that way. After Holger left her, her desire for sensory deprivation had only increased. She had drunk more. Taken more pills. Woken up without realizing that she'd been asleep. Fallen asleep without realizing she'd been awake. She had promised herself not to care too much about the contents of the file. Stupid, obviously. When had she ever been able to distance herself from anything in these cases? Her job. Well, it might be a job for other people, but not for Mia Krüger. Each case affected her far too deeply. They all reached right inside her soul, as if it were her own story, as if *she* were the victim. Kidnapped, raped, beaten with iron bars, burned with cigarettes, killed with a drug overdose, only six years old, hanged from a tree with a jump rope.

Why wasn't Pauline Olsen's name on the schoolbooks?

When everything else had been planned down to the last detail.

Fuck it.

She'd tried blanking out the image of the little girl hanging from the tree, but she could not get it out of her head. Everything seemed so staged. So theatrical. Almost like a game. A kind of message. But for whom? For whoever found the child? The police? Mia had trawled through her memories to discover if the name Toni had cropped up in any case she'd been involved with but had found nothing. This was exactly the kind of thing she used to be so brilliant at, but she no longer seemed to be able to function. And yet there was something here, something she could not quite put her finger on, and it irritated her. Mia watched the sun sink into the sea and tried to concentrate. A message? For the police? An old case? A cold case? There were only a few unsolved cases in her career history, thank God. Even so, one or two still troubled her. A rich elderly lady had been found dead in her apartment, but they had been unable to prove that it was murder even though Mia was fairly sure that one of the daughters was responsible for the old lady's death. She could not remember the name Toni in connection with that investigation. They had helped Ringerike Police in a missing-persons inquiry some years back. A baby had disappeared from the maternity ward, and a Swedish man had claimed responsibility and killed himself, but the baby had never been found. The case was shelved, even though Mia had fought to keep it active. No Toni in that investigation either, not as far as she could remember. Pauline. Six years. Hang on, wasn't it six years since that baby had disappeared? Mia drained the bottle and let her eyes rest on the horizon while she tried to guide her gaze inward. Backward. Six years back. There was something here. She could almost taste it. But it refused to rise to the surface.

Damn.

Mia rummaged around her pants pockets for more pills but found none. She had forgotten to bring more. Her medication was laid out on the dining table now. Everything she had left. Plenty of it. Ready for use. She had imagined waiting until dawn, until the light came. Better to travel in the light, had been her thinking. *If I travel in darkness, perhaps I'll end up in darkness,* but right now she did not care. All she had to do was wait until the clock passed midnight. When April 17 became 18.

Come to me, Mia, come.

It was not the ending she had imagined. She got up and hurled the empty bottle angrily into the sea. She regretted it immediately — she shouldn't litter; this rule had stayed with her since childhood. The lovely garden. Her parents. Her grandmother. Instead she should have written a message and put it in the bottle. Done something beautiful in her last few hours on earth. Helped someone in need. Solved a case. She wanted to go back to the house, but she could not get her legs to move. She stayed where she was, hugging herself, freezing, on the rocks.

Toni J. W. Smith. Toni J. W. Smith. Toni J. W. Smith. Toni J. W. Smith. Pauline. No, not Pauline. Toni J. W. Smith.

Oh, hell.

Mia Krüger suddenly woke up. As did her head, her legs, her arms, her blood, her breathing, her senses.

Toni J. W. Smith.

Of course. Of course. Of course. Oh, dear Lord, why had she not seen this earlier? It was so obvious. As clear as day. Mia ran toward the house, tripped in the darkness but got back on her feet, stormed into the living room without closing the door behind her. She continued into the kitchen. She knelt down by the cupboard below the utility sink and started going through the trash can. This was where she had tossed it, wasn't it? The cell phone he had left for her.

In case you change your mind.

She found the phone in the garbage and

rummaged around for the scrap of paper that had accompanied it. A yellow Post-it note with a PIN code and Holger's number. She went back to the living room, could hardly wait now, turned on the phone. Entered the code on the small screen with trembling fingers. Of course. Of course. No wonder it didn't add up. Everything had to add up. And it did. Toni J. W. Smith. Of course. She was an idiot.

Mia rang Holger's number and waited impatiently for him to pick up. The call went to voice mail, but she tried the number again. And again. And again, until she finally heard Holger's sleepy voice on the other end.

"Mia?" Holger yawned.

"I got it," Mia said breathlessly.

"What have you got? What time is it?"

"Who cares what time it is? I've got it."

"What?"

"Toni J. W. Smith."

"Seriously? What is it?"

"I think that J.W. is short for Joachim Wicklund. The Swedish suspect from the Hønefoss case. Do you remember him?"

"Of course I do," Munch mumbled.

"As for Toni Smith," Mia continued, "I think it's an anagram: *It's not him.* Joachim Wicklund didn't do it. It's the same perpe-

101

trator, Holger. As in the Hønefoss case."

Munch was silent for a long time. Mia could practically hear the cogs turn in his brain. It was almost too far out to be true, but even so. It had to be an anagram.

"Don't you think?" Mia said.

"But that's insane," Munch said at length. "Worst thing is, I think you might be right. So are you coming?"

"Yes," Mia replied. "But this case only. Then I quit. I have other things to do."

"Of course. It's up to you," Munch said.

"Are we back in Mariboesgate?"

"Yes."

"I'll catch the plane tomorrow."

"Great. See you there."

"You will."

"Drive carefully, will you?"

"I'm always careful, Holger."

"You're never careful, Mia."

"Screw you, Holger."

"I love you, too, Mia. Good to have you back. See you tomorrow."

Mia ended the call and stood for a moment smiling cautiously to herself. Now feeling calm, she walked into the living room and looked at all the pills she had lined up on the dining table.

Come to me, Mia, come.

In her mind she apologized to her twin

sister. Sigrid would have to wait a little longer. Mia Krüger had a job to do first.

II

13

Gabriel Mørk felt vaguely twitchy as he waited to be met in Mariboesgate. As far as he knew, Oslo Police had its headquarters in Grønland, so that was where he'd expected to go, but it turned out not to be the case. He had received a short text message: Go to Mariboesgate. Will pick you up at 11 a.m. No sender. Nothing. Strange, really. Come to think of it, his whole week had been strange — entertaining up to a point, sure, but Gabriel Mørk still did not know exactly what he had signed up for.

A job. He'd never had one of those before. Reporting to a boss. Working as part of a team. Joining the real world. Getting up in the morning. Becoming a responsible member of society. Not something this twenty-four-year-old was used to.

Gabriel Mørk liked staying up at night when the rest of the world was asleep. Much easier to think then. With the dark night outside and just the light from the screens glowing in his studio. Calling it a studio was a slight embellishment. Mørk was always reluctant to admit that he was still living at home. Yes, he had his own entrance and his own bathroom, but his mother lived in the same house. It wasn't very rock 'n' roll and definitely not something he would bring up on the rare occasions he met new people or bumped into old school friends. Not that it was a problem. He knew several hackers who did the same. Who still lived at home. But even so.

However, his situation was about to change. Completely out of the blue. It was all happening a little too quickly. Or was this what he'd been waiting for his whole life? He had met her online only seven months ago, and already she was pregnant. They were looking for a place together, and now he was standing in the street having gotten himself a job working for the police. Gabriel had never felt that he was very good at anything except computers. In that area few were better than him, but not in other aspects of life. At school he had kept mostly to himself. Blushed whenever a girl came over to invite him to join in something.

He glanced around nervously, but there was no sign of anyone coming to meet him.

Perhaps it had all been a joke? Working for the police? At first he'd thought some of his cyberfriends had been messing with him. He knew a couple of people who would think a prank like this would be hilarious. Screw with people. Hack their medical records. Hack lawyers' offices. Send messages to strangers telling them they were pregnant. Make false paternity claims. Wreak as much havoc as possible. Gabriel Mørk was not that kind of hacker, but he knew many who were. It was possible that someone was setting him up, but he didn't think so. The guy who'd called him had seemed very credible. They'd gotten his name from GCHQ in Great Britain. MI6. The intelligence service. Like most of his acquaintances, Mørk had had a go at Can You Crack It? — a challenge that had been posted on the Internet the previous autumn. To ordinary people it was a seemingly unbreakable code. One hundred and sixty pairs of numbers and letters with a clock counting down to zero to increase the tension. He had not been the first to solve the code, but neither had he been very far behind. The first to crack it had been a Russian, a black hacker, who cracked the code only a few hours after it had been uploaded to the Net. Mørk knew that the Russian had not cracked the code itself; he'd merely reverse-engineered it by hacking the website, canyoucrackit.co.uk, and found the HTML file, which was supposed to contain the solution. Kind of fun, but not really the point of the challenge.

Gabriel Mørk had spotted right away that it was machine code, x86, and that it implemented the RC4 algorithm. The creators of the code had put in place numerous obstacles, such as hiding a block of data inside a PNG file, so it was not enough merely to decrypt the numbers, but despite this it had taken him only a couple of nights. A fun challenge. The solution to the code itself was not quite as entertaining. The whole thing had turned out to be a PR stunt on behalf of GCHQ, a section of the British intelligence service, a test, a job application. *If you can break this code, you are smart enough to work for us.*

He had entered his name and explained how he'd cracked the code. Why not? He might as well. He had received a friendly reply that yes, his solution was correct, but unfortunately only British nationals could apply for jobs with the service.

Gabriel Mørk had thought nothing more of it. Not until his cell phone rang last Friday. Today was Thursday, and here he was with his computer under his arm, meeting a stranger before starting some kind of job. Working for the police.

"Gabriel Mørk?"

Gabriel almost jumped and turned around.

"Yes?"

"Hi, my name is Kim Kolsø."

The man who had spoken his name stuck out his hand. Gabriel had no idea where he'd appeared from. He looked very ordinary; perhaps that would explain it. Somehow he'd been expecting flashing blue lights and sirens, or a uniform, at the very least a brusque tone, but the man now standing in front of him could have been anyone. He was practically invisible. Ordinary trousers, ordinary shoes, an ordinary sweater in colors that didn't stand out from the crowd in any way, and then it struck Gabriel that this was precisely the point. He was a plainclothes police officer. He was trained to blend in. Not to stand out. To suddenly appear from nowhere.

"Please follow me, it's this way," said the man named Kim, and he led Gabriel across the street to a yellow office building.

The police officer produced a key card outside the front door and entered a code. The door opened. Gabriel followed the man to the elevator — same procedure here, you needed a card to operate the elevator as well. Gabriel watched the man furtively as he entered the code. He did not know exactly what to say or if he should say anything at all. He'd never had any dealings with the police. Nor had he ever taken an elevator that required a code. The police officer looked completely at ease, as if he did this all the time. Met new, unknown colleagues in the street. Entered codes in elevators. The two men were the same height, but the police officer was of a slimmer build, and despite his invisibility he looked in great physical shape. He had short dark hair and hadn't shaved recently. Gabriel was unable to tell if this was on purpose or whether the man just hadn't gotten around to it. He didn't want to stare, but he noticed out of the corner of his eye how the police officer suppressed a small yawn, so it was probably the latter. Long days. Heavy caseload would be Gabriel's guess.

The elevator stopped on the third floor, and the police officer got out first. Gabriel followed him down a long corridor until they reached another door, which also required a card and had a keypad. There were no explanatory signs anywhere. Nothing saying "Police" or listing the names of any other agencies. Total anonymity. The man opened a final door, and they had arrived. The offices were not large, but they were open and light. Some desks put together in an open-plan office, some smaller individual rooms here and there, most with glass walls, others with the curtains drawn. No one paid much attention to the two men who had just arrived, all busy with their own thing.

Gabriel followed the police officer through the open-plan office to a smaller room. One of those with glass walls. Gabriel would be on display, but at least he had his own office.

"This is where you'll be," Kim said, letting Gabriel enter first.

It was sparsely furnished. A desk, a lamp, a chair. Everything looked brand new.

"You submitted a list of the equipment you needed?"

Gabriel nodded.

"And that was a desk and a lamp from IKEA?"

For the first time, the police officer named Kim showed signs of emotion. He winked and slapped Gabriel on the back.

"Eh, no, there was more than that," Gabriel said.

"I'm just pulling your leg. The IT guys

are on their way. They'll get you up and running in the course of the day. I would have shown you around and introduced you to everyone, but we have a briefing in five minutes, so we won't have time for that. Do you smoke?"

"Smoke?"

"Yes, you know, cigarettes?"

"Er, no."

"Good for you. We don't have many rules here, but there is one that is quite important. When Holger Munch goes outside to the smoking terrace, nobody joins him. That's where Holger Munch thinks. That's when Holger Munch does not want to be disturbed, get it?"

The police officer pulled Gabriel out of his new office and pointed toward the terrace. Gabriel could see a man standing there, presumably Holger Munch, his new boss. The man who had called him and had casually, just ten minutes into the conversation, offered him a job. With the police. *Don't bother the boss when he's smoking, no problem.* Gabriel had no intention of disturbing anyone or doing anything except what he was told to do. Suddenly he spotted the woman standing next to Holger.

"Oh, wow!" he exclaimed.

He thought he'd said it to himself, but

Kim turned around. "Eh?"

"Is that Mia Krüger?"

"Do you know her?"

"What? No, not like that, but of course I have . . . well, I've heard about her."

"Yes, who hasn't?" Kim chuckled. "Mia is brilliant, no doubt about it. She's unique."

"Is it true that she only ever wears black and white?"

Gabriel had asked spontaneously, his curiosity having gotten the upper hand, but he regretted it immediately. Unprofessional. Like an amateur. He'd forgotten that they had already hired him. Kim probably thought he was a fan or something, which was partly true, but this was not how Gabriel Mørk wanted to come across to a colleague on his first day at work.

Kim studied him briefly before he replied. "Well, I don't remember ever seeing her in anything else. Why?"

Gabriel blushed faintly and stared at the floor for a moment. "Nothing, just something I read on the Net."

"You shouldn't believe everything you read." Kim smiled and took an envelope from his jacket pocket. "Here is your card. The code is your birthday, the incident room is at the end of the corridor. We start in five or ten minutes. Don't be late."

Kim slapped Gabriel on the shoulder once more and left him alone inside the small office.

Gabriel was at a loss. Should he stay where he was or sit down or maybe just run home and forget the whole thing had ever happened? Find another job, do something else. He felt like a fish out of water. And how could you be on time for a meeting that started in five or ten minutes?

He opened the envelope and was surprised to see a photograph of himself on the card.

Gabriel Mørk
Violent Crimes Section

He felt a sudden surge of pride. Secret doors. Secret codes. Specialist units. And he was on the inside. And Mia Krüger herself was standing outside on the terrace. He decided to make his way to the incident room in a few minutes. Being early had to be better than being late, whatever that meant in this mysterious place.

14

Tom Lauritz Larsen, a pig farmer from Tangen, had originally been dead set against the Internet. But when Jonas, the young farmhand, had moved into the spare bedroom, he had insisted that the sixty-year-old farmer get broadband or he would refuse to work for him. Tom Lauritz Larsen had been cross — that went without saying, as being grumpy was his default setting; there was never anything to smile about. And now he had managed to get this sickness in his lungs. Going on sick leave? What kind of nonsense was that? No one in his family had ever been on sick leave. What was this idiot doctor telling him? Was he suggesting that Tom Lauritz Larsen couldn't run his own farm? There had been three generations of pig farmers on Tangen, and no one had ever been on sick leave or taken disability payments from the state. What was the world coming to? But then he had started fainting without warning. Frequently and all over the place. The last time he fainted in the pigsty with the doors open. When he regained consciousness, he was surrounded by his neighbors, the pigs were at large in the village, and Tom Lauritz Larsen had been so embarrassed that he had taken his doctor's advice the next day. Attended appointments at the hospital in Hamar. Gone on sick leave. And found a farmhand through the employment office.

Nineteen-year-old Jonas from Stange had proved to be an exceptional worker. Tom Lauritz Larsen had taken to the boy right from the start. He was not one of those hobby farmers who did not know the meaning of hard work, no, this boy had what it took. Except for this business with the Internet, with which Tom Lauritz Larsen would have no truck. But he'd had it installed anyway because of the nineteen-year-old lad in the spare bedroom. It was something about a girlfriend and expensive telephone bills, and talking on the Internet was free, it would appear — they could even see each other and God knows what. What did he know? So Telenor had dispatched an engineer from Hamar, and now the Internet had been up and running for several months on the small farm.

Tom Lauritz Larsen poured himself another cup of breakfast coffee and searched the Norwegian Farmers Union's website. There was a very interesting article that he had looked at briefly the night before, but he wanted to reread it in depth. According to Norsvin, as many as one in four pig farmers in Hedmark had quit farming since 2007, saying pig rearing was no longer profitable. The average for those who remained was 53.2 pigs, where the figure the year before had been 51.1. It didn't take a genius to work out what was happening: the big farms grew bigger and the small ones went out of business.

Tom Lauritz Larsen got up for a refill but stopped at the kitchen window, still holding his cup as he saw Jonas run out of the pig barn as if the devil were at his heels. What was up with the boy this time? Larsen headed for the door and had just stepped outside when the young man reached him, sweating profusely, his face deathly pale and his eyes filled with panic, as if he had seen a ghost.

"What on earth is the matter?" Larsen said.

"Youuu . . . itttt . . . Kristi . . . Kristi . . ."

The lad was incapable of speech. He pointed and flapped his arms about like

119

some lunatic. He dragged Larsen, still wearing his slippers, still with his coffee cup in his hand, across the yard. He did not let go of him until they were inside the barn, standing by one of the sties. The sight that met the pig farmer was so extreme that for several months afterward he struggled to tell people what he had seen. He dropped his coffee cup and did not even feel the hot coffee scald his thigh.

One of his sows, Kristine, lay dead on the floor in the pen. Not the whole pig. Only her body remained. Someone had decapitated her. With a chain saw. Severed her neck completely. The pig was headless. Only the body remained.

"Call the police," Tom Lauritz Larsen managed to say to the lad, and that was the last he remembered before he fainted.

This time it was not because of his lungs.

15

Sarah Kiese was sitting in the reception area in her lawyer's office in Tøyen, growing increasingly irritated. She had expressly told the lawyer that she wanted absolutely nothing to do with her late husband's estate. What kind of inheritance was it anyway? More kids with other women? More letters from debt collectors demanding money and threatening to seize her belongings? Sarah Kiese was not perfect, far from it, but compared to her late husband she was a saint. Having a child with that loser had been a massive mistake. She had been ashamed of it then, and she still was. Not only had she had a child with him, she had even gone and married him — Christ, how stupid could you get? He had charmed her; she remembered the first time she saw him in a bar in Grønland, she had not fancied him right off, but she had been weak. He had bought her beers, drinks, yes, she'd been an idiot, but so what? It was over now. She would love her daughter forever, but she wanted nothing to do with that loser. When did he ever visit her? Whenever he wanted money. A loan for one of his schemes. He had claimed to be a builder, but he never had a steady job. Or started his own business. No, nothing like that, never any plans, no ambition either, just odd jobs here and there, a hand-to-mouth existence. And he would always come home smelling of other women. Didn't even bother to shower before slipping under her freshly washed sheets. Sarah Kiese felt sick just thinking about it, but at least it was over now. He had fallen from the tenth floor of one of the new developments down by the Oslo Opera House. She imagined he had gotten himself a job of some kind there — cash under the table, no doubt, that was how it usually was with him, casual night-time work. Sarah Kiese smirked when she thought how awful it must have been, falling ten floors from a construction site; she had chuckled with glee when she heard the news. A fifty-meter drop to his death, served him right. Surely he must have felt extreme terror while it happened. How long could that fall have lasted? Eight, ten seconds? Fantastic.

She glanced irritably at the clock in the reception area and then at the door to her lawyer's office. No, no, no, she had said when he called, I want nothing to do with that jerk, but the sleazy lawyer had insisted. Bunch of sharks, the lot of them. There would never be another man in her life unless he was the crown prince, and perhaps not even him. No more men for her. Just her and her daughter, now in their new small apartment in Carl Berner Square. Perfect. Just her own scent under the duvet, not fifty other cheap perfumes mixed with bad breath. Why had she even agreed to come here? She'd said no, hadn't she? Wasn't that what they'd practiced in that class she had been offered through Social Services: Say no, say no, build a ring around yourself, you're your own best friend, you need no one else. No, no, no, no.

"Sarah? Hi. Thanks for coming."

The dodgy lawyer with the comb-over stuck out his head and waved her into his office. He reminded her of a small mouse. Feeble, tiny eyes and hunched shoulders. No, not a mouse, a rat. A disgusting, cowardly sewer rat.

"I said no," Sarah said.

"I know," the sewer rat fawned. "And I'm all the more grateful for your making the trip. You see, it turns out . . ."

He cleared his throat.

"I overlooked something when I settled the estate, a small detail, that's all it is, my mistake obviously."

"More debt collectors? More court summonses?"

"Ha, no, no." The sewer rat coughed and pressed his fingertips together. "This is it."

He opened a drawer and placed a memory stick in front of her.

"What is it?"

"It's for you," the sewer rat said. "Your late husband left it with me some time ago, asked me to give it to you."

"Why didn't he give it to me himself?"

The sewer rat offered her a faint smile. "Possibly because he got a hot iron in his face the last time he showed up at your apartment?"

Sarah felt pleased with herself. Her husband had let himself into the apartment. Startled her. Suddenly he had appeared in her living room. Wanting to touch her, be all nice like he always used to be shortly before he would ask her to do him a favor. The iron had hit his gawking face with considerable force. He hadn't seen it coming, and it had floored him on the spot. She had not seen or heard anything from him since that day.

"I should have given it to you long ago, but we've been very busy," the rat said, sounding almost apologetic.

"You mean, he promised to pay you to do it but you never saw the money?" Sarah said.

The lawyer smiled at her. "At least that should conclude matters."

Sarah Kiese took the memory stick, put it into her handbag, and headed for the door. The rat half rose from his dusty chair and cleared his throat.

"Well, well. And how are you doing otherwise, Sarah? You and your daughter are all right and —"

"Fuck off," Sarah Kiese said, and left the office without closing the door behind her.

Several times on her way back to the new apartment in Carl Berner Square, she considered chucking the memory stick. Toss it in a garbage can and she would be finished with him, but for some reason she didn't. Not because she was curious, Sarah couldn't give a rat's ass about its contents; it was more about tying up loose ends. The lawyer was a rat, but he was still a lawyer. Her husband had been an idiot, but he'd had a last wish. Give that memory stick to Sarah and only to her.

She let herself into the apartment and

turned on her computer. Might as well deal with it sooner rather than later. The black laptop slowly roused itself. She inserted the memory stick and copied the contents to her hard drive. It contained only one file, which was called Sarah.mov. A film. Okay. So she would be forced to look at his ugly mug one more time, was that it? Even from beyond the grave, he was bothering her. She double-clicked the file to play the film.

He had recorded himself with a small camera. Possibly on his phone, she couldn't be sure. His horrible face was close to the lens, but it had an expression she hadn't seen before. He seemed scared out of his wits.

Sarah, I don't have much time, but I have to do this, I have to tell someone, because something here doesn't feel right.

He filmed his surroundings.

I was offered a job, and now I've built this. I'm far away in . . .

She heard noises, muffled, as if he were covering the microphone on his cell phone. She couldn't make out what he was saying. Her late husband continued filming his surroundings with trembling hands while he spoke, stuttering most of the time. So he had built something, so what?

. . . And I'm scared that . . . well, what did I

actually build? Look at this. I'm deep under-
ground. I thought that it might be a panic
room, but it's not. There's a small hatch. . . .

The voice disintegrated again while he
carried on filming. It was a kind of underground shelter.

. . . And no, it doesn't feel right, something
is going on here. Something . . . Take a look
at this. Just look. You can hoist things up and
down. Like an old service elevator or . . .

Her late husband suddenly jerked and
looked around. The whole scene reminded
her of a film she had seen years ago, *The
Blair Witch Project,* about some terrified
teenagers running around the forest filming
themselves.

. . . What the hell do I know, but I'm worried
that something might happen to me. I can feel
it. Have you any idea how far away I am?
Please, would you write down what I'm say-
ing, Sarah? Where I am and how I got this
job, and well, then you can go to the police if
anything should happen to me? I got the job
from someone who . . .

More scrambling. Sarah could not hear a
word of what her late husband was saying;
she could only see his frightened eyes and
trembling lips as he babbled away. This
lasted just over a minute. Then the film
ended.

So who did you have to sleep with to get this job? Or was it a job in return for sex? I certainly never saw any of that money. Help you? I don't think so.

The short film clip had been very unpleasant to watch, but she no longer had the energy to care. The whole thing could be nonsense for all she knew, some idiotic hoax. She had given up believing anything that idiot said a long time ago.

Sarah deleted the film from her computer, took out the memory stick, threw it in the trash can, went out into the stairwell, and threw the trash bag down the shaft. Just like that. The house was tidy once more. Only her. No trace of him.

Soon her daughter would come home from school. Life was wonderful. In this apartment Sarah was in charge. She went outside on the terrace and lit a cigarette. Put her feet on the table, smiled to herself, closed her eyes, and enjoyed a glimpse of the spring sunshine that had finally made an appearance.

Her life. No one else's. At last.

16

Gabriel Mørk was about to make his way to the incident room when there was a knock on his door.

"Yes?" he called out.

"Hello, Gabriel."

Holger Munch entered and closed the door behind him. Gabriel nodded hello and shook the large, warm hand.

"Er, right," Holger said, scratching his head. "I see your stuff hasn't arrived yet."

"No," Gabriel said. "But that guy . . . he . . ."

"Kim?"

"Yes, Kim, he said it was on its way."

"Great, great," Holger Munch said, now scratching his beard. "We had another guy doing your job, but he succumbed to temptation. Pity, but that's how it goes."

Gabriel wondered if he could ask what kind of temptation his predecessor had succumbed to, but he decided against it. There was something in Munch's eyes. Gabriel had seen the same expression in Kim's. The heavy, burdened expression of someone with a lot on his mind.

"I'm sorry about the somewhat unorthodox hiring process. I normally meet everyone I employ, but there was no time on this occasion, regrettably."

"It's fine," Gabriel replied.

"You came highly recommended." Munch nodded and patted Gabriel on the shoulder. "Again, I'm sorry about the rush, it's a bit . . . well, I don't know. Did Kim brief you?"

Gabriel shook his head.

"Okay, you'll learn on the job. Have you read today's papers?"

Gabriel nodded. "On the Net."

"Any particular news that stood out, in your opinion?"

"The two dead girls?"

Munch grunted. "Mia and I will brief everyone shortly, so you'll soon know what we're talking about. You have no previous experience with police work?"

Gabriel shook his head.

"Don't worry about it. I picked you because of what you know already," Munch told him. "Like I said, if we had more time, we would have sent you to an orientation course, a short version of the police academy, but there isn't, so it'll be learning by doing, and if you have any questions, then just come to me, okay?"

"Sure," Gabriel agreed.

"Fine," Munch muttered, looking absent-minded again. "By the way, what did you think?"

"About what?" Gabriel said.

"When you read the news today?"

"Oh, right," Gabriel replied, blushing slightly, feeling he should have realized what his new boss had asked him. "I guess I thought the same as everybody else, I presume. It was a bit of a shock. I'd been following the case about the two missing girls. Hoping they would turn up alive."

Gabriel thought about the stories in the papers.

Pauline and Johanne found killed . . .
Like two dolls in the trees . . .
Families in deep mourning . . .
White Citroën spotted . . .
Have you seen these clothes . . . ?

"Was that what you meant?"

"What?" Munch had been lost in thought.

"Should I say anything else?"

"No, that's fine," Munch replied, placing his hand on Gabriel's shoulder and turning to the door. "Or no, tell me a bit more."

Munch gestured for Gabriel to sit down while he continued to lean against the glass wall.

"Well, I don't really know," Gabriel began. "When I woke up this morning, I was an ordinary guy, I didn't know that this was the case I'd be . . . well, working on."

The words tasted strange in his mouth. Working. On a case. A murder investigation. The newspapers wrote of little else, same for the TV channels. Everyone was talking about the discovery of the bodies of two girls who had been missing for weeks. All of Norway had been hunting high and low for them. It was obvious that the police knew more than they were saying, but they were asking anyone who had seen the clothes to come forward. The dresses. The girls had been found wearing dolls' clothes. Between the lines a term was starting to appear, a term that had yet to be used, because this was Norway, not the United States or some other country where such things happened, and that term was "serial killer." It had not been printed anywhere, and yet it was what everyone thought.

"I thought it must be the same killer," Gabriel said.

"Aha. Go on."

"I thought it doesn't seem very Norwegian."

"Exactly. Go on."

"I was pleased they were not the children of someone I knew," Gabriel continued.

Munch gestured for him to carry on talking.

"It was strange that both of them were about to start school. At first I wondered if it might be about a teacher. Then I feared that perhaps more girls will disappear. Then I thought that if I had a six-year-old daughter, I would take extra care of her right now."

"What did you say?" Munch asked, and he seemed to come around momentarily.

"If I had a six-year-old daughter, I would take extra care of her."

"No, before that."

"Perhaps more girls will disappear?"

"Before that."

"I thought it might be about a teacher."

"Hmmm," Munch said, scratching his beard again. He reached for the door. "Incidentally, are you any good at code breaking?"

Gabriel smiled faintly. "I thought that was why you hired me."

"Oh, yes, so it was." Munch smiled, too.

He stuffed his hand into his trouser pocket and produced a scrap of paper on which he had scribbled something.

"This isn't a priority — it's a private matter — but I'm hoping you might be able to help me."

Munch handed Gabriel the note.

"I have several nerdy friends who like to challenge me. One of them sent me this, but I haven't been able to crack it."

Gabriel looked at the note Munch had just passed him.

Bwdybadynwbonnajgwpm=5

"Can you tell what it is?" Munch asked him with interest.

"Not at first glance," Gabriel said.

"She's been testing me for a few days." Munch sighed. "But I think I have to give up. Let me know if you make anything of it, would you? I hate it when these pals of mine get one over on me."

Munch chuckled and patted Gabriel on the shoulder again.

"But it's not a priority; it's just a private matter, okay?"

"Sure." Gabriel nodded.

Munch finally left, and this time he made it all the way out into the corridor before he popped his head around the doorframe again.

"Full briefing has been postponed. It'll be in just under an hour, okay?"

"Sure." Gabriel nodded once more and stayed in his chair, studying the challenge on the note Munch had just given him.

17

Benjamin Bache could not hide his disappointment as he flicked through today's edition of *VG* without spotting his own name. The paper had crowned this year's best-dressed men, and last year he had come in a respectable third, beaten only by Morten Harket and Ari Behn; this year, however, he hadn't even made the list. *Damn it.* The actor punched the wall in his dressing room but regretted it immediately. It hurt and made a noise. A moment later there was a knock on the door, and Susanne, the assistant director, appeared.

"Everything all right, Benjamin? I thought I heard something."

Benjamin Bache stuck his still-aching hand into his pocket and put on his best smile. After all, he was an actor.

"Everything here is just peachy. Perhaps it came from Trond Espen's dressing room?"

"Okay." Susanne smiled. "Rehearsals start

in fifteen minutes, act three from the beginning."

" 'To be or not to be, that is the question,' " Benjamin recited with a wink.

The assistant director giggled before she disappeared. Oh, yes, he still had it. But for the love of God, he had made the list last year; what had gone wrong this time? He'd taken such care with his appearance. He had even hired a PR firm and a stylist to advise him. Making sure he looked good. Having his pictures taken at all the right events. From all the right angles. He heaved a sigh and sat down in front of his dressing table. He hadn't aged much in one year. A few tiny wrinkles around his eyes. His temples were possibly slightly higher. He leaned forward and examined his hairline. There was cause for concern — it looked as if it had receded a bit since the last time he checked. He swept his hair to the side, as it looked thicker when he wore it like that. He began some vocal exercises. Warmed up his throat, pouted at himself in the mirror.

He had been hired by National Theater almost eight years ago. "A star is born," *Dagbladet* had written after his interpretation of Estragon in Samuel Beckett's *Waiting for Godot,* and from then on he'd been cast almost exclusively in leading roles, at least initially. He had played Romeo. He had played Peer Gynt. And now he was in Shakespeare's *Hamlet* on the main stage. He had hoped for the title role. Hamlet. *To be or not to be.* But instead he'd been cast as Horatio. The part of Hamlet had gone to Trond Espen because . . . well, it would, wouldn't it? Though he didn't really see why. He was obviously the better actor by far.

Oh, my dear Lord . . .

He was most put out. Acting in the shadow of Trond Espen. Bloody Horatio, a character ignored by practically everyone. It was pretty much only Hamlet who bothered to speak to him. Standing onstage, bowing his head, treating Trond Espen like a king . . . no, that really went against the grain. Benjamin Bache got up and studied his body in the mirror. He really was very good-looking. It put him in a slightly better mood. His recent workout routine was producing results. The yoga, too. As were the skin treatments. He could not see a flaw anywhere.

He returned to his chair and carried on with the vocal warm-up as the stage manager's voice crackled through the intercom.

"Ladies and gentlemen, we're ready to run act three. *Hamlet. Hamlet,* act three from the top starting in five minutes."

Benjamin Bache finished his vocal exercises, left his dressing room, and made his way to the main stage.

18

Gabriel Mørk was sitting at the back of the incident room waiting for the briefing to start. He had greeted everyone, shaken all their hands in turn, said "Hi . . . Hi" without being able to remember very many of their names. There was Kim, who had met him in the street, and a woman with long blond hair named Anette, and then there were three younger men whose names he could not remember and an older man whose name was . . . Ludvig, was it?

Holger Munch entered the room, closely followed by Mia Krüger. Mia took a seat in a chair at the front, while Holger turned on the projector and connected it to his laptop.

"Right, hello, everyone, today is the first briefing with everyone present. Full team in place, and that's what we need. We have some new faces, welcome to you. Those of you who have done this before, please help the newcomers settle in so that we get the best out of everyone. It's now ten days since we found the body of Pauline Olsen and eight days since we found Johanne Lange. After imposing a media blackout, we have decided to use the media to our advantage. As you have no doubt seen, we have today released pictures of the dresses the girls were found wearing."

Holger paused briefly and looked across the assembly. Gabriel Mørk thought he could detect a faint smile behind the grave eyes.

"We should really be celebrating being back here in Mariboesgate," Munch added. "But as you know, we have more important things to do, so that will have to wait."

Gabriel glanced around the room. Even though the mood was somber, he saw smiles and a couple of contented faces around him. There was no doubt that this team was pleased to be back together again.

"Some of you have been here from the start, but not all, so I'm going to give you a full briefing. I would like to add that this briefing is available as a PDF file on the server, which will be up and running later today. We ask that you share all information, and by that I mean absolutely everything you discover in the course of the investigation. Please upload it to the server so everyone has access to it. Things move faster this way, and it makes it easier to write reports later."

Munch hit a button on his laptop, and the first slide of his PowerPoint presentation appeared. These were not the same photographs that had been on the front pages of the newspapers, the two dolls' dresses. These were of the missing girls wearing the same dresses and hanging from two separate trees. Gabriel Mørk had never seen anything like it. It was at this point he suddenly realized what he had signed up for. This was not a movie. This was not just another TV program. This was real. Those two little girls no longer existed. Someone had killed them. In real life. They were no longer breathing. They would never talk again. They would never smile again. They would never start school. Mørk tried to stay calm and forced himself to look at the photographs even though his stomach churned. He feared that he stood out enough as it was. Fainting during his first briefing would not look good.

"Pauline Olsen and Johanne Lange," Munch said. "Both of them six years old. Due to start school this autumn. Pauline was reported missing four weeks ago. Johanne three weeks ago."

More photographs, some maps.

"Pauline disappeared from Skøyen Church Nursery School and was found in Maridalen. Johanne disappeared from Lille Ekeberg Nursery School and was found in Krokskogen. The times of their deaths have been difficult to pinpoint exactly, but evidence suggests that the girls were kept prisoners for a period of time before they were dressed in these costumes and left in a place where we would find them."

Munch again pressed a key on his computer, and fresh images appeared. Gabriel was unable to look at them and began glancing at the floor and at his shoes.

Dear God. What had he let himself in for? These girls were dead. The victims of some grotesque game.

He wished with all his heart he were back in his bed now. He felt that his life had changed in just a matter of minutes. He wished he had never seen these photographs. That he did not know that such people existed. People capable of such acts. Suddenly he felt utterly despondent. He was overcome by a sadness he had never previously known. Of course he knew that such things happened, and yet a part of him had refused to believe it. This was too unreal — no, it was far too real; it was reality bloody and brutal, that was what it was. Gabriel took a deep breath and concentrated very hard on sitting still.

"There was no sign of sexual assault," Munch continued. "The girls had recently been washed, their nails trimmed and cleaned, their hair brushed. Both girls had a sign from Norwegian Airlines hanging around their neck: *'I'm traveling alone.'* Both had backpacks on their backs. Both were killed with an overdose of anesthetics. There is no doubt that we are dealing with the same killer, and both the abductions and the murders were carefully planned. Pauline was found by a man named Walter Henriksen. He has a record, but not for anything like this. Two counts of driving under the influence some years ago, but we have no reason to think that he is involved. Johanne was found by two brothers, Tobias and Torben Iversen, aged thirteen and seven years old. The boys have a stepfather, Mikael Frank, who is also known to us. He served six months for minor offenses, but again there is no reason to think that any of them are involved. Door-to-door inquiries carried out in the vicinity of the crime scenes have not produced many leads, but as you know, a car was spotted that might turn out to be of interest, a white Citroën, the year unknown."

Munch hit the keyboard again, and the photographs from the newspapers appeared. He took a sip from a bottle of Farris mineral water that was sitting on the desk and carried on.

"The dresses are copies of dolls' clothes made especially to fit the girls. If the killer made them himself, we probably won't get any useful leads from them, but there is a chance that he or she got the job done by a third party who didn't know their intended purpose. That's why we went to the newspapers, in the hope that someone might recognize them. We haven't heard anything so far, Anette, is that right?" Munch turned to the blond woman.

"Nothing," Anette said. "But it's still early."

"Absolutely." Munch nodded. "For those of you who don't know, Anette is the link between us and police headquarters at Grønland. All communication with them must go through her. We don't want any leaks at our end. There's a reason we're hiding up here, isn't that right, Kim?"

"I thought it was so that you can smoke on the terrace."

There was muffled laughter among the small gathering.

"Thank you, Kim. Don't get hit by the door on your way out. But seriously, and I cannot stress this enough: We don't talk to anyone. Not to the press. Not to our colleagues down at Grønland. Not to family, friends, wives, girlfriends, roommates, mistresses, or in your case, Kim, your dog."

There was scattered laughter once more. Gabriel Mørk looked around. He could not see how anyone could laugh in these circumstances, but then it struck him that that was *all* they could do. Distance themselves emotionally. They had to detach themselves. If they didn't, then they wouldn't be able to think straight and do their jobs properly.

Don't feel too much. Don't get emotionally involved.

He took a deep breath and tried to join in the laughter but didn't manage to utter a sound.

"What we know," Munch continued, "we keep to ourselves. We'll get all the help we need — just ask Anette over there. Whatever you want, talk to Anette. We've been allocated unlimited resources for this."

"What do you mean by unlimited?" Kim asked.

"I mean no limits at all," Munch said. "Overtime, vehicles, tech, manpower — this investigation is not only a priority for us and Grønland, it's a case that concerns the whole nation. The orders are coming from the highest level, and I'm not talking about Mikkelson."

"The justice secretary?" asked one of the men whose name Gabriel did not think he had caught.

His head was shaved and he looked like a thug. He could easily play the villain in a movie.

"Among others," Munch allowed.

"The prime minister?" the man persisted.

"The prime minister's office has been informed," Munch said.

"Isn't this year an election year?" The man with the shaved head grinned.

Kim smiled. "It's always an election year, Curry."

Curry. So that was his name. Gabriel had thought the man had said "Kari."

"I don't give a damn what the two of you think about the prime minister," Munch continued in a more brusque tone of voice. "Those two girls could be our daughters, and we are not the only ones who feel that way, the whole country feels that way — look at the Net, at the news. We're a nation in mourning, in shock. We're not just solving this case to deliver justice to the girls' families. It's a state of emergency out there, people fearing for their lives, so I could not care less where you stand politically, Curry. A united government is backing this investigation with unlimited resources. It isn't our job to question political motives. We have to find the killer. *That's* our job, do you understand?"

For a moment the mood in the room was rather strained. Curry said nothing more, just bowed his head slightly and played with his fingers in his lap. Gabriel had not seen this side of Munch yet. On the telephone and in his office, the man had seemed incredibly kind and calm, affable, like a big teddy. Now he looked more like a grizzly bear. Dark were his eyes and dark was his purpose. Slowly Gabriel began to understand why Munch was the boss here, rather than any of the others.

"As you can all see, Mia is back," Munch continued, in his usual pleasant mood this time.

"Hello again," said Mia Krüger, who had been sitting quietly during the whole presentation but now got up and walked over to the screen.

There was scattered applause and the odd whistle from the room.

"Thank you, everyone, it's good to be back."

Gabriel glanced furtively at Mia; he was frightened of looking at her too often, scared that he wouldn't be able to stop staring. It was all getting to be too much for him. Pauline and Johanne hanging dead from the trees, and now Mia Krüger standing only a few meters away. Gabriel Mørk was not the only person who had had a crush on Mia Krüger. Mia Krüger had her own fan pages on Facebook. Or perhaps she didn't these days — he wasn't quite sure — but she used to. He had considered "liking" some of them, but as a hacker, Gabriel Mørk knew that all your online activity could be traced down to a single click, so he was very careful with anything he ever did. Rumor had it that Mia Krüger had set out to shoot and kill her sister's boyfriend, a junkie; the newspapers had been all over the case for a few weeks, until it had been overtaken by other events. Gabriel believed that the final police report had concluded that Mia Krüger had done nothing wrong, but even so, she had clearly been away for a while.

The skinny girl with the jet black hair was wearing a black-and-white turtleneck sweater and tight black trousers with zippers on the thighs. She looked exhausted, her eyes were dull, and she was much thinner than she'd looked in the photographs in the papers. *Mia Moonbeam.* That was what they'd called her on the Net. It was taken from a Belgian cartoon Gabriel did not know, something before his time, but he believed it was called *The Silver Arrow.* One of the characters had been a very beautiful Native American girl, Moonbeam, and during the eighties all the boys were supposed to have had a secret crush on her.

Even so, he couldn't help staring at her. Mia Krüger. There were not many famous Norwegian crime investigators. Perhaps that explained it. A beautiful, young, talented, blue-eyed Norwegian girl who looked like a Native American, caught up in a huge scandal — perfect tabloid fodder. He couldn't help feeling a little sorry for her now. She really did look exhausted. Her thin legs ended in a pair of big biker boots with buckles that rattled whenever she moved. She wore a silver charm bracelet around one wrist and a leather cord around the other. In chat forums on the Net, stories had been circulating about both items. The silver bracelet was supposedly a present from her sister, who had died from a drug overdose. She was said to have taken the leather cord from a Latvian man who was suspected of having murdered a young girl he'd trafficked to Norway as a sex slave. It had been early in her career, and the Latvian man had made her feel sorry for him. She allowed him to be interviewed without being handcuffed. He attacked her with a craft knife concealed in one of his boots. With blood all over her face, she managed to overpower him and then used his own craft knife to cut the leather cord off his wrist. It was said that she wore it to remind herself never to be weak. She had almost lost an eye in the attack. Gabriel could see the scar from where he was sitting. Rumors and stories. He didn't know if any of it was true, but even so, it was fascinating. Now she was standing right here in front of him. And they would be working together.

Mia Krüger hugged herself with one arm and spoke softly and cautiously; Gabriel had to strain to hear what she was saying.

"Most of you already know everything that we know. We're going to take a look at a few things you don't know about, which we believe are important."

Mia pressed a key on Holger's laptop, and another photograph appeared on the screen.

"The girls wore backpacks when they were found. The backpacks contained schoolbooks. A name had been written on the cover of the books. On Johanne Lange's books, it said Johanne Lange. However, on

Pauline's books it said Toni J. W. Smith."

Another photograph on the screen.

"Why?"

Mia Krüger smiled briefly. "Thanks, Curry, just as patient as always. Good to see you again."

"Let Mia finish," Munch said irritably.

"So on Johanne's books it said Johanne Lange. On Pauline's books, however, it said Toni J. W. Smith. As you can see, nothing in these cases is accidental. Everything seems to be planned down to the last detail. The killer knew what he was doing, he knew the girls' names. We have reason to think that he watched them for a long time before he abducted them, and we'll get back to that later, but as I was saying . . ."

Mia Krüger stopped for a moment, cleared her throat, and hugged herself more tightly. Munch got up and offered her his water bottle. Mia shook her head and continued in a low voice.

"As everyone knows, there's no doubt that these two cases are connected, but we now have reason to believe they are also connected to a third case, a case we didn't manage to solve some years ago."

She pressed a key on the computer again.

"In 2006 a baby disappeared from Høne-foss Hospital. A few weeks later, a Swedish nurse named Joachim Wicklund was found hanging in his studio apartment. On the floor below his body, we found a typed note in which he takes responsibility for the kidnapping. The baby was never found. The case was shelved."

Mia Krüger stopped again. Decided to drink some water after all. She was not in good shape. Everyone could see that. The normally fit and healthy woman was trembling slightly, and it looked as if she were struggling to make her head work properly.

"Holger and I," she continued after a short pause, "are convinced that the name on Pauline's book, Toni J. W. Smith, is a message from the killer. We're still not sure why he did it, but we think that 'J.W.' is short for Joachim Wicklund, and that 'Toni Smith' is an anagram: 'It's not him.' "

Low murmuring in the room. It was clear that everyone had huge respect for Mia Krüger and her intellect.

Munch took over again. "As a result we're reopening the Hønefoss investigation. Everything we discovered back then must be reviewed, every interview, every observation, and any names linked to that case must be revisited. I want you to take charge of this, Ludvig, because you worked with us back then, and take Curry with you, because he didn't. A pair of old eyes and a pair of fresh ones, that would be good, I think."

Both the older man named Ludvig Grønlie and the man with the shaved head, Curry, who had been so eager to comment on politicians, nodded.

"So that's our first lead, Hønefoss 2006, Ludvig and Curry. Our second lead, the dresses. Anette will coordinate any tip-offs received by Grønland and go over them with Mia and me. Ex-offenders and other likely suspects . . ." Holger looked up again. "Kyrre?"

A tall, slim man with short black hair and large glasses looked up from his notes.

"Yes. Trond and I are on it, but it's not a long list. What we have so far are sex offenders, assault cases. To be quite honest, I'm not really sure what we're looking for. Have we seen anything like this before? I mean, seriously? Not me, certainly. We have cross-referenced our lists with our friends down in Europe, especially in Belgium, with the names of everyone associated with Marc Dutroux, but again, that case involved serious sexual assaults, quite unlike this one. To tell you the truth, our colleagues abroad are shaking their heads at us, but we'll keep looking, of course."

"Good." Munch nodded. "Oh, I forgot to

tell you. We have a new database system that will be up and running later today. Everything we enter — names, observations, anything at all — will immediately be cross-referenced against all other available databases, ours and anyone else's. If anyone experiences any problem making it work, please talk to Gabriel Mørk, our new nerd. Have you all met Gabriel?"

Gabriel jumped when he heard his name spoken. He looked up and saw that everyone had turned to him.

"Hi, Gabriel," some of them said.

"Hello, everyone," Gabriel replied, sounding a little nervous.

He had the feeling of being back at school again. That soon he would have to stand up and say something, but fortunately he was not made to. He had no idea what database they were talking about. Munch looked at him and winked.

"A project I didn't have time to tell you about, but we'll do it later, okay?"

"Okay." Gabriel was relieved when Mia Krüger started talking again.

"I don't know how many of you have seen this." She pressed a key.

"But we discovered a number on the nail of the left little finger when we examined Pauline. It's the number one. As you can

155

see . . ."

Another photograph on the screen.

"Johanne had exactly the same, the number two, in the form of two lines on her left ring finger."

"Damn!" Ludvig exclaimed spontaneously. He was the older man with the round glasses.

"Yes, exactly." Mia looked at him.

"What the hell?" Curry said.

"There will be others," Anette said.

The room fell silent.

"We have cause to fear that Pauline and Johanne were only the beginning. That there will be others, unfortunately."

Munch had taken over again.

"So we pay special attention to any missing-persons cases. Girls aged six years, even if they have only been gone for thirty minutes, we turn up like gangbusters, do you understand?"

The assembly nodded.

"Now I feel the need for a cigarette, so we'll break for ten minutes and meet back here again."

Munch produced cigarettes from his jacket pocket and went outside on the smoking terrace, closely followed by Mia. Gabriel did not quite know what to do with himself. Seeing the photographs of the two girls had been overwhelming enough by itself. And they were saying there would be more? He breathed in and out deeply a couple of times to lower his pulse and went out into the corridor to get himself a cup of coffee.

19

Lukas was sitting in his usual place in the chapel, on the slightly raised chair close to the wall with a good view of the pulpit and the congregation. Pastor Simon had gone up in front of the altar but had yet to start speaking. It looked as if he were thinking about something important. Lukas and the rest of the congregation sat very still. You could have heard a pin drop in the large white room. Everyone waited with bated breath to hear what Pastor Simon had to say. The white-haired pastor was known for taking his time before preaching; it was about making contact with the Lord, opening the lines between God, himself, and the congregation, clearing the room of anything that might obstruct the celestial dialogue. The whole service was beautiful, angelic, almost meditative, Lukas thought as he sat very calmly with his hands folded in his lap.

Lukas loved listening to Pastor Simon. He

had first heard him by chance twelve years ago at a campsite in Sørlandet. His foster parents had sent him on holiday with their neighbors; either they couldn't afford to take Lukas with them or didn't want to go on holiday with him themselves. Lukas could not remember where they themselves were going — to the Mediterranean, something like that. It no longer mattered. He had been fifteen years old and initially felt very uncomfortable at the campsite, as everyone else there was very old compared to him. It was not the first time he'd felt like an outsider; he'd felt that way his whole life. He had been moved in and out of foster care ever since Social Services had removed him from the place that was supposed to be his home, and he had never settled down. Not at school either. No difficulties with the subjects. The problem was the other pupils. And the teachers. Or maybe people in general. Lukas gazed in admiration at Pastor Simon, who was still standing with his eyes closed and both palms facing the sky. Lukas could feel the heat. The glowing heat and the soft, bright light that filled his body and made him feel safe. He remembered the first time he'd had this feeling, at that campsite in Sørlandet twelve years ago. Not to begin with; at first he had felt like a fish out of water, as if everyone around him knew a secret that excluded him. The insecurity and the restlessness had affected him badly, and as always when this happened, the voices in his head started telling him to do things, things he could not say out loud. But then, as if God himself had lit up the path for him, he had found his way to one of the smaller tents on the outskirts of the campsite. A beam of light directed him to the white tent, and a Whisperer encouraged him to go there, one of the voices that was not so loud, not like the Shouters, he hated them, but it was not one of them, it was a nice Whisperer, calling softly in this foreign language. *"Sequere via ad caelum."* The kind voice in his ear and the compelling light drew him closer. *"Sequere via ad caelum. Follow the path to heaven."* Not long afterward he found himself standing inside the tent, mesmerized by the voices and the warmth and the light. And there, on a podium in the center, was Pastor Simon, his eyes shining, his voice powerful, and ever since that day Lukas had been saved.

Lukas looked across the congregation, which was still waiting silently for the pastor's sermon to begin. He recognized every face. Most had been members of the church for years, but none as long as Lukas. He had not returned to his foster parents that summer, and no one had seemed to mind. Twelve years later he had risen up the ranks, and though he had yet to turn twenty-seven, he was now Pastor Simon's right-hand man. His second-in-command. He helped Pastor Simon with all his activities, be they private or church-related. As far as Lukas was concerned, working for Pastor Simon was his mission in life. There was nothing Lukas would not do for him. Life was nothing compared to Pastor Simon, and if it came to it one day, he would gladly die for him. Death was no longer death, not for Pastor Simon's followers. It was just another step nearer to heaven. Lukas suppressed a small smile as the warmth and the beautiful light filled him again.

He had not heard the voices in his head for a while now. From time to time, sure, but not loud and not often, not like when he was younger, when the voices, especially the Shouters, had told him to do things he knew he should not do. Even though he tried to resist, it had been futile, and deep down he knew that the Shouters would never give up. He had to obey them. Get it over with. Hope for the best. It had occurred to Lukas that the Whisperers and the Shouters were like God and the devil. Pastor Simon had explained to him once how one could not exist without the other. That these two poles of the universe and eternity were inseparable. That you should not be scared, because the path of light would always guide you. Succumbing to the devil's commands from time to time was not mortal sin; it constituted proof of God's existence, proof that sometimes God spoke in the devil's voice to test you. It was a trial. Even so, Lukas was pleased that the voices, especially the Shouters' voices, did not visit him so often now.

Deo sic per diabolum.

The path to God is through the devil.

Lukas was well aware that this was not the official position of their church. It would not be well received by the amateurs. You had to be one of the initiated in order to understand. But the amateurs were only there to be used, like the people now sitting in front of him in reverent silence. The initiated were the people who mattered. Those who had understood what Pastor Simon really meant about the path toward the light. And Lukas was one of them.

Tonight was amateur night. Lukas could feel how much he was looking forward to the coming weekend, when they would return to the forest and meet up with the other initiated. Deep down, Lukas could not understand why Pastor Simon insisted on holding meetings for the amateurs anymore — after all, they had more important work to do — but he would obviously never contradict the pastor. The pastor was in contact with God and knew exactly what needed doing. *Lux domus.* Wait until the weekend. Lukas had to press his lips together again so as not to sigh with pleasure as the warmth and the light flowed through his body once more.

At last Pastor Simon opened his mouth, and God was in the room. The members of the congregation sat as if glued to their seats and let themselves be filled with bliss. Lukas had heard this sermon before — it was written for the amateurs; it was fine, but simple — and besides, his mind was on the upcoming weekend. *Lux domus.* Another step closer to heaven. He shut his eyes and let the pastor's words fill him, and then soon afterward it was over and the pastor was standing by the exit. Grateful hands and bowed heads proceeded past him on their way out of the hall, and then Lukas and the pastor were alone again, just the two of them, in the large white space.

Lukas followed the pastor into his office

and helped him out of his cassock. He turned away so as not to see the pastor in his underwear, then helped him put on the suit he normally wore. Poured him a cup of freshly brewed coffee. He said nothing until the pastor had sat down in his chair behind the huge desk and indicated that God had left the room and that they were permitted to speak again.

"Another name has come forward." Lukas cleared his throat and produced the envelope he'd kept in his inside jacket pocket during the whole service.

"Ah?" The pastor looked up at him and took the envelope. It contained a single white sheet of paper. Lukas did not know what it said, only that it was a name. He did not know what name it was; that was for the pastor's eyes only. His task was to collect the envelope and give it to the pastor. Not to open it. He was merely a messenger, like an angel.

As usual, the pastor said nothing. He read the name, folded the sheet, and locked the envelope in the safe under the small table by the window.

"Thank you, Lukas. Was there anything else?" The pastor looked up at him.

Lukas smiled back at the kind, luminous

gaze. "No, nothing. Oh, yes, your brother is here."

"Nils? He's here now?"

Lukas nodded. "He came right before the service. I asked him to wait in the back garden."

"Good, Lukas, good. You can tell him to come in now."

Lukas bowed and went to fetch the visitor.

"Why did you keep me waiting so long? I told you it was important."

Simon's brother, Nils, was also a high-ranking member of the church. Lukas had met him for the first time in the tent on Sør-landet, but even though he had been with them just as long, Nils was not quite up there by the pastor's side. Lukas knew that there had been some arguing and dissenting voices when he had been given the role of second-in-command; many people felt that place belonged to Nils, but, as always, no one challenged the pastor. After all, he was the one who had been entrusted with the key to heaven.

"You know it's important for the pastor to help the amateurs. He's ready for you now."

"Lux domus," the brother with the short hair muttered.

"Lux domus." Lukas smiled and showed

him the way.

The pastor rose when they entered. His guest bowed and went up to his older brother. Kissed his hand and both cheeks.

"Sit, sit, my brother," the pastor said, and resumed his seat behind the desk.

Nils glanced briefly at Lukas.

"Would you like me to leave?" Lukas offered immediately.

"No, no, stay."

The pastor gestured casually to indicate that Lukas should sit down. He was one of the initiated; there was no reason for him to leave the room.

Lukas thought he detected a certain amount of irritation from Nils at the decision, but he said nothing.

"How are you all up there?" the pastor asked when the three of them were seated.

"All is well," his brother replied.

"And the fence?"

"More than halfway finished."

"Will it be as high as we discussed?"

"Yes." His brother nodded.

"So what's the reason you're no longer up there?"

"What do you mean?"

"Why are you here when you have work to do there?"

Nils glanced at Lukas again. He appeared

to have something on his mind but did not dare say it while Lukas was in the room.

"The flock nearly lost a member," he muttered at length with his head bowed; it looked as if he were ashamed.

"What do you mean, lost a member?"

"We had an accident with one of the younger members."

"What do you mean by an accident?"

"Just an accident. A mistake. It has been taken care of."

"Who was it?"

"Rakel."

"Rakel the good one? My Rakel?"

The brother acknowledged this, his neck bowed even more. "She disappeared from us one night. But she's back now."

"So everything is all right?"

"Yes, everything is all right."

"So I ask you again, my brother, why are you down here when you have work to do up there?"

Nils looked up at the pastor, his big brother. Even though Nils was a man well past fifty, he seemed almost like a little boy who had just been told off by his father. "You asked me to keep you updated."

"As long as everything is all right, then everything is all right, is it not?"

Nils nodded obediently. "It might have

been easier if we'd had a telephone," he said tentatively after a small pause.

The pastor leaned back in his chair and pressed his fingertips together. "Do you have any other suggestions? Any other opinions? Are you dissatisfied with what God has given you?"

"No, no . . . that's not what I . . . I just wanted . . ."

Nils struggled to find the words, and his face grew red. The pastor shook his head briefly, and a strange silence spread across the room. It was not awkward for Lukas — he was always on the pastor's side — but it was uncomfortable for the brother, and he deserved it. How dare he question the pastor's orders? The brother stood, still keeping his eyes on the floor.

"You'll be coming up on Saturday?"

"We'll be there on Saturday."

"Good. See you then." The pastor's brother dipped his head and left the room.

Lux domus," Lukas said when only he and the pastor were left. That was how he liked it best, just the two of them.

The pastor smiled and looked at him. "Do you think we have done the right thing?"

"Absolutely," Lukas agreed.

"Sometimes I'm not so sure," the pastor said, pressing his fingertips together again.

168

"There is something I have to tell you," Lukas said.

"Yes?"

"You know that it's my job to take care of you."

"Is it, Lukas? Is it?" The pastor smiled.

Lukas blushed faintly. He knew the pastor so well. He knew his voice. He knew when he was being praised.

"I don't know if you're aware, but we might have a problem with the congregation."

"You mean this one?"

"Yes, the amateurs."

"And what is the problem?"

"Well, that's up to you to decide. I'm only here to tell you what I see and to take care of you."

"Yes, so you say, Lukas, and I appreciate that. What is it?"

Lukas coughed slightly before he continued. "One of our regular supporters has a somewhat unfortunate association."

The pastor shook his head. "You're speaking in tongues now, Lukas. Spit it out."

"An elderly lady in a wheelchair, glasses, she usually sits at the back."

"Hildur?"

Lukas nodded.

"What about her?"

169

"She's the mother of Holger Munch."

"Who?"

"Holger Munch. He's a police officer."

"Oh, is he? I did not know that."

Lukas was somewhat taken aback, because he knew that the pastor had heard of Holger Munch, but he said nothing.

"Hildur is his mother," he said again.

"And why would that present a problem for us?"

"I just wanted you to be aware."

"Are you thinking about the contents of the envelope now?"

Lukas nodded cautiously.

"Thank you very much, Lukas, but I don't think that we need to worry about Holger Munch. We have more important things to think about right now, don't we?"

"Yes, we have." Lukas quietly got up.

"*Lux domus,* my friend." The pastor smiled amicably.

"*Lux domus,*" Lukas said, smiling back at him.

He bowed deeply and left the pastor's office without saying anything else.

20

Mia Krüger was sitting in her office, fidgeting with the tablets she kept in her pants pocket. She had promised herself not to take any with her, to leave them all behind in her house on the island until she had finished this case, until she needed them again, but she hadn't quite succeeded. She had stuffed a few pills into her pocket, just in case. She was longing to take one now. She was itching all over. She had pushed it so far away that she'd forgotten what it was like to be exposed to the real world. After all, she hadn't expected to have to deal with it for much longer, but then Munch had turned up and ruined her plans.

Mia Krüger hadn't had a drink for four days either, not since she returned to Oslo. Several times she'd been tempted to attack the minibar in her hotel room, but she'd managed to restrain herself. Holger had offered her a government apartment, but she insisted on a hotel room and was happy to pay for it out of her own pocket. She did not want to come back. She was not coming back. An impersonal hotel room was all she needed. A transition room. A waiting room. She did not want to get too close to everyday life. Just solve this case. Then she would go back again. To Hitra. To Sigrid. She'd been searching for a new, symbolic date. April 18, the tenth anniversary, had passed. The next one was their birthday, November 11. When they would both turn thirty-three. Would have turned thirty-three. November seemed incredibly far off. Much too far. She had to find a nearer date. Or maybe she didn't need one. It could be anytime. The most important thing was that it happened. That she was spared this. These people. She stuck her hand into her pocket and placed a pill on her tongue. Changed her mind. Spit it out and put it back in her pocket.

"Someone has called about the clothes."

Anette had suddenly appeared in her office.

"What?"

"We have a hit on the dolls' dresses."

"So soon?"

"Yep." The blond woman smiled, waving a piece of paper in her hand. "Jenny, from

Jenny's Sewing Room in Sandvika, called. She apologized for not calling sooner, but she hadn't gotten around to reading the papers until now. Do you want to come with me?"

"Yes, please. Where is Munch?"

"He had to pick up his granddaughter from nursery school."

"Do you want to drive, or shall I?" Anette said, dangling a set of car keys in front of her.

"You had better drive." Mia smiled and followed her colleague down to the underground garage.

"So what did she say?" Mia asked when they had left the city center.

She'd worked with Anette on several cases in the past, but it had not resulted in a close relationship. Mia didn't quite know why. There was nothing wrong with Anette. She was quick-thinking and always friendly. She had trained as a lawyer, and she was incredibly clever and the perfect member of the special unit. It was probably because Mia was not close to any of her colleagues. Except Holger Munch, of course, but that was different. Was she close to anyone these days? She had not spoken to her friends from Åsgårdstrand for years. After Sigrid left, she had isolated herself more and more.

173

Perhaps that hadn't been such a smart move. Perhaps it would have done her good to have a life outside of work. It made no difference now. Solve this case, then go back to Hitra. Back to Sigrid. She caressed the S dangling from the charm bracelet. It made her feel safe.

"I didn't speak to her myself. A colleague down at police headquarters reported it to me. But I think we have the right one."

"She knew about the writing on the collar?"

Anette nodded and changed lanes.

"Mark 10:14. 'Suffer the little children to come unto me.' Do you think we're dealing with a religious maniac?"

"It's too early to say," Mia said, putting on her sunglasses.

The light outside was bright; other people might regard it as pale spring sunshine, but not her. Her body felt as if it could not handle any kind of sensory input. She had tried to watch television last night, but it had given her a headache. She'd even had to ask Holger to turn off the radio in his office. They drove in silence. Mia was aware that Anette wanted to ask questions but ignored it. The others had been just the same. Polite smiles behind curious eyes. Except for the people who knew her best —

Curry, Kim, Ludvig — or maybe them as well. *How are you? How have you been? Are you feeling better, Mia? We heard that you had had a breakdown? Shaved your head? Tried to kill yourself on an island in the middle of the sea?* Out of the corner of her eye, she noticed Anette glancing at her. The car was full of unanswered questions, just like the offices in Mariboesgate, but Mia did not have the energy for that right now. She decided she would put it right later. She really liked Anette. Perhaps they could go out one evening and have a beer together. Or maybe not. Why this and why that?

Come to me, Mia, come.

Why are you out there alone?

The rain set in just as they turned off toward Sandvika. It drummed on the windshield, but Mia kept her sunglasses on. She closed her eyes behind the lenses and listened to the sounds. The raindrops hitting the windshield. The droning of the engine.

"We have arrived," Anette announced finally, and got out.

Mia placed her sunglasses on the dashboard and followed her. The rain had ceased. It had been only a little local shower, and now the mild spring sun peeked out from behind the clouds once more and showed them the way to a small shop painted yellow, here on the outskirts of Sandvika.

It said JENNY'S SEWING ROOM on the window. In the door hung an old-fashioned sign: CLOSED. Mia knocked, and a kind but anxious old face appeared behind the curtains.

"Yes?" the woman said through the closed door.

"Mia Krüger, Oslo Police, Violent Crimes Section," Mia said, holding up her ID card to the glass to reassure the old woman.

"You're police?" the woman said, looking incredulously at both of them.

"Yes," Mia replied kindly. "Please, may we come in?"

It was clear that reading the newspapers had given the elderly woman quite a shock, as it took her some time to unlock the door. Shaky old fingers struggled to turn the key, but at last she succeeded. Mia entered calmly and showed the woman her ID card again. The woman closed the door behind them and locked it immediately. She stayed in the middle of the small, colorful room, not knowing quite what to do with herself.

"You're Jenny?" Mia asked.

"Yes, and I'm sorry, I'm forgetting my manners. Phew, what a day, I'm shaking all over. Jenny Midthun," she introduced herself, holding out a small, delicate hand to Mia.

"Is this your shop?" Anette said, taking a look around.

There were tailor's dummies in the windows wearing homemade clothes. The walls and the shelves were filled with items that Jenny had clearly made herself. Tablecloths, dresses, one wall covered with patchwork quilts — the whole shop exuded good old-fashioned craftsmanship.

"Yes, we have had it since 1972," Jenny Midthun told them. "My husband and I started it together, but he's no longer with us. He died in '89. It was his idea to call it Jenny's Sewing Room. I thought it would have been more appropriate to call it Jenny and Arild's, but he insisted, so . . . well . . ." Jenny Midthun's voice petered out.

"Did you make these dresses?"

Mia took out the photographs from her inside pocket and placed them on the counter. Jenny Midthun put on her glasses, which hung from a cord around her neck, and examined the photographs before she nodded.

"Yes, I made both of them. What about them? Am I in trouble? Have I done something wrong?"

"Not at all, Jenny. We have no reason to think that you've done anything wrong. Who was the customer?" Mia said.

Jenny Midthun walked behind the counter and took a ring binder from one of the bookshelves.

"It's all in here," she said, tapping the ring binder with her finger.

"What's all there?"

"All my orders. I write everything down. Measurements, fabric, price, due date — everything is here."

"Would you mind if we borrowed that?" Mia asked.

"No, no, of course not, take whatever you want. Oh, it's terrible, oh, no, I don't know if I can . . . I had such a shock when . . . Yes, it was one of my neighbors who dropped by with the papers. . . ."

"Who ordered the dresses?" Mia said.

"A man."

"Do you have a name?"

"No, I never got his name. He brought in photographs. Of dolls. Said he wanted the dresses made to fit children."

"Did he say what the dresses were for?"

"No, and I didn't ask either. Had I known that . . . But I didn't know that . . ."

Jenny Midthun clutched her head. She had to sit down on a chair. Anette disappeared into the back room and returned with a glass of water.

"Thank you," the old woman said, her voice shaking.

"When was the order placed?"

"About a year ago. Last summer. The first one, I mean."

"Did he visit more than once?"

"Oh, yes." Jenny nodded. "He came here many times. Payment was never a problem. Always cash, always on time. A good price. No problems there."

"How many dresses did you make?"

"Ten."

The old woman stared at the floor. Anette looked at Mia and raised her eyebrows.

There will be others. Ten dresses.

"When did you last see him?"

"It's not that long ago, not really. Perhaps a month. Yes, I think so. In the middle of March. That's when he came to pick up the last two."

"Can you tell us what he looked like? Are you feeling well enough to do that?" Anette said.

"Completely ordinary."

"What does 'completely ordinary' mean to you?"

"He was well dressed. Nice clothes. A suit and a hat. Nice, newly polished shoes. Not so tall, as tall as Arild perhaps, my late husband, medium height. Neither fat nor thin, completely ordinary."

"Any regional accent?"

"What? No."

"Did he speak like us?" Anette said.

"Oh, yes, he was Norwegian. From Oslo. Perhaps forty-five or thereabouts. A completely ordinary man. Very nice. And very well dressed. How was I to know . . . ? I mean . . . If I had known then . . ."

"You've been very helpful, Jenny," Mia said, gently patting the old woman's hand. "And a great help. Now, I want you to think carefully: Was there anything about him that was unusual. Something that stood out?"

"I don't know what that would be. Do you mean his tattoo?"

Anette looked at Mia again and smiled faintly. "He had a tattoo?"

Jenny Midthun nodded. "Here," she said, touching her neck. "Usually he would wear a turtleneck sweater, so you couldn't see it, but once he didn't or he didn't quite cover it up properly, if you know what I mean — it was loose around the collar." She touched her own collar to illustrate.

"Was it a big tattoo?" Anette wanted to know.

"Oh, yes, it was. Covered practically

everything from here and then down to —"

"Did you see what kind of tattoo it was?"

"Yes, it was an eagle."

"He had an eagle tattooed on his neck?"

Jenny Midthun nodded tentatively.

"Call it in immediately," Mia said.

Anette got out her cell phone. She went outside into the street to make the call.

"Have I been helpful?" Jenny Midthun looked up at Mia with frightened eyes. "Am I going to go to prison?"

Mia patted her shoulder. "No, you're not. But I would like you to come into town so that we can get an official statement from you. It doesn't have to be right now, but in the next few days, would that be all right?"

Jenny Midthun agreed and walked Mia to the door. Mia produced a business card from the back pocket of her jeans and handed it to the woman.

"If you remember anything else, I want you to call me, okay?"

"I will. But I'm not in trouble, am I?"

"No, definitely not." Mia smiled. "Many thanks for your help."

She heard the door being locked behind her when she stepped out into the street. Poor thing. The old woman really was terrified. Mia saw the old woman's face peer out from behind the curtains and hoped that she would not be alone for the rest of the day, that there was someone she could phone. Mia turned when Anette had ended the call. "Did you speak to Holger?"

"No, he didn't answer his phone. I spoke to Kim. He'll follow it up."

"Good." Mia smiled.

The two police officers got into the car and drove back to Oslo quickly.

21

Holger Munch was sitting in Peppe's Pizza being given a lesson in how to brush a doll's hair. They had just finished eating, he and Marion — that is to say he had done the eating, Marion had spent most of her time drinking soda and playing. To his daughter's great despair, he could not help himself, could not resist his granddaughter's cute eyes and her pleading voice. He had never been able to. He had showered Marion with presents from the day she was born, teddies and dolls; her bedroom looked like a toy shop. Finally Miriam had put her foot down and told him that enough was enough. They were trying to bring up their daughter to be an independent and sensible girl, not a spoiled brat.

"Oh, Granddad, look. Monster High!"

"Monster what?"

"Monster High. That's where they go to school. Look, that's Jackson Jekyll. He's a boy. Look at his nice yellow shirt. That's because he's a monster. Please, can I have him?"

"We had better not buy anything today, Marion. You remember what your mom said: we have to wait until it's your birthday."

"But that's a trillion days away! And anyhow, when I'm with you, Mom's rules don't apply."

"Really? Says who?"

"Says me. Just now."

"Is that right?"

"I get to make the decisions, because I'm six years old and I'm going to go to Lilleborg School soon, and then no one can tell me what to do anymore. *I'm* in charge."

Now, who did she remind him of? Sweet and lovely, but incredibly stubborn and willful?

"Oh, that's Draculaura! Look, Granddad, Draculaura! And Frankie Stein! Frankie Stein, Granddad! Oh, please, can we buy them, Granddad?"

Marion got her way in the end, as she always did. Two dolls. Jackson Jekyll and Frankie Stein. Both students at some kind of monster school about which Holger Munch did not know the first thing, not that it mattered. But the smile in her eyes and her warm, soft arms wrapping themselves around his neck did. Who cared what school a couple of dolls went to and whether her mother would get annoyed?

"Jackson Jekyll wants to be Frankie Stein's boyfriend, but she doesn't want to go out with him, because she's a tough girl who has big plans for the future."

"You mean she's independent?"

Marion looked up at him with her bright blue eyes. "Yes, that's what I mean."

Holger smiled to himself. It was like hearing his daughter's voice all over again. Little Marion was a true copy of Miriam and then some. Holger Munch was reminded of when they had walked Miriam to school for her first day. How proud he had been. His little girl had grown up and was going out into the world. How did she suddenly turn into a heavily made-up fifteen-year-old, listening to loud music behind a closed bedroom door, definitely no Daddy's girl anymore. Not to mention the next leap to twenty-five — how did *that* happen? The little girl who had clung to his leg, scared of all the other children, was now being fitted for her wedding dress, about to marry Marion's father, Johannes, who was a newly qualified doctor from Fredrikstad and a man whom Holger barely knew. Holger

Munch switched his attention back to his grandchild, who still thought he was the best grandfather in all the world and still wanted a hug and to sit on his lap.

"Now *you* be Jackson Jekyll," Marion said.

"What did you say, sweetheart?"

"Now you're Jackson Jekyll and I'm Frankie Stein."

"Don't you want a bit more pizza?"

"Frankie Stein doesn't want to eat anything, because she's on a diet. Please take the doll, Granddad."

Holger accepted the doll reluctantly while trying not to be distracted by all the messages that kept arriving on his cell phone. He was determined not to make the same mistakes twice. When he was with Marion, she would have his full attention. That was the way it was going to be, and the rest of the world would just have to wait.

"Say something, Granddad," Marion urged impatiently, balancing the thin monster doll on the table between leftover pizza slices.

"What do you want me to say?"

" 'Hey, Jackson, how are you?' " Marion said in her doll's voice.

"Do you want to go see a film?"

"Yes, that sounds like fun. What's on?"

"Pippi Longstocking," Holger Munch said.

186

"But that's a kids' movie." Frankie Stein sighed. "And that's not the voice you used before, Granddad."

"I'm sorry," Holger said, stroking his granddaughter's hair.

Holger saw a chance to sneak a peek at his phone. Anette had called and sent a text message. Kim had sent two text messages. And Kurt Eriksen, his family lawyer, had called several times. Holger wondered what he wanted. Marion was absorbed in playing, so he seized the opportunity to read the message from Anette.

We have the woman who made the dresses. And the customer. A man with an eagle tattoo on his neck. Have spoken to Kim. Call me.

So soon? Munch felt his policeman's heart beat a little faster. Sometimes the media could be useful — they'd gotten a hit almost immediately. He quickly skimmed the two messages from Kim.

Might have something on the eagle tattoo guy. Curry thinks he knows who it is. Call me.

And then just:

"Hi, where is Marion?"

Holger snapped back to reality to discover his daughter standing in front of him with a mildly irritated expression.

"Hello, Miriam. Marion? She's —"

Marion was not in her chair.

"She was just . . ."

He never managed to complete the sentence. Miriam had already gone to retrieve Marion, who had wandered farther into the restaurant as part of her game.

"Didn't we have a talk about buying her fewer toys?"

"Yes, but —"

"Get your things, Marion, we're going home."

"Already? But me and Granddad were going to get ice cream."

"That'll have to be some other day. Come on."

Miriam started packing up Marion's things. Holger got up to help.

"So how did the fitting go? Is everything all right?"

"It's not really what I wanted." Miriam sighed. "But they have a tailor, so we can alter it. I just hope they'll get it done in time."

"Yes, May twelfth is not far away."

"No, you can say that again. Come on, Marion, we have to run now. Daddy is parked illegally. Say bye-bye to Granddad."

"Bye-bye, Granddad." The little girl smiled and gave him a big hug. "Promise you'll practice playing for next time?"

"I promise." Holger returned her smile.

"Will you be going on your own?" Miriam said.

"To what?"

"To the wedding. Will you be on your own, or will you be bringing someone?"

Bring someone to the wedding? It hadn't even crossed his mind. He didn't quite know why, but suddenly Karen from the nursing home sprang to mind. Her face lit up every time he visited. But take someone to a wedding for your first date? No, that would be completely wrong.

"I'm coming on my own," Holger said.

"Why don't you bring Mia? I heard she's back. I would love her to come. I've tried calling her, but her cell phone doesn't seem to work."

Bring Mia, now there was a thought. And he knew that Miriam and Mia liked each other.

"She has a new phone," he said. "But I don't mind asking her myself. In fact, it's a very good idea."

"Good, then I'll add her to the list," Miriam said, and almost smiled before she became her usual serious self. "And another thing. It looks like Johannes and I may have to take a trip to Fredrikstad next weekend. Could you have Marion?"

"Of course. She can spend the whole weekend with me. It would be great."

"Okay, I'll call you."

Miriam herded Marion toward the exit.

"Bye-bye, Granddad."

"Bye-bye, Marion."

Holger Munch waved good-bye until the door slammed shut behind them. Then he went to pay the bill.

Once he got outside, he could barely wait to call his colleagues. His break from the world had lasted long enough. They had news about the dresses.

Kim answered his phone after the first ring. "Hello?"

"What have we got?" Munch said.

"Anette and Mia found the woman who made the dresses. A seamstress from Sandvika."

"And?"

"The customer was a man in his mid-forties. Eagle tattoo on his neck. Ten dresses."

"Ten dresses?"

"Correct."

Damn.

"And we know who he is?"

"Curry thinks so. Like I said, we're not a hundred percent, but how many people in their mid-forties have a large eagle tattoo on their neck? He fits the description. Roger Bakken. He doesn't have a record, but Curry ran into him once when he was working on the Drug Squad."

"What kind of guy are we talking about?"

"A drug runner. Picking up and delivering packages, you know."

"That sounds like it could be the break we've been waiting for."

"I should say so."

"Do we have an address?"

"Last known address is a hostel down in Grønland. That is, if we're talking about the same Roger Bakken."

"Have we dispatched a team?"

"Mia and Anette are there now."

"I'll be there in five minutes," Holger said, hanging up.

22

Mia held the door open for Anette and followed her inside the dark reception area.
Over the years Mia Krüger had seen her
fair share of hostels, and, like all of them,
this one had the familiar oppressive feeling
of hopelessness within its walls. Last stop
before the final destination. A place you
ended up only once nobody wanted you.

"Hello?" Anette called out behind the
counter in the faded lobby, but no one came
out.

"Can't we just go straight up?"

Mia walked across to a door that appeared
to lead upstairs and pushed on the handle;
it was locked.

"I think we have to be buzzed in," Anette
said, and she peered behind the reception
desk. "Doesn't a place like this usually have
an entry phone? Surely they would want to
have some control over who's coming and
going?"

Mia Krüger looked around. The lobby was sparsely furnished. A small table. Two spindle-back chairs. A dried-out palm in a corner.

"Hello?" Anette called again. "This is the police. Is anyone here?"

Finally a door opened behind the counter and a skinny, elderly man appeared.

"What do you want?"

"Police. Violent Crimes Section," Mia said, placing her ID card on the counter.

The man looked at the two women with skepticism. He glanced at the photograph of Mia while he polished off the sandwich he held in his hand.

"Uh-huh," the man said, picking at his teeth with his finger. "What can I do for you?"

"We're looking for a man named Roger Bakken," Anette said.

"Bakken, hmmm," the man said, glancing at a ledger lying in front of him.

"Roger Bakken," Mia said impatiently. "Mid-forties, large eagle tattoo on his neck."

"Oh, him," the skinny man said, now sucking at his teeth with his tongue. "I'm afraid you're too late."

"What do you mean?"

The thin man smirked slightly. He seemed almost pleased to throw a monkey wrench into their plans. Clearly not a big fan of the police.

"Checked out about a month ago."

"Checked out?"

"Dead. All gone. Suicide," the thin man said as he took a seat behind the counter.

"Are you messing with us?" Mia said irritably. "By the way, I assume everything here is in order? Nobody staying here who shouldn't be? And you don't allow drugs here, do you?"

The thin man got up again, smilier and more obliging now. "No, of course we don't. He killed himself, jumped from the roof and hit the tarmac. That is, if we're talking about the same guy."

"Roger Bakken. Mid-forties. A tattoo on his neck."

"That sounds like him." The man nodded. "Tragic story, but he wouldn't be the first one. That's life. Or it is for these guys."

"How did it happen?" Anette asked.

"Jumped from the balcony in the lounge on the eighth floor."

"You have a balcony? What kind of place is this?"

The thin man gave a shrug. "What can we do? Nail the windows shut? People have a right to make decisions about their own lives, even if they don't belong to the upper echelons of society, don't you think?"

Mia decided to ignore the sarcasm. "Please can we see his room?"

"Sorry, someone else's already living there. We have a waiting list of several months."

"Did he have any family? Has anyone been by to collect his things?"

"Nope," the thin man said. "We called the police, and someone came to pick up the body. Not many of our residents have family. Or if they do, then the family doesn't want to know about them."

"Do you still have his stuff?"

"It's in a box in the basement, as far as I know."

"Thank you," Mia said impatiently.

"You're welcome," the thin man said.

Mia drummed her fingers on the counter. She had forgotten all of this. What it was like. To be a police officer in the capital. To be back in the world. She missed her house. Her island. The view of the sea.

Come to me, Mia, come.

"I was thanking you for your help," she said at length.

"You what?"

"For getting his stuff and handing it over without us having to waste the whole day."

The thin man looked surly, but then he

nodded and shuffled to the back room.

"Shit," Mia muttered under her breath.

"What's wrong?" Anette said.

"What do you mean?"

"You don't normally let people like that get to you."

"I slept badly," Mia said by way of excuse.

At that very moment, the door opened and Holger Munch appeared.

"What have we got?" He sounded breathless as he reached the counter.

"Bad news."

"What is it?"

"Roger Bakken killed himself a month ago." Anette heaved a sigh.

"Before Pauline disappeared?"

Mia nodded.

"Damn!" Holger exclaimed.

His cell rang. He stared at the display for a moment before he decided to answer the call. The thin man reappeared from the back room carrying a box.

"Here we are. That was all he had." He placed the box on the counter in front of them.

"Is there a cell phone? Computer?"

The thin man shrugged his shoulders again. "Never checked."

Mia produced a card from her back pocket and put it on the counter.

"We'll be taking it with us," she said. "Call me if you have any questions."

"What the hell?"

Anette and Mia turned simultaneously, startled at Holger's sudden outburst on the phone. He ended the call and turned to them with a grim expression on his face.

"Is that all?" he asked, nodding toward the box.

"Yep."

"Who were you talking to?" Mia asked curiously.

"My family lawyer."

"Problem?"

"I have to go see him now. I'll meet you at the office."

Holger Munch slipped his cell phone into the pocket of his duffel coat and held the door open for his two colleagues.

23

As Lukas rode his bicycle, he felt the lovely spring air on his face. He was in high spirits today; he had risen early, carried out his chores, morning prayer and housework. It was his responsibility to keep the chapel nice and tidy, an important job that he valued. To describe morning prayer as a chore was wrong. Morning prayer was a joy. Sometimes he would even start praying the moment he woke up, while he was still in bed, even though he really ought to get dressed and have his breakfast first. But he just couldn't help himself. It felt so right. Talking to God. For that to be his first activity as soon as he had opened his eyes. He started every prayer by expressing gratitude. He thanked God for taking care of his nearest and dearest. For Pastor Simon. For everyone up in the forest. Occasionally he wondered if he ought to have included his former families in his thanks, but to be honest he could no longer remember their faces. His birth family who had given him up, his foster family who hadn't cared about him all that much, he was not angry with any of them — why on earth would he be angry? *Forgive them, Father, they know not what they do.* It was a no-brainer as far as Lukas was concerned. If he had not grown up the way he had, he never would have ended up at the campsite in Sørlandet, never had the chance to be completely happy in union with God and Pastor Simon. Lukas grinned from ear to ear and trod harder on the bike pedals. Why would he be dissatisfied with anything? He had no cause. Life was wonderful. Perfect. He chuckled to himself and whispered a short prayer. A thank-you. Thank you, God, for the birds in the trees and this fine road. Thank you, God, for spring and all the other seasons. Thank you, God, for making me important, for finding Pastor Simon for me, because I wake up and fall asleep every day with joy in my heart. He said this last part out loud as he felt the warmth and the light course through his blood. The pastor was in direct contact with God; Lukas could bear witness to that himself, it was not nonsense. He had seen it happen several times. He had seen God in the room. Thank you, God, for purifying me. Thank you, God, for the beautiful wildflowers along the road. Thank you, God, for the Whisperers. Thank you, God, for the Shouters. Thank you, God, for making my life complete.

Lukas got off his bicycle, deployed the kickstand, and sat down on a rock. They met in various places, and this was one of them. Not that they'd met many times. This was perhaps the eighth time, wasn't it? The woman came by car. The last time had been some weeks ago. Normally she would turn up, open the window, hand him the envelope, and drive off without saying anything. However, the last time had been different. She'd gotten out of the car, lit a cigarette, and chatted with him briefly, not about anything important, just about the weather and things like that. He did not know how old she was — thirty-five or thereabouts. She was always quite well dressed, with ankle boots and a coat or a smart jacket, and she wore bright red lipstick and had a lovely smile. She had long dark hair and a straight nose, and she always wore sunglasses whatever the weather. The woman was clearly not one of the initiated, Lukas had no doubt about that. You could tell from the way she dressed. Lipstick and ankle boots and sunglasses, even cigarettes.

In the Bible she would have been a whore, but it was exactly as Pastor Simon had said: *Sometimes the path to the light goes through silent darkness.* Lukas felt that he and the woman balanced each other out, with her on one side, himself on the other. Both messengers. Brought together by God, for God. He got up and stretched his arms, kicked a pebble on the ground into the bushes. Hummed a little to himself. He'd started doing that recently. He did not sing out loud, just quietly to himself, a melodious chant. *Eternity has already begun.* He clearly remembered the first time Pastor Simon had said it. It was the third day of the Sørlandet camp, after Lukas had been saved and found God. *Eternity has already begun.* Lukas went on humming and looked up at the trees again. A nuthatch was fluffing its feathers. Farther in, he could hear a woodpecker hammering away. Last Saturday he had seen an owl up at the house in the forest. *Lux domus.* Many people did not like owls, they regarded them as birds of ill omen, but Lukas knew better. The weekend had been just as rewarding as he had expected, perhaps even better. Nils had done a good job in the forest. It really had become a paradise.

A car pulled up and stopped a short

distance from him. It was not the same car as the last time, but it was her; he recognized her through the windshield. Her long dark hair, drawn back into a ponytail, lipstick, but no sunglasses this time. It looked as if she had no intention of getting out of the car today. She simply summoned him, opened the window, and stuck out the envelope. She scooted around a little nervously, as if something were wrong. As if she were in a hurry and just wanted to get this over and done with as quickly as possible. Lukas held out his hand for the envelope, and at that moment she turned to him, glanced at him briefly before turning away again.

Lukas's heart skipped a beat. *Her eyes were two different colors. One was brown. The other blue.* Lukas had never seen anything like it in his whole life. He stood frozen holding the envelope, unable to utter a single word, and for the first time in a very, very long time, he felt a kind of terror creep over him, drops of something dark in his happy blood. The woman with the different-colored eyes closed the window and rejoined the traffic on Maridalsveien. Soon she was gone again, just as quickly as she had appeared.

24

Mia Krüger hauled the large cardboard box into the office and closed the door behind her. The usually busy offices were quiet; no one was there. She had lost Anette along the way — Anette had to help her daughter with something and would come back later. Mia had said that there was no need, she was happy to go through the items on her own. Anette had reeked of guilt, like everyone torn between the demands of family and work, but Mia had reassured her that it wasn't a problem. She had promised to call if she found anything important. The truth was that Mia preferred to work alone. It made thinking easier. Going deep. Seeing the connection. She had nothing against Anette or indeed any of her colleagues — they did an excellent job — but every now and again being surrounded by people got to be too much for her and her brain refused to work as it should.

Mia carried the box to the incident room and put it on the table. She sat down and stared at the wall. As always, Ludvig had put up pictures from both cases, Post-it notes and arrows, names and questions. Pauline and Johanne. *Dresses? Who?* At least they knew the answer to that now, even though they'd gotten no further than a cardboard box left behind by a dead man with an eagle tattoo on his neck. Mia removed the lid and spread out the box's contents on the large table. There was not much in it. A few photographs. One showing a dog. A golden retriever. A guy on a fishing trip, his face not included in the photograph, only the large salmon he held in his hands. A car. *Who on earth keeps a photograph of their car?* Mia thought as she delved deeper into the box. Underneath a pile of bills, she found what she was looking for. A laptop and an iPhone. She tried turning on the iPhone. The battery was dead. She searched the box for the charger but didn't find one, nor one for the laptop; when she tried turning that on, it, too, had run out of power.

Mia was heading to her office to fetch her own charger when she heard noise from one of the offices farther down the corridor. It would appear that not everyone had gone home after all. The new nerd was still there . . . what was his name again? Gabriel. Gabriel, that was it. Mia was annoyed that her brain still refused to work properly, her diet of pills and alcohol on the island having left its traces, nausea and dizziness, no appetite, and jumbled thoughts that refused to straighten out. She walked down the corridor to Gabriel's office and made up her mind to start exercising again. She used to be in great shape once, but that was a long time ago. She wondered if Chen was still in town. Probably. But he was pissed off with her. Or was *she* pissed off with *him*? She couldn't remember. She made a mental note. Call Chen. Get back to exercising. Get the blood flowing through her muscles. Get her brain working again.

"Hello, are you still here?"

Mia popped her head around without knocking. The young man with the blond hair jumped.

"Oh, I didn't hear you," he said apologetically.

Mia thought she detected a hint of blushing in his cheeks.

"Sorry, my mistake." She smiled. "I was just wondering if you could help me with something."

"Of course." Gabriel nodded. "Do you

mind if I finish connecting these?" He pointed to some cables lying on the floor.

"Take all the time you need," Mia said.

"I thought the police were supposed to be experts," Gabriel told her as he crawled under the desk with the cables in his hand. "But whoever installed this had no idea what they were doing."

"Don't ask me, I don't know anything about computers. I'm down in the incident room."

"Okay, I'll be with you in a minute."

Mia stopped by her own office on her way back and picked up the chargers, for both the laptop and the iPhone. Who keeps photographs of their car and their dog? Mia had no photographs at the office. She had put everything she owned into storage when she moved to Hitra. Paid three years' rental in advance. She did not want to have to think about her personal possessions now. Her photographs, her parents, or Sigrid. She pushed the thought aside and continued to the incident room. She connected Roger Bakken's laptop and phone to the chargers and went out on Munch's smoking terrace to get a bit of fresh air. The evening twilight was descending over the city, and the air was growing colder. She pulled her leather jacket around herself more tightly and missed her knitted cap. Why was she acting like this? Behaving like a spoiled brat? Was she starting to feel sorry for herself? Now? She'd never complained a single day in her life. She had a sudden urge for a cigarette. She'd never smoked, but it seemed the right thing to do up here. Smoking in order to think, that was what Holger did. And where was he anyway? She checked her watch; it was two hours since he had gone to see his lawyer. She hoped it was nothing serious; they had enough on their plate as it was.

"Ahem, Mia?"

Gabriel had appeared in the incident room. Mia went back inside to join him. Suddenly she felt bad for the guy, new to working with the police. Had anyone bothered showing him the ropes? Told him what he was here to do?

"How are you, Gabriel?" she said, sitting down on the big table.

The young hacker looked away and then at the floor; it definitely looked as if he was blushing. He really was a delicate little petal, Mia thought and produced a packet of lozenges from her pocket.

"Oh, I'm all right," Gabriel said.

"You're settling in? Do you have everything you need?"

"I've just finished installing the equipment. Looks good. In fact, I'm going to a meeting in Grønland later. Orientation. Someone named Møller?"

"Ah, yes, we call him Hat Trick," Mia said. "He's good."

"Excellent." Gabriel nodded. "I haven't seen police databases before. It'll be fun to see how they work."

Mia smiled. "You're a hacker and you've never had a look at our databases? I find that hard to believe. Or sneaked a peek at Interpol? Come on, you must have done that."

Gabriel reddened again and looked tongue-tied. "I don't know. . . ."

"I'm just pulling your leg, relax. I don't care. Do I look as if I care?"

Mia offered him a lozenge. Gabriel took one and sat down on a chair. Mia liked this boy. Nice and clever. Polite and shy. It was good to be around such people again. In fact, she was starting to feel better. Her brain was recalibrating.

"What can I do for you?"

"Those two," Mia said, pointing to the laptop and the iPhone currently charging.

"Whose are they?"

"Roger Bakken. The guy who ordered the dresses the girls were wearing."

"The one with the tattoo?" Gabriel asked.

"Yes. You're well informed."

Gabriel smiled. "I record all the unit's phone calls, text messages, and conversations. Everything shows up on my computer."

Mia took another lozenge. "Really? Anything new?"

Gabriel gave her a strange look. "Are *you* asking *me*? I haven't been here long."

"It's been a while since I was last here," she said. "But seriously? Everything anyone says and all our text messages?"

"Yep. Plus, all our cell phones have a tracker so I can see where everyone is. Security and hypercommunication."

"Good God. Quite useful, though."

"Absolutely," the young man agreed.

"So when Curry calls gay chat lines at night, we'll know about it the next day, is that right?"

Gabriel looked uncomfortable. He wasn't sure if she was joking or she was up to something.

"In theory, yes," he said, his cheeks rather red once more.

"I'm just kidding."

She got up and gave him a pat on the shoulder. Gabriel went over to the laptop and the cell phone, sat down on the floor, and turned on both devices. He continued to stare at them while they slowly came to life. The iPhone was up and running first, asking for a PIN code. The laptop followed soon after; that, too, was password-protected.

"Will it be easy to access it?"

"Yes."

"Can you do it?"

"Now?"

"Yes, please."

"Sure."

Gabriel got up, went to his office, and returned with a memory stick. Mia watched as the young hacker went to work on the computer.

"I have a program called Ophcrack on this," Gabriel said as he inserted the memory stick into the laptop. "All I have to do is change the start-up sequence so that it reads the memory stick before it reads the hard drive, understand?"

Mia nodded. She was not the sharpest person in the world when it came to computers, but this much she understood. Gabriel turned off the laptop and turned it back on again.

"There, as it starts up, it'll first read the memory stick, and then it'll load Ophcrack."

Mia watched while Gabriel worked.

"Right. As you can see, this machine has two users, Roger and Randi."

"Who is Randi?"

Gabriel shrugged. "Perhaps he had a girl-friend?"

"Remind me to check that out. Randi."

"Will do. Which password do you want me to crack?"

"Let's start with Roger."

"Okay," Gabriel said, pointing to the screen. "Take a look at the columns saying 'LM Pwd 1' and 'LM Pwd 2.' If the password is more than seven characters long, and it probably is, the first seven characters will appear in the column LM Pwd 1 and the rest in LM Pwd 2. Now all I have to do is select the user."

Gabriel selected *"Roger"* and clicked a command in the program, *"Crack."*

"And presto."

Mia waited in tense anticipation for a few seconds while the program ran. Soon the password appeared on the screen in front of them:

"FordMustang67."

The car in the photograph. If she hadn't had this young genius to help her, she probably could have cracked it herself. Not in a few seconds, obviously, but eventually.

"Is this something everyone can do?" Mia

wanted to know.

"Ophcrack is freeware. It's available on the Net, so as long as you know what you're looking for, then yes, everyone can do it." Gabriel turned the computer on and off again.

The log-in screen appeared, and he was about to type in the password when Mia's phone rang. The display said it was Holger Munch. She went out on the smoking terrace to answer it.

"Mia here."

"Hi, Mia, it's Holger."

"Where are you?"

"In the car. Listen, there's something we need to talk about."

"Okay, right, go on, then."

"Not on the phone. Let's go for a beer."

"You want a beer?"

"No, I don't want a beer, but I do need to talk to you. It's personal. Not work. You can have a beer; I'll have a Farris."

"Okay," Mia said. "Where do you want to meet?"

"Are you at work?"

"Yes."

"How about Justisen in a few minutes?"

"No problem, Holger. See you there."

"See you soon," Holger said, and ended the call.

How strange. Holger had never minded discussing problems on the phone before, Mia thought. Then she remembered what Gabriel had just told her. Their phones were being monitored — for their own safety, of course. Once again she hoped that nothing serious had happened.

"I'm afraid I need to leave," she told Gabriel when she came back inside.

"Okay." The hacker nodded. "The laptop is up and running now. You want me to crack the iPhone as well?"

"That would be super," Mia said with a smile. "Will you be working late?"

"I'll stick around for a while," Gabriel said. "I prefer to work nights anyway, and there's a lot for me to learn."

"If something spectacular crops up, then call me, okay? If not, we'll go over it tomorrow."

"Understood," Gabriel said.

"Thanks for your help," Mia said.

She walked down the steps, pulled the jacket around herself more tightly, and made her way to Møllergata.

25

Holger Munch was sitting in Justisen's beer garden under one of the heat lamps. He had just lit a cigarette and was looking anxiously at his phone, typing a message, but put it down the moment Mia appeared.

"Hello, Mia."

"Hello, Holger."

"Is it all right with you that we're outside? I've already ordered."

"Sure," Mia said, pulling out a chair.

It was an Oslo evening at the end of April and, truth be told, still too cold to be sitting outside, but the heat lamp helped. Mia knew there was very little point in sitting indoors with Holger. He smoked nonstop, so she might as well make herself comfortable outside from the start. She took a blanket and covered her legs.

"What have you ordered?"

"Just a Farris and a sandwich for me and a beer for you. I didn't know if you wanted anything else."

"No thanks, a beer would be great," Mia said.

Holger glanced around the charming, rustic beer garden. "I haven't been here for ages."

"Me either." Mia smiled.

They both knew when the last time had been, but neither was prepared to say. A glance and a nod were enough. They had sat here, at the same table, two years ago while the allegations against her were being investigated. Mia had been down in the dumps, and Holger was the only person she could talk to. Somehow a photographer from *Dagbladet* had found them and started taking photographs, refusing to leave them alone. Holger had politely but very firmly escorted the photographer out of the bar. Mia had to smile at the memory. He really had been very chivalrous. She'd needed him then. This time he needed her.

"I wasn't trying to make a drama out of it. I just haven't got the energy to do this on the phone. It's not serious — I mean, it's not as important as the case — but all the same I would like your advice," Holger said.

A waitress appeared with their order. A bottle of mineral water and a prawn sand-wich for Holger, a beer for Mia.

215

"Hope you enjoy it, and just let me know if you need anything else," the waitress said before she disappeared.

"And besides, we haven't yet celebrated that we're back." Holger smiled and raised his glass. "Cheers."

"Cheers." Mia smiled, too, and took a sip of her beer.

She was loath to admit it, but it tasted wonderful. It hit just the right spot. She had to be careful, she was only too aware of it, but at this moment in time it was the way it was going to be. She deserved to relax. Holger ate his prawn sandwich without saying very much. He pushed his plate aside when he'd finished and lit another cigarette.

"Did you find anything useful among Bakken's belongings?"

"A laptop and an iPhone," Mia told him.

"Good. Anything of interest?"

"Don't know yet. Gabriel is checking them out as we speak."

"What do you make of him?"

Mia gave a light shrug and took another sip of her beer. "I haven't had time to talk to him all that much, but he seems like a nice guy. Young, of course, but that's not necessarily bad."

"I have a good feeling about him," Holger said, blowing smoke up into the air. "Sometimes it can be wise to recruit from the outside. A fresh pair of eyes not tainted by police thinking. We tend to develop tunnel vision, don't you agree?"

"You might be right." Mia nodded. "Certainly seems like he knows his stuff."

Holger chuckled. "Ha, ha, yes, he's not underqualified, to put it mildly. I got his name from MI6 in London. He cracked the code, you know, that challenge they posted on the Net last year?"

Mia shrugged her shoulders again. "So you went to see your lawyer?"

"Yes, damn him." Holger heaved a sigh. "Don't really know where to start. Like I said, it's not difficult, but even so, I've had a lot going on recently. Miriam is getting married, and —"

"Good God, that's wonderful, I didn't know."

Mia realized it made her really happy. She liked Miriam enormously. They had hit it off the moment they met. She knew that the relationship between Miriam and her father was strained, but she had always imagined that it would work itself out, given time.

"Oh, yes, it's great," Holger agreed.

"Am I right in thinking she's still with

217

Johannes? Has he finished medical school now?"

Holger nodded.

"So are we playing Twenty Questions?" Mia teased.

"What do you mean?"

"Do you want me to guess what it is you wanted to talk to me about? Is that how it works?"

Holger chuckled to himself. "You haven't changed much, have you? Just as lippy, still not showing respect, eh? I *am* your boss — you know that, don't you? The way this works is that you shut up and do whatever I tell you."

"That's not going to happen," Mia assured him.

"It's a bit awkward. I don't know how to say it. It really bugs me."

"Okay, start at the beginning," Mia said.

"Right," Holger said, taking another drag of his cigarette. "You know my mother?"

"Yes, what about her?"

"You know I moved her to a home a few years ago?"

"Yes, what about it? Is she not well?"

"Oh, no, there's nothing wrong with her. Her legs aren't so good, so at times she uses a wheelchair, but that's not the problem."

"Does she not like it up there?"

"She didn't to begin with, but that changed quickly. She met other people in the same situation, made friends, joined a sewing club, so no, that's not it. Only she has suddenly gotten it into her head that she's a Christian."

"What do you mean? Christian Christian? Has she found God?"

Holger nodded.

"Wow, I thought you came from a family of atheists."

"That's what's so strange, I've never heard her talk about religion or anything like that, but then she changed from one day to the next. Started to attend services every week at some church, along with friends of hers from the sewing circle."

"It might be her age," Mia said. "What would we know about getting old? Perhaps there's no harm in it? Having something to believe in?"

Holger stubbed out the cigarette and lit another one. "She has decided to leave all her money to the church."

"No shit?"

"Quite." He threw up his hands. "So do I go along with it?"

"Are we talking about a lot of money?"

"No, not a whole lot, but even so. There is her apartment in Majorstua. Her cabin in

Larvik. And she has plenty in the bank — she hasn't spent any of the money my father left her. It's not that I care about the money, but I had always imagined that it would be passed on . . . you know, to Marion, so that she's provided for. Family inheritance and all that."

Mia understood. Holger had a lovely but dangerously close relationship to his granddaughter. Mia was convinced that if anyone told him to cut off his arm for her, he would do it without hesitation. Without an anesthetic. Here you are, one arm, do you need another one?

"Ouch, that's a tricky one," she said aloud.

"Yes, it is, isn't it? So do I go along with it?"

"Well, it's complicated."

"I do understand that it's just money, and seriously, we have more important things to worry about. Two six-year-old girls are dead and another eight dresses are out there. It's a goddamned nightmare. I don't even want to think about it. I'm constantly looking over my shoulder, I can barely sleep, I lie awake waiting for the phone to ring telling me that another girl has disappeared. Do you understand?"

Of course she did. She felt exactly the same.

"So that's why I didn't want to do this on the phone. It's hardly relevant in the greater scheme of things. And I didn't want anyone to know that I'm spending my time on anything other than catching this bastard."

"Let's hope we're talking about just the one," Mia said.

"Do you think there could be more?"

'Well, we need to keep an open mind. I have been a bit —" Mia said, but interrupted herself.

"Been what?"

"Oh, I don't know what you would call it . . . not quite focused. I can't get into it. I can't see the picture. There's something behind the pattern, I know it, it's screaming at me, it's as clear as daylight, but I can't see it — if you understand what I mean."

"It'll come," Munch reassured her. "You've been out of the loop. That's all it is."

"Probably," Mia said softly. "Let's hope so. To be honest, I feel a bit useless. I feel sorry for myself. I act like a brat. That's not me. I hate myself when I'm like this. If it turns out I can't focus, promise me you'll take me off the case?"

"I need you, Mia," Munch said. "There's a reason I brought you back."

"To sort out your family problems?"

"You know something, Mia? Screw you."

"Screw you, too, Holger. I was doing fine where I was."

The two colleagues exchanged an affectionate look that needed no further explanation.

Holger lit another cigarette while Mia took another sip of her beer and tightened the blanket around her.

"Hønefoss was in 2006, wasn't it?" she asked.

"September," Holger replied. "Why?"

"If she were still alive, she would have started school this year. Have you thought about that?"

"The thought had occurred to me," Holger said. "Gabriel said something that got me thinking."

"What was it?"

"That we might be looking for a teacher, something along those lines."

"That's not a bad idea. Perhaps he has the makings of a police officer after all."

"You don't think she's still alive?" Holger asked.

"What do you mean?"

"It was the way you said it: 'If she were still alive.' The girl who disappeared. We never found her. She *might* still be alive."

"No," Mia said.

"You sound so sure."

"She's not alive."

Holger glanced at his cell phone. "I have to run. Got some paperwork to do before I go to bed. Mikkelson is pestering me."

"I thought Anette was dealing with that side of things."

"She does as much as she can." Holger got up and took out his wallet.

"My treat," Mia insisted.

"Are you sure?"

"Of course. I understand your family is about to run out of money, it's the least I can do."

"Ha, ha," he laughed.

"Will there be a full briefing tomorrow morning?"

"I hadn't planned on one. Let's see what we get from the laptop and the iPhone."

"I'll keep you posted," Mia promised.

"Yes, please. See you later."

She stayed behind contemplating the empty beer glass on the table in front of her after Munch had left. She fancied another one but wasn't convinced that it was a wise move. The hotel room would be a better option. Go to bed early in clean sheets. She drummed her fingers on the edge of the glass while she ran the case through her head to make her brain wake up.

"Can I get you anything else?"

The waitress was back, regarding Mia with a smile on her lips.

"Yes, another beer, please. And a shot of Ratzeputz schnapps."

"Certainly." The girl turned and disappeared.

"Mia?"

A familiar and yet unknown face appeared behind a glowing cigarette in the courtyard. A woman Mia's own age came over to her table.

"Don't you recognize me? Susanne. From Åsgårdstrand?"

The woman bent down and gave Mia a warm hug. Of course. Susanne Hval. She had lived a few doors down the street. One year younger than Sigrid and Mia. A long time ago, the three of them had been close friends.

"Hi, Susanne. Sorry, I was completely lost in my work."

"I understand. I hope I'm not intruding. Is it all right if I sit down?"

"Yes, of course," Mia said, gesturing to the chair Holger had just vacated.

"Well, who would have thought it?" Susanne laughed. "How long has it been?"

"Far too long."

Her old friend gazed at Mia with a big

smile on her face. "I haven't seen you since . . . Well, I saw you in the newspaper — do you mind my bringing that up?"

"No, no, it's fine," Mia assured her.

"So what happened? After the investigation and everything?"

"I went on holiday."

Mia had thought about Susanne several times over the years, especially after Sigrid died. They had met again at Sigrid's funeral, but Mia hadn't seen her since or contacted her either. There had just been so much to do. It felt good to see her old friend again.

The waitress returned with the beer and the Ratzeputz schnapps.

"Do you want anything?" she asked.

Susanne shook her head. "I have a beer inside. I'm here with some people from work."

She said the latter to Mia with a hint of pride in her voice.

"So you've moved to Oslo?" Mia asked.

"Yes, four years ago."

"Great, what do you do?"

"I work at the National Theater." Susanne smiled.

"Wow, congratulations."

Mia could vaguely remember Susanne being very keen for her to join an amateur theater group in Horten, but fortunately

Mia had managed to get out of it. Being onstage was most definitely not for her. The very thought made her shudder.

"I'm only an assistant director, but even so, it's a lot of fun. We're about to open with *Hamlet*. Stein Winge is directing. It's going to be a hit, I think. You should go. I have spare tickets for the first night. Would you like to?"

Mia smiled faintly. She recognized Susanne now. The energetic, open girl everyone liked so much. The warm gaze it had always been difficult to say no to.

"Perhaps," she hedged. "I'm quite busy at work at the moment, but let's see if I can find the time."

Susanne laughed. "God, it's so good to see you. Listen, why don't I go get my beer? The actors only care about themselves. They'll never notice if I'm gone."

"You do that." Mia smiled.

"You wait here, don't go away."

Susanne quickly stubbed out her cigarette and half ran into the bar to fetch her drink.

26

Tobias Iversen had set the alarm clock for six and woken up as soon as it sounded. He quickly reached over to the bedside table to turn it off, as he didn't want the shrill noise to wake anyone else in the house. His younger brother, Torben, was not at home. He was having a sleepover with a friend from school. Tobias slipped out of bed and got dressed as quietly as he could. Everything was ready; he had been planning this trip for several days. His knapsack was all packed and waiting at the foot of his bed. He didn't know for how long he would be away, but he had brought extra supplies just to be on the safe side. He had a tent that slept two people, his sleeping bag, a camping stove and some food, his knife, a spare pair of socks and spare sweater, in case it got cold, his compass, and an old map he'd found in the loft. He was all set to go exploring and could not wait to get out of the house.

In the days after he and his brother had found the girl hanging from the tree in the forest, being at home had been slightly less bad. His mother and stepfather had had a lot of visitors, mostly police officers, who asked questions and kept probing, and his mother and stepfather had been on their best behavior; they had even tidied the house. The living room looked completely different now — it even smelled nice. The police officers had been really kind. Treated him almost like a hero, told him how good he'd been, how he'd done all the right things. Tobias had been almost embarrassed. He wasn't used to so much praise. The police officers had been around for several days — not during the nights but from early in the morning to late at night. They had cordoned off the area with red-and-white plastic tape that said POLICE to keep nosy people at bay. And there were plenty of those, from both the village and elsewhere. Farther down the road, there'd been cars from TV stations, there'd been helicopters in the air and plenty of journalists and photographers around, and several of them had wanted to talk to Tobias. In the days following the discovery, the family's phone did not stop ringing, and he had heard his mother talk to somebody about money, that they would get paid lots if the boys were prepared to be interviewed, but the police had said no, prohibited it, and, to be honest, Tobias was relieved at that. People had already started to treat him differently during break time at school. Most of them, especially the girls, thought it was cool — he'd become a kind of local celebrity — but it had also sparked trouble, because some of the boys, especially the two new ones from Oslo, had grown jealous and started saying bad things about him. Tobias asked his mother if he could take a few days off school, because the journalists would come to his school as well, taking pictures of him while he kicked a football around and calling out to him to come over to the fence. He didn't, obviously; the police had told him not to talk to anyone about what he'd seen, and he wanted to do as the police officers said. Dressed in white plastic hazmat suits, they had searched the whole forest. Tobias sat on a chair outside watching them. No one else was allowed to do that. Even NRK and TV2 and everyone else had to wait at the end of the road behind the cordon and could only shout whenever someone drove past. But he was the one who had found her, and he knew every tree stump in the forest, and he soon got to know the police officers. There was one named Kim, one named Curry, and another one named Anette, and then there was their boss, who had a beard and whose name was Holger. The boss had not been there very often, only once, but it was he who had interviewed Tobias and he who'd decided that no one was allowed to talk to anyone about what the boys had seen. Tobias had spoken mostly to the police officer named Kim, and quite a lot with the one named Curry. Tobias liked them both enormously. They hadn't treated him like a child, but more like a grown-up. Often they would leave the forest and walk down to the yard where he sat to ask him questions. Were there usually many people in the woods? Had he built the little hut inside? Questions about their neighbors. Did he remember seeing anything suspicious recently? On the first evening, a psychologist had visited the house with an offer of counseling, so he'd chatted with her for a little while. That had been all right, but he had not been particularly upset at finding the girl, because it had taken a few days before the truth of what he'd seen began to sink in. That was when it hit him. He'd been sitting on the steps when it dawned on him. That it was real.

That the girl in the tree, whose name was Johanne, had had parents, and a sister, and aunts and uncles and grandparents and friends and neighbors, and that now she was gone and they would never see her again. And that someone had done this to her on purpose, not far from his house, and Tobias had shuddered at the thought that it could have been him hanging from the tree. Or his younger brother. He had felt really bad inside and had to go upstairs to lie down in his bed, and that night he'd had terrible nightmares. About people putting a jump rope around his neck and hanging him and shooting sharp arrows at him, and he'd heard Torben calling out for help, but he was unable to free himself, he was trapped, and he struggled frantically, unable to breathe. Tobias had woken up covered in sweat and with his hair plastered to the pillow.

The police had spent several days in the area, and then they appeared to have finished and they left again. The cordons down the road had also been removed, and some of the journalists came to their house and rang the doorbell, but his mother did not let them in. Tobias was convinced that she really wanted to, he believed some of them had offered a lot of money, but the senior police officer, Holger, the fat one with the beard and the nice eyes, had been very strict.

Now, Tobias had been planning this trip for a long time, and his timing was perfect. He was off from school, and for once his younger brother wasn't at home. When he was ready, he put on his knapsack and crept out the back door without making a sound.

He'd been to Litjønna before, so he knew the route, but he'd packed the map and the compass just to be on the safe side. He might decide to make a detour along the way. Matches? Had he remembered the matches? He took off the knapsack and checked the side pockets. Yes, there they were. Matches were important. The nights would be cold without a campfire. Not that he intended to be gone all night, but you never knew. He might decide to stay in the forest and never return to this gloomy house. How about that? Never go back. That would serve them right. It was a silly idea, and he knew it. His younger brother would be back tomorrow. Tobias loved being with his brother, but it was nice to have some time to himself.

Tobias put the knapsack on again and closed the door softly behind him. The fresh spring air struck him outside in the yard.

He moved quickly across the open terrain and entered the forest. He chose a different route from his usual one so that he did not have to pass their homemade hut or the place where they'd found the girl. He didn't want to think about that right now, he did not want to feel scared again, he had to be tough now, he was on his own and embarking on an expedition, he could not afford to be scared. Tobias chose the route along the river until he reached a path he could follow quite a long way into the forest. When he'd been walking for about an hour, he took off his knapsack and ate some breakfast. It was important to keep his energy levels up, and he hadn't wanted to make any noise in the kitchen back home. The forest was nice and dry; it had not been raining for a while. He sat down on a tree stump and enjoyed the view while he munched his sandwich and drank some juice from a bottle he'd packed. Tobias loved spring. Seeing winter release its grip, it felt as if fresh possibilities opened up, another chance that something new would happen, that the world would be different. He had often thought that New Year's Eve ought to be in spring, not in the middle of winter. The day after December 31 was never any different, but in spring everything was different. The beautiful green of newly opened leaves on the trees, flowers and plants growing on the forest floor, the birds coming back to chirp between the branches. Tobias finished his breakfast and hummed softly as he carried on with his journey toward the ridge. He had promised himself to find out more about the Christian girls, no more making stuff up, but discover for himself what was really going on, and finally he was on his way. He began to regret not having packed his book, in case he decided to stay the night. It would be nice to sit by the campfire reading, right in the middle of the forest. He had started the next book on Emilie's list; he had already finished *Lord of the Flies,* he had raced through it and swallowed every word. He didn't know if he had understood all of it, but that made no difference. It had been good. It had made him happy. The new book was more difficult to read: *One Flew Over the Cuckoo's Nest.* It was in a more adult language, and Emilie had said that if he found it too difficult to just swap it for another one, but he intended to read all of it. It was very exciting so far. The book was about a Native American, Chief Bromden, who had been admitted to a hospital he could not leave. The boss, a woman, was incredibly strict, a proper witch. Chief Bromden pretended to be a deaf-mute, someone who could not hear or say anything in order to . . . Well, Tobias wasn't quite sure exactly why Chief Bromden was behaving like this, but the book was exciting all the same. He should have brought it. Leaving it behind had been a mistake.

At the top of the ridge, he had a better view of the landscape. He could make out Litjønna in the distance. Another hour or two, perhaps, and he would be there. Tobias realized he was looking forward to it, but he also had a lurching feeling in his stomach. Everyone was talking about the Christians, but nobody knew anything about them. What if they were dangerous? Or not dangerous, but perhaps they didn't like visitors? On the other hand, what if they were really nice? Perhaps they would welcome him with open arms and give him chicken and fizzy drinks and he would make a lot of new friends, and maybe they would want him to stay there, and perhaps Torben could come, too, and everything would be all right, just like snapping your fingers and all your problems would be solved in an instant.

It was probably best not to approach them immediately. After all, you never could tell. Perhaps he should set up camp some distance away, in a place with a view. Lie on the ground with his binoculars, perhaps camouflage his body, so he could spy on them. Pick his moment.

He smiled to himself. That was a good plan. Set up camp where he had a view. Do some spying. He should have brought his book, he should definitely have done that, but it was too late to turn around now. He would have to be the Indian instead. Chief Tobias Bromden on a secret mission.

It had grown a little warmer. The sun was peeping out from behind a cloud, almost lighting up the path in front of him — that was a good sign. Tobias took off his jacket, put it in his knapsack, and continued his hike through the forest.

He didn't see the fence until he was just a short distance away from it. He must have been lost in a world of his own. His mind had been filled with camouflage and camping. He had visited this farm before and knew of a good location for watching it. He'd heard that the town had sold the old farm and the land that belonged to it. The town had used the farm as a facility for drug addicts, where they could do farming jobs and go for walks in the forest and so on, because it was supposed to do them good. But then the town had run out of money or decided to spend it on something else or something Tobias didn't really understand, but the upshot was that the place for drug addicts had been closed down. The farm had been empty for a while. And now some Christians had bought it. Tobias had been there twice before, once when the junkies were staying there and once when it had been uninhabited. He'd been there with Jon-Marius, his best friend, who sadly had moved to Sweden with his mother in the middle of sixth grade. Anyway, they had found the perfect place from which to do their spying, a mound not far from the farm with a good view of most things that were going on.

But he did not remember this fence, and now he had almost walked right into it. A mesh fence, the kind that ought to have barbed wire running along the top. Tobias quickly stepped back and hid behind the trees while he took a good look at this unexpected obstacle. There was no barbed wire on the top, but it was high. Much taller than him, more than twice his height. The fence looked brand new. As if it had just been put up. Tobias looked at the top of the fence and sized it up. He could probably scale it, but not without being spotted. He could see it now, the farm far behind it.

Strange things had happened there; the farm had changed almost beyond recognition. They had put up new buildings. Extended outward and upward so it no longer looked like a farmhouse but more like a small church. It had a spire, and was that a greenhouse next to it? He shielded his eyes with his hand, but he could not see that far. The area between the fence and the building was open and offered few places to hide. The mound from which he was going to do his spying lay on the other side. In order to reach it, he would have to follow the new fence all the way around. It would be much quicker to climb it, but having reviewed his options, he decided it wasn't worth the risk. Not that he thought the people behind the fence wouldn't be nice, but even so. What would he say if he were caught? And after all, he had found a small girl in a doll's dress hanging from a tree with a sign around her neck, not so far from here, so perhaps it was best to err on the side of caution.

He could always walk home again; that was another option. He had seen something now. They'd built a new house and put up a fence. A kind of Christian campsite. That would be worth telling people about. Tobias briefly considered turning back, but his curiosity was greater than his fear. It would be exciting to have more to tell. He might catch a glimpse of the people living there. He wandered back into the forest. Enough for the trees to hide him, but he could still see the fence. It looked as if the shortest distance would involve going around to the left — he could make out the edge of the fence there; to his right it simply carried on, and he couldn't estimate how far the walk would be in that direction. Tobias pulled up the hood of his hoodie and contemplated his next move. Hiding inside the hoodie felt good. It also added to the excitement. He was a secret agent on a mission. With a knife and a flashlight in his knapsack and a riddle to solve. He crouched, made himself as small as he could, and followed the fence through the woods. Tobias moved as quietly as possible, in short sprints. He would lean forward, half run through the forest for a few hundred meters before throwing himself to the ground and checking out the terrain. No one in sight. Someone had dug a hole inside the fenced-off area. Tobias could see a vehicle now, a tractor parked farther away. He repeated his maneuver. Crouched down, half ran, found a suitable spot, and threw himself on the heather. This time he got a slightly better view. He'd been right, it was a greenhouse — two, in fact, both fairly big.

Tobias knew that the children who lived there did not go to school. Perhaps they did not go to the shops either? Perhaps they grew all their own food, so they never had to go anywhere? He eased out his binoculars from the knapsack. He could see the greenhouses very clearly now. And the tractor. An old, green Massey Ferguson.

Tobias's heart started to pound as a person appeared in the binoculars. A man. No, a woman. Wearing a gray dress with something white on her head. She went inside one of the greenhouses. Then she was gone. He scanned the area with the binoculars again, trying to spot more people, but everything had gone quiet. He dropped the binoculars, let them dangle from the strap around his neck, and got to his feet. Risked running a longer distance. This time he could not wait to get to a higher vantage point — his fear had completely evaporated, his curiosity had gotten the better of him now. He threw himself on the heather again as the door to the greenhouse opened and someone appeared, two people this time. The same woman and . . . ? He adjusted the binoculars in order to see better. A man. A woman and a man. The man was also wearing gray clothes but had nothing on his head. Perhaps only the women had to wear something on their heads. That would make a good story, wouldn't it? All the women wear white hats while the men have nothing. No, maybe not. After all, what did it mean? He had to get closer. This was nothing.

Tobias had just sat up again, ready to run the next stretch, when he suddenly noticed the girl behind the fence. He was so surprised that he completely forgot to throw himself to the ground; he just stood there, right in front of her, without moving. She was around his age, maybe a little younger. She was dressed just like the woman by the greenhouse, in a thick, gray woolen dress with a white bonnet on her head. She was kneeling in a vegetable patch. It looked as if she was pulling up weeds. Perhaps they grew carrots in the vegetable beds, or lettuce or something, it was hard to tell. Tobias squatted on his haunches and made himself a little more invisible. The girl sat up and straightened her back. Brushed dust off her knees. She looked weary. She was not far away from him, perhaps only ten meters. Tobias held his breath while the girl knelt on the ground again and continued weeding. She touched her neck and wiped her forehead. Tobias completely forgot that he was a spy and that he had to remain unseen.

The girl looked so tired and thirsty. What would be the harm in offering her a drink? After all, he had a big bottle of water in his knapsack.

Tobias cleared his throat. The girl went on weeding without noticing him. Tobias glanced around and spotted a couple of old pinecones on the ground. Carefully, he threw one of them in her direction, but it didn't get very far, didn't even reach the fence. He half rose, threw the second cone harder, and this time he succeeded. He hit the middle section of the fence, and it rang out. The sound was far too loud, and he regretted it immediately, threw himself on the heather, and lay as still as he could.

When he looked up again, the girl was standing near the fence. She had heard the sound. She was looking at him. He could see her eyes. She was looking straight at him. Tobias placed his finger in front of his lips. Shhh. The girl was very surprised, but even so, she obeyed his instruction and said nothing. She looked around. First to one side, then to the other. Then she nodded cautiously. Tobias looked around, too, and moved closer to the fence. He opened his knapsack, took out the water bottle, slipped it under the fence, and swiftly retreated to his hiding place. The girl in the gray dress glanced around again. There was no one in sight. She quickly got up, ran to the water bottle, snatched it, hid it in the folds of her dress, and raced back to the patch she'd been weeding. Tobias saw her unscrew the cap and drink practically the whole bottle. She must be very thirsty. The girl with the white bonnet kept looking around. She seemed nervous. Frightened that someone might come. Tobias's courage grew, and he walked all the way up to the fence. The girl also came closer, quietly, but she kept looking over her shoulder. He could see her face more clearly now. She had blue eyes and many freckles. Her strange bonnet and heavy dress made her look almost like an old lady, but she wasn't. If she'd been wearing ordinary clothes, she would have looked just like the other girls in his class. The girl held up the bottle to him as if to ask him whether he wanted it back. Tobias shook his head. The girl knelt down and took out something from the pocket of her dress. It was a notepad and a small pencil. She wrote something on a piece of paper and folded it carefully. Then she got up, half ran to the fence, and stuck the paper through it. She glanced around nervously and ran just as quickly back to her original position and went on pulling up weeds. Tobias elbowed his way to the fence to take the paper. He crawled back and opened it. *"Thank you,"* it said. He looked at the girl and smiled. He tried to work out how to signal "You're welcome" without speaking, but it was far from easy. The girl glanced over her shoulder and wrote something else. She ran to the fence again, except this time she did not fold the piece of paper, but left the whole notepad and the pencil by the fence. Tobias hastily crouched down and made his way back to the fence, took the notepad and the pencil, and returned to his hiding place. *"My name is Rakel,"* it said on the notepad. *"I am not allowed to talk. What is your name?"* Tobias looked toward the girl. Not allowed to talk? What kind of rule was that? And why had she been so thirsty? And why was she out here all alone? Tobias thought about it and wrote a reply. *"My name is Tobias. Do you live here? Why can't you talk?"* He crept back to the fence with the notepad and resumed his position. Writing "Do you live here?" might have been a bit stupid, because she obviously did, it was plain to see, but he hadn't known what else to write. The girl smiled slightly when she saw the notepad and wrote a speedy reply. She was still very wary. She glanced over her shoulder several times before she risked passing the new message through the fence. *"I live here. Lux Domus. Can't tell you why (not talking)."* She tried to signal something with her hands when he had read the note. As if she wanted to add something but did not know how. Tobias smiled to her and wrote a reply back. *"I live at the edge of this forest. We are neighbors."* He added a smiley face. Then he wrote, *"What does Lux Domus mean?"* The girl got the notepad back. Again she smiled faintly. After a fresh check to make sure that no one was watching her, she wrote her reply and ran to the fence to leave the notepad there before running back to the vegetable bed. *"Lux Domus = House of Light. It's very kind of you to help me. Thank you."* Tobias frowned at the second half of her message. He did not think he'd done that much to help her. All he'd done was give her some water. He wondered what to write back. Words seemed really important now that he wasn't allowed to say them out loud. He had to think very carefully. He chewed the pencil for a while before he realized what he wanted to write. *"Do you need any more help?"* he wrote, and slipped the notepad through the fence.

Suddenly something happened up by the main house. The girl glanced uneasily over her shoulder and wrote another fast reply.

She tore off the paper this time and folded it as she had done with her first message. People were coming now, several were emerging from the house, quite a few. It looked as if they had just finished something inside the church. The girl got up swiftly and pushed the note for him through the fence. Now Tobias could hear voices as well. They were calling her name.

"Rakel!"

He could no longer see her eyes, as she had bowed her head now. She picked up the hoe and walked quietly toward the voices calling her. Tobias lay completely still, too scared to move before the crowd had dispersed. Once the girl joined them, everyone went inside one of the greenhouses. Once more the farm was silent. Tobias emerged from his hiding place to pick up the final note. He stuffed it into his pocket and didn't take it out until he'd found a better hiding place, deeper inside the forest. His fingers were trembling as he unfolded the paper. He had a shock when he saw what she had written.

"Yes. Help me. Please."

Slowly he crept back toward the fence. There was still total silence on the other side. Tobias did not know exactly what to do. He'd planned to go on a secret mission, but that had been just a silly idea in his head.

This was different.

This was real.

The girl in the gray dress existed. The girl who was thirsty but not allowed to talk. And now she had asked him for help.

Tobias put on his knapsack and walked calmly to the mound from where he would have a clearer view.

27

Mia Krüger woke up with a feeling that there was someone in her hotel room. She was unable to open her eyes properly, enveloped in a fog, half asleep, half awake. She forced open her eyelids enough to establish that she was alone. There was no one there, just her. A depressing thought. Her life was reduced to this? A hotel room and a murder case. Not that it really mattered. This was only temporary.

Come to me, Mia, come.

She would be gone soon. Why fret about it? Why think? Why this? Why that?

For some inexplicable reason, Mia had a headache. After her consumption of various drugs in the last six months, she thought she'd become immune to low-level pain like this. Her evening with Susanne had gone on longer than planned — well, "planned" was an exaggeration; it had been a chance meeting — but the bottom line was that she'd had too much to drink. When her cell rang, she reached out sleepily, pressed the screen, and started to talk before she was fully conscious.

"Yes? Mia speaking."

"Sorry, did I wake you?"

It was Gabriel Mørk. The new guy. The cute one who blushed. The hacker.

"No," Mia said, sitting up in her bed.

"Now, I know I'm not a bona fide police officer," Gabriel said, sounding apologetic. "So I'm not sure if this is important or not."

"You're doing fine." Mia yawned. "Just tell me."

"Okay," Gabriel went on. "You know that the laptop had two users?"

"Roger and Randi."

"Yes, Roger and Randi. And this is where it gets weird."

"Why?"

"Let's start with Roger. No surprises there. Did not use his laptop all that much. He wasn't a computer freak."

"Why not?"

"He only used it for the usual guy stuff."

"Which is what?"

"Emails. Cars and motorbikes. What we would expect, basically."

"Who did he email? Anyone interesting?"

"Not really. There were hardly any private

emails. I mean, from people he knew. He had ordered some biker magazines. Bills, e-invoices. Junk mail. A fairly sad life, judging by his email account."

"Not everyone lives their life on the Net, Gabriel," Mia said.

"No, you're right, but even so. The absence of personal stuff is odd, but that's not the interesting bit."

"Could you hang on two seconds?"

"Okay."

Mia put the cell on hold and made her way to the hotel telephone on the bedside table. She called reception and ordered breakfast to be sent to her room. She had tried going to the dining room for breakfast yesterday, and that had been a mistake. Too many people.

"I'm back."

"Okay," Gabriel said again. "I'll check out this Roger user a bit more, but I wanted to tell you what I found on the other one."

"Randi?"

"Yes."

"Who is she?"

"That's the weird part."

"What?"

Gabriel fell silent for a little while. "I think you need to see it for yourself, but I'm quite sure that it's the same person."

"What do you mean?"

"Roger and Randi. They're one and the same."

"Roger Bakken was two people?"

"Yes . . . or no. Or yes. He liked to be a woman."

"Are you kidding me?"

"No, it's the truth."

"How do you know?"

"Under the Roger username, he's a man. He has photographs of motorbikes and cars. He goes fishing and drinks alcohol. As Randi he's completely different. He's a woman. Bookmarks on the browser are blogs about crocheting and interior design. He has photographs of himself wearing women's clothing. It looks like he lived a double life."

"And you're quite sure about this?"

She heard Gabriel sigh on the other end.

"I know I'm not a police officer, but I am capable of spotting a man dressed like a woman."

"Sorry," Mia said. "It just sounds so weird."

"I agree," Gabriel said. "But it is him. One hundred percent. You can see for yourself when you get here."

"I'll be there shortly," Mia said. "What about his cell phone?"

"That's also a bit odd."

"What do you mean?"

"Practically all the messages had been deleted, and he had no stored numbers. I don't know what this guy was up to, but he's done everything he could to erase every trace of himself."

"Apart from the photographs of himself dressed as a woman."

"Yes, except for that, but like I said, they were on the laptop."

"You said that practically all the text messages had been deleted. Are you telling me you do have some?"

"Yes, a few cryptic ones."

"Let me hear them."

"Now?"

"Yes, now." Mia couldn't help smiling.

"Okay."

Gabriel cleared his throat and prepared to read aloud what he had found. "There are three text messages. All are dated March twentieth."

"The day he died."

"Was it?"

"Yes, let me have them."

There was a knock on the hotel door. Mia put on one of the hotel's dressing gowns and took in her breakfast while Gabriel opened the text messages.

"Okay, the first one is short."

"Who sent it?"

"The sender is anonymous."

"How is that possible? Can you really hide your number when you're texting?"

"Yes, that's easy," Gabriel replied.

"I know I probably sound like your granny right now, but how do you do that?" Mia asked him, and took a sip of her coffee.

It was bitter. She spit it out, muttering curses under her breath. How could people not learn to make proper coffee? The scrambled eggs and the bacon on the plate didn't look very appetizing either.

"You send it via the Net using TxtEmNow.com or some similar site. There are lots of them where you don't have to register. You just type in the number and the message, and off it goes, usually with advertising — that's how they finance it."

"And what did the message say?"

"There are three."

"Let me have them."

" 'It is unwise to fly too near the sun.' "

"Again, please."

Mia was unable to eat anything. She carried the tray to the windowsill.

" 'It is unwise to fly too near the sun.' That's the first message."

"What did he reply?"

"He didn't. You can't reply to a text message when there's no sender."

Mia sat down on the bed and leaned her head against the wall. Her headache was starting to lift. Fly too near the sun. The eagle tattoo. Wings. Icarus with his wings. He flew too near the sun, and the wings melted. Hubris. Arrogance. Roger Bakken had stepped out of line.

"Are you there?"

"Yes, sorry, Gabriel, just had to think."

"Are you ready for the next one?"

"Sure."

" 'Who's there?' "

"Was that the full message?"

"Yes. Do you want the final one?"

"Yes."

" 'Bye, bye, birdie.' "

Mia closed her eyes, but nothing came to her. *Who's there? Bye, bye, birdie.* Right now it made no sense. She got up from the bed and went to the bathroom. Caught a glimpse of herself in the mirror and did not like what she saw. She looked exhausted. Practically dead. Ghostly. She bent down and started running the bath.

"Mia? You still there?"

"Yes, sorry, Gabriel. I was just trying to work out if the two latter ones made any sense."

"And?"

"No, not right now. I'll be there in a while, all right?"

"That's fine, I'll stay where I am."

"Great, Gabriel, good job so far."

She returned to the bedroom. Put her cell phone on the windowsill and tried eating some of her breakfast. She could not get anything down. Never mind. She would get herself a coffee and a scone on the way.

Who's there? Bye, bye, birdie.

Mia undressed and got into the bath. The warm water enveloped her body and calmed her. Being out with Susanne had been great. Really great. In fact, they had arranged to meet up again, hadn't they? Mia could not quite remember — she'd been a little drunk toward the end.

She leaned her head against the rim of the bath and closed her eyes.

Who's there? Bye, bye, birdie.

It wasn't much, but at least it was a start.

28

Cecilie Mykle had slept so soundly that it almost hurt to wake up. Force of habit made her reach for the alarm clock, but for some reason it wasn't ringing. Cecilie tried and failed to open her eyes. Her body felt so heavy and comfortable and warm, almost as if she were lying on a soft cloud with another lovely cloud covering her. She pulled the duvet more tightly around herself and turned over onto her stomach. Pressed her face into the pillow. Tried to obey her body. *Go back to sleep, go back to sleep. Forget what your head and your mind are telling you. You need to sleep now, sleep, sleep, Cecilie, sleep.* It was for this reason that the doctor had prescribed her the pills. Cecilie had been against it; she'd never taken sleeping pills in her life. She did not like medication. She liked to be alert. She hated the thought of something controlling her body. Cecilie Mykle was very keen on being in control. Underneath the duvet her hand reached out again, automatically trying to switch off the alarm clock, at six-fifteen as always, but it had still not begun to ring. A tiny part of her brain wondered why, but it was quickly overruled by the rest of her brain, which could not care less, swayed by the aftereffects of the sleeping pills; she snuggled up under the duvet and pressed her head against the lovely soft pillow.

"This is not a suggestion, it's an order," her doctor had said. "You have to take these pills because you need some sleep. You need to sleep. How many times do I have to tell you before you understand?"

The best doctor in the world. Who knew what she needed and was a bit strict with her, who had told her to take care of herself. Something Cecilie Mykle was not very good at. *You have to take care of yourself,* people told her all the time, but Cecilie Mykle thought that was easier said than done. She had grown up with a mother unable to do that, who had always put other people's needs first. It was a difficult pattern to break.

She was a worrier. That's why she was unable to sleep. She couldn't remember the last time she'd had a good night's sleep. Her nights were largely restless: she would doze a little, then get up, watch some late-night TV, have a cup of tea, and then perhaps catnap for a few minutes before the alarm went off and it was six-fifteen again. There were always so many things that could go wrong, and Cecilie was the sort of person who worried more than most.

"You're worrying yourself unnecessarily," her husband would say, as he had the time they bought the terraced house in Skullerud.

"Are you sure we can afford it?"

"We'll manage," her husband had said, and he'd been right. They'd managed fine, especially once he started working on the North Sea oil rigs.

Six weeks on, six weeks off. She missed her husband, of course, the weeks he was away, but the money did come in very handy. And when he was at home, he was at home the whole time. Cecilie Mykle loved her husband. He was perfect; she could not have wished for a better friend or lover. He was not like many of his friends who also worked on the oil rigs, men who would come home with money in their pockets and then hit the town. Six weeks at work, six weeks of drinking. No, he was not like them at all. When her husband was at home, he was at home.

Cecilie Mykle stretched her arms toward the ceiling and finally managed to open her eyes. She decided to stay in bed for a little bit longer while she came around. She felt lethargic, but still also incredibly rested after a good night's sleep, her skin warm, her body soft and calm. She hadn't had any dreams last night either, as she had recently — violent, almost feverish nightmares — but last night nothing. Just total relaxation.

She was awake now. Suddenly she surfaced in the dark bedroom and started to feel anxious again. What time was it really? She reached out to switch on the bedside lamp. It would not come on. Why was everything dark? And cold? Had they had a power cut? Cecilie Mykle pressed the button that lit up the small alarm clock and had a shock when she realized what time it was. A quarter to ten? Gosh, she should have been up hours ago. She should have taken Karoline to nursery school by now. Cecilie swung her legs over the edge of the bed but stayed sitting with her head buried in her hands. It felt like a lump of lead. She could barely keep her eyes open. She staggered to the light switch by the door and tried turning on the ceiling light, but it would not come on either. The house was cold and strangely quiet. Cecilie fumbled her way to the window and opened the curtains. Spring light poured into the bedroom, enough for her to see by.

Cecilie stumbled out into the passage. She had to wake Karoline. Her legs were heavy, almost incapable of supporting her down the dark hallway. She had forgotten to put on socks, and the floor was cold. Cecilie felt her way along the wall to Karoline's room.

"Karoline?"

Her voice was feeble and weak. It, too, refused to wake up.

"Karoline, are you awake?"

There was no reply from her daughter's bedroom. At a quarter to ten? Karoline was usually up by seven, or at least awake. Often she would pad to her parents' bedroom with her teddy in tow. Best time of the day, really. Quiet mornings in bed with Karoline and her teddy.

"Karoline?"

Cecilie continued to feel her way around, her eyes slowly acclimating to the darkness. Suddenly she felt something wet and sticky under her feet. What on earth? She stopped and raised her foot. Carefully, she touched the sole. There was something yucky on the floor. But she had washed it only the day before. Cecilie made her way gingerly across the sticky floor and entered Karoline's room. She pressed the light switch, but again the light did not come on.

"Karoline?"

She quickly crossed the room and opened the curtains. The light poured in, and it was at this point that Cecilie Mykle started to worry in earnest.

"Karoline?"

She could not believe her own eyes. Karoline wasn't in her bed. There was blood on the floor. Cecilie could not be awake. She had stepped in the blood. So she must be dreaming. She was still asleep. She should never have taken that sleeping pill, but her doctor had insisted. Cecilie Mykle stayed in her daughter's bedroom while she waited to wake up. She did not like this dream. Karoline was not in her bed. It was a quarter to ten in the morning. There was blood on the floor. There was no electricity. The house was dark. Cecilie had goose pimples on her arms under her sweater. She really wanted to wake up now. *The alarm clock will go off any moment now,* she thought, and chewed her lip.

This is just a dream.

Cecilie Mykle was in shock. She did not even hear the distant ringing of the telephone.

29

Mia Krüger sat at the café drinking her second cortado of the day. She had eaten a scone and drunk a glass of orange juice and was suffering from a surprisingly bad hangover, and yet her body was slowly but surely starting to recover after last night's excesses with Susanne. She normally never read the newspapers, but for some reason she had done so today, even though she found the front pages tasteless. "The Babes in the Woods Murders" seemed to be what the papers had decided to call them. Mia hated it when the media did this, coined names and logos for murder investigations, the hunt for missing people, civil unrest, war, or indeed any form of tragedy. Did they not realize the effect it had on their readers? Did they not care that they fueled people's fears, terrified them? Damn them all to hell.

She put down the newspaper and had knocked back the last of her cortado just as her phone rang.

"Yes, Mia speaking."

"It's Holger. Where are you?"

"The café on Storgata. What is it?"

"Another girl has gone missing."

Mia felt the hairs on her arms stand up. She put on her leather jacket and was out the door in a matter of seconds.

"Are you at the office?" she asked him.

"I'm just about to leave."

"Pick me up outside 7-Eleven on Pløensgate."

"Okay."

Mia ended the call and ran. Damn. Number three. *Three lines on the nail of her left little finger.* No, not this time. This time they had a head start. Another girl had gone missing, but they were on the case. There would be no more Paulines. Mia did not know who this new girl was, but she had already made up her mind as she pushed through the crowds on her way down Torggata, that they would find this girl before it was too late.

She arrived at the corner just as Holger's black Audi drove down Pløensgate. She jumped into the passenger seat and slammed the door shut.

"Where are we going?" she panted.

"Disen," Munch replied briefly. "Disen-

263

veien. The call came in ten minutes ago. Andrea Lyng. She wasn't in her bed when her father woke up."

Munch put the flashing blue light on the roof and pressed the accelerator.

"He has only just woken up?" She checked the clock on her cell.

"So it would seem," Munch muttered.

"Who is up there?"

"Kim and Anette. Curry is on his way."

Munch sounded the horn irritably at a tram and a couple of pedestrians who had failed to get out of his way. "Damn idiots."

"She disappeared from her home?"

Munch nodded.

"How odd. The other two disappeared from their nursery school."

"Get out of the goddamn way!"

Munch sounded the horn again, finally managed to extricate himself from the traffic, and headed toward Sinsen.

"So only the father was at home? Where's the mother?"

"No idea," Munch muttered.

His phone rang, and he answered the call. His voice was brusque. This was not one of his good days.

"Yes? . . . Damn! . . . Yes, cordon off the area. And send Forensics up there immediately. . . . What? No, I don't give a crap

264

about that, we have priority. . . . No, of course we're treating it as a crime scene. We'll be there in five minutes."

He ended the call and shook his head.

"Anette?"

"Kim."

"Found something?"

"Blood."

"Blood?"

Munch nodded grimly.

"So perhaps it's not our guy," Mia suggested. "The MO is completely different."

"You think so?"

He said this without looking at her. A six-year-old girl had gone missing from her bedroom in Disen. Mia found a lozenge in the pocket of her leather jacket. They could always hope that the two cases were not connected. *Three lines on the nail of the left little finger. Please, not again. This time they wouldn't be too late.*

Munch sounded the horn again; he had practically come to a standstill because of a couple of punk rockers who saw no reason to increase their speed as they sauntered through a pedestrian crossing despite the flashing blue lights.

"The girl's blood?" Mia asked.

"Too early to say. Forensics are on their way."

"Did you hear the news about Bakken?"

"The eagle tattoo, yes. Roger and Randi? An interesting situation. Was he a transvestite?"

"Sounds like it."

"That's not what I need right now. I really don't need that."

This remark was not aimed at her. Munch muttered it to himself through gritted teeth as he steered toward Disen. Disenveien itself was made up of small red terraced houses that had woken up to a day out of the ordinary.

"What have we got?" Munch said as soon as they were out of the car.

"Andrea Lyng. Aged six. Missing from her bedroom. Traces of blood all the way from the bottom of the stairs and up to her bedroom. Blood in the bed."

Kim scratched his head and looked grave.

"Where's the father?"

"Living room." Kim pointed. "He's completely beside himself."

"Is the doctor here?"

Kim said he was and showed them to the front door. They had just reached the gravel path leading to the house when Anette turned up. She had her cell phone in her hand and was looking anxious.

"We have another one."

"What?" Munch burst out. "Another missing girl?"

Anette nodded. "The call has just come in. Karoline Mykle. Aged six. Disappeared from her bedroom in Skullerud."

"Damn," Munch said.

"Blood?" Mia asked.

Anette nodded once more.

"Okay," Munch said. "You two go to Skullerud. Kim and I will stay here. Get a team from Forensics to join you."

"They're already on their way," Anette told him.

Munch glanced at Mia. He did not say anything, but she knew what he was thinking.

Two in one day?

Two at the same time?

"We'll take my car," Anette said, running ahead of Mia to the red Peugeot parked along the curb.

30

Mikkel Wold, a journalist with *Aftenposten,* had just had one of his articles uploaded to the Internet, and he was very pleased with the result. Everything was happening so fast these days that he'd barely had time to proofread it before it was published. He had skimmed through the article a few times as it appeared online — no typos, phew, everything looked fine. "Final Farewell to Pauline." He had covered the funeral the previous day along with two of his colleagues. They'd been responsible for the main feature in the printed version of the paper, while his task had been to find another angle. Reporters working on the printed and the Internet editions of *Aftenposten* usually worked independently of one another, but not in this case. "Do it all and do it first" was the motto now, and he had noticed that their rivals did exactly the same.

Skøyen Church had been filled to the

rafters with mourners. The family had requested that all press remain outside, but not everyone respected their request. Mikkel Wold had watched as several reporters from other newspapers talked their way into the church, mixing with the family, neighbors, and friends. Yes, of course they worked in a competitive industry, but surely there had to be some boundaries. *Aftenposten* had a good team working on the story. Talented people. Skilled journalists. They had not discussed it, but there was a tacit understanding at the paper to keep it low-key. Not shout fire in a crowded theater. Show consideration. Not prod deep wounds with their dirty, intrusive fingers. Like some of their competitors did.

Mikkel Wold had been offered a job with a rival newspaper some months before. He was approaching forty and had worked for *Aftenposten* for almost twelve years; the new job sounded exciting, and who knew when he would get another offer? But he was pleased that he'd said no. "Final Farewell to Pauline." He had interviewed a friend of Pauline's from nursery school and her parents. Was it borderline good taste? Possibly, but he had decided it was responsible journalism. Relevant. Profound grief following the loss of her friend. They had taken a picture of the little girl crying, holding a bunch of flowers in one hand and a drawing she'd made for Pauline in the other. It was beautiful and moving. Well within press regulations, surely? Or perhaps it wasn't. Mikkel Wold sighed and stretched his arms. He hadn't had much sleep since the girls' bodies had been found. Was he starting to lose his sense of perspective? Would he have written this article ten years ago? Five years ago? He dismissed his moral qualms and went to the kitchen to get himself a cup of coffee. The offices were buzzing. It was a long time since they'd had a story like this — in fact, had they ever seen anything quite like it? A serial killer who dressed up girls like dolls, put backpacks on them and hung them from trees? He shook his head and sipped his coffee. The whole thing seemed surreal. Like a case from the United States or something on their TV perhaps, but not here in Norway. Mikkel Wold had struggled to keep his emotions in check when he saw the crowd of mourners leave the church. The small white coffin. The grim faces. Grieving. *Final Farewell to Pauline.* He hoped he'd managed to stay within the guidelines. Yes, he had. It was a fine article.

Silje popped her head into the kitchen. "They're off again."

"Where are they going this time?" Mikkel put down his cup on the counter and followed the young journalist into the next room. They had started listening to the police radio around the clock in order not to miss out on anything.

"Skullerud."

"Another girl?"

"It's difficult to tell," Silje said, turning up the volume a fraction.

Grung, their editor, entered the room, ruddy and unshaven as usual. He did not look as if he'd had much sleep recently either. "What have we got?"

"Several units have been dispatched to Skullerud," Silje said.

"Skullerud? I thought they were going to Disenveien?" Grung asked.

"Both locations," Silje answered.

"Disen?" Mikkel Wold said. He'd not been aware of that.

"A few minutes ago." Grung nodded. "Erik and Tove are there now." He turned to Silje again. "Do we have an address for Skullerud?"

"Welding Olsens Vei. Not far from Skullerud School."

"I'll go," Mikkel said.

"Good," Grung agreed. "Keep me updated as it unfolds, will you?"

Mikkel Wold ran back to his desk and grabbed his bag. "Do we have a photographer?"

Grung shouted across the room, "I think John is available."

"No, he has gone to Disen," Silje said.

"Call Nina," Mikkel Wold said, heading for the exit. "Tell her to meet me up there."

He took the elevator down to the ground floor, ran to the taxi stand, and got into one. He took out his cell phone and called Erik Rønning, his fellow reporter who had gone to Disen.

"Erik speaking."

"What's happening?"

"They've blocked the area off so we can't get access. It's chaos. Nobody knows what's going on."

"Are we the only ones there?"

"You wish." His colleague chortled to himself.

"Oh, no, the whole pack has turned up. Mia! Mia!"

Mikkel's colleague disappeared for a moment. Then he was back on the phone.

"What's happening?" Wold asked.

"Munch and Krüger have just arrived. Looks like we're in the right place. Mia! Mia!"

His colleague disappeared once more, this

272

time for good. Mikkel Wold made eye contact with the cabdriver and told him to speed up. He was hoping he'd be one of the first reporters to get to Skullerud, that the other journalists would not have heard the call going out over the police radio. Mikkel tried to phone Erik back, but his call went straight to voice mail. Holger Munch and Mia Krüger had turned up. Something big must have happened.

Mikkel Wold arrived at Welding Olsens Vei only to discover that police had already cordoned off that area as well. He paid the cabdriver, jumped out of the car, and made his way through the small crowd of onlookers that had already assembled. Cordons out so soon? It was happening more and more these days. Even though they listened to the police radio, they were still too late. He had heard several journalists discuss it. Have we lost our touch? Rumor had it that the police were trying out something new, a different means of communication, but so far no one had been able to work out what it was.

Mikkel Wold pushed his way right to the cordon and spotted a reporter from *VG.*

"What's going on?"

"Don't know yet." The *VG* journalist lit a cigarette and gestured toward the road. "I think it's number three or number five. One of the yellow row houses over there. None of the heavyweights has turned up yet, just the foot soldiers. I don't know what's happening."

Mikkel Wold looked about him. New people kept arriving. He could see NRK and TV2. He nodded to a reporter from *Dagsavisen* just as his cell phone rang.

"Mikkel speaking."

"It's Grung. What have we got?"

"Nothing so far, but everyone is here."

"Why the hell are we always playing catch-up?" Grung snapped.

"It's a problem, I know. We need to do something about it," Wold said.

Grung fell silent. The editor did not like being told how to do his job.

"Munch and Krüger have gone to Disen," Mikkel said, to change the subject. He didn't want to get on the wrong side of Grung. He'd seen what happened to people who did, and it was not pleasant. He had no wish to be demoted to covering missing-cat stories in Sandvika.

"Krüger has just left Disen," Grung told him. "I bet she's on her way up to Skullerud."

"Did you get hold of Nina?"

"Yes, she's coming. I've got Erik on the

other line. I'll call you back."

"Okay," Mikkel said, hanging up.

He walked back to the cordons and tried to get a handle on the situation. The police had cordoned off the whole street, not just one of the houses. Munch and Krüger were in Disen, and Krüger might be coming up here now. It had to be something major. It had to be several girls. Two at the same time? That would be tomorrow's front page. He would bet on it. He looked around the street, trying to see if there was a gap he could sneak through. Surely there had to be another way in? He went back to the spot where he'd gotten out of the taxi. Should he stay where he was or try to explore? He was interrupted by his phone ringing again; this time the display showed that the number had been withheld.

"Hello, Mikkel here."

There was total silence at the other end.

"This is Mikkel Wold, who is this?"

He covered his free ear with his hand in order to hear better. Many people had arrived by now, and the area was filling up with cars and curious passersby.

"It's not fair, is it?"

A strange voice in his ear. It grated. There was some kind of distortion. He did not recognize the caller.

"Who is this?" he said again.

"It's not fair, is it?" the voice repeated.

Wold moved farther away from the crowd, crossed the street, and found a quieter location.

"What's not fair?" he asked.

Again there was silence from the other end.

"Hello?" Wold could feel himself growing irritated. "Hello? Listen, whoever you are, I haven't got time for this."

"It's not fair, is it?" the strange voice said again.

"What's not fair? Who is this?"

"It's not fair that you have to stand so far away," the voice said.

At that moment a red Peugeot arrived. Mikkel caught a glimpse of Mia Krüger and one of her colleagues. The Peugeot drove up to the cordon and was let in by a police officer guarding it.

"Damn," Mikkel said.

Where was the photographer? He needed pictures of this.

"Listen, find someone else to pester," he snarled into the phone. "I'm busy."

He was just about to hit the OFF button when the grating voice came back.

"Number three," the voice said.

"What do you mean?"

"It's number three," the voice said again. "Her name is Karoline. Are you still going to hang up?"

With this the caller got Mikkel Wold's full attention.

"Who are you?"

"Donald Duck. Who do you think I am?" the voice mocked him.

"No, I meant —"

The voice laughed briefly.

"Do you want me to call one of the others? Rønning from *Dagbladet*? Ruud from *VG*? One of those?"

"No, no, no . . ." Mikkel Wold said. "I'm right here."

He retreated even farther from the crowd.

"That's good," the voice said.

Mikkel tried to get out his notepad and pen from his pocket.

"Are you going to be my friend?" the grating voice said.

"Perhaps," Mikkel replied.

"Perhaps?"

"Yes, I would like to . . . to be your friend," he stuttered. "Who is Karoline?"

"Who do you think Karoline is?"

"Is she . . . number three?"

"No, Karoline is number four. Andrea was number three. Don't you pay attention? Haven't you been to Disenveien?"

Something was happening over by the cordons. Another vehicle was on its way in. Forensics.

"How do I know that —"

"How do you know what?" the voice said.

"I mean . . ."

Mikkel was unable to think of anything else to say. His forehead was hot and his palms were sweaty.

"They're so cute when they're asleep, aren't they?" the voice said.

"Who is?"

"The little ones."

"How do I know that you're not just messing with me?"

"Do you want me to send you a finger in the post?"

Mikkel Wold felt a shiver down his spine. He was trying to keep calm, but it was getting harder.

"No, absolutely not," he stammered.

The voice chuckled to itself again.

"You have to ask the right questions," the voice said.

"What do you mean?"

"At press conferences, why don't you ask the right questions?"

"What are the right questions?" Wold said.

"Why did the pig drip all over the floor?" the voice said.

"Why did the . . . ? What did you say?"

Mikkel tried desperately to get out his notepad without dropping his phone.

"Tick-tock," the grating voice said, and ended the call.

31

Holger Munch peeled off the thin latex
gloves and went outside on the terrace to
have a cigarette. Christ Almighty, what a
start to the day. *Two girls in one day?* He lit
his cigarette and peered into the house
through the window. The crime-scene technicians were still at work, and the girl's
father had been driven down to police
headquarters in Grønland. They had yet to
trace the mother, as the father had been in
shock and had made little sense. It would
appear that the two of them were no longer
together, that they had separated, that it
was his week with the daughter, that the
mother had gone to a cabin with some
female friends where there was no cell
coverage. The glass in the French windows
to the terrace had been smashed. There
were traces of blood on the ground floor,
on the stairs, and in the little girl's bedroom.
Andrea. Someone had taken her from her

bedroom. Munch took a deep drag of his cigarette and tried to fight off a budding headache. He called Mia. She answered after only a few seconds.

"What have you got?" Munch asked her.

"Karoline Mykle, aged six, missing from her home."

"Any sign of a break-in?"

"No, the key was under the mat."

Dear Lord. Munch heaved a sigh. Under the mat. Did people still do that these days? "Blood?"

"Traces of blood from the passage and into the bedroom."

"Parents?"

"Cecilie and John-Erik Mykle. Neither of them has a record. He works on the oil rigs. We're trying to contact him. She's a teacher."

"A teacher?"

"Yes, but it's not her. She's in a state of complete shock. I've sent her off to Ullevål Hospital. She didn't even know where she was. She kept saying she didn't have time to talk to us. She had to take Karoline to nursery school."

"I see," Munch said.

"We're about to start door-to-door inquiries to ask if anyone saw anything."

"Yes, that's what we're about to do as

281

well," Munch said.

"ALPHA1 procedure on this one?"

Munch nodded.

"Holger?"

"What? Yes, I want everyone working on this. Everyone. And when I say everyone, I mean everyone. I want them to check every single road, every fucking footpath, understand?"

"Understand," Mia said, and ended the call.

Holger took another deep drag of his cigarette. His headache was arriving with a vengeance. Some water. He needed fluids. And food. His phone rang again.

"Yes, Munch here."

"It's Gabriel Mørk. Is it a bad time?"

"Depends what it is," Munch growled.

"You know that private job you gave me?"

Munch rubbed his forehead.

"The code," Gabriel continued.

Munch sifted through his memories before the penny dropped. The math puzzle he'd been unable to solve. The one the Swedish girl had sent him on the Net.

"Did you crack it?"

Munch walked back inside the house. He took care not to contaminate any of the bloodstains or touch anything. The technicians were still at work.

"I think I understand what it is, but I need more."

"What do you mean, more?"

"Do you want to talk about it later?"

Munch walked through to the front of the house, went outside, and lit another cigarette. They had moved the police tape farther down the street now. Keeping the press at bay for as long as they could. He dreaded reporting the latest developments to Mikkelson. Two dead girls. No suspects. And now another two were missing. There would be hell to pay down at Grønland.

"I think it's a Gronsfeld," Gabriel said.

"A what?"

"A Gronsfeld cipher. A code language. It's a variant of Vigenère, but it uses numbers rather than letters. However, I need more. Did you get anything else?"

Munch struggled to concentrate. "More? I'm not sure. What would that be?"

"Letters and numbers. The way Gronsfeld works is that both parties, both the sender and recipient, possess the same combination of letters and numbers. It makes it impossible for an outsider to crack the code."

"I can't think of anything," Munch said just as Kim walked through the gate. "We'll have to do it later."

"Okay," Gabriel said, and hung up.

"Anything?" Munch asked.

Kim shook his head. "Most people are out at work at this time, so we'll do another round in the early evening."

"Nothing? Damn, surely somebody must have seen something?"

"Not so far."

"Do it again," Munch said.

"But we've just —"

"I said do it again."

The young police officer nodded and walked back out through the gate.

Munch was just about to return to the house when Mia called again. "Yes?"

He could tell from her voice that they had discovered something.

"It's a woman," was all she said.

"We have a witness?"

"A senior citizen living right opposite. Trouble sleeping. He looked out his window, he thinks it was about four o'clock in the morning. Saw someone hanging around a mailbox. So he went outside to check."

"Tough senior."

"Absolutely."

"What did he say?"

"He shouted at her. She ran away."

"And he's quite sure that it was a woman?"

"He's a hundred percent sure. He was only a few meters away from her."

"Bloody hell."

"I told you so, didn't I?" Mia said eagerly. "I knew it."

"Yes, you told me so. Is he with you now?"

"We're bringing him in."

"See you at the office in ten minutes?"

"Sure," Mia said, and hung up.

Munch did not exactly run, but it was not far short. A woman. He quickly got behind the wheel and drove toward the cordon. There was a sea of flashes when he passed the huge crowd of journalists and reporters. At least they had something for the vultures.

A woman.

Munch placed the blue flashing light on the roof and drove to the city center as fast as he could.

III

32

Tom-Erik Sørlie, a Norwegian veteran of Afghanistan, was sitting by his living-room window when two police cars pulled up on the road below his house and started erecting barriers. He picked up his binoculars from the coffee table and adjusted the lenses until the officers came into focus. He had listened to the police radio all day as he always did, and he knew that something had happened. Two little girls had been killed, he believed another two had gone missing, and now police had decided to check all the roads going out of Oslo. He adjusted the lenses again. Armed police officers with helmets and machine pistols, Heckler & Koch MP5s — he knew the gun well, had used it many times himself. The armed officers had finished setting up the checkpoint and were now stopping cars. Fortunately for the drivers, it was early in the day. Most of the traffic was heading into the capital, not out.

He put down the binoculars and turned up the sound of the news. His TV was always on. As was his computer. And the police radio. He liked keeping himself informed. It was his way to feel alive now that he was no longer part of the action.

Lex, his puppy, stirred in its basket before it padded over to him. It settled by his feet with its head to one side and its tongue hanging out. The German shepherd wanted to go for a walk. Tom-Erik Sørlie stroked the dog's head and tried to keep an eye on the screens. A TV2 reporter holding a microphone appeared in front of a camera. A residential development in Skullerud could be seen in the background. Police cordons. A girl had gone missing from there. He'd heard the news one hour ago. He got up and grabbed the puppy by the collar. Guided it out onto the steps, into the garden, and attached it to the tie-out line. He didn't have the energy to go for a walk now. His head was hurting.

It had grown dark outside before the police took down the barriers in the road. A whole day. Someone in the department must have written them a blank check. He ate his dinner in front of the television. A police sketch appeared on the screen. A

woman. A witness had seen her in Skullerud. *Good luck,* Tom-Erik Sørlie thought.
It could be anyone. Footage from a press
conference. A female public prosecutor. The
girls were still missing. No leads. Two
murder investigators getting into a car. A
bearded man in a beige duffel coat. A
woman with long black hair. Both were
sharp-eyed. The man in the duffel coat
flapped his hand to make the journalists go
away. No comment.

Tom-Erik Sørlie turned down the volume
on the television and got up to make himself
a cup of coffee. Was that a noise he heard?
Was there someone in the garden? He put
on his shoes and went outside. The dog was
no longer attached to the tie-out line.

"Lex?"

He walked around the house to the back
garden and had a shock when he saw the
apple tree.

Someone had killed his dog and hanged it
by its neck from a jump rope.

33

Mia Krüger crossed the road and started walking up Tøyengata. She tried to ignore the newspaper headlines. She passed yet another kiosk that had her life on display. MYSTERY WOMAN: STILL NO LEADS. The police sketch of the woman seen by the retiree on the front page. There was nothing wrong with the police sketch. Just as there was nothing wrong with the witness observation. The only problem was that it could be anyone. Nine hundred phone calls, and that was just on day one. People thought it was their neighbor, their colleague, their niece, someone they'd seen on line for a ferry the day before. The switchboard at police headquarters had been jammed; they'd had to shut it down, take a break. Rumor had it that waiting time to get through had been up to two hours. HAVE YOU SEEN KAROLINE OR ANDREA? New front pages, big photographs of the girls, blown up as if to mock her. *You can't do your job. This is your responsibility. If those girls die, it'll be your fault.*

And what was all that blood about? Mia Krüger did not understand it. It made no sense. It did not fit with the other evidence. They'd tested the blood, and it belonged to neither of the girls. It wasn't even human. It came from a pig. The killer was taunting them, that was what she was doing. Or he. Mia Krüger was starting to have doubts. Something did not add up. With the woman seen in Skullerud. With the police sketch. She got the feeling that the whole thing was a game. *Look how easy it all is for me. I can do whatever I want.*

I win. You lose.

Mia tightened her jacket around her and crossed the street again. They had nothing on the white Citroën. Nothing from the list of previous offenders. Ludvig and Curry had reviewed the Hønefoss case in detail. One of the offices in Mariboesgate was covered from floor to ceiling with photographs and notes, but despite their efforts they hadn't discovered anything so far. After all, there'd been nearly eight hundred sixty staff members at the hospital where the baby had been taken. Not to mention everyone with easy access: patients, visitors, relatives. It all added up to thousands of potential suspects. Nor had the surveillance cameras picked up anything. There'd been no cameras in the maternity unit itself in those days, only near the exit. Mia remembered watching hours of recordings without success. Nothing. Crates of interviews and statements. Doctors, nurses, patients, social workers, relatives, receptionists, cleaners — she had personally spoken to nearly a hundred people. All of them had been equally upset. How could it happen? How could someone just walk into a maternity unit and walk out with a baby without being challenged? She remembered how high-ranking officers at police headquarters had jumped for joy when the young Swede had "confessed" and then killed himself. They could not shelve the case fast enough. Sweep it under the rug. A blot on the force. It was a question of moving on.

Mia Krüger crossed the street again and entered a courtyard. It had been a long time since her last visit, but the place was still there. The green door without a sign, hidden away in an invisible corner of the city. She knocked and waited for someone to open it. They had decided to offer a reward now, the girls' families and their supporters. Munch and Mia had been against it. It would only increase the number of time wasters, telephone calls, block the lines for people with important information, but after consulting their lawyers they had decided to go ahead nevertheless. The police could do nothing to prevent it. Perhaps they might even benefit from it. Maybe the right amount of money would entice someone out from the shadows.

A small hatch opened in the door, and a man's face appeared.

"Yes?"

"Mia Krüger," Mia said. "Is Charlie here?"

The hatch was shut again. A couple of minutes passed, and then the man returned. He opened the door for her and let her in. The security guard was new, someone she hadn't seen before. A typical choice for Charlie: a bodybuilder, big with a square body, tattooed biceps bigger than her thighs.

"He's down there." The man nodded, pointing farther into the room.

Charlie Brown was standing behind the bar with a big smile on his face when she appeared. He hadn't changed. Perhaps a tiny bit older and his eyes a little wearier, but as colorful as always. Heavily made up and wearing a bright green sequin dress with a feather boa around his neck.

"Mia Moonbeam!" Charlie laughed and

came out from behind the bar to give her a hug. "It's been absolutely ages! How the devil are you, girl?"

"I'm good," Mia told him, and sat down.

There were only six or seven men in the club, most of them wearing women's clothing. Leopard-print leggings and high heels. White dresses and long silk gloves. At Charlie's you could be anyone you wanted to be — no one cared. The lighting was soft. The mood relaxed. A jukebox in the corner played Edith Piaf.

"You look terrible," Charlie Brown said, shaking his head. "Do you want a beer?"

"What, you finally got a license to serve alcohol?"

"Tut-tut, girl. We don't use words like that here." Charlie winked at her and pulled her a beer. "Do you want a small one or . . . ?"

"What's a small one in this place in the daytime?" Mia smiled and took a sip of her beer.

"It's whatever size you want it to be." Charlie winked again and wiped the counter in front of her.

"Sadly," he continued, "the place isn't buzzing the way it used to. We're getting old, or at least Charlie is."

He flung the green feather boa around his neck and reached for a bottle on the shelf.

"How about a Jäger?"

Mia nodded and took off her knitted cap and leather jacket. It was good to be indoors where it was warm. Hide from the world for a while. She had hung out at Charlie's back in the days when the investigation into her had been all over the media. Mia had discovered this place by accident and felt at home immediately. No prying eyes. Tranquillity and security, almost a second family. It seemed a very long time ago, in another life. She didn't recognize any of the men wearing ladies' clothes sitting in the booths over by the red wall.

Charlie found two glasses and poured them each a Jägermeister. "Cheers, darling. Good to see you again."

"Likewise." Mia smiled.

"Goes without saying you don't look a day older," Charlie said.

He cupped Mia's face in his hands and studied it.

"Those cheekbones, girl. You shouldn't have been a police officer. You should have been a model. But seriously, how about embracing healthy living for the sake of your skin? And you are allowed to put on a bit of makeup every now and then, even though you're a girl. Right, I've got it off my chest. Mama Charlie always tells it like it is."

"Thank you." Mia knocked back her Jägermeister. It warmed her all the way down her throat.

"Could we have a bottle of champagne over here, Charlie?" someone called.

"What have I said to you about shouting, Linda?"

Charlie was addressing a man at one of the tables. He was wearing a pink minidress, ankle boots, gloves, and a string of pearls. He might be in his forties, but he moved his body and his arms like a fifteen-year-old girl.

"Oh, come on, Charlie. Be a dear."

"This is a respectable establishment, not some Turkish brothel. Do you need fresh glasses?"

"No, we'll use the ones we already have," the man whose name was Linda said with a giggle.

"No class." Charlie sighed and rolled his eyes.

He fetched a bottle of champagne from the back room and brought it to the table. Opened it with a bang to the delight of the men-girls who clapped and cheered.

"Right," Charlie said when he came back. "I thought we had lost you."

"Rumors of my demise have been greatly exaggerated," Mia said.

"A bit of rouge, a touch of foundation, and I would agree." Charlie tittered. "Oh, that was naughty of me. What a naughty girl I am."

Charlie Brown leaned over the counter and gave her a big hug. Mia had to smile. It was a long time since she'd been hugged by a bear in women's clothing. It felt good.

"*Was* I being naughty? You look absolutely gorgeous, you do. A million dollars."

Mia laughed. "That's quite all right."

"Two million."

"That's enough, Charlie."

"Ten million. Another Jäger?"

Mia gave him a thumbs-up.

"So what's up?" Charlie said when they'd both emptied their glasses.

"I need your help," Mia said, and she produced a photograph from the inside pocket of her jacket.

She slid the picture across the counter. Charlie put on a pair of bifocals and held the photograph close to a candle.

"Ah, Randi." Charlie nodded. "Tragic story."

"Was he one of your customers? Sorry, I mean she."

Charlie took off his spectacles and pushed the photograph back across the counter.

"Yes, Randi used to come here," he told

her. "From time to time. Sometimes she would come often, and then several months would pass before we saw her again. Roger was one of those who . . . well, how do I put it? Who wasn't comfortable with who he was. I think he tried really hard not to be Randi, but you know what it's like, he couldn't help himself. He had to get very drunk in order to let himself go. Sometimes we had to ask her to leave when she started bothering the other guests."

"Any idea why?"

"Why he jumped?" Charlie heaved a sigh. "No idea. It's a tough world out there, that's all I can say. It's hard enough to be normal. It's even tougher when society wants you to be one person while your body tells you something else."

"No one is more normal than you," Mia said, and raised her beer glass from the counter.

Charlie chuckled. "Me? Christ, I gave all that up thirty years ago, but not everybody is like me, you know. Some are riddled with guilt, shame, and a bad conscience. We can get the Internet on our cell phones and send rockets to Mars, but mentally and emotionally we still live as we did back in the Dark Ages. Then again, you would know all about that."

"Would I?" Mia said.

"Yes, because you're smart, and that's why I like you so much. And pretty — that helps obviously — but smart. I don't need to explain everything to you. Why don't you become prime minister, Mia? Teach this country a thing or two?"

"Oh, I don't think that would be a good idea."

"You may be right. You're far too nice."

Charlie laughed and poured them each another Jäger.

"Did she always come here alone?" Mia asked.

"Who? Randi?"

"Yes."

"Mostly. She brought a female friend a couple of times, but I never spoke to her."

"A man?"

"No, a woman."

"What did she look like?"

"Strict. Straight-backed. Dark hair pulled tightly into a ponytail. Rather odd eyes."

"What do you mean by odd eyes?"

"They were different colors."

"Really?"

"Really. One was blue and one was brown. She looked a bit freaky. Callous. Serious. I was quite pleased when he stopped bringing her, to be frank. She gave me the creeps."

"When was this?"

"Oh, I can't remember." Charlie found a cloth and started wiping off the bar again. "Some months after you stopped coming here, I guess. By the way, where have you been?"

"I left the world for a while."

"Well, it's good to have you back. I've missed you." Charlie raised her shot glass. "Do you want me to throw out the other guests? Then we can have a proper drink like we used to in the old days?"

"Some other time, Charlie." Mia put on her jacket. "Too much to do right now."

She found a pen in her pocket and scribbled her number on a napkin.

"Call me if you remember anything else, will you?"

Charlie leaned over the counter and kissed her good-bye on both cheeks. "Don't be a stranger."

"I promise." Mia smiled.

She pulled her cap well over her head and stepped out into the rainy Oslo evening. She scouted for a taxi but saw none. Never mind. She wasn't in a hurry. It was not as if anyone were waiting for her back at the hotel. She'd pulled the hood of her jacket over her cap and had started walking back to the city center just as her phone rang. It was Gabriel Mørk.

"Hi," Mia said.

"Hi, it's Gabriel. Is now a good time?"

"Absolutely," she replied. "Are you still at the office?"

"Yes."

"You don't actually have to be there 24/7 — you *are* allowed to go home, you know. Has Holger told you that?"

"No, I know that, but there's quite a lot to learn." Gabriel sounded a little weary.

"So any news for me?"

"Yes, as a matter of fact, there is. It occurred to me that there must be a way to retrieve deleted text messages, so I called a buddy of mine, an Apple freak."

"And?"

"Simple. I found them."

"Everything that was on Roger's cell phone?"

"Yep."

"Wow, that's brilliant!" Mia said. "So what have we got?"

"Good news and bad. I found the deleted messages, but there weren't many of them. His phone must have been quite new. I'm starting to get cross-eyed, and I don't have the energy to read them all out loud. Do

303

you think you could look at them tomorrow?"

"Sure. Am I right in thinking there was no
sender this time either?"

"No, I have a number."

"Whose is it?"

"It's not listed. That's why I'm calling.
I'm going to have to hack several databases
to find out who owns it."

"How many are we talking about?"

For a moment there was silence from Gabriel's end. "As many as I have to."

"And?"

"Er, it's illegal. We should really get a
court order first. What do you think?"

"Have you spoken to Holger?"

"He's not answering his phone."

"We can't wait for that," Mia said. "Go
ahead."

"Are you sure?"

"Yes."

"Okay," Gabriel said.

"Are you starting now?"

"I thought I might hit the sheets first."

"As you wish. I'm sure it can wait until
tomorrow morning."

"Or I could do it now."

"Now is fine. I'm staying awake."

"Okay."

Mia ended the call and continued toward

the city center. The streets were practically deserted. She could see people through the windows, the glare from their television screens. Suddenly her hotel seemed even less attractive than it had earlier. There was no reason to go there. She wouldn't be able to sleep anyway. She might as well have another beer. Try to focus her mind.

Fortunately, Justisen wasn't busy. Mia ordered a beer and found a table in a quiet corner. She took out pen and paper and sat staring at the blank sheet in front of her. Four girls. Six years old. Pauline. Johanne. Karoline. Andrea. She wrote down their names at the top of the sheet. Pauline. Went missing from her nursery school. Found in Maridalen. Johanne. Went missing from her nursery school. Found by Hadelandsveien. Karoline and Andrea. Taken from their homes. Where would they be found? She could see no pattern. The answer had to be there somewhere. Roger Bakken/Randi. The text messages. *It is unwise to fly too near the sun. Who's there? Bye, bye, birdie.*

First message. Icarus. Roger had done something he shouldn't have. Second message. Who's there? She seemed to remember a series of jokes that started like this. *Knock-knock jokes. Knock, knock. Who's there? Doris. Doris who? Doris locked, that's why I'm*

305

knocking. It made no sense. Bye, bye, birdie. That was easier. *Bye Bye Birdie* was a musical popular with gay men. The eagle tattoo. *See you later, birdie.*

Mia got a foul taste in her mouth and ordered another Jäger to wash it away. The alcohol made her feel good. She was starting to get a little drunk, but that made it easier to think. She found another piece of paper and placed it alongside the first. Backpacks. Books. Paper. The names on the books. Dolls' dresses. I'm traveling alone. *"These go together,"* she quickly scribbled. *"They add up."* Pig's blood. Who's there? *"They don't add up,"* she wrote below it. Two from nursery school. Two in their homes. Ten dresses. A woman. Mia ordered another beer. It was happening now. Her head was clearer. The transvestite. A woman. Gender. Playing with gender? Gender confusion? Shame. Guilt. I'm traveling alone. The first symbols were clear proof of intelligence. Backpack. Sign. Dolls' dresses. The others didn't fit in with the rest; they were just white noise. Pig's blood? Who's there? She tore off another sheet and placed it next to the first two. Knocked back her beer and ordered another beer and chaser. This was it. She was onto something. She wrote *"Woman"* at the top of the third piece of

306

paper. *"Hønefoss. Maternity ward. Washed and got the girls ready. Anesthesia. Care. Nurse? Police sketch. Looks like everyone else.* Invisible? *How can you hide in plain sight?"* She left a section of the paper blank and wrote something at the bottom. *"Callous. Serious. Different-colored eyes. One brown and one blue. One in Maridalen. One near Hadelandsveien. Forest. Hidden. Have to search. Have to work. Have to hunt. On display and yet hidden. She wants to show us what she has done but not make it so obvious that we don't have to look. Pig's blood?* Who's there? *Why so clean first? Serious? Why so unclean later?"* Mia ordered more alcohol and found another sheet of paper. It was starting to flow now, there was something there. Something was taking shape, but it refused to come into focus. *"Pride. Look at me. Look at what I've done. Toni J. W. Smith. You're useless, and I'm going to prove it. It's me against you. A game. Why so clean first and then so unclean? Blood? Pig's blood? Staged. So theatrical. Fake. Ignore it."* It was loosening up inside her now. A rush of unstoppable thoughts. That was it. *"Fake. Ignore it."* Mia scribbled so furiously that she almost forgot her drinks. *"Ignore it. Not everything matters. Not the staged elements.*

307

Not the theatricality. It is dishonest. Fake. It does not add up. Look at what does add up. What is true. Which symbols point where? What do we need to address and what can we disregard? Is that the game?"

That is the game.

Mia smiled to herself but was unaware of it. She was miles away. Deep inside herself. The city did not exist. Justisen did not exist. The table did not exist. Beer did not exist. Jump rope, yes. Satchels, yes. Dolls' dresses, yes. I'm traveling alone, yes. Anesthesia, yes. Pig's blood, no, fake. Bye, bye, birdie, no, not important. Fly too near the sun, no, not important. Who's there?

"Mia?"

Mia was so startled that she leaped from her chair. She looked around, dazed, not knowing where she was.

"Sorry, am I disturbing you?"

Reality slowly returned. Her beer came back. The room came back. And there was Susanne standing next to her table with frizzy hair, her jacket soaked from the rain, looking upset.

"Hi, are you all right?"

"Do you mind if I sit down? I can see that you're working. I don't want to intrude."

Mia didn't have time to reply. Susanne took off her jacket and collapsed on the chair like a drowned rat.

"Sit down," Mia said. "No, it's fine. Is it raining outside?"

"Inside and out." Susanne heaved a sigh and buried her face in her hands. "I didn't know where to go. I thought you might be here."

"And I was," Mia said. "Do you want a beer?"

Susanne nodded softly. Mia went up to the bar. She came back to the table with two beers and two Jägermeisters.

"Are you writing a novel?" Susanne said, mustering up a feeble smile under her bangs.

"No, it's just work," Mia said.

"Good, because that title has already been taken," Susanne said, pointing to one of the sheets. " 'Who's there?' "

"What do you mean, taken? Where is it from?"

"It's the opening line of *Hamlet*." Susanne brushed her hair behind her ear and drank some of her beer.

"Are you sure?"

Susanne laughed. "Yes, I should hope so. I mean, I'm the assistant director. I practically know the script by heart."

"Sorry, I didn't mean it like that," Mia said. "Is it really?"

Susanne coughed slightly and suddenly switched to Drama Susanne from Åsgård-strand. " 'Who's there? Nay, answer me: stand, and unfold yourself. Long live the king!' "

She took another sip of her beer and suddenly seemed a little embarrassed.

"It's not original. We can ignore it," Mia said quietly.

"Ignore what?" Susanne said.

"Oh, nothing. So what has happened? Why are you looking so miserable?"

Susanne sighed again. Pulled out her hair from behind her ear and tried to hide behind it. "The same old story. I'm an idiot."

It was not until now that Mia realized that her friend had had quite a lot to drink already. She was slurring her words and struggled to steer the beer glass to her lips.

"Actors. Never trust them," she continued. "One day they tell you they love you, and then the next day they don't, and then they love you again, and then you believe them, and they sleep with one of the girls from the lighting crew. What's wrong with them?"

"Two faces," Mia said. "It's hard to know which one is real."

Two faces?

Playing with gender?

310

An actor?

"Lying bastards," Susanne said, quite loud.

Mia was starting to feel pretty drunk herself. She drained her beer and watched as Susanne tried to drink the rest of hers.

"I always end up going home alone," Susanne said, wiping away a tear.

Mia's cell rang. It was Gabriel Mørk again. "Yes. What have we got?"

"Another dead end."

"You didn't find anything?"

"Yes, the number is registered to a Veronica Bache."

"Excellent, Gabriel. Who is she?"

"The question you should be asking me is who *was* she? Veronica Bache lived to be ninety-four. She died in 2010."

34

The woman with one blue and one brown eye was standing in front of one of the mirrors in her bathroom. She opened the bathroom cabinet and took out the lenses. Blue today. Blue eyes at work. Not different-colored eyes. Not at work. At work she was not her true self. *At work nobody knows who I am.* And anyway, it wasn't her real job, was it? It was just a cover. Just for appearance's sake. She pulled her hair into a tight ponytail and bent forward toward the mirror. Placed the lenses carefully against her eyes and blinked. She put on a fake smile and studied herself. Hi, I'm Malin. Malin Stoltz. I work here. You think you know me, but you have no idea who I really am. Look how good I am at lying. Smiling. Pretending that I care what you're talking about. Oh, your dog is sick? How awful. I hope it's feeling better now. A glass of OJ, of course, no problem, Mrs. Olsen. Now, let me change your bedlinen as well, make it more comfortable for you. There's nothing nicer than fresh linen. The woman with one blue and one brown eye left the bathroom and went to her bedroom, opened her wardrobe, and took out her uniform. Staff wore white, a good rule. When everyone wears the same, we become invisible. Unless our eyes are different colors. And now they aren't. Now they are blue. As blue as the sea. Norwegian eyes. Beautiful eyes. Normal eyes. Sandwiches in the break room. Totally, I completely agree with you. She should have been kicked off the show, I certainly didn't vote for her, that woman has two left feet. Dead faces. Empty. Vacant. Empty words. Lips moving below dead eyes. Did he really say that? Your ex-husband? How dare he? Yes, of course I'm on Facebook. Coffee. Eight o'clock. Sometimes I work night shifts. I park in the garage. But it's not my real job, is it? Not really? No, reality is completely different.

The woman with one blue and one brown eye went out into the hall, picked up her bag and her coat, walked downstairs, and got into her car. She started the engine and turned on the radio. They are missing, but no one will find them, will they? Not everyone is capable of having children. Who gets

313

to decide? Who decides who can have a child? Some people lose a child. Who gets to decide? Who decides who will lose a child? It's not my real job. Not this. No, no one can say what my real job is. Yes, some people know, but they won't tell.

The woman with one blue and one brown eye changed radio stations. It was the same everywhere. The girls are still missing, and nobody knows where they are. Where are those girls? Are they still alive? Is someone holding them captive? How many girls do you need? How many children do you have to have? Two point three, isn't that the norm? Normal? So you are not normal if you don't have children? What if you can't have children? The woman with one blue and one brown eye drove slowly out of the city center. It is important to drive slowly if you want to be invisible. If someone were to stop your car, he might discover that it isn't yours. That your name isn't Malin Stoltz. That it is something completely different. That would not be good. Slow is better. Sometimes you can hide in plain sight — at work, for example. Some people think you need an education in order to get a job. You don't. You just need papers. Papers are easy to fake. You just need references. References are easy to fake. The woman with one blue and one brown eye turned off Drammensveien and drove up to the white brick building. She parked her car and made her way to the entrance. Ten minutes to eight. If you arrive on time and do your job, nobody asks any questions.

She opened the door and went to the staff changing room. Hung up her coat and left her bag in her locker and looked in the mirror again. *I have two blue eyes. I'm a little girl with blue eyes. This is just for fun. My real job is completely different. As long as nobody says anything, everything will be just fine. Sometimes you can hide in plain sight.* The woman with one blue and one brown eye tightened her ponytail and went to the nurses' station.

"Hi, Malin."

"Hi, Eva."

"How are you?"

"I'm really good. And you?"

"It was a long night. Helen Olsen felt unwell again. I had to call the ambulance."

"Oh, dear, I do hope she's feeling better."

"It's fine. She's coming back today."

"Good. That's good. How is your dog?"

"Better. It wasn't as serious as we first feared."

I'm not ill. You're ill.

"Who is on duty today?"

315

"You and Birgitte and Karen."

I'm not ill. You're ill.

"What is this?"

The woman with one blue and one brown eye looked at the notice above the coffee machine.

HØVIKVEIEN NURSING HOME CELE-BRATES 10 YEARS!

"Oh, that'll be nice. Big party on Friday."

"Yes, it'll be fun, won't it?"

"Will you be there?"

"Yes, of course. Of course I'll be there."

You're all sick. This isn't reality.

"Some of the girls talked about getting together for a drink beforehand. Are you in?"

"Of course I'm in, sounds like fun. Do you want me to bring anything?"

"Talk to Birgitte, she's organizing it."

"Right, I will."

"Can't wait!"

"Neither can I."

"Have a good shift, Malin."

"Thanks. Drive safely. Say hi to your husband."

"Thank you, I will."

The woman with one blue and one brown eye poured herself a cup of coffee, sat down, and pretended to read the newspaper.

35

Mia was standing outside the hotel, already regretting having agreed to go with Munch to Høvikveien Nursing Home. Talk to his mother — surely Munch could handle that on his own? For a moment Mia fantasized about being back on her island. The sunrise and the sea. She needed more sleep. She had stayed up far too late, had far too much to drink. She felt childishly sick and remorseful. Had she drunk-dialed Holger? A nagging feeling at the back of her head told her that she had decided that she absolutely must tell him what she'd discovered, that it could not wait.

Holger Munch looked grim, but Mia didn't have the energy to ask.

"You need to get yourself another cell phone," Munch said.

"Why?" Mia asked.

"You called me last night."

"Damn, I thought I might have."

"Drunk?"

"I bumped into an old friend from Ås-gårdstrand."

"I understand," Munch said. "You know that all our calls are being monitored, don't you?"

Mia made no reply. She tried to recall what she'd said, but it refused to come back to her. Never mind.

"So what did you find out?" Munch wanted to know.

"Roger Bakken had a female friend. Someone he spent a lot of time with when he was Randi."

"Anyone we know?"

Mia shook her head. "No, but I believe her eyes are different colors."

"What do you mean?" asked Munch, intrigued. "Is that possible?"

"Yes, one blue and one brown. I believe it's a genetic quirk."

"How is that useful?"

"We have to explore everything, don't you think?"

"Yes, true."

Munch opened the window and lit a cigarette. Mia hated people smoking in the car, especially in the state she was in today, but she didn't say anything. Munch seemed exhausted. Introverted.

"Anything else?"

"Yes," Mia said. "Gabriel managed to retrieve a number from Bakken's cell."

"Yes, I heard." Munch nodded. "Veronica Bache. Died in 2010."

"Have you found out anything more about her?"

"Not very much. Last known address was in Vika, lived with her great-grandson, a Benjamin Bache, he's an actor. Do you know who that is?"

"No."

"National Theater. *Hello!* magazine. A celeb, as they say."

"Someone has been using her cell phone for two years. Paid every bill so that the contract was never terminated. That must be what happened, am I right?" Mia said.

"Yes, that's the only way," Munch agreed.

"So what do you think? The great-grandson with access to the bills? The actor?"

"It's a possibility, certainly. I tried to get hold of him today, but he was going to some kind of rehearsal. We'll need to talk to him at the earliest opportunity. I think I'm onto something. Maybe."

"What?" Munch turned off Drammensveien and onto Høvikveien.

"You know all the symbolism?" Mia continued.

"Yes?"

"Wouldn't you say that it's a bit obvious?"

"Possibly," Munch said. "That's your area of expertise."

"No, seriously, Holger, I mean it."

"Yes, I understand, only I can't follow all the twists and turns of your brain. It makes me dizzy."

He muttered this as he parked outside Høvikveien Nursing Home.

"Here we go." He sighed, turning off the ignition.

Mia was convinced that if he'd been a Christian, he would have made the sign of the cross. It was clear that Holger Munch was dreading this conversation.

"It'll be fine," Mia said. "Just relax."

"I need one more cigarette," Munch said, and he got out of the car.

Mia followed him and took off her sunglasses. She was starting to feel slightly better. And being here in Høvik was fine. She was glad she'd come with him after all.

"Go on, try me," Munch said, and lit a cigarette.

"Now?"

"Yes, why not? Make me see inside your head."

"Okay," Mia said, sitting down on the hood of the car. "What was the first sign he left us?"

"I thought we were looking for a woman?"

"Never mind that now, what was the first clue?"

Munch shrugged his shoulders. "The dresses?"

"No."

"The backpacks?"

"No."

"Mark 10:14, 'Suffer the little children'?"

"No."

"Go on, then, enlighten me." Munch sighed and took another drag of his cigarette.

"Toni J. W. Smith," Mia said.

"And why is that the first clue?"

"Because it doesn't quite fit. Everything else fits, doesn't it? It's a part of the bigger picture, but it's not what we need to look at. We need to look beyond it."

"Ah?" Munch said, clearly intrigued now. "So the first clue that didn't fit?"

"The name on the book?"

"Exactly. A clear sign, wouldn't you say?"

"A sign of what?"

"Of intent, Holger. Come on, try again."

"Intent?"

"Oh, I give up." Mia heaved a sigh.

Holger took another long drag of his cigarette and blew smoke at the spring sun.

"Okay, intent," he said. "All the other symbols are fake. Washing the girls. The dresses. The school items. Toni J. W. Smith was invented by someone with an agenda? By someone with a plan?"

"Good, Holger." Mia clapped her hands somewhat ironically.

"Yes, yes, I haven't lost it completely."

"And what does Toni J. W. Smith mean?"

"Hønefoss."

"Precisely. And what about the other symbols?"

"The pig's blood?"

"No, that was the third."

"What was the second?"

"Do you remember Roger Bakken's three text messages?"

"Yes?"

"Which one of them did not fit?"

"Did any of them fit?"

"Yes, of course, try again, Holger. 'Icarus flew too near the sun.' Eagle wings. 'Bye, bye, birdie,' a gay musical. Roger Bakken was a gay man with a bird tattoo. Everything fits, but not 'Who's there?' It's the odd one out."

"That was clue number two? 'Who's there?' "

Mia nodded.

"And what does that mean?"

"I'm not sure, but I discovered yesterday that it's the opening line of *Hamlet.*"

Munch lit another cigarette and glanced nervously toward the entrance. Mia was sorely tempted to laugh. A grown man, the head of a special unit, and yet he was frightened to confront his own mother.

"And *Hamlet* is about to open at the National Theater? Veronica Bache's cell phone? Her great-grandson? Is that where we should be looking?"

"Not sure," Mia said, and she thought about it. "I've worked out *what* we should be looking for, but not *why.* That's as far as I've got."

"And the pig's blood was number three?"

Mia nodded.

"And that means what?"

"I don't know yet."

There could be little doubt that Høvikveien Nursing Home was a facility for the more affluent. A typical West Oslo place, Mia thought as they walked through the doors and into the light, airy reception area. The place was spotless. Clean and pleasant, with new furniture, modern light fixtures, original prints on the walls. Mia recognized

323

several of the artists. Her mother, Eva, had been very interested in art and had taken the girls to a wide range of exhibitions whenever the opportunity arose.

There were photographs of different activities on the walls. A display cabinet filled with trophies. Trips around Norway and abroad. Bridge tournaments. Bowling. Even though it was the last stop on life's journey, there was nothing here to suggest it. At Høvikveien Nursing Home, life was not over until you had swum in the Dead Sea or won a prize for growing pumpkins.

"Wish me luck." Holger sighed as he disappeared down one of the corridors.

To a private room, Mia guessed. With an en suite bathroom, a television, a radio, and round-the-clock service. She was about to pick up a magazine when she noticed a certificate on the wall. HØVIKVEIEN NURSING HOME 2009 CANASTA CHRISTMAS TOURNAMENT. WINNER: VERONICA BACHE. Mia got up to have a closer look. Yes indeed, it did say Veronica Bache. It had to be the same woman. She went over to the glass counter and rang a small bell. A few seconds later, one of the employees appeared from a back office.

"Hi, can I help you?"

The woman matched the rest of the nursing home. Gentle, pretty, with glowing cheeks. Perhaps they only hired people who matched the interior design, Mia mused. No worn-out staff clustered behind the kitchen puffing on hand-rolled cigarettes here. The woman was about Mia's age. Good posture and attractive, with bright blue eyes and her black hair in a swishy ponytail.

"My name is Mia Krüger," Mia said. She considered producing her ID card but decided against it.

"I'm Malin. And who are you here to see?" the gentle girl asked.

"I'm here with a friend, Holger Munch. He's visiting his mother."

"Hildur, yes." The girl with the blue eyes smiled. "Great lady."

"Absolutely," Mia agreed. "I couldn't help noticing that Hildur's acquaintance Veronica won the canasta tournament. It says so on one of the certificates over there."

"That's right," the girl confirmed. "We have a tournament every Christmas. I think Veronica won the last three before she passed."

"I've never played canasta," Mia said.

"Me either," the soft-spoken girl said with a laugh. "But the old people seem to enjoy it."

"That's the most important thing," Mia said. "Listen, something has occurred to me, and pardon me for asking, because you might not be allowed to tell me, but was Bache related to that good-looking actor by any chance?"

"Benjamin Bache?"

"Yes, that's the one."

The girl with the blue eyes looked at her for a moment. "Hmm, I'm not supposed to say anything," she said.

"I understand," Mia said. "Did he used to visit often? Did you see him? Is he just as handsome in real life?"

The woman with the ponytail relented. "He didn't come here that often, only a few times a year. And just between us, he's better looking on TV."

"I see."

The woman with the blue eyes disappeared into the back office. There was a small television in one corner. Mia looked for the remote control and found it next to the screen.

They had scheduled a press conference for today at twelve noon. Mia Krüger shook her head and turned up the volume another notch. Two anchormen in the studio, a reporter in front of the stairs at Grønland. The press conference would appear to have

326

been postponed. Mia turned off the TV, went outside, and dialed Gabriel's number.

"Hi."

"Why has it been postponed? Has anything happened?"

"No, we're about to begin."

"Will Anette be taking it today?"

"Yes, I think so, along with the public prosecutor. The one with the short hair."

"Hilde."

"Might be."

"Did you discover anything else about Veronica Bache?"

"Was I supposed to?"

"No, but I've stumbled across something," Mia continued. "Please, would you check it out for me?"

Gabriel sighed. "Of course. What is it?"

"What's wrong?"

"Nothing, only it's a lot to get your head around. And besides . . ."

"And besides what?"

"No, it's nothing. My girlfriend is pregnant."

"Is she? Congratulations."

"Er, thank you. . . . What did you want me to look up for you?"

"I'm not quite sure, it's just a hunch I have. I would like access to Høvikveien Nursing Home's . . . now what do you call it . . . ?"

"Waiting list? Are you thinking of moving in?"

Mia laughed. "Good God, it didn't take you long to settle in!"

"Sorry," Gabriel said. "I'm having a bit of a crap day."

"Well, don't take it out on me. It's not my fault that your girlfriend is pregnant," Mia teased him. "You only have yourself to blame for that."

"Yes, I guess so. Is it normal to want things in the middle of the night?"

"What things?"

"Soft-serve ice cream."

"I've heard it said that pregnant women get bizarre cravings," Mia said.

"Have you any idea just how difficult it is to find soft-serve ice cream in the middle of the night?"

Mia laughed.

"That's right, ha-freakin'-ha," Gabriel said.

"A list of staff. And guests."

"Guests?"

"Or what you call people who live in a nursing home. Inmates? Residents?"

"I know what you mean. I think we refer to them as staff and clients."

"Great, can you get it for me?"

"Legally?"

"No."

"If I get into trouble for this, I expect you to cover my back."

"You've been taking that class with Hat Trick, I can tell."

"Yes, indeed I have." Gabriel sighed once again.

"Of course I'll take responsibility," Mia said. "Høvikveien Nursing Home. Do you need the address?"

"No, I can find it. Am I looking for anything in particular?"

"No idea. Like I said, it's just a hunch. Munch's mother and Veronica Bache lived at the same nursing home. I mean, it's worth checking out."

"Munch's mother?"

"Did I say that out loud?"

"Damn, am I going to have to lie to Munch now?" Gabriel said. "I don't suppose he's supposed to know anything about this."

"Good boy," Mia said. "I've got to run. When is our next full briefing?"

"Three o'clock."

"Good, talk to you later."

Mia ended the call just as Munch appeared on the steps. She was about to join him but stopped when she noticed that he wasn't alone. A female caregiver in the same white uniform as the girl with the blue eyes was standing next to him. Pretty and slim with long, wavy, strawberry-blond hair. She laughed out loud and touched Munch, who, for his part, acted like a teenager, with his cheeks flushed and his hands stuffed into his trouser pockets.

"How did it go?" Mia asked when Munch came down to the car.

"Don't ask," he said, and lit a cigarette.

"Who was she?"

"Who?" Munch said.

"Who do you think?"

He got into the car without putting out his cigarette. "Oh, her. That's . . . I think she's named Karen. She looks after my mother. I just had to . . ."

He started the car and pulled out on Høvikveien.

"Yes? You just had to do what?"

"Any news?" he said, changing the subject.

"The press conference is on now."

Munch turned on the radio. Mia heard Anette's voice. *No news, we're still looking. We would welcome any information.* They had nothing new to announce. Even so, the world demanded a press conference.

Mia glanced at Munch, who was still lost in a world of his own. She wondered if she should tell him that Veronica Bache had shared a nursing home with his mother, but she decided to let it lie for now. Gabriel was on the case, and Munch looked as if he had enough on his plate.

"You have to see a psychologist," Munch said out of the blue when they were back on Drammensveien.

"What do you mean?"

He took a business card from his jacket pocket and handed it to her. "You have to see a psychologist."

"Says who?"

"Mikkelson."

"Screw that."

"Don't look at me. They heard your call last night. They don't think you're all there."

"Well, they can forget about that," Mia snarled.

"That's exactly what I told them."

"Then we agree."

She opened the glove compartment and tossed the business card in without looking at it. "Damn nerve."

"What did you expect?"

"How about a bit of respect?"

"Good luck with that." Munch sighed. "Why don't we stop for a burger on the way back?"

"Fine by me," Mia said.

He found an exit and pulled up at a gas station, just as it started to rain.

36

The rain was dripping down outside the windows of *Aftenposten*'s editorial offices. The staff had gathered in Grung's office to watch the press conference, which was scheduled for twelve noon but had been postponed for ten minutes. Present were Mikkel Wold, Silje Olsen, Erik Rønning, and Grung, their editor, and although Mikkel did not like to think of it in such terms, for once he'd been given the VIP seat, a leather chair next to Grung. There'd been a shift since that phone call at Skullerud. He had moved up the ranks. Suddenly he was at the center of events. Grung turned down the TV volume and opened the meeting.

They had kept it in-house that the killer had contacted them. They hadn't run a story on it. Not yet. This was the agenda for the meeting. Should they use it? And if they did, then how?

"I say we wait," Silje said, taking a bite of

her apple.

"Why?" Grung said.

"Because we don't know if he or she will go underground if we go public with it."

"I say we run it. Why the hell not?" Erik said.

The twenty-six-year-old highly talented journalist had been the apple of Grung's eye ever since Grung had first hired him, and he usually got the chair that Mikkel was now occupying. If the young lad was jealous or envious, he was hiding it well. He sat relaxed, with his legs apart, but he was playing with a rubber stress ball.

"What's to stop the killer from calling *VG* tomorrow? Or *Dagbladet* tonight?" he went on. "We have the chance of a scoop, but we have to act now."

Mikkel Wold rolled his eyes. Erik had started using the word "scoop" quite a lot after winning the Scoop Prize last year for a series of features about the homeless in Oslo.

"So why hasn't the killer called them yet?" Silje sparred.

Silje and Erik were like day and night. She twenty-something, loud, pierced lip, with vociferous, left-wing liberal views — certainly left-wing for someone working for *Aftenposten*. He calm, levelheaded, usually dressed in a suit, neatly combed hair, every mother-in-law's dream, with a pleasing smile and a twinkle in his eye. Whenever there was a discussion at the office, the two of them were usually on opposite sides of the argument.

Mikkel Wold was more a journalist of the old school. Notepad and paper and close to his sources, he had never written about anything or anyone he hadn't met in person or at least been in contact with. These days it was mostly in the form of a press release and a quick phone call, sometimes not even a quick phone call. In terms of dress style, he sided with neither Silje nor Erik. He was halfway between the two, and perhaps he was a little dull. He wondered about it sometimes. If he should make the effort to buy some smarter clothes, which would — now, what was it the magazine his sister always had on display would say? — "bring out his personality." But he never had. The clothes in his wardrobe had been there for almost ten years. It was because — he didn't quite know how to put it — well, because a vain, self-obsessed appearance, whatever your style of choice, just did not fit in with a serious job like his. And he'd been proved right. The killer had called him. Not one of the others.

"You're right," Erik said. "Let's run the risk."

"Oh, please, Erik, passive-aggressive arguing is the preserve of us ladies, isn't that right?"

"Was I being passive-aggressive just now?"

"Oh, Jesus, give me a break." Silje laughed.

"What do you think, Mikkel?" Grung said, turning to him.

For once the other two fell silent. Everyone wanted to know his opinion. He was loath to admit it, but the mysterious caller had inadvertently done him a favor.

"I'm not sure." Mikkel cleared his throat. "On the one hand, I know that we could run a story on it, no doubt about that."

"And it would be an exclusive," Erik interjected, rolling the stress ball along the table in front of him. "Just us. No one else. I say go."

"But on the other hand," Mikkel continued, "it would be silly to blow it on a headline or two and then lose the source. We might actually be able to help."

There was silence around the table again.

"Help?" Silje said. "Do you mean go to the cops?"

"The police." Grung sighed. "This isn't the *Socialist Worker,* you know. We work for *Aftenposten.*"

336

"Does that mean we can't call them cops?" Silje argued back, and took another bite of her apple.

"Whatever," Grung said. "It's something we have to make a decision about."

"What is?" Erik said.

"Whether we go to the police with what we know."

"What good would that do?" Erik sighed. "Number one, we haven't got anything. No hard evidence. Not something the police can use but *we* can, wouldn't you agree?"

Silje nodded. "It feels strange to hear myself say it, but on this point I actually agree with Erik. Not that we shouldn't go to the cops —"

"The police," Grung corrected her.

"— but that we don't have anything they can use. Not yet."

"That's what I said," Erik chimed in.

"But that doesn't mean we should blow it," Silje went on. "If we run the story now, who knows what we'll lose out on? And besides, hello, three days ago? Old news? What —"

"No, it isn't," Erik interrupted her. "It's still fresh."

"Shhh, it's starting," Grung said, turning up the volume on the TV.

It was Anette Goli who was giving the

press conference today, together with Hilde Simonsen, the public prosecutor.

"Goli and Simonsen," Erik said with a sigh, and started fidgeting with his stress ball again. "Why don't they bring out Munch or Krüger? I fancy writing another feature on Krüger."

"Hah," Silje laughed scornfully. "We all know what you fancy doing to Krüger. A feature? Is that what they call it now?"

"Hush," Grung said, turning up the volume even more.

Anette Goli had just welcomed everyone to the press conference when Mikkel Wold's phone rang. The meeting room fell completely quiet.

UNKNOWN NUMBER.

"Let it ring twice!"

"Answer it!" said Erik and Silje in unison. Grung pressed the MUTE button on the remote control and mimed, *Put it on speaker,* to Mikkel Wold. Mikkel sat up in his chair, cleared his throat, and answered the call.

"Yes, hello, Mikkel Wold, *Aftenposten.*"

Crackling noises in the handset. They could not hear anyone on the other end.

"Wold, *Aftenposten,*" Mikkel said again, rather more nervous now.

Still nothing. Just hissing.

"Is anyone there?" Erik said impatiently.

Grung and Silje both grimaced.

Shut up, Grung mouthed across the table.

A few seconds passed. Then a grating, metallic voice could be heard.

"We're not alone, I gather?" it said.

Even Erik fell quiet at this; he had also stopped messing with his rubber ball, just sat with his eyes wide open and his mouth gaping. To a large extent, they had assumed that it must be a prank. The killer calling — what was that about? Every journalist's dream, surely, and why should Wold be the lucky one? Now there could be no doubt. This was real. Silje spit out the apple bite and placed it carefully on the desk.

"No," Wold said. "You're on speakerphone."

"Good heavens, what an honor," the metallic voice said archly. "*Aftenposten* listens to its readers, but that's quite all right. It means more of you can take responsibility."

"For what?" Mikkel Wold croaked.

"We'll get to that later," the voice said. "By the way, I thought you were going to the press conference. Didn't you have a question to ask?"

"Why did the pig drip on the floor?" Wold said nervously.

"Good boy, you remembered it," the voice said.

"I know how to do my job. I don't ask questions I didn't come up with and can't explain," Wold said.

He looked across to Grung, who was frantically shaking his head to signal that Wold had given the wrong answer. They had to play along with the caller, not antagonize him — they'd agreed on that in advance. There was silence from the other end.

The voice laughed after a lengthy pause. "A journalist with integrity."

"Yes," Mikkel said.

"You're very sweet," the voice said scornfully. "But everyone knows there is no such thing as a journalist with integrity. It's just something you like to think you have. You are aware, aren't you, that journalists came in at the bottom in a survey last year? About which professions we trust? You were beaten by lawyers, advertising agencies, and used-car salesmen. Did you not see it?"

The metallic voice laughed again, almost heartily this time. Erik Rønning shook his head and made a rude gesture at the cell phone on the table. Grung glared furiously at him.

"But that's not why we're here," the voice said icily.

"So why *are* we here?" Mikkel Wold demanded to know.

"My, my, you are on the ball tonight. Did you think of that question all by yourself?"

"Stop fooling around!" Erik burst out, unable to restrain himself any longer. "How do we know you're not just some time-wasting weirdo who likes playing games?"

Grung's face turned puce, and he kicked Erik under the table. Another silence followed, but the voice did not go away.

"That's a good question," the voice said drily. "To whom do I have the honor of speaking?"

"Erik Rønning," Erik said.

"Good heavens! Would you believe it, Erik Rønning himself. The winner of the 2011 Scoop Prize. Congratulations."

"Thank you," Erik said.

"How does it feel to write about the homeless before going home to Frogner to drink chardonnay in the hot tub? You call that journalistic integrity?"

Erik was about to say something but thought better of it.

"But obviously, Rønning, you're quite right. How can you be sure that I am who I say I am? Why don't we play a little game?"

Erik cleared his throat. "What kind of game?"

"I call it 'Being in the News.' Want to play?"

There was total silence around the table. No one dared say a word.

"Why don't I explain the rules before you make up your mind?" the metallic voice said. "You people always report the news, so I thought you might be getting a little bored. Why not *be* the news for once? How's that for a kick?"

"What does it involve?" Mikkel Wold asked.

"You get to decide," the voice said.

"What do we get to decide?"

"Who lives and who dies."

The four journalists stared at one another.

"What do you mean?"

The voice laughed briefly. "What do you *think* I mean? I have yet to make up my mind. Andrea or Karoline? You get to decide. How cool is that? I'm letting you join in."

"Y-you can't be serious," Silje said.

"Oh, a girl as well, how nice. Who are you?"

"S-S-Silje Olsen," Silje stuttered.

She was clearly intimidated by the gravity of the situation.

"So what do *you* make of it all, Silje Olsen?" the voice said.

"What do I make of what?"

The voice laughed again. "A woman. Do you believe it?"

"Yes," Silje said tentatively.

"You're so naïve. It's very simple. It's far *too* simple, really. I'm bored. I really am. This is boring. I had expected more of a challenge. Come on, Mikkel, did you believe it?"

"Yes," Mikkel said, having paused to think about it.

"Oh, please, do I have to be better than anyone else? A woman. A senior citizen claims to have seen a woman. How about a transvestite? Did anyone think of that? How about a homeless person? Erik, that's your area. What do you think a homeless person would do for two thousand kroner? Put on a hoodie and turn up in a street in Skullerud in the middle of the night, especially if he gets a lift there and back? Would you have said yes, Erik, if *you* were homeless?"

"You're not a woman — is that what you're telling us?" Erik said feebly.

"Christ Almighty, you're so much stupider than I'd expected," the chilling voice said. "I actually had some faith in you. Never mind. Okay, this is how we play: You have one minute to pick a name. Andrea or Karoline. Whoever you pick will die tonight. The

343

other gets to live. She'll be returned to her home within twenty-four hours. If you don't give me a name, they both die. It makes no difference to me. One will die. One will live. You decide. Are you clear about the rules?"

"But you can't do this," Grung protested.

"I'll call you back in one minute. Good luck."

"N-n-no," Silje stuttered.

"Tick-tock," the voice said, and ended the call.

37

Lukas was in heaven. Or at least it felt like it. He had been looking forward to this visit for days, his third to the house in the forest. Lux Domus, *the House of Light,* or as Pastor Simon liked to call it, Porta Caeli, Heaven's Gate. How was it possible for anything to be so beautiful? Porta Caeli. Heaven's Gate. His body had been tingling with excitement all day, and finally they had arrived; he was so near to heaven he could barely contain himself, but he forced himself to sit completely still on the spindle-back chair by the window while the pastor read to the children.

God had spoken to the pastor. Told him to build this place. A new ark. Not for animals this time but for his chosen people. The initiated. The House of Light. Heaven's Gate. They would travel together on the Day of Judgment. No one else. Only them. Forty people, no more. There were several arks across the world, God had said to the pastor, but the congregation had not been told where the others were. Only that they existed, that was enough; these people would meet the other chosen ones in heaven, so there was no rush. In heaven. God's Kingdom. Where turquoise water flowed in fresh streams and everything was made of gold, on a carpet of bright white clouds. Eternity. The chosen ones. Forever.

Lukas closed his eyes and let the pastor's voice fill him. God's voice, that was what it was. The children mattered most, God had said, they were pure. It was important that children be pure and clean, as innocent as they had been in their mother's womb, not tarnished after years on earth. No, pure, they must be purified. Even if it took fire. The flames of hell. The pastor spoke with a mild and calm voice, firm like God's own hand, hard on the outside and soft on the inside. Water was flowing inside Lukas's head now. Clean, fresh rivers winding their way through green forests and across white fields in front of a house of gold.

"My children, I will manifest myself in front of you to guide my people from the darkness to the light," the pastor said. "I will reveal the reality of hell, so that you can be saved and renounce your evil ways before it is too late. Your souls will be taken from your bodies, by me, the Lord Jesus Christ, and sent into hell. I will also offer you visions of heaven, and many other revelations."

The pastor fell silent and gazed across the assembly. He liked doing this. Looking into everyone's eyes. It was important. So that the people could see God's eyes behind his. Lukas opened his own eyes and smiled. His house would lie right next to the pastor's — God himself had promised that. There were not all that many children here, only eight. The pastor had chosen them himself. Five girls and three boys, almost entirely pure. A few sessions with the pastor's kind voice and they would be ready.

Lukas looked around to see if Rakel, the special girl, was here. The children looked very similar. That was the point — *we are all equal before God* — but he spotted her eventually. Blue eyes and plenty of freckles. They'd had a few problems with her. Lukas could not understand why the pastor made such a fuss over one little girl. What made her so special? If she wanted to run away from the House of Light and spend eternity in hell, then let her go. Why waste time on her? There were plenty of other good candidates in the congregation.

It was not an opinion Lukas had voiced, obviously. The pastor always knew what was best. Why had he even had this thought to begin with? Lukas shook his head at his own idiocy and closed his eyes again. Once more the pastor's voice filled him. He pressed his lips together hard so as not to emit even a small sigh.

"One night as I was praying in my house, I was visited by the Lord Jesus Christ," the pastor continued. "I had been deep in prayer for days, and suddenly I felt God come to me. His strength and glory filled the whole house. A brilliant light lit up the room around me, and I was overcome by a feeling of beauty and completeness. The light flooded in, rolling in and out like waves. It was a wondrous sight. And then the Lord started talking to me. He said, 'I am your Lord Jesus Christ, and I will reveal to you how you should prepare the faithful for my return and how to punish the sinners. The forces of darkness are real, and my judgment is true. My child, I will take you into hell with the strength of my spirit, and I will show you many things that I want the world to see. I will reveal myself to you many times; I will take your spirit out of your body, and I will take you into hell.' 'Dear Lord,' I cried out, 'what do you wish me to do?' My whole being wanted to call out to Jesus in gratitude at his presence. It was the most beautiful, serene, blissful, powerful love I have ever felt. Praises of God flowed from my lips. Immediately I wanted to devote my whole life to him, so that he could use it to save others from their sin. I knew, by his spirit, that it really was Jesus, the Son of God, who was in the room with me. 'Look, my child,' Jesus said, 'with my spirit I will take you into hell, so you can describe it, so that you can lead the lost souls out of the darkness and into the light of the Gospel of Jesus Christ!' Straightaway my soul was taken out of my body. Then I traveled with Jesus out of my house and up to heaven."

The pastor rose and told the children to do likewise. They formed a circle in the middle of the floor. The pastor nodded to Lukas to indicate that he should join them. Lukas rose softly from his chair and took two of the children by the hand.

"Let us pray," the pastor said, and bowed his head.

Soon the small room was full of murmuring voices.

" 'Our Father, who art in heaven, hallowed be thy name. Thy kingdom come, thy will be done on earth as it is in heaven. Give us this day our daily bread. And forgive us our trespasses, as we forgive those who trespass against us. And lead us not into temptation, but deliver us from evil. For thine is the kingdom, and the power, and the glory, for ever and ever. Amen.' "

"Amen," Lukas said again. He could not help himself.

Porta Caeli, Heaven's Gate. And now they were here to prepare for the day that would soon arrive.

The pastor opened the door and let out all the children. All except Rakel. He always kept Rakel back for an extra chat. Perhaps it was like the lamb that had gotten separated from the flock. Of course it was. The lost sheep and the shepherd. Yet again Lukas felt bad for having doubted the pastor's wisdom.

"I think that Rakel needs a little time alone with God and with me," the pastor said, and he signaled to Lukas to leave the room.

Lukas nodded, smiled, and left.

"Make sure that no one comes in and disturbs us, would you, Lukas?"

"Of course," Lukas said with a bow.

He closed the door softly behind him. It had started to grow dark outside now; he could see stars in the sky. He smiled broadly to himself and felt another warm rush through his veins. That was where they were going. To heaven. He could hardly wait. He was so looking forward to it. Indeed, it was hard to describe how excited he was. A huge, wonderful, constantly tingling feeling from the top of his head to the tips of his fingers and into his toes. Turquoise rivers and houses made from gold. Was that really possible? That he could be so blessed? Lukas folded his arms across his chest, still grinning from ear to ear, and he started humming a new hymn he had just taught himself.

38

It was undoubtedly the longest minute in Mikkel Wold's life. And the shortest. The shortest and the longest minute. It was as if time had stopped. And yet it was slipping away between his fingers. Time had acquired a new meaning. Time had no meaning. They spent the first five seconds just staring at one another. Mikkel stared at Silje, whose jaw had dropped and whose eyes looked as if they'd just seen a UFO. Silje stared desperately at Grung, like a young member of the flock seeking comfort from one of the older ones, but there was no help to be found in Grung. The normally resourceful editor stared alternately at the cell phone lying on the table between them and Mikkel Wold, who was now staring at Erik Rønning.

Erik had ground to a halt. He was no longer functioning. There was not a single movement or expression to be found in his face. The rubber ball sat half squeezed in his hand. His mouth was half open. A witty or sarcastic comment had stopped on its journey out into the room and was now going back inside his head. All four of them. Dumbstruck. Frozen. In total shock. So went the first five seconds.

The next fifteen seconds were the total opposite. They all started talking over one another simultaneously. Like four children in a tunnel who had just realized that the freight train was coming toward them and that they could not get off the tracks, that there was just one way out and that was to run, even though deep down they all knew that it could only end in tragedy, but still they ran, out of instinct. Random words bounced around the room.

"Christ Almighty."

"We have to pick one."

"Jesus."

"What if it's a hoax?"

"I think I'm going to be sick."

"But what the hell. We can't just . . . ?"

"What if we don't pick one?"

"Oh, my God."

"We have to pick one."

"We can't."

"This can't be happening."

"Grung?"

"Mikkel?"

"What are we going to do?"

"We can't kill another human being."

"I think I'm going to throw up. I feel sick."

"We can save a human being."

"Erik?"

"Silje?"

"What happens if we do nothing?"

"They both die."

"We can't kill a little girl."

"Shit."

"We can save a little girl."

"Shit."

"What are we going to do?"

"Shit."

Twenty seconds had passed now. The clock in the office had no second hand. It still said 12:16. It was not helping. It did not count the seconds. That was the one thing they needed right now, not hours, not minutes, just seconds. The next ten were spent trying to work out how much time had passed. At this point panic was spreading around the room like wildfire.

"How much time has passed?" Silje's face was deathly pale. "How much time is left?"

Grung had stood up and was resting the palms of his hands against the table. "Did someone make a note of the time?"

Mikkel Wold looked at his phone, at the

clock on the wall. Without the second hand, the numbers might as well have been painted on the wall. Four children on the railway tracks in a tunnel who can feel the vibrations of the train thundering toward them.

"Let's not waste time working out how much time has passed!" Erik said tightly.

He had gotten up, too, and banged his fist against the table. Once. Twice. Three times.

Grung had moved his hands from the table and started pulling at his hair. "How much time *has* passed?"

This part took ten seconds. By now thirty seconds had passed.

"We have to think now!" Erik shouted. "There's no point shouting over each other."

"We can't just shout each other down!" Silje shouted.

"We must decide!" Mikkel Wold shouted.

"What are we going to do?" Grung shouted, still tearing his hair out.

"Everyone calm down!" Erik shouted.

"Let's all calm down!" Silje shouted.

By now forty seconds had passed. Every single one of the last twenty seconds felt like an entire minute in itself. Or an hour. Or a whole year. It was as if the hands had stopped moving and yet were running away at the same time. Erik was the first person to make a sensible suggestion.

"Let's vote."

"What?"

"Don't say anything. We're voting now. Hands up, everyone who thinks we ought to do something."

Erik held up his hand. Grung held up his hand. Mikkel Wold held up his hand without quite knowing why, his reaction pure reflex. Silje's hands remained on the desk.

Forty-nine seconds had passed.

"Three against one."

"But," Silje protested, but Erik was not listening to her.

"Hands up, everyone who votes to save Karoline."

"You mean kill Andrea?" Silje wailed.

"Hands up!" Erik shouted.

By now fifty-three seconds had passed.

"Hands up if you think we ought to save Karoline!" Erik shouted again, desperate now. The train was nipping at his heels — this was the only way out, make it stop or derail it.

He raised his hand and stared at Grung. Grung copied him and looked desperately at Silje.

"No!" Silje sobbed. "No, no, no!"

Fifty-seven seconds had passed.

Grung and Erik were standing with their hands in the air now. They both looked at Mikkel Wold.

"Yes or no?" Erik demanded.

Mikkel Wold tried to raise his arm from his lap, but it refused to move. It felt leaden. His arm had never been that heavy before. It refused to obey him. Or maybe that was exactly what it did. His brain didn't know.

Fifty-nine seconds had passed.

"Come on!" Erik roared. "Do we save Karoline or not?"

"We kill Andrea!" Silje sobbed. "We can't do that!"

"Yes or no?" Grung bellowed.

He had clumps of hair in his hand, which was raised in the air. Mikkel Wold tried to lift his hand again, but it was still stuck to his lap.

Then his phone rang.

The room fell completely silent. Their time was up. The phone rang again. Mikkel Wold was staring at it, yet he had no idea where it was. He could not see it clearly. It could have been in another room. Or on the moon. He did not know what to do. Finally Erik Rønning leaned over and pressed the screen.

"Hello again," the metallic voice said.

There was total silence around the table.

"I'm very excited," the voice said. "What did you decide?"

None of them were capable of uttering a single word.

"Is anyone there?" the voice asked.

Silje looked at Grung, who looked at Erik, who looked at Mikkel Wold, who looked at his fingers.

The metallic voice cackled. "Has the cat got your tongue? I need an answer now. Time is running out. Tick-tock."

Erik Rønning cleared his throat. "We . . ."

"Andrea?" the chilling voice asked. "Or Karoline? Who gets to go home? One girl dies, one girl lives. How hard can it be?"

"They both live!" Silje sobbed.

The metallic voice laughed again. "Oh, no, Miss Olsen, that's not how we play. One lives, one dies. *You* get to decide who lives and who dies. It feels good, doesn't it? Being master of life and death. It's a bit like being God. Isn't it fun to play God, Rønning?"

The room fell completely silent again. The seconds crawled past at a snail's pace. Mikkel Wold's brain had stopped working. Silje was hugging herself. Grung was standing up with both hands in the air. Erik Rønning opened his mouth and was just about to say something.

"Right," the cold voice said. "Both of them it is. It's a shame, really, but if that's what you want, who am I to argue? Thanks for playing."

"No!" Silje cried out, lunging for the phone with both hands, a last desperate attempt to knock some humanity into the icy, metallic being, but it was too late.

The voice had already gone.

39

Mia Krüger was sitting on the smoking terrace watching Munch destroy his lungs. They had just finished today's briefing, and Munch was in a particularly bad mood.

"How is that possible?" he kept repeating, rubbing his eyes.

None of the team had slept much in the past week, but Munch looked as if he might have slept even less than the others. Mia had been waiting for the right moment to tell him what was on her mind, but she was having second thoughts. She couldn't be sure. It was just a hunch. But a hunch that had grown stronger as the day went by.

"How is that possible?" Munch said again, lighting his next cigarette with his current one.

"What are you talking about?" Mia said.

"Eh?" Munch grunted, turning to her.

When he realized who he was talking to, his eyes softened.

"All of it," he said, rubbing his eyes again. "Surely someone must have seen them. Two six-year-old girls don't just vanish into thin air."

"Have we had a ransom demand yet?"

"We've got nada. The families have offered a reward of half a million, I believe. You'd have thought that amount of money would make someone come forward."

"Will they increase it to a million?"

Munch nodded. "They're announcing it tomorrow. We'll just have to cross our fingers."

"And hope that not every nutjob in the world jams our switchboard," Mia said.

"That's the risk we run." Munch sighed, taking a long drag of his cigarette. "Did you manage to contact Benjamin Bache?"

"I'm meeting him at four-thirty at the theater. He could only spare me half an hour. I think he's doing *Karius and Bactus, the Tooth Trolls* as well as rehearsing *Hamlet*. Do you want to come along?"

Munch shook his head. "No, you take that one. Does he live in his great-grandmother's apartment? Is that the address where the bills are sent? You know the drill."

"No problem," Mia said.

"I just refuse to believe it," Munch said. "Someone must have seen something. Our killer getting in and out of a car? Going into or out of a cabin? In or out of a basement? The girls have to be fed — our killer buying extra food? Our killer . . ." He continued to stare at the tip of his cigarette.

"If it's so well planned, then we need a lucky break. You must be aware of that," Mia said quietly.

"And it does seem well planned, doesn't it?" Munch agreed.

"Yes, I'm afraid so," Mia said. "It could have been years in the preparation, for all the evidence we have."

"And we know what that means," Munch said. "The girls will be dead if we don't find them soon."

Mia said nothing. She, too, stayed where she was, staring down at the street. Sometimes she envied the people down there. Normal people. Who owned a corner shop or bought shoes for their kids. Who did not have to deal with stuff like this. She braced herself for what she had to say. "There's something I have to tell you," she said to Munch.

"Spit it out," he said.

Mia paused as she struggled to find the right words.

"What is it?" Munch urged her.

"I think that you're involved," she said at length.

"Involved?"

"I think you were part of the planning."

"What are you talking about, Mia?"

They were interrupted by a timid Gabriel Mørk, who popped his head through the door to the terrace.

"Sorry to disturb you, but —"

"What do you want?" Munch barked at him.

"Oh, it's just . . . Mia, I found . . . well, you know the information you asked for earlier today? What do you want me to do with it?"

"I want you to give all the names to Kim and Ludvig and get them to cross-reference them with the Hønefoss case. I have a hunch we might find something there."

"Will do," the young man said, and he quickly closed the door without ever once looking at Munch.

"Just what did you mean when you said that I was part of the planning?"

"I think," Mia said pensively, "that this is about you."

"About me?"

"I think so."

They were interrupted once more, this time by an agitated Anette Goli, who didn't even bother knocking.

"You have to come right now," she said to Munch.

"What is it?"

"We have a breakthrough. We've just had a call from a lawyer —" She looked at a Post-it note in her hand. "His name is Livold. He represents *Aftenposten.* They've been contacted by the killer."

"Shit," Munch said. He got up and stubbed out his cigarette. "When?"

"Several times, I believe. Some days ago. Most recently lunchtime today."

"And they call us now?" Munch was fuming. "Now? Morons."

"They've clearly spent a day or two taking legal advice."

"Goddamn fools, where are they?"

"The Postgirobygget building. They're waiting for us now. I have a car downstairs."

Munch turned to Mia. "Are you coming?"

She shook her head. "I'm off to see Benjamin Bache."

"Yes, of course." He gave her a strange look. "We'll have to do this later, but soon. I have absolutely no idea what you're talking about."

"I'll meet you at Justisen afterward," Mia said.

"Fine," Munch said, and he half ran after Anette out of the office.

40

Benjamin Bache was sitting on the steps outside the National Theater when Mia arrived. He seemed restless; he checked his watch, played with his phone, lit a cigarette, drummed his fingers on his thigh, glanced around as if he were nervous that someone might notice him. It wasn't the smartest place to hang out if you didn't want to be seen, Mia thought, stopping behind the statue of Henrik Ibsen so she could spend some time observing Bache.

She had seen him somewhere before, but it took a while before she could place him. Not in *Se og Hør* — she never read that, couldn't even be bothered to flick through such magazines when she was at the dentist's. Not that she had anything against them; it was just that their features held very little interest for her. The press had turned its attention to her when the storm raging around her was at its worst, but she had refused them all. "The truth about Mia Krüger" was pretty much how the journalist had put it when he called her. Could such people even be called journalists? How did it work? Were you a journalist if you wrote about people's breasts and where they spent their holidays? Surely there had to be some sort of professional standard. She'd declined politely even though he offered her "a great holiday in the sun for you and your boyfriend — are you seeing anyone right now?" Mia chuckled to herself and took a bite of the apple she had bought from the Narvesen kiosk up the street. A holiday in the sun, seriously. Was that the best they could do? Was that their best offer? In return for which she would lay bare her private life? A holiday in the sun?

Benjamin Bache sat with a cigarette dangling from the corner of his mouth and one eye narrowed while he tapped the screen on his phone. He put the phone in his pocket, rolled the cigarette between his fingers, went back to drumming his thigh before he suddenly took out the phone again and pressed the screen once more. That was when it came back to her. A scene from a film at the Contemplation by the Sea Festival. He'd been playing a police officer. He was supposed to be her, or rather not her but pos-

sibly Kim or Curry, a male detective who
was not the boss but a member of a unit.
He had seemed uncomfortable in the role.
Mia took a last bite of the apple, tossed the
core into a trash can, and walked up to the
steps.

Benjamin Bache rose when he saw her and
came toward her with a broad smile on his
face.

"Hi, Mia, great to see you," he said, and
offered her a firm handshake.

"Hello," Mia said, somewhat surprised
that he acted as if he knew her.

Perhaps that was what they did in his
circles. *Those of us who appear on TV and
are featured in the newspapers are in the
same boat, we're a community, and we stick
together.* It was so not Mia's cup of tea, but
she decided to ignore it.

"I've booked us a table at Theatercaféen,
is that all right?" Benjamin said, stubbing
out his cigarette.

"Fine." Mia smiled. "But I don't think it'll
take that long."

"Indulge me." Benjamin winked at her
and punched her arm gently. "I need food.
I've been rehearsing all day, and now I need
to go and do some children's theater before
more rehearsals tonight."

"Sure." Mia nodded. "I'm not hungry, but

I can watch you eat."

"Sounds great." Benjamin gestured for her to follow him across the street.

She was not surprised to discover that Benjamin Bache was on a first-name basis with the waitress at Theatercaféen and chatted with her all the way to the table he had reserved by the window. He even introduced her to Mia. The girl was clearly embarrassed at having to shake Mia's hand and introduce herself, and again Mia forced a smile. Everyone was so chummy. It was a form of manipulation, she knew that, but she couldn't tell if Benjamin Bache was bright enough to realize it. Perhaps that was just how things were done in his line of work. Everything was personal, intimate, we know each other, we're on the same team, cast me, I can play this part.

He was a huge flirt, no doubt about that. Mia could only hope that Susanne hadn't been dumb enough to get involved with a guy like him. That she hadn't shed tears over him. No, he was unlikely to be the one. Susanne preferred older men. Men who could take care of her. Though Mia was quite sure that Benjamin Bache could play the strong, caring type if he had to. Now he was playing the part of . . . well, what would she call it? The innocent young guy?

"I must say I was surprised when you called," Benjamin said once he had ordered. "What is this really about?"

Mia realized he had said almost the same line in the film she'd seen.

"It's pure routine," Mia said, and took a sip of her water.

"Fire away," Benjamin Bache said.

He raked his hand through his hair in a knowing way. He really was a flirt. She made a mental note to tell Susanne to stay well clear of him the next time they saw each other.

"It's about your great-grandmother, Veronica Bache."

"I see," Benjamin said, raising his eyebrows.

"She was your great-grandmother, wasn't she? Veronica Bache, Hansteensgate 20. She passed away two years ago?"

"That's correct," Benjamin said.

"She was living there when she died?"

"No, no," Benjamin said. "She was in a home for many years."

"Høvikveien Nursing Home?"

"Yes, that's right. What is this really about?"

"Who lives at the Hansteensgate 20 address?"

"It's my apartment. I've lived there for

seven years."

"Since your great-grandmother went into nursing care?"

"Yes."

"Did you inherit it? Is it in your name?"

"No, it's in my father's name. What's happened? Why are you asking me this, Mia?"

Again this first-name business. She was tempted to confide in him, open up. It really was a very effective technique. She would have to try it out sometime.

"Like I said, it's just routine," Mia said, taking another sip of water. "What's the production you're doing?"

"What? Er, *Hamlet*," Benjamin Bache said. "Or rather we're still rehearsing. I'm in a children's play right now, but I'm also rehearsing an incredibly exciting new project, a young Norwegian dramatist, only twenty-two, hugely talented. A group of us have come together to support her, pro bono, if you know what I mean — raw, underground, edgy."

"I understand," Mia said. "Where was her mail sent to?"

"Whose mail?"

"Veronica Bache's."

"What about her mail?"

"I'm asking if her mail was sent to the nursing home or to your address?"

Benjamin Bache seemed perplexed.

"Eh, most of it went to Høvikveien Nursing Home. What kind of mail do you mean? Some of it was sent to me, but I either forwarded it to the nursing home or took it with me when I visited her. What kind of mail are we talking about?"

Mia took out a piece of paper from her jacket pocket and slipped it across the white tablecloth. "Was this her cell-phone number?"

Benjamin stared at the number and, if possible, looked even more confused. "I haven't got a clue what you're talking about."

"This number. Did it used to be hers?"

"My great-grandmother never owned a cell phone in her life," Benjamin said. "She hated them. And why would she want one? All the residents had their own private landlines."

Mia took back the piece of paper and stuffed it into her pocket.

"Thank you," she said, getting up. "That was all I needed to know. Thanks for your time."

"Was that all?" Benjamin Bache said, seeming almost disappointed.

"Yes. Oh, no, there *was* one more thing," Mia said, sitting down again. "Who inherited from your great-grandmother?"

"My father," Benjamin said.

"Was there ever any talk . . . How do I put this? Did she leave any of her money to a church?"

Benjamin Bache fell silent. He stuck a toothpick in his mouth and gazed out the window.

"Do I have to answer that?" he said at length.

"No, of course you don't," Mia said, patting his hand. "It's just that I'm working on a major case and . . . well, her name cropped up, and I know I shouldn't tell you this, Benjamin, but . . ."

She leaned toward to him.

"We're so close to cracking this case, and if you're able to help me, perhaps I can solve it as early as tonight."

"A major case?" Benjamin, too, moved forward as he whispered it to her.

Mia nodded and placed her finger against her lips. Benjamin nodded back. Then he sat upright again and, as the accomplished actor he was, pretended that nothing had happened.

"This will be just between the two of us, okay?" he said, looking around casually.

"Absolutely," Mia whispered.

Benjamin cleared his throat. "My father is

a very proud man, so if this were to come out, then . . ."

"It'll stay between you and me," Mia assured him.

"We agreed to a settlement," Benjamin said quickly.

"What kind of settlement?"

"She changed her will just before she died."

"How much would the church get?"

"Everything." He coughed.

"But you managed to put a stop to it?"

He nodded. "My father contacted the church. Threatened to sue them. He offered them some money. And that was the end of it."

"How much money?"

"Enough," Benjamin mumbled.

Mia studied the actor for a while. He seemed genuine and innocent, but then again he was an actor, wasn't he? He could have taken out a cell-phone contract in Veronica Bache's name, and hadn't he just told her that he was rehearsing *Hamlet*?

Who's there?

She thought about taking him to the station for a more formal interview but decided it would be better to have him followed. That would soon tell them if Benjamin Bache was who he said he was.

"Thank you so much," Mia said, taking his hand again. "You've been a great help."

She stood and zipped up her leather jacket.

"Was that all? Don't you want something to eat?"

"No, but thanks for offering. See you later, Benjamin."

"Yes, see you later, Mia."

Mia put on her cap and left Theatercaféen with a smile on her lips.

41

Tobias Iversen made himself as small as possible as he crept toward the edge of the mound. From this position he would have a good view of the farm in the forest. He had pitched his tent farther back, in between some trees where no one could see him, and spent the night there. His original plan had been to go home, but since meeting the girl in the gray dress he simply had to stay. Rakel. That was her name. She had written him a note asking for his help. That made it more important to stay in the forest than go home to the dark house where no one ever smiled. Tobias was just thirteen years old, but he felt much older. He'd been old for a long time. He'd been subjected to things no child should ever experience, but right now it didn't matter. Out here he could do what he wanted.

Tobias wormed his way to the edge and raised the binoculars to his eyes. The farmyard was quiet. He didn't know what time it was, but it had to be early, because it was not properly light yet. He could see everything much more clearly now; last night he'd only been able to make out silhouettes. There was no doubt that they were busy with several building projects. There were materials everywhere, different-sized planks, sacks that might contain cement — he could see a cement mixer, a small tractor, and a small backhoe. The farm was made up of seven buildings, all white. There was the main house, a small church with a cross on the top, two greenhouses, and then three smaller houses, plus a shed. Tobias had lain in the same place last night until it grew too dark to see anything through the binoculars. He had made a small sketch of the area, noting the locations of all the buildings, where the field was, the piles of sand, the bigger stacks of timber, and the gate. The tall fence, through which they had passed notes, surrounded the whole area, and as far as he could see, there was only the one way in. The gate. He could not see whether it was locked, but it was closed, he could see that much. He had watched a man open it the night before. A car had arrived right before dusk. A large black car, possibly a Land Rover or a Honda CR-V. Tobias didn't know much about cars. He wasn't terribly interested in them; he preferred mopeds and motorbikes, preferably those with cross-country tires that could go off-road, but he knew a little.

There had been two people in the car, and they'd been received as if one of them were the king or the prime minister. There was a young man with short blond hair, who must be a servant or a guard or something because he jumped out of the car first and opened the door for the other man, who was older and had plenty of white hair and carried a kind of stick, almost like Gandalf from *Lord of the Rings*.

Everyone on the farm had emerged from the buildings and bowed and curtsied in front of the new arrivals, and some had stepped forward and greeted the man with the shock of white hair, and then they all went inside the large building with the cross at the top. After that it grew dark, and Tobias hadn't been able to see much more. The light was on behind the windows, but they were covered with something like glass, only it was not glass but a sort of material that obscured — Tobias didn't know what it was called. Afterward he ate his sandwiches and heated some soup on the camp stove inside the tent. He had been very careful —

he knew you should never use propane inside a tent, but he didn't want to light it outside in case it gave him away. Besides, he had seen on TV that Børge Ousland, the North Pole explorer, had done it, *he* had lit his propane stove inside the tent because it was too cold outside, or there'd been a polar bear around or something; at any rate *he'd* been okay.

At first Tobias was unable to asleep. He kept thinking about the girl. Rakel. She was so different from the girls in his school. According to Emilie, his Norwegian teacher, being a girl these days was not easy; they'd had a discussion in class once because some of the girls had worn skimpy clothes. Emilie had spent a whole lesson discussing not Norwegian or books but stuff like girls wearing too much makeup or showing their midriffs or wearing too-short skirts. Emilie had said it was important to remember that they were only thirteen years old, but she could understand why they did it, because all the women they admired on TV often wore just a bra and panties and fishnet stockings while they sang. Afterward they'd agreed on some rules about what was allowed and what was not, and things had improved a little, but the girls at school still wore completely different clothes from Rakel.

Help me. Please.

She had looked so frightened. For real. Not like when he and his brother played Indians and were trying to catch bison. The bison were imaginary, and they weren't real Indians either. *This* was real. He was Tobias, and she was Rakel. And she was frightened for real, and now he was here to help her. Tobias Iversen stuck a twig in his mouth and chewed it while he scanned the area with his binoculars to see if he'd missed anything on the sketch he made the night before.

Tobias aimed his binoculars at the gate and focused them as sharply as he could. The gate was made from the same material as the fence, wire netting or whatever it was called, and it had a large hinged gate that opened inward. There appeared to be a chain in the middle and probably also a lock. Tobias set down the binoculars in the heather and unwrapped the packed lunch he had in his jacket. There were two sandwiches left; he had saved them from last night, one with brown cheese and one with salami. He ate the one with brown cheese and drank from his water bottle, which he'd refilled from the river. He had to make a plan now — that was important. First he had to get a clearer idea of the area; he'd learned that from a film he saw about some men who wanted to rob a bank — no, a casino in Las Vegas. They had lots of maps and blueprints and held many meetings where everything was discussed. He already had a map. Now all he needed was a plan.

Tobias was just about to eat his salami sandwich when something happened down on the farm. He grabbed his binoculars. A door was flung open, and a figure emerged outside. A girl in a gray dress. His heart leaped underneath his sweater. *It was Rakel.* She was running as fast as she could, heading for the section of the fence where they had spoken the day before. She tripped on the hem of her dress, fell, and got back on her feet. She hoisted up her dress to make it easier, but she still wasn't very fast. Right behind her, out of the same door, four — no, five men gave chase. Tobias's heart pounded in his chest, so hard that he could barely keep his binoculars steady in front of his eyes. Rakel turned around, glanced back, and stumbled a second time. The men were gaining on her, they were not far behind her now, Tobias could see them waving their hands, shouting something. Rakel neared the fence, and finally she reached it. She started to climb it, but it looked like she was having trouble. The holes in the mesh were small, and her heavy dress didn't help. The men approached rapidly, one of them reached the fence and managed to grab her foot; they pulled her down while she kicked and screamed, then carried her back to the house between them, and everything fell quiet again.

Tobias felt icy cold. Not on the outside, but underneath his skin. His thoughts ran amok, and he started hyperventilating, even though he was lying completely still. *What on earth was going on down there?* He scrambled to his feet. There was no time to make a plan. Nor was there any time to pack. He raced back to the tent, picked up his knife and the map he'd drawn, and made his way stealthily down the mound, toward the farm.

42

Mia was sitting in Justisen toying with the idea of ordering a beer, but she ended up getting a Farris. Some minutes later Holger arrived and collapsed breathlessly on the chair opposite her.

"What happened?" Mia asked.

"The killer contacted *Aftenposten* some days ago. He called a journalist named Mikkel Wold. Distorted voice. Gave information about Karoline."

"Why didn't they come to us?"

"Because they're a bunch of selfish bastards who only care about selling newspapers." Munch was visibly agitated.

"So now what?"

"I'm not sure," he fumed. "Their lawyer kept stressing that they had done nothing wrong and that we couldn't charge them with anything."

"Surely we can bring them in, if nothing else?" Mia said.

"Mikkelson said he would think about it but that my interviewing them would probably suffice."

"Seriously?"

"Damn politicians," Munch snarled. "Always feathering their own nests."

He ordered a prawn sandwich and a cola and took off his jacket.

"So what did you get?" Mia asked.

"A verbal statement. They'll send us a written one tomorrow."

"Anything useful?"

"Not really, no," Munch said, shaking his head in despair. "What did Bache say?"

"Bingo," Mia said.

"What do you mean?"

"I think you *are* involved."

Munch raised his eyebrows. "I heard you. What do you mean by it?"

"I think this is about you."

Munch got his food and took a sip of his cola.

"It's a bit difficult to explain. Like I said, I have this hunch," Mia continued.

"Try me," Munch said.

"Okay," she said. "The killer points us to Hønefoss and the missing baby. Who was responsible for that investigation?"

"I was," Munch said.

"Correct."

"Hamlet," Mia said. "What's *Hamlet* about?"

"True love?" Munch ventured.

"That's *Romeo and Juliet.* Try again, Holger — *Hamlet*?"

"You were the one who studied literature, Mia."

"Three lectures in two terms and no exam doesn't make me an expert," Mia said.

"I don't know Shakespeare very well." Munch sighed.

"Okay, never mind. Revenge. *Hamlet* is about revenge. There's more to it than that, obviously, but that's the main theme."

"Right. Baby disappears. I'm in charge of the investigation. The Swede hangs himself. We shelve the case. The baby is still missing. Presumed dead. The killer tells us the Swede didn't do it."

"Toni J. W. Smith."

"Exactly, and points us to *Hamlet.* So this is about revenge?"

"Something like that."

"But now what? Okay, I can follow you some of the way. The baby is missing, yes. I'm responsible, yes. *Hamlet,* revenge, yes. But why kill ten girls? What does that have to do with me? Surely you can hear it sounds a bit far-fetched, Mia."

Mia drank her mineral water and thought

about it. "Benjamin Bache's great-grandmother."

"Veronica Bache, what about her?"

"She lived at the same nursing home as your mother. What do you make of that?"

Munch's eyes widened. "Did she? How do you know that?"

"I discovered it earlier today. Ludvig is cross-referencing all staff members, residents, and names associated with the nursing home with the Hønefoss case as we speak. I don't think Benjamin Bache is our guy, but we need to remember that a cell phone registered to Veronica Bache was used to send those messages. By someone at the nursing home? Or are we being played? I have to admit that I'm not clear about that right now. I've asked Ludvig to look into it."

"And?"

"Nothing yet. And oh, the nursing home isn't the only link between your mother and Veronica Bache."

"What more is there?"

"A church."

"Bache was a member of it?"

"More than that. She was going to leave it all her money."

"What?"

"Do you see it now? Do you understand

what I'm saying?"

"Good job, Mia," Munch muttered. "This is good."

He became lost in his own world. Tried to process the information she'd given him.

"Why?" Mia said.

"Yes, why?"

"I don't know that yet, but there are too many coincidences, wouldn't you say? What is the common denominator here, Munch?"

"The church."

"Precisely."

"But —" Munch frowned.

"I know, I don't really understand it either. It's too messy. I almost think that's the point, that we're supposed to get lost. A million dead ends. I know that it sounds weird, but he's doing a good job. The killer, I mean. I would have done it the same way."

Munch sent her a sideways glance.

"You know what I mean. If I were on the other side. Symbols everywhere, changing the MO — we're running around in circles. We're sent this way, then that way. It's how you play tennis, isn't it?"

"Tennis?"

"The player who serves always has the advantage. As long as you keep pressing your opponent so hard that all he can do is return the ball, you're in the driver's seat.

Unless you make a mistake, you'll win."

"So the killer is serving?"

"Yes."

"I'm not sure I get the comparison," Munch said. "How do you rob a bank without getting noticed?"

"You blow up the building across the street. I know." Mia sighed.

"Sorry." Munch smiled and rubbed his eyes. "It's been a long week. I lost my temper with my lawyer today. Why won't people ever take responsibility for their own actions? So where do we go with this?"

"That was what I wanted to ask you about."

"The church?"

"That goes without saying."

"You and me tomorrow morning?"

"Absolutely."

"Is Gabriel still at the office?"

"I think so."

"Send him a text. Ask him to check up on the church so we're prepared when we get there. I can't remember what they call themselves, but the address is on Bogerudveien in Bøler."

"Okay," Mia said, taking out her phone.

"By the way," Munch said, lighting a fresh cigarette with his current one. "What did you say just now?"

"About tennis?"

"Yes, that if you're serving, then you'll win."

"Unless you make a mistake . . ."

They both fell silent and looked at each other.

"It's a nice idea, isn't it?" Munch said.

"Definitely." Mia nodded.

"Putting pressure on the killer," Munch said.

"I'll see what I can come up with."

"You do that. Meanwhile I'll put together a list of the sons of bitches who want my money."

Munch got up, stubbed out his cigarette, and left.

Mia again considered having a beer, but she willed herself to order another Farris instead. She took out her pen and her papers, which she spread across the table as she usually did when she wanted to get her thinking in order. In the past she had seen everything so clearly and worked much faster; at her peak all she had to do was close her eyes and everything would play out in her head, but that was a long time ago. The Tryvann incident. The months on Hitra. It was as if her eyes were veiled. A kind of fog clouded her brain cells. She'd been told to rest. Plenty of rest for a long time. Not to subject herself to any kind of pressure. Her response had been to drug herself. Almost to the point of death. And now she was paying the price. She started making notes on the sheets in front of her. Trying to get the pen to do the work. Impose some kind of order on the chaos. Thinking was almost painful. Two girls were dead. Two girls were missing. It was her responsibility. Munch. Munch was definitely involved somehow. She was sure of it. Or was she? Something that had been so easy for her a few years ago now seemed impossible. She should never have agreed to leave the island. She should have stuck with her plan.

Come to me, Mia, come.

She wrote down the names at the top of the sheet again. Pauline. Johanne. Karoline. Andrea. Six years old. About to start school this autumn. Mark 10:14. Suffer the little children to come unto me. I'm traveling alone. Jump rope. From the trees. The forest. Clean clothes. Freshly washed bodies. Shakespeare. *Hamlet.* Satchels. Schoolbooks. It was coming now. Toni J. W. Smith. Hønefoss. The baby, who was never found. I'm traveling alone.

Come, Pauline, come.

Come, Johanne, come.

Come, Karoline, come.
Come, Andrea, come.

Mia was roused from her reverie when the waitress suddenly appeared next to her. *Damn.* She'd been on her way. To the place where she had to go. A place she hadn't visited for a long time.

"Can I get you anything else?"

"Yes, get me a beer, please," Mia muttered irritably. "And a Ratzeputz. Make that two Ratzeputzes."

She needed help to get back to the place where she needed to be.

43

Mia Krüger was drunk, but she couldn't fall asleep. She had drunk too much. She had not drunk enough. The hotel room seemed colder and even more impersonal than usual. She had chosen this room because it didn't remind her of anything, but now she was missing home. A home. Something familiar. Something safe. Someone who could take care of her. Perhaps Mikkelson had been right after all. Perhaps she should go see a psychologist. Perhaps she needed to be admitted. She had balanced on a knife's edge for a long time, recovered a little, been positive, felt strong, but now she was spiraling downward once more.

Her body spun around the large bed, and she clung to it. She'd been on her way, hadn't she? To the place where she belonged? Get behind the façade. Her specialty. Seeing what no one else saw.

She walked barefoot across the floor and found her pants on a chair. Her pills were still in the pocket. She took one of them with her to the window and swallowed it with a mouthful of water. She sat for a long time staring at the traffic lights until she could no longer distinguish the colors. She staggered back to her cold bed and rested her head on the pillow.

Her cell phone rang just as she had managed to fall asleep. She did her best to ignore it. It started ringing again. Then it stopped. Her leaden body lay on the white sheet. When her phone rang for the third time, she could no longer leave it alone.

"Mia?" It was Munch.

"What time is it?" she mumbled.

"Five," Munch said.

"What is it?"

"They've found the girls."

"What?"

"I'll pick you up outside the hotel. Can you be ready in ten minutes? We have a long drive ahead of us."

"Damn," Mia heard her own voice say. "I'll be ready."

44

Tobias Iversen was lying behind a tree, waiting for darkness to fall. He had eaten his last sandwich a long time ago and was starting to feel hungry, but he couldn't go home now; he had more important things to do. His plan had been to try the gate first, but that had proved impossible. It was locked with a chain, and besides, it was far too visible. The men had carried Rakel inside one of the small houses, and ever since then the farm had been quiet. A few times someone had emerged from the church and gone to the greenhouse, but apart from that he hadn't seen anyone. The place seemed deserted. Almost like a graveyard. The wind rustled the trees above him. Tobias tightened his jacket around him and took out his binoculars again. Perhaps going home was a better option. Contact the police? After all, he had seen them restrain her. Surely that was against the law. Or was it? They hadn't hurt her, they'd carried her across the yard. A naughty child who had refused to do as she was told. And wouldn't the police need a warrant? They always had to have one in American movies. If they didn't have one, they weren't allowed to enter people's houses to search them. Tobias didn't exactly know how things were in Norway, but perhaps it was the same. Suddenly he no longer felt quite so tough. It had started out as a game. All he wanted was to take a closer look. A small expedition. He'd never imagined meeting someone in need of help. He thought about Torben, who was probably back home now and wondering where his big brother was. About his mother and stepfather, who wouldn't know what to tell him. He didn't like the thought of his little brother being at home without him. The temptation to go home grew stronger. After all, Tobias didn't know this girl. What if she were just a spoiled brat? Perhaps she was just like Elin, a girl who was in his class last year; she had broken into the headmaster's office and stolen money and bitten the hand of one of the teachers during break time when he caught her smoking in the playground. She, too, had seemed very nice, or at least she had been toward Tobias, but then she was expelled and no one had seen her since. Rakel might be just like her. Perhaps he was making a mountain out of a molehill. His mom often told him to stop making things up. It wasn't a good thing to do. Making stuff up. It was bad. It was getting colder now. It was supposed to be nearing spring, but it wasn't really, certainly not in the evenings. He regretted not bringing his camping gear. The tent and the sleeping bag and his knapsack were still on the mound where he'd spent the night. He hadn't brought his flashlight either. What a stupid thing to do. *Where is your head?* his mom would often say. *Is anyone at home?* He was starting to feel a little ashamed. He had behaved like an idiot. Soon it would be too dark to get back to the tent. Too dark for him to find his way through the forest. If he left now, he could do it. At least he could reach the tent. He would be able to walk home as long as he had his flashlight. It was probably for the best. Pack up his stuff. Make for home. And Torben. Tobias got up from his hiding place and looked around just as one of the doors opened and something happened. He raised the binoculars to his eyes and stood very still. Two men had appeared from one of the houses with a figure between them. Rakel. It was her. Her head was covered. They had put a hood over her head. The two men were holding her arms, one on each side and slightly behind, frog-marching her. They disappeared behind the church and reappeared slightly farther ahead. Tobias's heart was racing. He could barely believe his own eyes. It was like a movie. They had captured her. Tied her hands in front and pulled a hood over her head. The two men continued walking in the direction where Tobias was hiding, still pushing the girl between them. Past the tractor and the small shed, across the field, and what were they doing now? Tobias plucked up his courage and moved closer to the fence. The two men had stopped. One bent down toward the ground. He did something; Tobias could not see what it was. Then suddenly she was no longer there. She was gone. Only the two men were left, and they began to make their way back to the house.

Tobias made a spur-of-the-moment decision. His plan had been to wait until it was completely dark, but now there was no time to lose. He crept all the way up to the fence and started scaling it. You were not allowed to treat a child like that. You were not allowed to be cruel to children, no matter what they had done — no grown-ups should be allowed to get away with it. His courage was swelling now. He was angry. He grabbed hold of the wire netting, sticking his fingers through the holes. He managed to get a foothold, and presto, almost before he knew it, he had climbed over the tall fence and was inside the compound. He stayed crouched on the ground to catch his breath while he glanced around. The farm was quiet again. The ground was cold and wet underneath him. Where could she be? They had dragged her into the middle of a flat area, and then she disappeared. Tobias ought to have been scared, but he wasn't. He was livid. He was furious with all the adults who hurt children. Children should be free. To play. To feel safe. Not stand with their heads bowed in the kitchen. It hurt to be told you were stupid. It hurt to have your arms grabbed. It hurt not to be able to answer back because you didn't know what would happen to your baby brother if you said the wrong thing. Tobias started creeping across the ground. The man had bent down about a hundred meters away. Then Rakel had disappeared. Why did adults have children if they weren't going to treat them properly? One day after Norwegian class, Emilie had asked him why he had marks on his neck. Bruises on his arms. *You can tell me,* she'd said. She had been very nice, stroked his shoulder. *You can tell me, it's safe to tell me.* But he hadn't said anything. It wasn't her fault. She was just trying to help. But she didn't know what it was like. She wouldn't be there when he came home from school and they found out that he had told tales, would she? Telling would only make it worse. Everything would be worse — oh, yes, he knew exactly how it would be. It was a question of endurance. Survival. Making sure that his younger brother didn't suffer the same treatment. Take the beatings. *Is anyone in there? Are you thick or something?*

Tobias crouched in the damp grass, trying to make himself as small as possible. His knees got wet, but he didn't care. He could take it. He was tough. It was important to keep your mouth shut. Never argue back; that only made it worse. Nod. Bow your head. Say yes. He wasn't afraid. He was no longer scared. They had put a hood over her head. You weren't allowed to do that. Adults were not allowed to do this to children. He sneaked forward, pausing every now and then to make sure everything was safe, that no doors had opened, that no one had spotted him. In five years he would be eighteen. When you were eighteen, you got to decide everything for yourself. He would move out, perhaps find himself a job, maybe take his brother with him even though Torben would be only twelve. *Is everything okay at home, Tobias? Please tell your mother to come to Parents' Evening. I really want to talk to her. She hasn't been to a Parents' Evening for a long time, and it's important that she comes. Please, would you tell her? Have you hurt your hand? What happened to your ear? Is there anything I can help you with, Tobias? You can trust me, you know that.*

Tobias reached the place where Rakel had disappeared from sight. It was dark outside now. The church soared toward the sky, poking its spire into the moon and the clouds. Almost like an old-fashioned horror movie. *Frankenstein* or *Dracula,* one of those. He should be scared, but he wasn't. He was angry. He had seen her eyes under the white bonnet. They were adults, and she was a child. You weren't allowed to hurt children. Yet again Tobias regretted not bringing his flashlight. He could barely see the ground in front of him; the moon provided him with a little light, but it appeared only a few seconds at a time. He wasn't an idiot. She could not just simply have vanished into thin air. There had to be a hole in the ground somewhere. A hatch. Something. What kind of adult puts a child into a hole in the ground?

Tobias bent and started patting the earth around him. Suddenly a light was turned on inside the church. Tobias reacted instinctively, threw himself down and lay flat on the wet ground. He could smell soil and grass. He lay like this for a while, but no one came outside. He steeled himself and got up into a kneeling position, the light from the windows making it easier for him to see. He was looking for a hatch. People don't just disappear.

It didn't take long before he found it. It was brand new, pale planks fixed together in a square measuring a meter by a meter, a hatch leading right into the earth. It was padlocked. Not with a big padlock, a small one, gold-colored like the one his PE teacher used for the ball cupboard, so no one would take the soccer balls without asking for permission first. He glanced around again. There was no one in sight. There were voices coming from the church now. Singing, the people inside the church were singing. They did some other things as well as sing. Prayed to God, or whatever it was. They didn't know that he was out here. That someone was out here trying to help Rakel. Pick the padlock. Release her. Tobias couldn't help smiling. The PE teacher had never worked out why the soccer balls kept going missing. He didn't know how easy it is to pick a padlock. Tobias had done it many times. Nearly all the boys in his class knew how to pick a padlock. It was even easier than cheating on a test. They had made picklocks during metalwork when the teacher went outside to have a cigarette. All you needed was a strip of metal — a nail file like the ones the girls used was a good starting point. You trimmed the tip with metal cutters and filed it down until the tip became very thin. It was a bit tricky, obviously, and someone had to show you how to do it, but once you knew how, it was easy. Tobias took out his keys from the zippered pocket in his jacket and found the picklock. Held the padlock so that the keyhole was widest to the right. Inserted the picklock, pressed it hard to the left until he felt it make contact with the metal inside. He flicked it, pulling the lock toward him, pressed it, and then turned it hard to the right. Tobias heard a small click as the lock opened. He removed it and lifted up the heavy hatch. A ladder. There was a long ladder leading into a hole. Carefully he stuck his head inside the hole and whispered:

"Hello? Rakel? Are you there?"

45

Munch was already waiting outside the hotel when Mia appeared. She got into the black Audi and tried to force herself to wake up. The pill she'd taken was still in her system, making her slow and lethargic. Munch didn't look as if he had slept much either. He was wearing the same clothes as yesterday, the brown corduroy jacket with the leather patches on the elbows and a stained shirt. He had bags under his eyes and deep frown lines on his forehead. Suddenly Mia felt a little sorry for him. He really needed company. A woman in his life. Someone who could take care of him, the way he always took care of everybody else.

"What have we got?" she said.

"Isegran Fort."

"Where is that?"

"Fredrikstad."

Mia frowned. The two other girls had been found near Oslo. In the woods. The killer had changed MO again.

"Who found them?"

"A couple of students." Munch sighed. "I believe the area is fenced off, but they crept in to make out or something, what do I know?"

"Who have we got down there?"

"The local police. Curry and Anette are on their way. They should arrive soon."

"And what do we know so far?"

"Both girls were lying on the ground on either side of a stake."

"A stake?"

Munch nodded.

"What kind of stake?"

"A wooden one. With a pig's head on top."

"What do you mean?"

"What I said. The girls were lying on the grass on either side of a wooden stake with a pig's head stuck on top."

"A real pig's head?"

Munch nodded again.

"Jesus Christ." Mia let out a sigh.

"What do you think it means?" Munch turned on the heat and took the tunnel by Rådhusplassen to get out of the city center.

"It's hard to say," Mia replied.

The heat inside the car made her sleepy. She was in need of her morning coffee but didn't want to ask Munch to stop.

"It has to mean something."

"Lord of the Flies," Mia said quietly.

"What?"

"It's from a book. *Lord of the Flies.* Some kids wash up on a desert island, no adults present. They think a monster lives there. They place a pig's head on a spike as an offering."

"Christ Almighty." Munch sighed. "We're dealing with a monster, is that it?"

"Could be."

"There's a bag of mints in there," Munch said, pointing to the glove compartment.

"And?"

"You need one," Munch said as he turned onto Drammensveien.

Mia felt a flash of irritation, but it passed quickly. She opened the glove compartment and took out the bag of mints. Put two in her month before stuffing the whole bag into the pocket of her leather jacket.

"Why Fredrikstad of all places?" Munch wondered out loud. "It makes no damn sense. And it's so public."

"We're too slow on the uptake," Mia said, taking out her cell phone.

"What do you mean?"

"The killer is telling us we're doing a bad job."

"Dear Lord."

Mia found Gabriel Mørk in her list of contacts.

"Gabriel speaking."

"Hi, it's Mia, are you at work?"

"Yep."

"Tell me what you have on Isegran Fort in Fredrikstad."

"Now?"

"Yes, Munch and I are on our way there. They've found the girls."

"I heard."

There was silence from the other end. Mia could hear Gabriel type on his keyboard.

"Have you found something?"

"What am I looking for?"

"Anything."

"Right, here we go," the young man said. "Isegran Fort. Fortification on a small island outside Fredrikstad. It divides the Glomma Estuary into two. It was built at the end of the twelfth century by the Earl of Borgsyssel, whoever he was. A stone-and-wood building. Destroyed in 1287 by some king or other. New fortress built in the sixteenth century. Peter Wessel Tordenskiold used the place as a base during the Great Nordic War, whenever that was. The name Isegran means . . . the wise men seem to be in disagreement here, but it could be from the French Île Grande, 'Big Island.'

Does any of this help?"

"Not really," Mia said. "Is there anything else? Something contemporary? What is it used for today?"

"Hang on."

Mia wedged the phone between her ear and shoulder and popped another mint. She could still feel the taste of alcohol at the back of her throat.

"There's not much here. Wedding photographs taken at Isegran Fort. It's a popular destination for retirees on a day out."

"Is that all?"

"Yes. No, wait."

There was silence again.

"What have you got?"

"I don't know if this is useful, but a monument will be unveiled there in 2013. Not on the fort itself but on the seaside promenade."

"What kind of monument?"

"It's called *Munch's Mothers.* Bronze statues of Edvard Munch's mother and aunt."

"Of course," Mia muttered to herself.

"Was that any help?"

"Absolutely, Gabriel, thank you so much."

She was about to hang up, but Gabriel stopped her. "Is Munch there with you?"

"Yes."

"What kind of mood is he in?"

"So-so, why?"

"Please could I speak to him?"

"Okay."

Mia passed her phone to Munch.

"Yes, Munch speaking."

Munch's Mothers. She'd been right after all.

"Yes, I understand," Munch said on the phone. "But don't worry about it. Like I said, it's personal. We have other, more important things to do. . . . What? . . . Yes, it can drive you crazy, but I — What? . . . Yes, I got it from a friend online. From Sweden . . . What? She calls herself Margrete_08. Don't worry about it. . . . Yes, yes, I understand. Talk to you later."

Munch laughed briefly to himself before handing the phone back to Mia.

"What was that about?"

"Nothing important, just a private matter."

"He's good," she said.

"Who? Gabriel? Yes, absolutely. I like him. I'm glad we hired him."

Mia opened the window slightly.

"Did you get anything from him? About Isegran Fort?" Munch asked.

"Absolutely." She repeated what Gabriel had just told her.

"Damn," Munch swore softly to himself. "So this is about me? It's my fault that these girls are dying?" He narrowed his eyes and banged the steering wheel hard.

"We don't know that for sure," Mia said. "How long before we get there?"

"An hour and a half," Munch said.

"I think I'll take a nap," she said.

"Good idea," he agreed. "Have one for me, too, while you're at it."

46

The sun was rising when they reached the police cordon. Munch showed them his ID card and they were waved through by a young police officer with messy hair who looked as if he had just gotten out of bed. They parked the car outside a small red building with a sign that said CAFÉ GALEIEN where they were met by Curry, who guided them along the old stone wall. Mia could make out the seaside promenade on the other side where the bronze statues would be located. Edvard Munch's mother and aunt. Laura Cathrine Munch and Karen Bjølstad. Mia knew a lot about Edvard Munch. Most people from Åsgårdstrand did. Their little town had always been proud that he'd lived there, even though the fine ladies back in the day had twirled their parasols in disgust when they encountered the disreputable artist. Typical, wasn't it, Mia thought, as she spotted the white plastic tent that the crime-scene officers had erected. Back then they despised him, but today we conveniently forget all about that.

Curry seemed surprisingly wound up and kept talking all the way to the tent. The experienced police officer could come across as cold and hard, with his shaved head and muscular body, but Mia knew better. Curry was extremely talented and had a big heart, even though he looked and acted like a bulldog.

"Two students found them. A couple. From Glemmen College. They were very upset, so we sent them home."

"Anything to do with this?" Munch asked.

"No, no, they could barely get a word out. I've never seen two kids sober up so quickly in all my life. I think the discovery evaporated the alcohol right out of them."

"Any observations from the neighborhood?" Mia asked.

"Not yet," Curry said. "Fredrikstad Police are doing door-to-door inquiries now. But I doubt that they'll come back with anything."

"Why not?" Mia said.

"Is that a serious question?" Curry smiled wryly.

"It's not exactly amateur hour, is it?"

They reached the tent just as an older man in a white plastic coverall emerged from it.

411

Mia was surprised to see a familiar face. She had worked several cases with criminal pathologist Ernst Hugo Vik, but she thought he had retired by now.

"Munch. Mia." Vik nodded to them as they arrived.

"Hello, Ernst," Munch said. "Did they drag you all the way from Oslo for this?"

"No." Vik sighed. "I was hiding in my cabin, trying to get some peace, not that it did me any good."

"What have we got?" Mia asked.

Vik pulled down the white plastic hood and peeled off his gloves. He lit a cigarette and kicked a bit of dirt off his boots.

"They haven't been lying there long. One hour max before they were found would be my guess."

"And the time of deaths?"

"The same," Vik told her.

"They were killed in situ?"

"It looks like it. But I can't tell you for certain until we get them on the table. What's going on, Munch? I have to say it's one of the weirdest cases I've ever seen. Rigorous."

"What do you mean?" Mia said.

"Well," Vik said, taking another drag of his cigarette. "What can I say? For a ritual murder, it's very tidy. The girls are neat and

412

clean. Dressed. Backpacks. And then there's this pig's head? Damned if I know. You take a look for yourself, I need a break."

The old man stuffed the gloves into his pocket and shuffled toward the parking lot. Munch and Mia put on the white coveralls that had been set out for them and entered the tent.

Karoline Mykle was lying on the ground with her hands folded across her chest. She was wearing a yellow doll's dress. A backpack had been placed by her feet. Andrea Lyng lay only a few meters away, and she, too, had her hands folded on her chest and a backpack near her white shoes. Both girls wore identical signs around their necks, just like Pauline and Johanne: *I'm traveling alone.* An almost religious scene with a grotesque pig's head placed in the middle. Mia Krüger put on her gloves and bent over Andrea. She held up the girl's small white hand and studied her fingernails.

"Three." She nodded.

She carefully replaced the hand on the girl's chest and went over to Karoline.

"Four."

At that moment Munch's phone rang. He looked at the display but ignored the call. The phone rang again.

"I don't fucking believe it," he said, and

413

pressed the red button for the second time.

"Language," Mia said.

She angled her head in the direction of the girls and got up again.

"Sorry," Munch said as the phone rang for the third time.

He pressed the red button again, and almost immediately Mia's phone started to ring. She saw Gabriel's name on the display.

"Gabriel?" Munch whispered.

Mia indicated that it was and pressed the button to ignore the call. "Did he just call you?"

Munch said that he had as Mia's phone rang yet again. She stepped outside the tent to answer the call.

"This had better be important," she snarled.

Gabriel sounded upset, almost out of breath. "I have to talk to Munch," he panted.

"He's busy, what is it?"

"I've decoded the message, and —" Gabriel started.

"What message?"

"He got an email. A challenge. A coded message. Margrete_08. I've cracked it. The Gronsfeld cipher. I've decoded it."

Mia sighed. "Surely it can wait?"

"No, it definitely can't!" The young hacker

was practically screaming through the phone now. "You have to tell him! Now!"

"Tell him what? What was the message?"

Gabriel fell silent for a moment, almost as if he were too scared to say what he'd found out.

"Gabriel?" Mia said impatiently.

"Tick-tock little Marion = 5."

"What?"

"Tick-tock little Marion is number five."

"Christ!" Mia exclaimed, and ran into the tent to tell Holger Munch.

IV

47

Miriam Munch was sitting in the back of her father's Audi trying to keep her emotions in check. On orders from her father, she wore a woolly cap pulled over her ears and large sunglasses. Marion was lying on the seat next to her, curled up under a blanket that completely concealed the little girl. Miriam had not understood very much when her father woke her two days ago and told her to lock all the doors. Don't let anyone in. Keep Marion home from nursery school.

What do you mean, keep her home from nursery school?

For God's sake, Miriam, just do as I say!

The thought had occurred to her, obviously. Miriam Munch wasn't stupid. Quite the contrary. Miriam Munch had always been one of the smartest girls in school. Ever since she was little, she found it incredibly easy to do what others struggled with.

Rivers in Asia. Capitals of South America. Fractions. Algebra. English. Norwegian. She'd soon learned to keep quiet about her cleverness, not to come in first on every test, not to raise her hand too often. She also possessed emotional intelligence. She wanted to have friends. She did not want to be thought of as better than anyone else.

So of course the possibility had crossed her mind. Her daughter was due to start school this autumn. And her father was heading the investigation into the murder of four girls. She wasn't an idiot. But she had been stubborn. There was no way she would allow herself to be intimidated. Her life would not be destroyed by some madman. She'd taken precautions, of course — who hadn't? She took Marion to and from nursery school herself. She had already said no to letting Marion go to birthday parties, to her daughter's great despair. She had organized a meeting at the nursery school with staff and parents of all girls due to start school this autumn. Some of the parents had taken time off work, too frightened to send their children to nursery school, some thought the nursery school ought to shut temporarily, others wanted to be with their children — it was mayhem, but Miriam had managed to calm them down. Convinced them that it was about living as normal a life as possible. Not least for the girls' sake. But all the time there'd been a nagging voice at the back of her head: *You might be at greater risk. You have the most to fear.* And now this.

Miriam wrapped the blanket more tightly around her daughter, who was sound asleep. It was dark outside, and the black Audi drove smoothly through the almost deserted streets. Miriam Munch was not frightened, but she was concerned. And sad. And frustrated. And irritated. And outraged.

"Is everything okay in the back?"

Mia Krüger turned to look at her. They had yet to tell Miriam why she was being moved again, the second time in as many days, but deep down they guessed she knew.

"We're fine," Miriam assured her. "Where are we going this time?"

"An apartment we have at our disposal," her father said, glancing at her in the rearview mirror.

"Isn't it about time someone told me what's going on?" Miriam said.

She tried sounding stern, but she was exhausted. She had barely slept for two days.

"It's for your own good," her father said, looking up at her in the mirror again.

"Has the killer made a threat against

Marion? Are you doing this just to be on the safe side? I have a right to know what's going on, don't I?"

"You're safe as long as you do what I say," her father said, jumping a red light at an intersection.

She knew what her father was like once he'd made up his mind about something, so she didn't push him. Suddenly she felt fourteen again. He had been incredibly strict when she was younger, but he'd mellowed with age. Back in those days, there was no point in trying to talk to him. *No, Miriam, you can't wear that to school, that skirt is far too short. No, Miriam, you have to be home by ten. No, Miriam, I don't like you seeing that Robert, I don't think he's good for you.* Her paranoid police-officer father micromanaging her teenage life. It had raised her status among her friends, though. Those who had it toughest at home got the most sympathy from the other students at school. Besides, she knew how to pull the wool over her father's eyes, no matter how good a police officer he was. Toward the end he'd barely been at home, which meant he rarely presented a problem for her. Her mother, too, had been bound up in her own concerns. Christ Almighty, adults, parents — did they really think their children didn't know what was going on? Miriam had known about Rolf before the eruption at home. Her mother, whose routine you could set your watch by. Who suddenly had to "see a friend"? Who suddenly got a lot of calls, which turned out to be "wrong numbers"? Please.

"Is she asleep?"

Mia Krüger turned around again and looked at Marion, who was still curled up under the blanket.

Miriam nodded. She liked Mia, always had. There was something about her personality. She was charismatic. She had great presence. At times she might seem a little distant and eccentric, but not to Miriam. Mia reminded her of herself, perhaps that was why Miriam had taken to her. Intelligent and strong, but also quite vulnerable.

"Your father received a coded message via a website," Mia said.

"Mia!" Munch hissed, but Mia simply continued.

"The sender pretended to be a Swedish mathematician named Margrete. When we cracked the code, it turned out to be a direct threat against Marion."

Miriam could see her father's face grow redder.

"Seriously?" Miriam said.

To her surprise, she realized that she was intrigued rather than scared.

"And how long have you been in contact with her? Online, I mean?"

Her father made no reply. His jaw was clenched and his knuckles white around the steering wheel.

"Almost two years," Mia said.

"Two years? Two whole years?"

Miriam could not believe her ears.

"Have you been in contact with this person for two years, Dad? Is that true? Have you been communicating with a killer for two years without realizing it?"

Munch still made no reply. His face was puce now, and he pressed the accelerator hard.

"He couldn't have known," Mia said. "Everyone on that website was anonymous. It could have been anyone."

"That's enough, Mia," Holger Munch hissed.

"What?" Mia said. "Maybe Miriam knows something. If the killer has been in contact with you for two years, he might have contacted her as well. We have to know."

Without warning, Holger Munch slammed on the brakes and pulled over, turning off the engine.

"You, stay where you are," he ordered

Miriam in the mirror. "You, out."

"But, Holger," Mia protested.

"Out. Get out of the car."

Mia unbuckled her seat belt and left the Audi, against her better judgment. Holger Munch opened the driver's door and followed her out onto the pavement. Miriam couldn't hear the exact words, but it was clear that her father was incandescent with rage. He waved his arms about and was practically frothing at the mouth. She could see that Mia was trying to say something, but Munch did not let her get a word in edgewise. He jabbed his finger right up in her face, and for one moment Miriam feared that he might slap Mia. He ranted at length, and eventually Mia stopped talking. She was just nodding now. Then the two police officers got back inside the car. Munch started the engine, and nothing more was said. The mood in the car was tense. Miriam thought it best not to say anything. Two years? Her father had been in touch with a killer that long? No wonder he was livid. Someone had tricked him. And now four girls were dead. Was Marion meant to be number five? Had that been the message? Was that why they had to go into hiding? Miriam tightened the blanket around her daughter even more and stroked

the girl's hair while the black Audi continued through the night to a safe house whose
location not even she knew.

48

Mia was standing on the pavement outside the gray apartment building in West Oslo, wondering if someone was watching her. It wasn't the first time the thought had crossed her mind. Ever since she'd returned to Oslo, she had this horrible feeling of being followed. She'd dismissed it as paranoia. Quite normal for someone in her situation. It was vital not to give in to it. She was not anxious by nature, so that wasn't the problem, but even so, she couldn't shrug it off. She glanced about her, but she didn't see anyone. The streets around her were completely quiet.

They had moved Miriam and her daughter to a safe apartment in Frogner. Safe in the sense that it wasn't listed anywhere. Not in official archives. The night before, they'd kept mother and daughter in an apartment farther east, but Munch didn't feel safe there and decided to move them again. The apartment they were using now was reserved for politicians and other important visitors who needed protection, but Munch had pulled a few strings on the QT so that only a small number of people were involved. He was getting really paranoid now, but she could see his point.

Mia glanced up and down the street. Still no one there. No cars. Not even a newspaper boy. She was all alone, and she was quite sure that no one had seen Miriam and her daughter enter the apartment.

A few minutes later, Munch appeared in the street. He lit a cigarette and raked a hand through his hair.

"Sorry," Mia said.

"Don't apologize, it was my fault," he said. "I just wanted to . . . well, you know."

"Don't worry about it," Mia said.

"Are we alone?"

"I think so. I haven't seen anyone. Is everything okay up there?"

Munch took a deep drag of his cigarette and glanced up toward the third floor. "Everything is fine. Miriam is pissed off with me, but I understand. I hope she realizes that I'm only trying to help her."

"Of course she understands," Mia reassured him. "It's just a bit too much for her right now. She'll thank you when it's all over."

"I'm not so sure about that. I had to tell her that she can't get married."

"You told her to cancel her wedding?"

"Yes, of course."

"That's taking it too far," Mia objected.

"A hundred people in the same church? And everyone with a connection to me? We couldn't allow that," Munch said.

It was a game to the killer, nothing more. He or she was playing with them. How do you rob a bank? You blow up the building across the street. The killer knew exactly what he was doing. What she was doing. This was about more than four girls. Than ten girls. Someone had been watching Munch for years. And knew exactly how to hit him where it hurt. How to create maximum confusion. Chaos. Terror. Mia had not slept more than four hours in the last three days, and it was starting to get to her now, she could feel it. She was struggling to think straight.

"Who's at the office?" Munch asked when they were back in the car.

"Ludvig, Gabriel, Curry, I think," Mia said.

"Mikkelson will take me off the case," Munch said, lighting another cigarette without opening the window.

"How do you know?"

"What would you have done?" He looked at her without expression.

"Taken you off the case," Mia said.

"Of course you would," he said, and drove toward Mariboesgate.

"What's your opinion?" Mia asked him.

"What do you mean?"

"It's a legitimate question. We're investigating a major incident. The killer is coming after you personally. Will you be able to stay objective? Keep your emotions in check? I don't think so."

Munch snorted. "Remind me again whose side you're on."

"Your side, obviously," Mia said. "But someone is bound to ask that question."

"It's personal now," Munch said, narrowing his eyes. "No one goes after my family and gets away with it."

"My point exactly."

"What?"

"One comment like that in front of Mikkelson and you're out." She ran her finger across her throat to illustrate.

"Ha," Munch scoffed. "Who else would they put in charge?"

"Wenngård."

"Yes, all right."

430

"Klokkervold."

"For Christ's sake, Mia! Whose side *are* you on?"

"I'm just telling you, Holger. There are others. It is possible for you to step aside."

Munch mulled it over before he replied. "What would you have done? If it were a member of your family?"

"You already know the answer to that."

"Exactly. So let's say no more about it."

"Don't you think you ought to get some sleep?"

"Maybe, but it's not going to happen." Munch sighed before finally opening his window. "Contact everyone. Office in one hour. Those who don't show can start looking for another job. We're going over everything again. We turn over every stone until we find that bloody cockroach, even if it's the last thing I do."

Mia took out her phone.

49

"What have we got?" Munch said when everyone was gathered in the incident room. "And don't say nothing, because that's impossible. Somebody out there must have seen something. I know that you've all been working around the clock, but from now on we need to work twice as hard. Who wants to start? Ludvig?"

Mia looked around the room. A sea of tired faces stared back at her. It was agony. Everyone had put in a ridiculous number of hours in the last few weeks, but still they had almost nothing to show for it. Curry had grown a beard. Gabriel Mørk's face was deathly pale, and he had big bags under his eyes.

"We've cross-referenced most of the names from Høvikveien Nursing Home with the Hønefoss case. So far we haven't found anything, but we still have a few names to check."

"Keep on with that, there might be something there," Munch said. "Anything else?"

"I carried out a background check on the church you mentioned," Gabriel said.

Munch glanced quickly at Mia, who simply shrugged. They had let the church slip to the bottom of their list. Too slow off the mark. They'd been planning to go there when the girls' bodies were found at Isegran Fort, and immediately after that they'd discovered the threat to Marion.

"What have you found?"

"It's a bit odd," Gabriel said. "They call themselves the Methuselah Church, but I found no companies or religious organizations registered under that name. They don't have a website or anything, it seems — either they haven't quite entered the digital age or they've decided not to join, I don't know."

"Is that all you have?"

"No, there's an individual whose registered address is the same place." Gabriel checked the information on his iPad. "A Lukas Walner. I did a quick search, but he didn't show up anywhere else."

"Okay," Munch said, scratching his beard. "I've visited the church myself, and as far as I remember, there were at least two people there. An elderly man with white hair and a man with short blond hair, possibly in his mid-twenties. We have to dig deeper, and it's important that we do it quickly. The killer caught us unawares, and we need to regain the initiative. My mother attends services there, so I'll see what I can get out of her, okay?"

"I'll get on it as soon as we're finished here," Gabriel replied.

"Good," Munch said, looking out over his team again. "Anything else?"

"We're keeping Benjamin Bache under surveillance, but so far there's nothing to suggest that he has anything to do with this," Kyrre said.

"Okay," Munch said. "We have plenty of resources, so just keep up the surveillance until we're quite sure. Anything else?"

"I've run a trace on the account Margrete_08," Gabriel said. "It's a Hotmail address created on" — the young man looked at the iPad in front of him — "March second, 2010. A few days before you got the first email from her, isn't that right?"

Gabriel glanced up at Munch, who looked uncomfortable. Not only was his mother's name mixed up in the investigation, but the killer had also been in contact with him privately. And Munch had allowed himself to be used. Mia knew him well enough to see what was going on behind his furrowed brow. He was trying to pull himself together to avoid giving the rest of the team the impression that he was letting it get to him.

"That's correct," Munch said.

"This email account was only ever used to send emails to you. It's been accessed from three different IP addresses."

"Norwegian, please." Curry yawned.

"IP addresses. Internet protocol addresses. Each device connected to the Internet has its own address that tells you where it is. Country, region, broadband supplier."

"Its exact location?" Munch said.

"Yes." Gabriel nodded, looking down at his iPad again. "Like I said, it was accessed from three different addresses. All Burger King outlets in Karl Johan, Ullevål Stadium, and Oslo Central Station. Using a laptop. Impossible to trace, to be honest. I've pinged it, but there's no reply, so I guess it's not connected anymore. The user probably tossed it — that's what I would have done."

"You can get Internet at Burger King?" Curry said.

"We've received just under two thousand calls," Anette said, ignoring her tired colleague. "Most of them regarding the police sketch of the woman from Skullerud. I'm sorry to have to tell you this, but so far we haven't received anything useful. The police sketch is too vague. It could be anyone. As for the reward . . . well, you know how this goes. You wouldn't believe how many people like the idea of having a million kroner and think their neighbor looks a bit suspicious."

Munch combed his hand through his beard. "Offenders with a similar MO?"

Kyrre just shook his head.

"Damn it, come on, people! We must have something! Someone must have seen something! Heard something!"

Mia gave Munch a hard stare. *Calm down.* Although this was a tight-knit team, she knew there would always be some who were keen to further their careers. She imagined that Mikkelson had a hotline to several of them.

She cleared her throat and got up. Walked over to the board to divert attention from Munch.

"I'm not sure if everyone is aware of what we know so far, so let me go over it again. Not everything is proved — some things are just ideas in my head, hunches, and I need your help with them. Tell me what you think, believe, feel. No suggestion is too stupid, everything is useful, okay?"

Mia looked around the room. They were

quiet now. Everyone's eyes were on her.

"This is the story as I see it. In 2006 someone takes a baby from Hønefoss Hospital. There are two main reasons to take a baby. One is blackmail, but no demands have ever been made, so we'll ignore that. The second is that somebody wants a baby. That's what I believe. Somebody wants a baby. I've thought all along, or perhaps felt it rather, that the killer is female. A woman wants a baby. Let's imagine the following scenario: This woman has access to the maternity ward. As we've seen, and saw back then, it's frightening how much easier it is to steal a baby than you would think. Especially a baby with no parents. Right, so this woman steals a baby. There's outrage, obviously, everyone starts looking for the baby — the media, us, everyone. No one can withstand that much pressure. The woman finds a scapegoat, Joachim Wicklund. Very conveniently, he goes and hangs himself. Very convenient for us. The autopsy report tells us nothing, because no postmortem was ever carried out. Wicklund hanged himself. He confessed. Case closed. Everyone can move on."

She drew breath and drank some of her Farris. She hadn't planned what to say. She was talking just as much to herself as to the rest of the team.

"It occurs to me now that if we had carried out a full postmortem, there's a good chance we would've found a needle mark in Wicklund's neck. Very convenient and clever, isn't it? An overdose in the neck, right under the rope, very hard to spot unless there was suspicion of foul play. Well, that's one theory. So we have a woman. With a baby. Who knows how to perform injections. Who has access to drugs."

"A nurse?" Ludvig suggested.

"A definite possibility." Mia nodded and went on. "But we found no suspects among the nurses at Hønefoss. So we have a woman who has stolen a baby. And everything is fine. The media is no longer writing about the kidnapping. We have given up. Then something goes wrong. Maybe the baby dies. Baby dies and she decides to come after us. It's our fault that the baby died. We should have found her. We should have found the baby. And Munch is responsible. So she decides to come after Munch."

She cleared her throat and took another sip of her mineral water. The room had gone very quiet now. Everyone knew that Mia was good at this. No one wanted to interrupt her now that she was in full flow.

"This woman is incredibly clever," Mia

438

continued. "But crazy. She thinks it's acceptable to steal a child and has no problem with killing. It feels morally right for her, so this woman must have experienced something, something . . ."

She struggled to find the words.

"I don't know what exactly, but it could have been any number of things. She's logical and yet not seeing straight at the same time. Or at least she doesn't see the world the way we do. She loved the baby, who is now dead. Perhaps. The baby was due to start school in the autumn. Now the baby is dead. I think that's how she sees it. *I'm traveling alone.* The sign. The girls are going on a journey. Yes, it's a journey. Mark 10:14, 'Suffer the little children to come unto me.' The girls are traveling to heaven."

Mia was increasingly talking to herself. Her knotted thoughts began to unravel, all the things that had lain concealed in the shadows of her mind.

"This woman is incredibly caring. She loves children. She wants to protect them. She washes them and she gets them ready. It's not going to hurt. Now, two things."

Mia coughed slightly. She felt exhausted, but she had to go on.

"Two things. This was what confused me to begin with. The chaos, the symbols, I didn't see at first, so many traps and hints, and yes . . . well, I didn't see this initially, but I think we're dealing with two separate issues. One is the girls. She doesn't want the baby to be alone. That's it, that's it. It was her fault that the baby died. She was responsible. She wants to make amends. Find some friends for the baby. But that was our mistake. We should have stopped her. Damn, I'm losing my train of thought here."

"Two things," Curry prompted her gently.

"Yes, thank you. Two things. Number one: She kills the girls so that the baby, who is now six years old, won't have to be alone. In heaven. Number two: She wants to get Munch. Sorry, it was obvious all along. But that's why it was so muddled to begin with. That's why we made such a mess of it. We need to look at everything from both of those angles even though she's mixing two motives to confuse us. Number one: She kills the girls so that the girl she stole won't have to be alone in heaven. Number two: She wants to get her own back on the police. Take revenge. Get Munch. Somehow she killed the baby, but she blames Munch. I think . . ."

Mia Krüger was completely exhausted now. She was barely able to talk.

"What do you think, Mia?" Munch said to support her.

"She wants to be caught," Anette said.

"What do you mean?" Munch said.

"She wants to be caught," Anette continued. "She shows us what she's doing. Toni J. W. Smith. The girls at the fort. Calling the journalists. She wants to be caught, doesn't she, Mia?"

Mia nodded. "I agree. Good thinking. She wants to be stopped. She's almost reckless. She's revealing more and more to us. Because she's going up there, too. To heaven. To be with her baby again. She's going to be . . ."

"Are you all right?"

Mia nodded again slowly.

"This is starting to make sense," Munch said, turning to the team. "It's damned brilliant. A woman. I believe it. I can see it. So which women have we already considered?"

"The woman with two different-colored eyes," Ludvig said.

"Someone from the church?" Curry said.

"Staff at Høvikveien Nursing Home," Gabriel said.

Mia looked at Ludvig Grønlie. "Anything? Any links? Veronica Bache's cell phone?"

"I'm sorry, nothing yet, we're still working on it," Ludvig said.

"Oh, Christ, I'm slow!" Mia burst out.

"What is it?"

"Charlie. Charlie Brown."

"Who?" Munch said.

"A friend. He runs a transvestite club in Tøyen. He told me about her. The woman with different-colored eyes. He's seen her several times. God, I'm an idiot!"

"Bring him in," Munch said. "We have to find this woman. Perhaps she's the woman from the police sketch, the one our eyewitness saw in Skullerud. God knows it's a long shot, but why not give it a go? We'll let this Charlie meet every woman whose name has cropped up in the investigation, who would have been in a position to pay Veronica Bache's cell-phone bills after her death, all staff at the nursing home, and anyone connected to this church. And if we get a hit, check with the old man and see if it's the same woman."

As Mia was heading out the door, Anette pulled her to one side.

"Are you sure about this?" Anette whispered.

"About what?"

"This whole setup? You don't think Munch is too close? I mean, a threat has been made against his grandchild. His mother might be involved. Shouldn't he step aside? Let someone else take charge?"

"Holger knows what he's doing," Mia said sharply.

"Let's hope so," Anette said.

50

"What do you think?" Charlie said, twirling in front of Mia in the bedroom.

He was dressed as a dandy in a black suit with a pink tie and patent-leather shoes. He looked like a cross between James Bond and Jimmy Cagney.

"What do you think?"

Charlie smiled and spun around once more.

"Stunning," Mia said.

"Am I man enough now?"

"Very manly. The ladies at the nursing home will throw roses at you."

"Do you think so?" Charlie chuckled.

"I'm sure of it," Mia said. "Now, come on."

Charlie followed her out to the waiting car. On their way to Høvik, Mia wondered if she should tell Charlie that he was not going there to perform but simply to look at photographs of the staff on a computer. She decided against it. The police had called the nursing home in advance, and fortunately they had photographs of all staff members on record. New security requirements made it essential for all staff to carry photo ID; it would make their work so much easier.

Holger Munch was waiting outside the nursing home for them when they arrived.

Charlie bowed and greeted him politely.

"Nice to meet you," Munch said, smiling slightly. "Like the suit. Has Mia explained to you why we're here?"

"I'm working undercover, isn't that right?" Charlie winked.

"Yes, exactly. What we need you to do is to look through some photographs on a computer here, tell us if you recognize Roger Bakken's friend."

"I can do that," Charlie said.

"Her eyes were different colors, am I right?"

"Yes," Charlie confirmed. "One brown and one blue. I knew there was something mysterious about her."

"Well, that might be going a bit far," Munch said. "We just want to have a word with her, that's all."

"I understand." Charlie nodded. "Top-secret police business."

At that moment the door opened and the

woman Holger had been talking to outside the last time they were here came out.

"This is Karen Nylund," Holger said.

The woman, who looked to be in her late thirties, was slim, with long, strawberry-blond hair and a beautiful smile. Charlie bowed and took her hand.

"This is Charlie, he's helping us today. And this is Mia, my colleague."

Mia shook Karen's hand.

"Nice to meet you," Karen said. "I've been trying to get hold of Karianne, but she's not answering her phone. She's quite strict about things like that. She doesn't want to be disturbed when she's off work."

Mia did not ask but concluded that Karianne must be the manager of the nursing home.

"But is it all right if we take a look?" Holger said.

"Yes, I don't see why not," Karen agreed. "I'm glad to be of service."

Mia still said nothing. She'd been a little worried about the paperwork; they needed a warrant, and these things usually took time, but she expected that Holger must have called in a favor from the staff at the nursing home because they already knew him.

"Excellent," Holger said. "Shall we go inside?"

They followed Karen inside the nursing home and into one of the offices. Charlie strutted like a peacock through the corridors, bowing politely right and left.

"Here we are," Karen said, indicating a computer on a table.

Suddenly she looked a little hesitant.

"This is a shared computer used by all staff members, and none of the residents have access to it, but I guess it's okay for you to look at it. I mean, you are the police."

Karen glanced at Holger, who nodded to reassure her. Mia suppressed a smile.

"It'll be fine, Karen," he said, patting her tentatively on the shoulder. "I'll take responsibility, so you don't have to worry about a thing."

"Do you want me to stay?" she asked.

"Yes, that would be good. In case we have any questions."

"Not a problem," Karen said. "We'll be serving lunch in a little while."

"Good," Holger said, taking a seat in the chair next to Charlie. He grabbed the mouse and clicked on the file Karen had found for him. "Do we scroll down?"

"Just use the arrows," Karen told him, pointing to the keyboard.

Holger pressed the arrow key, and the first picture appeared. The caption identified her as Birgitte Lundamo.

"No," Charlie said, looking very grave to prove that he was taking the job seriously.

Holger pressed the key again. This time a picture of a Guro Olsen appeared.

"No," Charlie said again.

"How many employees have you got?" Mia asked.

"We have fifty-eight residents and twenty-two — no, twenty-three staff in total. Some work full-time, others part-time, and in addition we have a list of temps we call on when someone's off sick."

"And they're all in the file?"

"Yes, we have details of everyone," Karen said.

"No," Charlie said.

Holger Munch pressed again. This time the name Malin Stoltz came up on the screen.

"That's her," Charlie said with a nod.

"Are you sure?" Mia said.

"Absolutely," Charlie said.

"But her eyes aren't different colors."

"It's her," Charlie insisted.

Mia swore softly. She had met this girl. It was the girl with the long, raven-black hair she'd chatted with the first time she was here while she waited for Holger.

"Do you know her, Karen?"

"Yes, I do." Karen looked slightly frightened for the first time. "What has she done?"

"It's too early to say," Holger said, noting down the address on the screen.

"How well do you know her?" Mia asked.

"Really well," Karen said. "But only through work. She's nice enough. All the residents like her."

"Have you ever been to her home?"

"No, I haven't. Please tell me why you're looking for her. It makes me feel . . . well, it makes me feel a bit scared." She looked at Munch, who rose to reassure her.

"She's just a witness, Karen."

"Ugh." Karen shuddered and shook her head.

"Like I said, just a witness."

"Have we got her address?" Mia asked.

Munch glanced over Karen's shoulder and passed Mia a note with the address. He gestured for her to go outside to make the call so as not to upset Karen further.

Charlie sat there looking slightly put out. "Was that all?"

"It was," Munch confirmed. "Well done, Charlie."

"Good job, Charlie," Mia said, half running outside to call Curry.

"Yes?" Curry answered.

"We have a name and an address," Mia told him.

She could barely conceal her excitement.

"Malin Stoltz. Born in 1977. Long, pitch-black hair. About five six, weighs about one forty." She read out the address on the note to him.

"Is that her?" Curry said.

"Yes, Charlie identified her immediately."

She could hear Curry shout orders into the room before he came back on the phone. "We're on our way now. I'll see you there."

Mia had spoken to her. Stood very close to her. Not realized it. She'd had blue eyes. Contacts, probably. Damn, how stupid could you get?

Charlie appeared outside on the steps, closely followed by Munch and Karen, who was still looking anxious.

"I'll call you," Munch said, taking Karen's hand.

"Thanks for your help, Karen," Mia said.

"Oh, don't mention it," said the woman with the strawberry-blond hair, trying to muster a smile and not quite succeeding.

Munch said good-bye to Karen and walked quickly to his car. "Are you coming

450

with me, Mia?"

"Yes." Mia nodded, following him.

"What about me?" Charlie said, flinging out his arms.

"He'll give you a lift home," Mia said, pointing to the police officer who had driven her and Charlie up here.

"Not even a cup of coffee?"

"Next time!" Mia shouted as she jumped into the car.

Munch hit the accelerator and pulled out on Høvikveien so fast the tires squealed on the asphalt.

51

Malin Stoltz had slept badly. She'd had such bizarre dreams. That an angel had come to carry her off. That it was all over. *Now I can stop doing this,* she had thought in her sleep or in her dream — she wasn't sure which was real and which was not. But an angel had come to her. A beautiful, white angel girl. The angel had held out her hand to Malin and told her to follow. She could leave the earth now. She would never have to do this again. And Malin Stoltz had been so relieved and so happy that when she woke up, she was unable to go back to sleep. She had different-colored eyes today. One brown and one blue. This was who she was. For real. She had been teased about it when she was little. People had called her a freak and a weirdo. Only cats had different-colored eyes. *You look like a stupid cat.* And they hadn't meant a nice cat either, but a stray. Whose fur fell off in clumps because it was riddled with disease. Even though her doctor had said it was a common condition. Heterochromia. No, not common. It was not common, but neither was it as unusual as many people thought. The doctor had explained to her that it was a genetic fault. No, not a fault. When genes changed at the embryonic stage, a mutation might occur where the gene for blue eyes might partly dominate in an individual who was meant to have two brown eyes. A mutation. A mutant. The doctor had called her a mutant. She was a mutant with different-colored eyes, and that explained why she was not herself. Why she should have been someone else. That was what the doctor said. Or had she read it somewhere? The doctor had said nothing of the sort. She'd read about it on the Internet. And in *Science Illustrated.* The doctor had issues of *Science Illustrated* in his office when she came to find out if she was able to have children. The doctor had said that she could not have children because she was a mutant. That she was not supposed to be who she was, that she should have been someone else. Even though many celebrities had different-colored eyes. Dan Aykroyd. David Bowie. Jane Seymour. Christopher Walken. None of them had to be anyone else, even though some of them had changed their names, too. Malin Stoltz had dreamed that an angel had come for her, that she would not need to do this ever again, and she'd been so happy that she had woken up. Afterward she couldn't fall asleep again. She had spent a couple of hours in front of the bathroom mirror. The doctor had given her pills. Told her she was not normal. That she was a mutant who had to take pills. Malin did not like the pills. She took them only occasionally, when she heard voices in her head, but she did not take them often enough to be normal.

Malin Stoltz stood in front of the stove. She was hungry. She hadn't eaten for a long time, and she'd slept badly. And she'd forgotten to buy eggs even though she put them on the list yesterday. Malin Stoltz was good at faking. She was good at being someone other than herself. As long as she was someone other than herself, everything was fine. Finding work was easy. As long as she was not herself. She returned to the bathroom without knowing why, so she went back to the kitchen and opened the fridge. The clock near the kitchen window showed eight. She was not going to work today, and that was good, because she had slept badly.

Malin Stoltz decided to get dressed and

go to the shops. Going shopping was easy as long as you remembered to get dressed. The shops opened early today. It was easy to buy eggs as long as you remembered to put them in your basket, pay for them, and take them home in a bag. Malin Stoltz went to her bedroom to find some clothes, but when she opened the door to her closet, it was full of dairy products. Milk, butter, and cream. She closed the door again and discovered that she was in the supermarket. There was a sour smell. It was very early, and people had slept badly — that explained the smell. Malin Stoltz had dreamed that an angel had come for her, told her she did not have to be on earth any longer, but now she was in the supermarket buying eggs because she was hungry. Not all days were bad. There were things she could do to make herself feel better. Pretending to be someone else, that made everything better. When she was herself, things did not go so well, just like today, but she had to be herself now, because today was a day off, and she was hungry. She hadn't had a day off for a long time. She had been good, worked hard, been Malin Stoltz, who was polite and normal and had the same color in both eyes. Soon she would stop being Malin Stoltz, she would become someone else, and she was looking forward to that.

She closed the door to the dairy cabinet and found the place where they kept the eggs. She put four boxes in her basket. Her basket was blue, she could see that, if she closed the eye that was brown. If she closed the eye that was blue, the basket turned brown. It was not true, but everything was possible if you just pretended. Four times twelve eggs equals forty-eight. She tried but failed to remember what else was on her list. Yes, bread. She went to the bread counter and chose a whole-wheat loaf. There was still a sour smell in the shop, so sour she had to pinch her nose. Carrying the basket with the eggs with one hand was difficult. The boy behind the register also smelled sour. He, too, had slept badly — that must be the explanation. She had money in her bank account. It said "approved" on the terminal. The shop really was starting to reek now. She just about managed to put the eggs in her shopping bag and run outside into the open air before the whole shop rotted behind her. She sat on some steps for a moment until the air felt fresh again. Then she picked up the bag with her right hand and started walking home.

52

Munch had just parked a short distance from the apartment building, with a view of the entrance, when Mia's phone rang.

"Yes?"

"It's Curry."

"Is she at home?"

"No, there's no reply. We're waiting for you, can you see us?"

Mia glanced down the road and spotted the black Audi. "Yes."

"What do we do?"

She looked at Munch. "Do we go in?"

Munch shook his head. "We must remember that this woman might be innocent. All that we know is that she used to know Roger Bakken and that she might have had access to Veronica Bache's cell phone. I'm not putting my neck on the line with as little to go on as this."

"No, we'll wait a little longer," Mia said on the phone. "Do we have units on all streets?"

"Yes."

"Send in Kim," Munch said quietly.

"Send in Kim," Mia repeated into the phone. "See if one of the neighbors will let him in."

"Okay," Curry said.

Soon afterward the back door of another Audi opened and they saw Kim head for the entrance. He rang a couple of the bells before the door was opened, and he disappeared inside.

"He's in," Curry said.

"Yes, we saw," Mia said.

They had done this many times before. Both during training and in real life. One or two men would go inside while the rest waited outside, in cars or on foot. Now there was a knock on Mia's window. She opened it. Kyrre slipped a small bag inside and disappeared again. Mia opened the bag and handed the second set of earphones to Munch.

"We're up and running," she said, ending the phone call. "Kim, can you hear me?"

"Yes."

"What's on the inside?"

"Door to the basement. Elevator. Stairwell."

"Take the stairs to the second floor,"

Munch said.

"Okay."

They waited until Kim reported back.

"I'm here."

"Is it the right door?"

"The sign says 'M. Stoltz,' " Kim confirmed.

"Ring the doorbell."

They waited a few more seconds.

"There's no reply. Do I go in?"

Mia and Munch looked at each other.

"Yes," Munch said.

Mia was reminded of Anette's warning. Perhaps Munch was too close. Was he capable of making the right call?

"I'm in," Kim said.

"What have you got?"

There was silence for a moment.

"Oh, my God," Kim finally said.

"What is it?" Munch demanded, louder this time.

"This is just . . . You have to see this for yourselves."

"What is it?!"

Munch was shouting now, but Kim did not reply.

53

Malin Stoltz suddenly became aware again and discovered she had a plastic shopping bag in her hand. She must have been to the shops. She did not even remember going outside. She looked around. She was outdoors. The last thing she remembered was a strange dream. An angel had come for her. She would not have to be here much longer, it was just as she had planned, but after that she did not remember very much. She opened the bag and peered inside it. Four boxes of eggs and a loaf of bread. Good Lord.

It wasn't the first time this had happened, but it scared her just as much all the same. One time she woke up on a tram. Another time she'd been on her way to Tøyenbadet Swimming Pool. She took a deep breath and sat down on a bench. Perhaps she ought to go see her doctor again. She hated going to the doctor's, but perhaps it was about time.

The blackouts had become more frequent, especially on the days she didn't go to work; as long as she was at work, she could manage, but at home was another matter. Where she had to be herself. That was the tricky part. She was pleased that it would soon be all over. Not long to go now. Soon she could rest. Soon she wouldn't have to go on being Malin Stoltz. Or Maiken Storvik. Or Marit Stoltenberg. She tried focusing on the walk home, but images kept cropping up in her head. She tried concentrating on her shopping bag instead. She touched the plastic. That was tangible, wasn't it? It was here? Yes, it felt real. She looked down at herself. Matching shoes. Very good. Pants. Excellent. T-shirt and a thin sweater over it. She had done well. She hadn't gone outside naked. She'd gotten herself dressed. She was a little cold, that was all, but at least she was dressed. She patted herself to warm up and tried once again to conjure up images of how to get from the bench back to her apartment. She looked at the shopping bag again. It said REMA SUPERMARKET. She had been to Rema. To get home from Rema, she had to walk past the pizzeria. She looked around and saw a neon sign on the corner. Pizzeria Milano. She knew the way from there. Well, kind of. She rose quickly from the bench and crossed the street. She was very chilly now. She wanted to get home as quickly as possible. She did not want to catch a cold. If she had a cold, she could not go to work — they were strict about that. The old people were frail. They could not have germs at the nursing home. She reached the pizzeria and paused while she scouted for the next landmark. The one-way street. Walk in the opposite direction of oncoming traffic. Down the street with the red sign with the white bar. She saw the sign and aimed for it, but then she stopped.

Something was wrong. Something was not right. The neighborhood seemed different. Different from how it usually was in the morning. There were no people in the parks. There were no people sitting in their cars, looking around. Slowly it dawned on her. Very slowly. Then she realized it.

She dropped the shopping bag on the pavement, spun around, and started running down the street in the opposite direction.

54

Sarah Kiese was standing outside a brick building in Mariboesgate, waiting for a woman named Anette. She had tried calling for several days, but the line had always been busy.

You have reached Oslo Police Incident Line. All our operators are busy taking calls. Please hold.

Eventually, after trying for three days, she got through. That last time she was on hold for more than forty minutes, but she didn't give up; she waited patiently, and finally her call was answered. She'd expected the voice on the phone to be pleasant, but it was not. The woman had sounded irritated. Abrupt, like, *What do you want?* Sarah Kiese was starting to think that she was doing the wrong thing. That the woman assumed she was calling because of the reward, but she was not. She didn't care about the money. *One million kroner for anyone who can provide information that leads to a conviction in this case.* She had read about the reward in the newspaper, and that was when it started to dawn on her.

Her husband had died almost a year ago. He'd fallen from an unsafe building that was under construction. Sarah Kiese was glad he was dead. He'd been a terrible husband. He had nearly ruined her life. She'd wanted nothing more to do with him. She hadn't even attended his funeral. The smell of other women. Money disappearing from her purse, from the jar on top of the fridge, money she had saved up to pay the bills. The disappointed expression on her daughter's face on the rare occasions he came home but refused to play with her or talk to her. A memory stick from a lawyer containing a blurry film about something he had built. An underground room. She'd put it out of her mind. Forgotten about it. She had her own life now. She had a new apartment. She was happy for the first time in years. But then it came back to her. The movie on the memory stick. The one she'd deleted. They were offering a reward of one million kroner. Perhaps she had lied to the surly woman on the Incident Line. Perhaps the reward *had* prompted her to call. It had certainly caught her attention. Her husband had seemed terrified. And he used to be a tough guy. His trembling voice had told her to go to the police should anything happen to him. He had built a room underground, in the middle of nowhere. With a service elevator and a fan. She had deleted the film. She wanted nothing more to do with him. She felt clammy just thinking about him. More than anything she wanted to throw up. She did not want him in her head or in her life anymore, so she'd deleted the film, and that made it all go away. Right until last week, when she saw the newspapers. A reward of one million kroner to anyone providing information leading to a conviction in the case. Pauline, Johanne, Karoline, and Andrea. And that was when it hit her.

Her husband had built the room where the girls had been held prisoner.

Sarah Kiese found some chewing gum in her handbag and glanced around. She'd been told to wait in the street. She thought Oslo Police had their headquarters in Grønland, but it would appear not. No, that was still true, but perhaps they had other offices. Suddenly a door opened and a tall woman with blond hair and plenty of freckles came toward her.

"Sarah Kiese?"

"Yes?"

"Hi, my name is Anette," the police officer said, showing Sarah her ID card.

"I'm sorry for not calling earlier," Sarah apologized. "The lines were busy the whole time, and . . . well, my husband and I weren't exactly friends."

"Don't worry about it," said the policewoman with the freckles. "It's great that you're here now. Did you bring the laptop you told us about?"

"Yes." Sarah Kiese nodded, showing the policewoman the bag.

"That's great. Follow me."

The policewoman named Anette gestured to a door in a yellow brick building and held her card up to a scanner.

They waited quietly in the elevator. Anette was much nicer than the woman on the telephone. Sarah was pleased about that. She'd been worried that she might be criticized for contacting them after such a long time. She had been criticized so much her whole life. She couldn't take any more.

"This way, please." Anette smiled and led the way down the corridor.

They reached another locked door, and Anette ran her card over another scanner. The door opened, and they entered a large, airy, modern office landscape. It was buzzing with activity; people were practically

466

running back and forth, and the phones rang nearly all the time.

"In here." The policewoman with the freckles smiled again and showed her into an office behind a glass wall.

A young man with short, tousled hair was sitting with his back to them in front of several computer screens. It looked almost like a scene from a movie, with all those screens and boxes and cables and small flashing lights and plenty of modern technology everywhere.

"This is Gabriel Mørk," Anette said. "Gabriel, meet Sarah Kiese."

The young man got up and shook her hand. "Hello, Sarah."

"Hello," Sarah said.

"Please take a seat," Anette said, sitting down herself in one of the chairs. "Please, would you tell us again why you called?"

"Yes." Sarah coughed.

She gave a brief account of her situation. The death of her husband. The lawyer. The memory stick. The movie. The room he'd built. How scared he'd been. That she was now thinking it might have been about the girls.

"And you deleted the film from your computer?" the young man asked her.

She nodded. "Was that wrong?"

"Well, it would have been better if you had kept it, but we'll find it. Did you bring your laptop?"

Sarah Kiese took the laptop out of her bag and gave it to the young man.

"And you obviously don't have the memory stick?"

"No, that went out with the garbage."

"Ha, ha, yes, unfortunately, I won't be able to find that," the young man said.

Sarah started to smile. They were so nice in here. She felt as if a huge weight had been lifted from her shoulders. She'd been scared that they would be strict, tell her off, like the woman on the phone.

"I would like to take a written statement. Is that all right with you?" Anette asked.

"Yes." Sarah nodded again.

"Would you like a cup of coffee?"

"Yes, please."

The police officer with the freckles smiled and left the room.

55

After morning prayers Pastor Simon told Lukas that the two of them would be spending the day together. Lukas could hardly believe his own ears. Together? Just the two of them? He felt flushed with excitement. Lukas was often near Pastor Simon, but the pastor was always busy with something or other, usually in conversation with God or preaching the word of God to the apostates who needed to hear it, and Lukas was mostly told to carry out other important tasks, such as washing the floor or doing the laundry or making sure that Pastor Simon had clean bedlinen. One evening some years ago, Pastor Simon had said that Lukas was the person closest to him, his second-in-command, and since that day Lukas had walked tall; he had stood by the pastor's side, his back straight and his chin up. But there was one thing he'd been longing for — not that he wanted to complain about the past, indeed not, that would never occur to him — but if there was one thing he was lacking, it was that he would also like to be by the pastor's side when it came to spiritual matters.

And that was what Pastor Simon had implied today. Lukas had seen it in his eyes. *Today you and I will be together, Lukas, just you and me.* That was what the pastor had meant. Today Lukas would be initiated. Today he would learn the secrets and hear God speak. He was sure of it. They had left the farm, Porta Caeli, after morning prayers and breakfast. The women on the farm really knew how to cook. Lukas was proud of Pastor Simon for picking such wonderful women. Fifteen women who obeyed the word of God, who could cook, keep house, and do laundry — they were hard workers. The kind of women they'd need when they got to heaven. Not self-obsessed, vain women who spent their time lying in front of the TV, painting themselves like whores, demanding that the men do all the work.

Lukas started the car and drove through the gate. God had given them lovely weather, the sun was high in the sky, and he was increasingly convinced that today was going to be the day. Today he would be initiated. He didn't know very much about it, for obvious reasons. The pastor had dropped a few hints, and Lukas had also overheard him talking to God several times. Lukas felt a little guilty for eavesdropping, but he couldn't help himself. The pastor would often talk to God in his office. Lukas always made sure he was washing the floor outside the pastor's office when he heard voices in there. In that way he could be on his knees scrubbing while at the same time being filled with the word of God without there being anything improper about it. It was the pastor who had paid for Lukas's driving lessons. He had also paid for everything else that Lukas had. A black suit for special occasions. A white suit for prayer meetings. Three pairs of shoes. And a bicycle. And his food, obviously, and his room in the attic of the chapel. The pastor was rich. God had given him money. Pastor Simon was not one of those people who didn't believe in money. Many people would preach about this very subject, how you would not need money if you had God, but the pastor knew better, obviously. *In the next world, you won't need any money. There we will be taken care of, but in this world different rules apply.* Lukas never read the newspapers, and he didn't watch television, but even so, he knew that this world was founded on money. Some people were poor and others were rich. Poverty was often a punishment from God. There could be many reasons that people had to be punished. They might be homosexuals, or drug addicts, or fornicators, or blasphemers, or they might have spoken ill of their parents. Sometimes God would punish whole nations or continents. Often with floods or droughts or other plagues, but mostly by making sure they were poor. It was not the case that all rich people had been given their money by God, Lukas knew that. Some of them had stolen the money from God. It was straightforward. All money belonged to God, and if someone had too much and had not been given it by God, as Pastor Simon had been, then that person had acquired it dishonestly and so needed to be punished.

Lukas drove according to Pastor Simon's directions. They were not going back to the chapel; instead they headed upward, deeper into the forest, to a small lake. Lukas parked the car and followed the pastor down to a bench by the water. He glanced furtively at the pastor. Pastor Simon's big white hair was like an aerial, Lukas had often thought. A kind of angelic aerial that put the pastor in direct contact with God. The sun was in the middle of the blue sky now, shining directly behind the pastor's head. Lukas's skin was prickling. His fingers were tingling. He could barely sit still, and he was grinning from ear to ear.

"Can you see the devil in the water?" the pastor said, pointing.

Lukas looked across the lake, but he could not see anything. The water was dark and quiet, not a ripple on the surface. He could hear the birds chirp in the trees around him. There was no sign of the devil.

"Where?" Lukas asked, looking even harder.

He did not want to say that he could not see him, that would be stupid. This might be a test to find out if he was ready to be initiated.

"Out there," the pastor said, pointing again.

Lukas still could not see anything. He didn't want to lie or to say no. So he tried his hardest. He stared and he stared, he narrowed his eyes in the hope that the devil would appear, but nothing happened.

"You don't see him, do you?" the pastor said at length.

"No," Lukas said, and hung his head in shame.

"Would you like to see him?"

Lukas had half expected to be told off for

not looking hard enough; the pastor could be like that sometimes toward people who were not close enough to God, but he didn't get angry. He simply continued.

"I believe you, Lukas," the pastor said in his warm, mild voice. "But we can't take anyone with us who can't see the devil, because if you can't see the devil, you can't see God either."

Lukas bowed his head even further and nodded silently.

"You want to come to heaven, don't you?"

"Yes, of course," Lukas mumbled.

"Would you like me to show you?" The pastor smiled.

"Show me?"

"The devil," the pastor answered.

Lukas felt happy and a little scared at the same time. Of course he wanted the pastor to show him, to help him see, but then again he'd heard a great deal about the devil and he wasn't sure that he was ready to face him.

"Take off your clothes and step out into the water," the pastor ordered him.

Lukas was taken aback. It was not a warm day. It was almost spring, and there were pretty green leaves on the trees around them, but the air was still quite chilly. The water was bound to be terribly cold.

"Well?" the pastor said with a frown.

Lukas rose slowly and started to undress. Soon he stood naked in front of the pastor. His skinny white body shivered in the cool air. The pastor watched him for a long time without saying anything. Sized him up from head to toe. Lukas felt a strong urge to cover himself — he felt really uncomfortable — but he believed that this must be a part of the initiation. He needed to go through this stage to reach a higher level, and for that he would just have to endure a bit of discomfort.

"Now go into the water," Pastor Simon said, gesturing.

Lukas nodded and walked down to the water's edge. He dipped one toe in but quickly withdrew it. The water was freezing. A big bird took off from a tree and flew up toward the clouds. Lukas hugged himself and wished that *he* could fly. Then he would fly straight up to God and stay there forever. Not that he didn't want to be on the Ark. Of course he wanted to be on the Ark — after all, they were God's chosen people on earth — but had he been able to fly, he would not have needed to do things like this in order to be included. He looked up at the pastor, who sat like a pillar of salt on the bench. Lukas steeled himself and stepped into the icy water. It hurt. It was like standing in ice cubes. He wanted to ask the pastor how far out he had to go, but the pastor said nothing. He had risen from the bench now and come down to the water's edge. He was only a few meters away, still with the sun like a halo around his big white hair.

"Can you see the devil?" the pastor asked him again.

"N-n-n-o-o-o," Lukas stuttered.

He forced himself to go farther in, felt the icy water against the part of his body he was not supposed to talk about, took another step so that the water reached up to his waist.

"Can you see him now?" the pastor said.

The voice was no longer as gentle as it had been earlier. It was colder now, icy like the water. Lukas could barely feel his body; it seemed to be disappearing. He bowed his head and shook it. He felt utterly useless. He couldn't see the devil. He saw nothing. Perhaps he did not deserve to go to heaven after all. Perhaps he would have to stay in this world with all the whores and thieves, and burn slowly so that his flesh would be scorched and fall off his bones while the others went up to God's eternal kingdom.

Suddenly the pastor moved; he leaped into the water in several great bounds, and Lukas felt a cold, hard hand on his neck. He tried to resist, but the pastor was too strong. The pastor pressed down his head, and suddenly Lukas was submerged. His head was underwater, and he couldn't breathe. He panicked and flailed his arms about. He had to get some air. But the pastor did not release his grip. He forced Lukas even deeper down.

"Can you see the devil!" Lukas heard the pastor shouting from above.

Lukas opened his eyes, and his body grew completely limp. He was going to die now. That was how it felt. It was his time to die. This was why the pastor had brought him out into the forest. To this lake. Not to be initiated but to die. Lukas made a final attempt to free himself from the pastor's grip, but he didn't stand a chance. The pastor seemed almost possessed. His hand, no longer human, was heavy like an iron claw. Lukas's eyes started to mist over. His lungs were screaming for air, but he could not shake off the pastor's death grip. He was submerged in water. He had been robbed of all power to make decisions about his own life. To move. To grieve. The water no longer felt cold. It was warm now. His body felt warmer. A little farther away, he watched his fingers twitch. The pastor kept shouting, but Lukas couldn't hear him. He had no idea how long he had been under, because time wasn't time anymore, it was just eternity. He was going to die now, it was his time to die. There was no point in fighting it.

Suddenly, out of nowhere, his head was yanked from the water and up into the cold spring air. Lukas coughed and spluttered, spewed up the remains of his breakfast, and his lungs felt as if they were about to explode. The pastor dragged him ashore by his neck. Lukas lay by the water's edge, panting. He could not feel his body.

The pastor knelt by his side and stroked his wet hair. Lukas looked up at him with huge, shocked eyes.

"Did you see the devil?" the pastor asked him again.

Lukas nodded. He nodded so hard that it felt as if his neck might snap.

"Good." The pastor smiled, softly stroking Lukas's cheek. "Then you're ready."

56

Mia Krüger was standing in Malin Stoltz's apartment, and she knew exactly why Kim had reacted the way he had.

"I've never seen so many mirrors in all my life," Kim said, still reeling. "Now do you see why I jumped when I came in here?"

Mia nodded. Malin Stoltz's apartment looked like a hall of mirrors at a carnival. There were mirrors everywhere. Every square inch of her apartment was covered with them. From floor to ceiling in every single room.

They'd waited outside for an hour, but no one had appeared. The decision to go in had been made by Munch. Mia had disagreed, but she'd said nothing. He was the boss. She would have preferred to stay in the car, wait a little longer. That would have been better. Now they had made their presence known. Munch had asked for a full team to search the apartment. Their police presence was broadcast across the whole neighborhood. Malin Stoltz would never come back now. Mia knew it, and Munch knew it. Even so, he had made the call. Perhaps Anette had been right after all. Perhaps Munch was too close to the case. With Miriam and Marion hidden away in a safe house in Frogner. With his mother linked to the church.

"Have you ever seen anything like it?" Kim asked.

Mia shook her head. She had not. She had never even come close. No matter where she went or turned, she saw her own reflection. She felt a strong sense of unease, but there was nowhere she could rest her eyes, there was no escape. She looked exhausted. She did not look like herself. The alcohol and the pills had left their traces, both in her skin and in her usually bright blue eyes. Mia wasn't vain, but she definitely did not like what she saw. And they had lost Malin Stoltz.

Munch entered the kitchen where the others were, and he did not look particularly pleased either. He heaved a sigh as he stood in front of the mirrored fridge; it was clear that he was not used to spending much time in front of a mirror. Mia could see him looking at himself. She wondered what he was thinking.

"We have issued a description," Munch said after a pause. "We have stationed people at Gardermoen Airport, Oslo Central Station, TORP Airport, and cars in strategic locations, but I have a feeling that she's tricked us again."

Munch scratched his beard and glanced at his face in the mirror once more. "What the hell is this about, Mia?"

Mia shrugged. She knew that everyone expected her to answer this question, but right now nothing came into her head. An apartment filled with mirrors? Who liked to look at themselves all the time? Someone who was frightened of disappearing? Who had to keep looking at herself to reassure herself that she existed? Something started to come into focus, but it refused to materialize fully. She was overtired. She strangled a yawn. She really had to get some sleep soon. It was apparent from multiple angles just how much she needed a rest.

The head of the search team, a short man in his fifties whose name Mia had forgotten, appeared in the doorway.

"Anything?" Munch said, sounding hopeful.

"Nothing," the short man said.

"What did we find?"

"No, I mean nothing. There's nothing here. No photographs. No personal belongings. No handwritten notes. No newspapers. No plants. Just some clothes in the wardrobe and quite a lot of makeup in the bathroom. It's almost as if she did not live here."

Mia had a sudden flashback to her house on Hitra. She had done exactly the same. No personal belongings. Just clothes, alcohol, pills, a coffee machine. It seemed so far away now. A distant memory, even though it had been barely three weeks since she'd raised her last toast to heaven, ready to disappear.

Come to me, Mia, come.

"She doesn't live here," Mia said.

"What?" Munch said.

Mia still felt incredibly tired, but she pulled herself together. "She doesn't live here. Malin Stoltz lives here, but that's not her. She lives elsewhere."

"What do you mean?" Kim said. "Is she not Malin Stoltz?"

"There is no Malin Stoltz registered anywhere. It's a false name," Munch said irritably.

"So where *does* she live?" Kim asked.

"Somewhere else, keep up," Munch snapped.

It was clear that he, too, was exhausted.

"There's nowhere here you could hide the girls," Mia said.

She sat down at the table. She was so exhausted she could no longer stand up. Her eyes were stinging. She could feel that she had to get out of this apartment soon, before all those mirror images got the better of her.

"Malin Stoltz lives here. Malin Stoltz isn't real. She keeps her personal stuff elsewhere. A place she can be herself. And that's where she keeps the girls. A cabin or an isolated house. Call off your people at Gardermoen and TORP. She's not going to leave the country."

"How do you know?" Munch said.

"She likes being at home." Mia sighed. "Don't ask me why."

"We'll have them stay there for the rest of the day," Munch said. "And we need to go back to the nursing home. Someone there must know something about Malin." He turned to Kim. "Would you organize that? Interviews with all staff members?"

Kim nodded.

"I'm going to need some sleep soon," Mia mumbled.

"Go home. I'll keep you informed."

"You need some sleep yourself."

"I'll be fine," Munch said cantankerously.

"So do you want us to pack up?" the short man asked.

"No," Mia said.

"Why not?"

"Something is missing. She has a place where she hides things."

"We've already searched the whole place," the short man said, a little vexed and in a tone suggesting that they knew how to do their job.

Mia did not have the energy to be polite. She was too tired now.

"The lenses," she said.

"Eh?"

"Her lenses. She wore contact lenses. If she left behind makeup and clothes, she would also have kept lenses here."

"How do you know that she wears contact lenses?" the short police officer said.

Mia could feel herself starting to lose patience with him.

"When I saw her, she had blue eyes. Others have seen her with different-colored eyes. There must be contact lenses here somewhere. If she has hidden them, we might find something else as well."

"But we have searched —" the short man began.

"Search harder," Munch barked.

"But where?"

"Contact lenses must be kept in a cool place," Mia said. "Check the mirrors."

"But —"

"Start in the bathroom," Mia said. "That's the place where people keep their contact lenses, isn't it? Try pushing the mirrors, push the damned mirrors."

She got up, and for a second she blacked out. Her legs buckled underneath her, but Kim managed to grab her before she hit the floor.

"Mia?"

"Mia, are you okay?"

She came around and straightened up. She hated looking weak. Not in front of her colleagues. Damn.

"I'm fine. I just need some sleep and some food. Call me, okay?"

She stumbled toward the door and felt much better the moment she reached the stairwell. An apartment full of mirrors. Every wall from floor to ceiling, nothing but mirrors — who the hell did that?

Mia Krüger staggered down the stairs and got one of the police officers to drive her home. "Home" was an exaggeration. What sort of home was this? It wasn't a home. She didn't have a home. She was staying in a hotel in Oslo, she had her belongings in storage, and she owned a house on Hitra.

That was who she was now. A nobody. That explained why seeing herself reflected in the mirrors had been so painful.

She fell facedown on the bed and slept with her clothes on.

57

"Mommy, what are you doing?"

Marion Munch looked across to her mother, who was sitting on the sofa by the window. Miriam had been told to keep the curtain closed at all times, but she could not take the isolation any longer. She had to sneak a peek, reassure herself that the world outside existed.

"I'm just having a look, darling. Why are you not in bed?"

Marion padded over to her mother and snuggled up on her lap. "I can't sleep."

"You need your sleep, you know," Miriam Munch said, stroking her daughter's hair.

"I know, but surely I can't sleep unless I'm asleep?" the little girl said, tilting her head slightly.

"It's called falling asleep for a reason, darling," Miriam said with a little smile.

Her daughter had become rather precocious and argumentative recently. Miriam had been given a reminder of what she'd been like when she was little. Stubborn and headstrong. Old for her age. She sighed and closed the curtains again. She had blocked out much of her childhood. After her parents split up, part of it seemed to have disappeared as if it had all been built on a lie. Her parents were divorcing. She remembered being fifteen and starting to have her doubts about them. She thought that they must have been lying to her for a long time. But that was all in the past now. She'd been angry. Very angry. Mostly at her father. Holger Munch, the homicide investigator. For years she'd been proud of him. *My dad is a police officer. He'll put your dad in prison if he does something bad.* But he had hurt her. He had pushed her mother into the arms of another man. A man Miriam had never really learned to like. She was older now, but it still gnawed at her. They'd been so close, the two of them. She and her father. She should have resolved it a long time ago. Gone to him and said, *Sorry, Dad, I'm sorry for giving you such a hard time,* but she'd been unable to. Stubborn and headstrong. She was starting to feel that the time had come. Soon. Soon she would talk to him.

"Yes, but then you have to tell me to, Mom."

"Okay, Marion, go to your bedroom and fall asleep. Can you do that?"

"But it's so hard," the little blond girl objected. "I keep thinking about Draculaura and Frankie Stein. They're home alone."

The dolls her grandfather had bought Marion recently.

"Oh, they'll be fine."

"How do you know?" Marion asked.

"I spoke to your daddy just now, and he said that they were both fine. He says they send their love."

Marion looked sly. "I think you're lying, Mom."

"Me, lying? No, why do you say that?" Miriam smiled.

"Dolls can't talk."

"They talk when *you* play with them."

"Oh, Mom, that's my voice, didn't you know?"

"Is it?" Miriam said, feigning surprise. "Your voice? I thought they could talk."

Marion giggled. "Sometimes it's very easy to trick you, Mommy."

"Is it?"

"Yes, it is."

"Do you trick me a lot?"

"Yes, I guess I do."

Marion reached for the blanket lying on the sofa and covered herself with it. She rested her head against her mother's chest. Miriam could feel her daughter's little heartbeat against her sweater.

"So when do you trick your mom?"

"When I say that I've cleaned my teeth."

"But you haven't cleaned them?"

"Yes, but not very well."

"So when I ask you, did you brush your teeth properly, then you haven't?"

"No." The little girl giggled again.

"Then how *did* you clean them?"

"Quite well, sort of."

Miriam smiled again and stroked her daughter's hair.

Marion rubbed her face against her mother's neck and closed her eyes. Her thumb was inching its way toward her mouth, but she stopped herself and returned it to her tummy. Good girl. They'd spent ages trying to make her stop sucking her thumb. It hadn't been easy. But now it looked as though she was succeeding. Miriam tucked the blanket close around her daughter and held her tight.

"Mom?"

"I thought you were falling asleep?"

"I can't fall asleep when I'm talking," Marion said, precocious once more.

Miriam laughed. "No, obviously not."

It was a mistake, no doubt about it. Laughing. Reacting would merely encourage her, but Miriam couldn't help it. To be honest, she liked her daughter being awake. The apartment was silent and empty when she slept.

"What did you want to ask me?"

"Why isn't Daddy here?"

Miriam didn't quite know what to say. For security reasons Johannes didn't know where they were. If the killer was capable of hanging little girls from trees, he or she would also be able to extract from him where they were hiding. She thought of her fiancé and felt warm all over. Her father had been adamant: the wedding must be canceled. And even though she had argued her hardest, she complied in the end. Her feelings said no, but her common sense knew better. They couldn't fill a church with family and friends right now. It would be irresponsible. No one would benefit. Not now that Marion was number five.

Tick-tock, little Marion is number five.

Her father had been incredibly angry with Mia, but Miriam was grateful for knowing. Better to know what they were talking about than to live in ignorance.

"Why don't you say something, Mom?"

"Daddy is at work, but he loves you very much, he told me to tell you that."

The little girl threw aside the blanket and got up. "I think I'm ready to go to bed now."

"That sounds good, Marion. Would you like me to walk you upstairs?"

"I'm not a baby anymore." Marion yawned. "I know perfectly well where it is."

Miriam smiled. "Clever girl. Give your mom a good-night hug, then."

The little girl bent down and gave her mother a long hug.

Her daughter skipped across the floor in her nightdress and up the stairs. Miriam got up from the sofa and went to the kitchen to make herself a cup of tea. She heard her cell phone beep and ran back to check who it was.

Sorry, Miriam, but we have to move you again tonight. Something has happened, will explain later. Am sending someone to get you now. OK? M.

Damn — now? Marion had only just gone back to bed. Oh, well. Her daughter was still light enough to be carried. Something had happened. What could it be? She replied:

OK. ☺

She went out into the hallway and found the suitcase. She hadn't packed much. A few changes of clothing for both of them. Toiletries. The bare essentials. It took only ten minutes to pack everything. She brought the mug of tea with her from the kitchen and sat down on the sofa again. She wondered where they were going this time. The first apartment had been small, no television, just one room, something that had driven her a little crazy, claustrophobic. This one was much bigger and furnished luxuriously. She believed it was used for visiting VIPs who didn't want to be seen. Very anonymous. Perfect for keeping nosy journalists at bay. Like her. Was that why she had dropped out of journalism school? Because being a journalist wasn't good enough? Because she would rather do something more useful? Help people? No, that wasn't it. There was nothing wrong with being a journalist; she didn't know where that idea had come from. There were different kinds of journalists, just as there were different kinds of teachers and police officers. Some journalists wrote about celebrities. Others uncovered injustices. That was the kind of journalist Miriam had wanted to be. Fight for something. Use her brain to enlighten people, rather than dull their minds with lists of who was best dressed and what celebrities ate for Christmas.

She'd just finished her tea when the doorbell rang. Miriam jumped up and pressed the intercom.

"Hello?"

"Hi, are you ready?"

"I'm ready, just come up."

She pressed the buzzer and put on her shoes. Went to the suitcase in the hallway and put on her jacket. She hoped that Marion wouldn't wake up during the car journey. She would be crotchety, and perhaps she wouldn't be able to go back to sleep again.

There was a soft knock on the door. No doorbell. *What a considerate police officer,* Miriam thought, for being aware that a child was asleep here. She went to open the door. There was someone outside. Wearing a kind of mask. And a wig. She had no time to react. The figure pressed a cloth into her face. She heard the words:

"Night-night."

And she was out cold.

58

Mia Krüger was sitting at a table by the window in a Kaffebrenneriet café, trying to force herself to wake up. She had passed out on the bed in her hotel room, having set the alarm first as she felt too guilty to allow herself more than a few hours' sleep. But her body disagreed; it wanted nothing more than to go back to bed, crawl under the duvet, keep on dreaming.

She strangled a yawn and called Kim Kolsø.

"Yes? Kim speaking."

"Did we get anything from the nursing-home staff?"

"No." He sighed. "No one knew her very well. Malin Stoltz would appear to have kept mostly to herself."

"Are you still up there?"

"No, we're coming back to town now. We need to contact any members of staff who weren't at work today. See if we can get anything from them."

"Keep me informed, will you?"

"Will do."

Mia strangled another yawn and went up to order another coffee. It was the only way she could jump-start herself. Coffee. And plenty of it. To get her head in gear again. Her body going. She had dreamed about a maze of mirrors and been unable to find her way out; she had felt utterly confused and trapped, and the feeling still weighed her down. She ordered a double espresso and was about to carry it back to her seat by the window when she suddenly noticed two women absorbed in an intimate but rather loud conversation at a table close to the counter.

She couldn't avoid overhearing what they were talking about.

"So we tried everything, but it didn't work," one of them said.

"Oh, I'm sorry, was it you or your husband who couldn't have them?" the other one said.

"They never found out," the first woman said.

"How awful for you," the second woman said.

"Yes, if it hadn't been for the support group, I never would've gotten over it. As for him, he just refused to talk about it," the first woman said.

"Have you thought about adoption?" the second woman said.

"I really want to, but he . . . well, I don't think he does. I can't make him talk about that either."

"How stupid. Surely helping a child with no parents benefits everyone? It's a win-win."

"Yes, that's exactly what I said, but he —"

"I'm sorry," Mia said, walking up to them. "I don't mean to intrude, but I couldn't help overhearing your conversation."

The two women stared at her.

"A support group?" Mia asked. "What kind of support group were you talking about?"

The first woman looked a little offended, but she replied nevertheless.

"A support group for women who can't have children. Why do you want to know?"

"I have a friend . . ." Mia began, but changed her mind. "I . . . I can't have children, sadly."

"Oh, I'm sorry," the first woman said, her attitude changing. She was no longer offended. Mia was a fellow club member — they were playing for the same team.

"Was that here in Oslo?" Mia continued.

"Yes." The woman nodded. "In Bøler."

"Are there many of them around?" Mia wanted to know.

"Yes, they're everywhere. Where do you live?"

"Thank you so much," Mia said. "I'll look for one."

"You're welcome," the woman said. "Have you thought about adoption?"

"I'm thinking about it," Mia said, picking up her coffee from the counter. "Thank you so much."

"We need to stick together." The woman gently squeezed Mia's arm.

"Yes, we do."

Mia carefully carried her coffee back to her table, just as her phone rang.

"Yes? Mia speaking."

"It's Ludvig, are you busy?"

"No."

"I've got something. On the church."

"What is it?"

"We investigated them some years ago. Hvelven Care Center in Hønefoss made a complaint."

"Go on."

"Looks like the church has done this before. Persuaded old people to leave them their money."

"In Hønefoss?"

"Yes, three cases. None of them went to court. They were resolved through mediation."

A nursing home in Hønefoss. The nursing home in Høvik. There had to be a link.

"Can you get me the names of all staff working there during the time frame we're talking about?"

"It's on its way," Ludvig said.

"Can you check another thing for me?"

"Uh-huh."

"Can you check if there was a support group for childless people in Hønefoss in the period before the baby disappeared?"

"Of course I can. I'll do it first thing tomorrow morning when everything opens again."

"Super. Any news about Malin Stoltz?"

"Still missing without a trace."

"We'll find her."

"If anyone can do it, it's you," Ludvig said.

"Thank you, Ludvig."

"You're welcome."

"See you tomorrow."

"See you tomorrow."

Mia ended the call, knocked back her coffee in one gulp, put on her leather jacket, and left the café with a smile on her lips.

59

Mia Krüger could only feel sorry for Holger Munch as he sat beside her while they drove to the chapel in Bøler. They'd worked together on countless cases, but she didn't remember ever seeing him so burdened. He drove in silence, with a cigarette dangling from the corner of his mouth, staring vacantly through the windshield with an empty, almost resigned expression. The pressure lay like a heavy cloak on top of the otherwise unruffled detective. This case had reached deep inside his private life. He was involved. Threats had been made against little Marion. Malin Stoltz had clearly managed to rattle Holger Munch to such an extent that he was no longer thinking straight.

"Nothing from the nursing home?" she asked in a calm voice.

Munch shook his head grimly. "It looks as if Malin Stoltz lived two lives," he told her.

"People knew her at work, but no one had any contact with her outside work."

"Did you manage to talk to your mother?"

Mia knew that this was a sensitive question, but it had to be asked. They had more important priorities than to worry about feelings now.

Munch nodded. "The man who heads the church is some dick by the name of Pastor Simon."

He just about managed to utter the name, Mia noticed. He seemed shaken to his very core. Perhaps Anette had been right after all. Perhaps he should have been taken off the case. At this moment in time, Mia was inclined to agree with her.

"That was all? No surname?"

Munch sighed and shook his head. "Pastor Simon, that was all. I've asked Gabriel to see if he can find out any more about him."

"And this Lukas Walner? Did she know who he was?"

Munch said, "I believe he's this Simon's assistant."

"And you've seen them both?"

Mia knew this was also not a question Munch wanted to hear, but it had to be asked.

"From a distance, yes," Munch replied briefly as he opened his window.

He tossed the cigarette out and lit a new one just as they arrived at the white chapel. If Mia hadn't known where they were going, she wouldn't have picked this as the building they were looking for. From the outside there was nothing to suggest that it was a place of worship; it looked like a Boy Scout hut or some other anonymous public facility. It wasn't until they'd walked through the gate and reached the door that she could see that they had indeed come to the right venue. It said METHUSELAH CHURCH on a small sign beside the front door, and above it there was a small crucifix. The place seemed deserted. The door was locked, and she could see no signs of activity anywhere.

Munch walked down the steps and along a gravel path that led to the back of the building. Mia was about to follow him when her phone rang. She briefly considered ignoring it — given the state that Munch was in, she really didn't want to let him out of her sight — but the whole unit was now on red alert, so she couldn't. She watched the back of his duffel coat disappear around the corner as she pressed the green button.

"Yes, Mia here."

"Are you Mia Krüger?"

The voice was unfamiliar.

"Yes, who am I talking to?"

"You're hard to track down." The voice let out a sigh.

"Is that right? Who is this, please?" Mia said.

"I'm sorry if this is a bad time," said the man on the other end. "I've been trying to get hold of you for a while, but as I said, it hasn't been easy."

Mia followed Munch around the corner and watched her colleague peer through a window.

"And what is this about?" Mia said impatiently.

"My name is Albert Wold," the man continued. "I'm the sexton of Borre Church."

Borre Church.

Her whole family was buried in its cemetery.

"Go on," Mia said.

"Like I said, I'm sorry for disturbing you," the sexton continued.

"Has anything happened?"

Munch moved away from the window and continued to walk around the white chapel.

"Yes. We discovered it a week ago, and the whole thing seems very strange. We didn't know what to do, apart from contacting you, obviously."

"And what has happened?"

"One of your family graves has been

desecrated," the sexton said.

"What?" Mia said. "How?"

"Well, that's the odd thing," the man continued. "It would appear that the only grave affected is your sister's."

Mia Krüger stopped in her tracks and forgot all about keeping an eye on Munch. "Sigrid's grave?"

"Yes, I'm afraid so," the sexton said sadly. "As far as we can see, none of the other graves has been touched."

"Desecrated. How?"

"I don't know how to tell you this," the man went on. "The whole business is really very unpleasant. Someone has deleted your sister's name."

"Deleted it? What do you mean?"

"With a can of spray paint. At first we thought it was just ordinary vandalism — it does happen, with these out-of-control teenagers we have here — but we soon noticed that this was different. What made it so odd."

Mia glanced around for Munch, but she couldn't see him anywhere.

"What do you mean, different?"

"Now it says your name instead."

"What?"

"Someone has painted over Sigrid's name and written yours instead."

A wave of unease washed over Mia Krüger just as she saw Munch reappear around the corner of the building. He gestured to her that they were going back to the car.

"Would it be possible for you to come up here?" the sexton asked.

Munch tapped his watch and waved irritably to her on his way to the Audi.

"I'll try to get there as soon as I can," Mia said, and ended the call.

"What do you think you're doing?" Munch shouted out to her. "This place seems deserted. We have to issue descriptions of both Lukas and this pastor."

"Pardon?" Mia responded distractedly.

Someone had been to Sigrid's grave.

"We have to issue a description," Munch said again, getting angrier. "We have to find these idiots and bring them in for questioning."

Munch started the car and drove down Bogerudveien. Mia was contemplating telling Munch about the conversation she'd just had when his cell rang. The conversation lasted less than ten seconds. When he disconnected, his face was if possible even whiter than it had been a moment ago.

"What is it?" Mia asked anxiously.

Munch was almost incapable of speech now. He could barely squeeze out the words.

"It was the nursing home. My mother has suddenly taken a turn for the worse. I have to go there right away."

"Oh, God!" Mia exclaimed.

"I'll drop you off in the center of town. You sort out the wanted notice."

"Of course," she agreed.

She searched for some way to show her sympathy but found none.

Munch switched on the flashing blue light, hit the accelerator, and sped toward the center of Oslo.

V

60

Emilie Isaksen was driving along Ringvoll-veien. She was new to this area — she'd lived in Hønefoss less than twelve months — and it suddenly struck her that she was taking a roundabout route. Emilie Isaksen taught Norwegian, and several of her pupils lived around here, a few kilometers outside the town center. She shifted down to second gear and turned off onto Gjermundboveien.

Emilie Isaksen had known that she wanted to be a teacher from the moment she started college. She found work right after completing her teacher training, and she had enjoyed her job from day one. Several of the teachers at the school had given her advice when she first started, and they meant well — how important it was to look after yourself, not take your work home with you, don't get too close to the pupils — but that wasn't the way Emilie did things. And that explained why she was in her car now.

Tobias Iversen.

She had noticed him from the first lesson, a good-looking, gangly boy with alert eyes. But something was wrong. Something she couldn't quite put her finger on. He was well liked, so popularity wasn't the issue. She hadn't grasped the problem initially, but it came to her in time. His mother never attended Parents' Evenings. Neither did his stepfather. They didn't reply to letters. They didn't answer their phone. She was quite simply unable to contact them. And then she'd started noticing the bruises. To his face. His hands. She didn't teach PE, so she hadn't seen his body, but she suspected that he was bruised all over. She'd had a quick word with his PE teacher, but he was the old-fashioned type. Kids fall down and they get hurt. Especially unruly boys — what was she implying? She'd tried to question Tobias tactfully. Was he all right? How were things at home? Tobias had refused to open up, but she saw it in his eyes. Something was not right. There might be teachers who were prepared to overlook something like this, who didn't want to get involved — the sanctity of the home and all that — but Emilie Isaksen was not one of them.

Tobias hadn't been to school for a week. She had tried calling his home, but there'd been no reply. She'd asked around, discreetly, and discovered that his younger brother hadn't been to school either. She had spoken to the school counselor without mentioning any names but asking for guidance. What was the policy? What action should she take? She'd been given rather vague messages; no one had wanted to tell her exactly what to do unless she had proof. You had to tread carefully. Emilie Isaksen had heard it all before, but she refused to let herself be put off. What harm could a visit do? She just wanted to drop off some homework. Have a quick chat with his mother. Perhaps arrange a meeting with his parents. There was no reason that meeting couldn't take place in Tobias's home if his mother found it difficult to leave the house. Unorthodox perhaps, but Emilie had made up her mind that it was worth the risk. She was going to be polite. She was not going to accuse anyone of anything. She was only trying to help. It would be fine. Perhaps they had gone away on holiday without asking the school if they could take the boys out. Perhaps both boys were ill; there'd been a spring bug going around the school, among both pupils and teachers. There could be so many reasons.

She drove up the old Ringvollveien until

she found the address. "Address" might be an exaggeration, since it was just a lane that led deeper into the forest. A mailbox at the bottom of the road said IVERSEN & FRANK. She decided to leave her car there and walk the last stretch up to the house. The house was red and small and surrounded by other, even smaller buildings. A long time ago, it might have been a nice little cottage, but now the whole place was more of a junkyard. There were several rusting cars sitting about and piles of what she would call junk in several places. She walked up to the front door and knocked. There was no reply. She knocked again and heard a noise from the other side. The door opened, and a small, filthy face appeared.

"Hello?" the little boy said.

"Hi," Emilie said, bending down so as not to tower over him. "Are you Torben?"

The little boy nodded. He had jam smeared around his mouth, and his hands were grubby.

"My name is Emilie, I'm Tobias's teacher. Perhaps you've heard about me?"

The boy nodded again.

"He likes you," Torben said, scratching his head.

"That's nice. I'm looking for Tobias? Is he at home?"

"No," the little boy said.

"Is your mother or your stepfather at home?"

"No," the little boy said again.

She could hear that he was almost on the verge of tears.

"So are you home alone?"

The boy nodded. "There's no more food," he said sadly.

"How long have you been home alone?"

"I don't know."

"How many nights has it been? How many times did it get dark?"

The little boy thought about it. "Six or seven," he said.

Emilie Isaksen could feel herself getting angry, but she decided not to show it. "Have you any idea where Tobias might be?"

"He's with the Christian girls."

"Where is that?"

"Up in the woods, by Litjønna. That's where we hunt bison. I'm really good at it."

"I'm sure you are. I bet that's fun. How do you know that's where he is?"

"He wrote me a note and left it in our secret hiding place."

"You have a secret hiding place?"

The boy smiled faintly. "Yes, we're the only ones who know about it."

"How exciting. Please, can I see the note?"

"Yes. Would you like to come in?"

Emilie considered her options. Technically, she was not allowed. She could not enter someone's home without permission. She glanced around. There was no sign of the adults anywhere. The little boy had been home alone for almost a week, and there was no food in the house. Surely that was reasonable cause.

"Yes, please." Emilie Isaksen smiled and followed the little boy into the house.

61

Holger Munch was standing outside his mother's room at Høvikveien Nursing Home struggling to get his thoughts in order. Too much had happened recently, far too much. The threat against Marion. His daughter and granddaughter being forced to go into hiding. They had found Malin Stoltz. They had lost Malin Stoltz. Mikkelson had called him countless times, and Munch had yet to call him back. He sat down on a chair and stretched his legs. He caught a whiff of something unpleasant and realized to his horror that the smell was coming from him. He had dozed a couple of hours in his office chair and had not had time to change his clothing. He rubbed his face and fought to keep his eyes open. Thank God he could afford for his mother to live in a place like this. They had a doctor on call, so she hadn't even had to leave her room. She was fine. Fortunately, her problem had turned out not to be as serious as it first seemed.

Fortunately.

Holger Munch found his cell phone and called Miriam, but for some reason there was no reply. He shook his head and tried again, only to get the same result. Typical. Stubborn girl. He had promised to bring them more food, fresh clothes, more toys for Marion, and now he was stuck here. He sent her a text message asking her to call him, and then he put his phone back in the pocket of his duffel coat. The corridor was warm. He found the air stuffy. He ought to take off his jacket, but he really did not smell very good. He got up and went to one of the lavatories. Stuck his mouth under the tap and drank some water. He caught a glimpse of himself in the mirror and didn't like what he saw. He looked dreadful. Malin Stoltz's apartment has been filled with mirrors from floor to ceiling. He'd never seen anything like it. Who lived like that? He had struggled just to stay in it for five minutes. Malin. Miriam. Marion. Mikkelson. Munch. So many *M*'s. He tried for a moment to be Mia. Nothing but *M*'s. Was it significant? He returned to the corridor and sat down again. Nothing but *M*'s? Nonsense. Perhaps Mikkelson was right after all. Perhaps he should step aside. Let someone else take over. His head was no longer working as it should. He hated to admit it, but she really had them over a barrel. Malin Stoltz. If that was her real name. She had hit them at their most vulnerable point, their private lives, rattled them. Rattled *him.* He was no longer thinking clearly. He couldn't tell the difference between emotion and reason. He was tempted to go outside for a cigarette but opted for a mint instead. Four girls dead and his family in hiding. At least they had a suspect now. And no more girls had disappeared — that was something. *It'll be over soon,* he thought, leaning back in the chair. *We'll find her, and then it will be over.* He wasn't aware of it, but his eyelids were closing. He realized it only when the door opened and the on-call doctor appeared, together with Karen, who had alerted him.

Munch quickly got up.

"How is she?"

"She's fine," the doctor said. "And I mean that. I found no signs of anything wrong. She must just have been a little tired. Perhaps she got up too quickly from her bed. It could be so many things, but there's really nothing to worry about. She's quite all right."

Munch breathed a sigh of relief. "Can I

see her?"

"I've given her something to make her sleep, so it's better that she rests. Perhaps this afternoon."

"Thank you." Munch shook the doctor's hand.

"And who else?" the doctor said, now addressing Karen.

"Torkel Binde," Karen said. "He's been complaining about his medication. His room is at the far end of this corridor. Let me show you the way."

Karen smiled tenderly at Munch and followed the doctor down the corridor. Munch got up and went outside. He lit a cigarette and called Gabriel Mørk.

"Yes?"

"It's Holger. I'm at the nursing home, had to deal with a private matter. Where are we?"

"I've found the movie on the laptop that Sarah Kiese brought in. It's a little damaged, especially the sound, but I have a friend who can fix it. Is it all right if I contact him?"

"Go ahead," Munch said.

"I'll call him at once," Gabriel said.

Munch next called Mia. She didn't answer her phone. He called her again, but there was still no reply. *What is it with these stubborn girls?* he thought, and sent her a text

518

message as well.

Call me!

He then tried Ludvig, who did reply.

"Yes?"

"Munch here, can you do me a favor?"

"Sure."

"Please send someone to the apartment in Frogner with some things for Miriam and Marion."

"Will do. What do they need?"

"I'll text you a list. And pick someone you trust, won't you?"

"Will do," Ludvig replied.

"Yes, and would you . . ."

"Yes?"

For a moment Munch forgot what he was going to say. He rubbed his eyes. He had to get some rest now. This was irresponsible.

"What do we have on Malin Stoltz?"

"Still missing, nothing to report. Nothing from Gardermoen Airport, ditto Oslo Central Station. Do you want to call it off?"

Munch remembered what Mia had said. That Stoltz would not try to escape. That she wanted to go home. *An apartment full of mirrors.* He shuddered. He was loath to admit it, but this particular detail gave him the creeps.

"Yes, we'll call it off. Please, would you do it?"

"Okay," Ludvig said.

"Did you circulate a description of the two men from the church?"

"That has already gone out," Ludvig said.

"Good."

Munch threw aside his cigarette and was about to light a fresh one when Karen appeared on the steps.

"Are you all right, Holger?" The strawberry-blond woman looked at him anxiously.

"Hi, Karen, yes, fine."

"I don't think you look too good. I mean, don't you think you should get some rest?"

She stood very close to him. He could smell her perfume. He got a strange feeling he couldn't quite identify until he realized what it was. She cared for him. She was looking after him. It had been a long time since someone had done that. Usually it was he, Holger Munch, who took care of everyone else.

"Are you busy?" Karen asked.

"I'm always busy." Munch laughed and coughed slightly.

"You couldn't spare just one hour?"

"What do you mean?"

"Come on," Karen said, grabbing the

sleeve of his duffel coat.

"Where are we going?"

"Hush," Karen said.

She pulled him up the steps, into the nursing home, down one of the corridors, and into an empty room.

"I haven't got time for this," Munch said, but Karen placed her finger on her lips.

"Do you see that bed over there?"

She pointed to a freshly made bed below the window. Munch nodded.

"And that door over there?"

Munch nodded a second time.

"Then I suggest that you take a shower. Afterward you lie down in that bed and get some sleep. I'll wake you in one hour. No one will disturb you here."

"No, I —"

"To be quite honest, you're badly in need of both," Karen said, wrinkling her nose. "You'll find towels in the bathroom," she added. "One hour, okay?"

She gave him a hug and left the room.

A one-hour nap. What harm could it do? Good for his brain. Good for his body. Good for everyone.

Munch sent a quick text to Ludvig with instructions about what Miriam and Marion needed in the apartment, passed on the shower, and collapsed on the bed, still fully dressed, and closed his eyes.

62

Marion Munch awoke not knowing where she was. She normally woke up at home, but the last few days had been different, and recently she had awakened in two strange places. A small apartment. And then a big apartment. Now she was in yet another new place.

"Mom?" she whispered tentatively, but there was no reply.

She sat up in her bed and looked around. The room was very nice. It was clearly a child's bedroom. The other places had been just for grownups — no toys, nothing belonging to a child anywhere.

"Mom?" she called again as she climbed out of bed and started to explore the room.

The walls were white, bright white, so white that she almost had to shield her eyes with her hand, and there were no windows in the room. Marion felt a little sorry for the girl who must surely live here. No windows, what a silly idea. From her bedroom window in Sagene, she could see all sorts of nice things. Cars and people and so on. The girl who lived here could not see anything at all. The strange thing was, there was no door in this bedroom either.

There was a desk in one corner. With a lamp. And a pad of paper and some pens and crayons. Her mother had promised her a desk like it now that she was starting school, and that was soon. It was in . . . well, it was soon anyway. On one wall there were small posters with letters of the alphabet. One had an *A* and a picture of an apple. Another had a *B* and a picture of a banana. She could not remember the next letter — oh yes, *C*. She remembered it now, and she recognized the drink on the picture, the one her mother disapproved of but that her granddad let her have, cola. She couldn't read yet, but she also recognized a few words: "cat," "ball," "car." Her mother had taught her a song about it, the ABC song; it was quite good, and it taught you the letters. The alphabet. She knew it was called that. Her mother had always stressed the importance of learning to read, and she did want to, but then she wondered what her teacher would say if she started school already knowing how to read, because then the teacher would have nothing to teach her and perhaps she might be bored. So she might as well wait, mightn't she? She could swim. Not everybody could. And she could ride her bicycle almost without her training wheels. She was the only one she knew who could do that. And she couldn't be expected to learn everything at once, now, could she?

It was then that Marion discovered that she wasn't wearing her own clothes. How very strange. Hadn't she had been wearing her light-blue nightdress earlier? The one with the tear in it, which her mother wanted to throw out but Marion refused to let her. She liked putting her finger through the hole, feeling the soft fabric around her finger; it made it easier for her to fall asleep now that she had stopped sucking her thumb. She had done really well, stopping that. It had been very hard to begin with, she had missed the thumb terribly, had lied to her parents a few times and sucked it after all. But then Christian at nursery school had told her that only babies suck their thumb, and that had made her stop. Because she was no longer a baby. After all, babies couldn't swim, could they? Indeed, could *any* of the others swim? Oh, no, they could not. But perhaps that wasn't surprising, because none of them spent as much time in Tøyenbadet Swimming Pool as she and her mother did; she had certainly never seen anyone she knew there. She glanced down and almost had to laugh. She looked as if she were going to a costume party. She was wearing a big, old-fashioned dress that made it hard to move around. Then she discovered the dolls on the shelf. There were five dolls sitting up there, dangling their feet. Not new dolls, not cool ones like Draculaura, but old-fashioned ones with hard white faces, the kind of dolls her grandmother had up in the attic. One of them was even wearing the same dress as the one Marion had on. A bright white dress with all sorts of bits of lace, or whatever it was called. Marion climbed up on her bed and took down the doll. It had a sign around its neck. Marion knew what the sign said. It said MARION. Her name. She recognized her own name. She knew how to read and write it. It was on her peg at nursery school where she hung up her coat. She looked up at the other dolls, which were also wearing dresses and had signs around their necks. She could not read any of the names — oh, yes, Johanne, she knew that one, a girl at her nursery school was named that. Her peg was right next to Marion's.

"Mom?" Marion said, a little louder this time.

There was still no reply. Perhaps she had gone to the bathroom? Marion realized that she needed the bathroom herself. Now, where *was* the bathroom in this place? She walked up to what could be a door — grooves in the wall but without a handle — and ran her tiny fingers along the grooves but could not open it.

"Mom?"

She really needed the bathroom now, she really did. How strange that the girl who lived here had a sign with her name on it. Perhaps she was really nice. Perhaps she had known that Marion would be staying here for a while, and maybe she'd made the sign to say that it was fine for Marion to borrow her room, that she was welcome, like it said on their neighbors' doormat, WELCOME. I welcome you, I live here. Go ahead, do some drawing and learn the alphabet if you like.

She was close to bursting now.

"Mommy?" she called out at the top of her voice.

Her voice flew around the room and slammed back into her ears.

No, she could hold it no longer.

Suddenly something happened to the wall.

A buzzing noise and some squeaking. Then it fell silent again, only for the sound to resume, coming closer and closer, almost as if someone were banging two saucepan lids together, like they did at nursery school once when they made an orchestra out of the things they already had.

Marion kept staring at the wall where the noise was coming from. She noticed a handle on the wall that she hadn't seen before. She reached out and grabbed the handle. It was a hatch, which opened. Marion pulled open the hatch and jumped when she saw what was behind it; she got goose pimples all over. Inside the hatch was a small monkey. A wind-up toy that banged two metal discs together to make a noise. There was a note with the monkey. She waited until the monkey had stopped moving before she stuck in her hand and quickly snatched the note.

It had letters on it. Some repeated more than once. *E.* She knew that one. *A.* She knew that one as well, they were in Elsa's name — she worked at nursery school. And *O.* She definitely knew that one. She really needed to pee now. She pressed her legs together and tried to read the note.

"Peekaboo."

She had no idea what it meant.

"Mom! I need to peeeee!"

She shouted louder, but there was still no reply. She could not hold it anymore. She lifted up the heavy dress. She was wearing strange underpants, really big ones. She looked around the room. There, under the desk. She pulled down the big underpants as quickly as she could and peed into the wastebasket.

63

Mia Krüger parked the car and walked the last stretch up to the church. Borre Church. The beautiful white brick building glowed in the sunlight and gave her palpitations. Four funerals in the same church. Three gravestones in the same cemetery. She was not sure that she could handle seeing them again. That was the reason she'd been procrastinating. And now someone had been there. Desecrated Sigrid's gravestone. Forced Mia to return before she was ready. She looked out for the sexton who had promised to meet her but couldn't see him anywhere, and so she walked, almost reluctantly and with heavy footsteps, toward the graves.

She had stopped on her drive here. Bought flowers. She didn't feel that she could turn up without something. The scent of the flowers made her nauseous. Flowers. A house filled with flowers. Friends and neighbors paying their respects. It was all she had left. Three gravestones and a house filled with flowers. She had sold the houses. Both her parents' and her grandmother's. Two nice white houses in the center of Åsgårdstrand, not far from where Edvard Munch had lived. Her family inheritance. But she couldn't cope with it. She didn't want them. All she wanted was to forget. She passed a tap with a green watering can next to it. She felt a little ashamed now. Three stones. Four members of her family. Sigrid, her grandmother, and her parents. All of her family was here, and she hadn't even bothered tending to their graves.

Sigrid Krüger
Sister, friend, and daughter
Born November 11, 1979.
Died April 18, 2002.
Much loved. Deeply missed.

It was exactly as the sexton had said. Someone had sprayed over Sigrid's name. Written hers instead.

Then she could not take any more. She dropped the green watering can, slumped onto her knees, and started to sob. Everything came out now, all the things she had pent up inside. She hadn't cried for a long time, had been afraid to give way to such extreme grief. She stayed on the ground while the tears poured down her cheeks.

Come to me, Mia, come.

Sigrid. Lovely, beautiful, darling Sigrid. What difference did it make that Mia had shot some junkie loser? Nothing. It made no difference at all. It had only triggered more tragedy. More grieving relatives. More darkness. She never meant to. She never meant to shoot him. She really never meant to shoot. She should be punished. She didn't deserve to live. She could feel it now. She deserved to die. All these years she'd been weighed down by the guilt of the survivor, only she had never managed to put it into words, but it came to her now. She was guilty. Guilty of being alive. She should be with her family. That was where she belonged. With Sigrid. Not here on this damned planet where evil and selfishness had the upper hand. There was no point in fighting it any longer, trying to understand, trying to do good. The world was a rubbish heap. People were rotten to the core. She wanted nothing more to do with it.

Someone had written her name on the gravestone. Was someone coming after her? Wanting her dead? She had enemies, of course she did — no police officer with her reputation got through a career without making some — but she couldn't think of anyone in particular. It was unpleasant to see her name on the gravestone, but the feeling of rage because someone had desecrated Sigrid's final place of rest was much worse.

She muttered curses at the unknown attacker, got up, and dried her tears. Cleared away the leaves and twigs, put the flowers in the vase, and continued tidying the graves. She dug her fingers into the soil, turning it over so that it would look fresher. It was nicer this way. Went back to where she had gotten the watering can and found a rake. Took off her leather jacket and her sweater. Dipped the sleeve of her sweater in the water from the watering can and tried to scrub off her own name from the gravestone. The spray paint refused to budge. She had to talk to someone about it, get it removed as quickly as possible. She hated its being there, mocking her. Mocking both of them. She raked away the last remains of dead foliage while she waited for the sexton. She should have come earlier. This was far too late. She mumbled, "Sorry, Sigrid, forgive me," through pressed lips, trying to hold back a fresh stream of tears.

There was a small yellow plastic container

behind the vase. She bent down and picked it up, took it to the nearest trash can, and dumped it. She was walking back toward the grave when she stopped in her tracks.

Could it be?

No, it was impossible.

She spun around, went back to the trash can, and retrieved the yellow container. She twisted it open.

There was a note inside.

Mia's hands shook as she unfurled the note.

"Peekaboo, Mia. Clever girl. But you're not as clever as you think you are. You think this is the real grave, but it isn't. Can you see me, Mia? Can you see me now?"

Mia Krüger ran as fast as she could down to her car to find her cell phone. She had dozens of missed calls but decided to ignore all of them. She wiped the tears from her eyes and called Munch.

64

Ludvig Grønlie stepped out onto Munch's smoking terrace to get a bit of fresh air. He let out a small sigh and stretched his body. He was tired, but he wasn't going to complain. Other members of the unit had worked almost twice as many hours as he had recently. Ludvig Grønlie was approaching sixty, and although no one had said it out loud, it was in the air. Long and loyal service. No one would reproach him if he didn't work twenty-three hours a day anymore. But it was not only the physical pressure that took its toll — the mental exertion was worse. Never any peace, always something that needed doing. As long as a serial killer was at large, none of them could truly rest.

His cell phone rang. He recognized the name on the display and answered the call.

"Grønlie speaking," Ludvig said, stretching again.

"Hello, Ludvig, it's Kjell."

"Hi, Kjell, did you find something?"

Kjell Martinssen was one of Ludvig's old colleagues. They had worked together in Oslo for years, but in contrast to Munch, Martinssen had chosen to be demoted. No, that was unfair — he'd made the decision to take it easy. He had met a woman. Requested a transfer to Ringerike Police. Ludvig's old colleague had made a wise move. He sounded relaxed and happy.

"Yes, as a matter of fact, I did."

"A support group for childless women?"

"Yes," his colleague said. "Only they call it talking therapy. Heidi does quite a lot of work for Ringerike Volunteer Service Bureau, so she pointed me in the right direction."

Heidi was the woman who had made Martinssen leave the city. The thought had sometimes crossed Ludvig's mind. Say good-bye to the stress in the capital and find himself a job in a small town. It had never happened, and now his retirement was only a few years away.

"It was active from 2005 to 2007. That was the time frame you were asking about, wasn't it?"

"That's correct." Ludvig nodded. "Do you have a list of names?"

"I can do better than that. I can get you a picture of every member as well as all their names and addresses."

"Good work, Kjell, good work," Ludvig said, returning to his desk. "Will you be faxing it over?"

He regretted his words immediately.

"Fax it, Ludvig?" his colleague chuckled. "Don't you have email?"

"Email me, I meant email me."

"I'll get someone to scan it and send it to you as soon as it's ready."

"Sounds great, Kjell, great job."

"Do you think you'll get him?" His colleague sounded more serious now. "People are talking up here. People worry."

"We'll get her," Ludvig said, then wondered if perhaps he'd given something away.

"Her? Stoltz? The one whose photo you sent us? Who's wanted for questioning?"

"We don't know yet," Ludvig said as an idea came into his head. "Is she in any of your pictures?"

"Might be, I haven't seen them yet. Heidi had to go down to the Volunteer Service Bureau to pick them up. She's on the way here now. Hey, Rune, is our scanner working?"

The latter was shouted out into the room at the other end of the phone. Ludvig's colleague got a positive response back.

"If Heidi is right and she finds it, you'll have it today, okay?"

"Excellent," Ludvig said.

He'd just finished the call when Gabriel Mørk popped his head through the door.

"Have you heard anything from Munch or Mia?"

"I spoke to Munch not long ago, but Mia isn't answering her phone. Why?"

"I just wanted to let her know that I think we'll have the movie sorted out sometime today. I've sent it to a buddy of mine who knows how to clean up noise."

"Great," Ludvig said, and suddenly he remembered what Munch had asked him. "You don't happen to want some fresh air, do you?"

"Why?"

"Munch's daughter needs some stuff. She's up in that apartment. Could you deal with it?"

"All right," the young man said. "What does she need?"

"Hang on," Ludvig said, checking his phone for the list Munch had sent him.

65

Emilie Isaksen could not believe her eyes when she stepped inside the small house. The hallway was dark and so full of junk that she had trouble navigating it. The rest of the house wasn't much better. Rotting food scraps, ashtrays, bags of trash that no one had disposed of. It was all she could do not to hold her nose. Even so, she tried putting on a brave face. She didn't want to make things any harder for the little boy than what he'd already been through. All alone for a whole week in this dump of a home, without food or anyone to look after him. Emilie Isaksen was outraged, but she managed a smile.

"Would you like to see our secret hiding place?" Torben asked her.

He seemed overjoyed to have a visitor. He had looked almost startled when he opened the door to her, scared and with large, tearful eyes, but now he was starting to liven up.

"Yes, please." Emilie followed the little boy up the stairs to the first floor.

The first floor was just as bad as the ground floor. Emilie struggled to make sense of it all. It was almost too much for her. Poverty was one thing, but this? It wasn't until they reached what was clearly the two boys' bedroom that the house began to resemble a home. It smelled clean inside, and the room was tidy and light.

"We hide things inside the mattress in case the baddies come," Torben explained, kneeling in front of the bed.

He unzipped the thin mattress and pulled it apart so that Emilie could see it.

"Is that the note from Tobias?" Emilie pointed at it.

"Yes." Torben nodded eagerly.

"Please, may I see it?"

"Of course."

He stuck a filthy hand into the secret hiding place and gave her the note.

"I'm going to spy on the Christian girls, I will be back soon. Tobias."

"Do you know when he wrote it?"

The little boy thought hard. "No. But it must have been before I came home, because it was here when I got back."

Emilie couldn't help laughing. "I'm sure

540

you're right. So when did you get back?"

"After the soccer match."

"Which soccer match was that? Do you remember?"

"Liverpool against Norwich. I watched it at my friend Clas's house. They get the soccer games on their TV — not just the Norwegian Cup Final but all kinds of games. Clas and I support Liverpool. They won."

"Would that have been last Saturday?"

"Probably, I guess." Torben nodded, scratching his hair.

The boy was covered in grime, and he didn't smell too good either. He needed a bath, clean clothes, food, fresh bedlinen. Today was Friday. He had been home alone since last Saturday evening. Emilie sat on the floor in the boys' bedroom somewhat at a loss. What was she going to do? She couldn't leave the boy here alone. Then again, she couldn't take him home either. Or could she?

"Do you want to see what else we keep in the secret hiding place?" Torben offered.

He acted almost as if he were scared that she would leave him now that she'd gotten what she came for.

"Yes, I would like to, but listen, Torben."

"Yes?"

"Are you saying that Tobias hasn't been back home since you found the note?"

"No, no one has been here."

"Hasn't anyone called you?"

The boy shook his head. "The landline doesn't work. There's no noise when I pick up the handset, and cell phones are really expensive, did you know that?"

Emilie nodded and stroked the boy's hair. "They *are* quite expensive, that's true, and you don't need to have one either."

"No, that's what Tobias says."

"Who are the Christian girls?"

"We don't know, we're just guessing," the little boy said. "Some say they eat people, though that's not true, but we know they don't go to our school — they have their own school."

Emilie Isaksen knew as much as everybody else did about the new residents up in the forest. Which was practically nothing. The teachers had discussed them in the staff room, but it had mostly been gossip after all. None of the children were registered with the school, so they were not the teachers' responsibility.

"So he went there last Saturday and no one has seen him since?"

"I don't know if he went there on Saturday. Liverpool won three to nothing. Luis

542

Suárez scored a hat trick, do you know what that is? Why don't all televisions show soccer? Did you bring me any food? I really like pizza."

"Do you want to have some pizza?"

"Yeah, I really do," Torben said. "But you have to see this first."

"Okay." Emilie smiled.

"This is a piece of rock that fell from the moon," Torben said, showing her a black stone with holes in it. "We kept it because the aliens might want it back. Cool, isn't it?"

"Yes, that really is cool," Emilie said, feeling herself start to grow a little impatient.

Tobias Iversen had been missing for seven days, and no one had sounded the alarm. She dreaded to think what could have happened to the handsome boy she'd come to like so much over the last year.

"And this is the secret number for a police officer that Tobias and I know. We can phone him whenever we need anything, or if we're in Oslo. Because we're heroes, did you know that?"

"Yes, so I've heard," Emilie said, stroking Torben's hair again.

She could only just get her fingers through it. He really needed a bath. And some food. And, not least, someone to talk to. The two brothers had found the second murder victim in the grotesque series of child murders that was all over the media. At school an assembly had been held the day after the discovery, with several psychologists present so the children could discuss the events with someone if they wanted to.

"This man is named Kim. It says so here." Torben pointed proudly. He handed her the business card and pointed at it again. "K-i-m, Kim, isn't that right?"

"Well done, Torben, I didn't know you could read!"

"Oh, I can." The boy grinned.

Emilie looked at the business card.

Kim Kolsø
Violent Crimes Section, Special Unit

"Do you know something, Torben?" Emilie said, getting up.

"What?"

"I think we should go get a pizza."

"Yes!" The little boy punched the air.

"But first I think you should have a shower and put on some clean clothes. Do you think you can manage that yourself, or do you want me to help you?"

"Sheesh, I can do it myself," he said, walking over to a wardrobe. "These are my clothes," he said, pointing to the three bottom shelves.

"Great." Emilie smiled. "You find what you need and then take a shower. Afterward we'll go get some pizza."

"Neat!" Torben said, kneeling down in front of the wardrobe to pick out the items he needed.

"I'm stepping outside to make a phone call, is that okay?"

"You're not leaving, are you?" The little boy looked at her with anxious eyes.

"No, no," Emilie said.

"Promise?"

"I promise, Torben." She stroked his hair again. "Now, you go shower, okay?"

"I will," Torben said, skipping out of the bedroom and into the bathroom.

Emilie did not want to know the state of the bathroom. She could barely conceal her despair any longer over these two brothers who had to live in these conditions without anyone taking care of them.

She waited until she heard the shower being turned on before she went downstairs and outside to make the call.

"Ringerike Police."

"Yes, hi, my name is Emilie Isaksen, I'm a teacher at Hønefoss School, and I would like to report a child missing."

"Hold on," the voice said. "I'm connecting you."

Emilie waited nervously while she was transferred through the system.

"Holm speaking."

Emilie introduced herself again and explained the situation.

"And where are his parents?" said the man on the phone.

"I don't know. I found his younger brother home alone. He's been on his own for a week."

"And the boy we're talking about — Tobias, was that his name?"

"Iversen. Tobias Iversen."

"When was he last seen?"

"I'm not sure, but he left behind a note that was found last Saturday. The note said he had gone into the woods to look for . . . well, it's a religious group that has bought the old rehab center up there. Perhaps you've heard about them?"

"We have," the police officer said.

He fell silent for a moment. It sounded as if he was covering the mouthpiece on his phone. Perhaps he was consulting some of his colleagues.

"So we're talking about the boy who you say is missing, and his parents are gone as well — is that what you're telling me?"

Emilie could feel that she was starting to dislike him. "Yes, that's what I'm saying," she said curtly.

"So how do you know that he's not with his parents?"

"I don't."

"So he could be with his parents?"

"No, he's up in the woods!"

"Says who?" the voice said.

"He left behind a note for his brother."

The man on the telephone heaved a sigh.

"Listen," Emilie said, losing her patience now. "I'm here with a seven-year-old boy who has been home alone for one week. His brother is gone. His parents are gone. And you're telling me that you can't . . . ?"

She could feel the rage surging now; she had to breathe deeply to keep the conversation going.

"I'll make a note of it, and we'll see what we can do about it tomorrow. Would it be possible for you to drop by the station sometime later today?"

"Tomorrow?" Emilie shouted. "Are you going to let a boy who's been in the woods for a whole week spend yet another night outside? What if something has happened to him?"

"I understand, but I can't just . . . I mean, what if the parents have gone on holiday

547

and taken the boy with them?"

"And left his seven-year-old brother home alone?"

"Worse things have happened," the police officer said. "I'll make a note of your number. I'll look into it, and someone will call you back."

"You do that," Emilie snarled.

She gave him her number and hung up.

66

Gabriel Mørk was standing outside the exclusive apartment building in Frogner, getting absolutely no response. He was starting to grow annoyed with Ludvig, who had dispatched him here. He had not realized that his job would involve shopping for groceries. He knew he wasn't a senior member of the special unit — after all, he had only just started — but to go shopping, surely someone else could have done that? He had more important things to deal with right now. He looked up at the apartments and rang the doorbell again. There was still no response. It was a fashionable development. The most desirable part of West Oslo. Each apartment had large windows and a terrace overlooking the park. He thought about his girlfriend and the baby she was carrying. He'd been so worried to begin with. Where would they live? How would they pay the bills when the baby came? They had to buy so much stuff, and he was embarrassed at how ignorant he'd been. He really hadn't known the first thing about becoming a father. Cribs and strollers, and that was only for starters. But not anymore. Now he had a job. Out of the blue. A cool job at that. An important job. He had never thought that something like this would turn up. The police had been . . . the enemy, to be blunt. To the other hackers he knew. But they had no idea what they were talking about. They hadn't met Mia Krüger. And Holger Munch. And Curry. And Anette. And Ludvig. And Kim and all the others. They didn't know what it was like to have colleagues. Going to work, being a part of something where people smiled and said hello and knew that you belonged to the team, who liked you and respected the work you did. He felt he was helping to make the news somehow. He had never cared much about the news before, not until now, but it was completely different when it was about your own work. Also, the equipment the technicians from Grønland had brought him was brilliant. He would never have been able to afford this himself; for the first few days he had almost felt like a little kid at Christmas.

He rang the doorbell yet again and waited.

He was just about to try it once more when the front door opened and an old lady came out. He smiled politely at her, held the door open, and slipped inside.

He carried the bags up the stairs and reached the second floor. Ludvig had explained that it was the apartment at the far end of the corridor. He was about to ring the bell when he noticed that the door was ajar.

"Hello?" he called out softly. "Is anyone here?"

He carried the shopping bags inside the foyer.

"Hello? I've brought you some things from Holger Munch."

That was when he discovered the body.

What the hell?

He threw down the bags, called 112, and knelt down by the woman lying on the floor.

67

Mia Krüger broke the speed limit, but so what? She'd been wrong, wrong all along. It was the wrong Munch. The killer was not coming after Holger. She was the target. Not the right Munch. Not Holger. But Edvard Munch. Åsgårdstrand. It was her. Mia Krüger. She was the target. Not Holger. She was ashamed. She'd been wrong. Damn, why didn't Munch pick up his phone? She passed a car, a camper, turned the steering wheel with one hand as she swerved back to the inside lane in the nick of time. She pressed the cell phone to her cheek, considered using the police radio but decided against it. You never knew who was listening in, and she didn't want anyone to hear what she had to say.

She was just about to try Munch once more but was interrupted when her phone rang. It was Gabriel.

"Where is Munch?" Mia said.

"Where are you?" Gabriel said.

"On my way to the office. Where is Munch?"

"God only knows," Gabriel said. "He's not answering his damn phone, Mia."

She realized how distraught he sounded. "What's happened?"

"Marion is gone."

"Jesus Christ!"

"She . . . she really is." The young man was almost stuttering now. "I went to the apartment with some groceries, and I found her on the floor."

"Who?"

"His daughter."

"Miriam?"

"Yes."

Fuck.

"Is she all right?"

Mia moved into the opposite lane again, passing three cars.

"She's unconscious, but she's breathing."

Miriam must have been drugged. Had Mia not *told* them they needed to have an officer posted outside 24/7?

"And no trace of Marion?"

"None," Gabriel said.

The young man was almost on the verge of tears now.

"Have you tracked Holger's phone? The

last time I talked to him, he was on his way to the nursing home. His mother had taken a turn for the worse."

"His mother?" Gabriel asked.

"Forget it, I need to speak to him right now."

"I'm not at the office," Gabriel said. "I'm at the apartment."

"Get back to the office," Mia said, sounding her horn at a motorbike that was hogging the lane in front of her.

"We . . . work . . . noise red . . ."

"You're breaking up," Mia said. "Say it again."

At last she had passed the biker and could hit the accelerator once more.

"We're working on the film right now, noise reduction," Gabriel said.

"Good, when will we have it?"

"As soon as it's ready."

"Yes, but when will that be?"

She was losing her temper and took a deep breath. This wasn't his fault. He'd done a good job.

"I can't say for sure," Gabriel said.

"Get yourself to the office and call me when you're there."

She ended the call and rang Ludvig.

"Where have you been?" her colleague wanted to know. "All hell has broken loose here. Haven't you heard?"

"Yes, I've heard. Where's Holger?"

"No idea, he's not answering his phone. Are you far away?"

"Twenty minutes, half an hour," Mia said.

"Damn. This is a total mess."

That was undoubtedly true. They'd had Marion under police protection, and now she was gone.

She ended the call and phoned information. It had started to rain now. The raindrops beat the windshield hard, and visibility was diminishing. She turned on the wipers but didn't take her foot off the accelerator.

"Number, please?"

"Please put me through to Høvikveien Nursing Home."

"Would you like me to inform you of the number?"

"No, damn it, just put me through!" Mia snarled, hitting the brakes when she realized that she was dangerously close to the shoulder.

It took a long time before anyone picked up.

"Høvikveien Nursing Home, Birgitte speaking."

"Yes, hello, this is Mia Krüger. You wouldn't happen to have Holger Munch there, would you?"

"He was here a while ago," the voice said.

"I know, but is he there now?"

"No, I haven't seen him."

Shit.

"Is Karen there?"

"Yes, Karen is here, hang on."

A million seconds passed. Mia felt like screaming into her phone. She had to turn the wipers up to max in order to be able to see out the window. A million more seconds passed before Karen finally arrived.

"Yes, Karen speaking."

"Hi, Karen, it's Mia Krüger."

"Hi, Mia, nice to hear from you."

"Have you seen Holger today?"

"Yes, he was here earlier. His mother had a turn, but fortunately it was nothing serious. The doctor gave her something to make her sleep and —"

"Yes, all right, fine," Mia interrupted her. "But is he there now?"

"No, he's left."

"Do you know where he went?"

"No, I don't. He was completely exhausted. I told him that . . ."

Mia swore under her breath. She did not have time for this.

". . . so I woke him an hour later. He

didn't look all that well when he left, but
—"

"But you don't know where he went?"

"No, he got a call and ran out. He didn't even say good-bye," Karen said.

"Okay," Mia said. "Thank you."

"Listen," Karen said just as Mia was about to disconnect.

"Yes?"

"I don't know if this is important, but her car is outside."

"Whose?"

"Malin. Malin Stoltz. Her car is here."

It was now raining so heavily that Mia was forced to slow down. The raindrops battered the windshield almost like hailstones. She could see the cars in front of her hit the brakes, their red lights glowing at her in a blur. She eased off the accelerator and exhaled. Holger had gotten a call. Who from? Someone had called him, and he ran. Holger never ran. He hadn't even said good-bye. But run? Who on earth made Holger Munch run?

The killer.

It was obvious. Marion had been abducted. The killer had called Holger. Holger for his part had not called anyone from the team. He'd run off without saying good-bye. It had to be Marion. He would never run for anyone else.

"Are you still there, Mia?"

"Sorry, Karen, what did you say?"

"Oh, it's probably not important. We can talk about it another time."

"No, what did you say? About her car?"

"It's downstairs in the underground parking garage. I don't know if it means anything, bu—"

"What kind of car is it?"

"It's a white Citroën."

A white Citroën.

Mia stared ahead of her. Trying to work out where she was. She saw a sign saying Slependen. She wasn't far from the nursing home.

"I'll be there shortly," she said. "Is the car locked?"

"I don't know," Karen said. "But she might have left a spare key in her locker in the staff room. She can be a little distracted, misplacing things. I think I heard her say that —"

"Great, Karen," Mia interrupted her again. "Please, would you find out for me. I'll be there soon, okay?"

She ended the call and dialed Anette.

"Anette speaking."

"Hi, it's Mia."

"Thank God, where have you been?"

"Åsgårdstrand. Has Munch called you?"

"No, have you heard?"

"Yes, what a nightmare."

"Yes, it certainly is. And Mikkelson is here. He's freaking out."

Mia realized that she didn't give a damn what Mikkelson thought.

"Who is in charge now?" she said, scouting for the exit.

"Mikkelson," Anette replied.

"But he doesn't have a clue about what's going on. Anette, you have to take over."

"What do you want me to do? By the way, where are you?"

"I'll be in Høvik soon. We've found Stoltz's car. Any news about her?"

"No, nothing. What do you want me to do?"

"Get hold of Gabriel and get the GPS location from that damn film. And make him put a trace on Munch's phone. I think the killer might have called him and that he's on his way to a meeting."

"Okay," Anette said. "Anything else?"

"We have to —"

Mia saw the exit for Høvik and turned off. The worst of the rain was easing up now, and she could actually see where she was going.

"Have to what?"

She couldn't think of anything else. "Just get that lousy film sorted out and trace Munch's phone."

"Okay," Anette said. "Oh, yes, Ludvig has something for you."

"What is it?"

"A photograph. The therapy group in Hønefoss."

Brilliant. Her hunch had proved to be spot-on.

"Ask him to forward it to my cell."

"But nothing on Stoltz?"

"Not a word."

"Okay, I'm just about to arrive. I'll be in touch if the car turns out to be interesting."

Mia ended the call and pulled into the nursing home.

68

Lukas was sitting on the bench by the lake, wrapped in a blanket. He was wearing dry clothes, but he still struggled to warm up. Pastor Simon had held him underwater. He had almost drowned. Pastor Simon had asked him if he could see the devil, but he could not, and then the pastor had pushed his head under the water. Lukas was confused. First the pastor nearly drowned him, then he brought him dry clothes. He had kept the dry clothes and the blanket in the car. The pastor must have planned this. Why?

Pastor Simon returned from the car with a packed lunch and a thermos. He sat on the bench of the picnic table facing Lukas. Brown-cheese sandwiches. He unscrewed the lid on the thermos and poured hot chocolate into the cup.

"Eat and drink," the pastor said.

Lukas took a sip of the cocoa and felt the

warmth flow down his throat. He ate the sandwiches slowly while the pastor watched him. The pastor did not say a single word. He sat on the bench with his hands folded in front of him, looking at Lukas with a soft, warm gaze. Lukas was still a little scared, but he was starting to feel much better. The pastor didn't take his eyes off him for one second. Usually he would look above his head, toward heaven, or at some other point — at any rate never directly at him, never fix his eyes on him like he did now. Slowly, Lukas's body began to warm up. He tried meeting the pastor's gaze but was only partly successful. He had eaten all the sandwiches and drunk three cups of hot chocolate before the pastor finally started talking.

"God sent his only son, Jesus Christ, to earth to take upon himself the sins of the world," the pastor said. "The people had the chance to save Jesus, but they chose Barabbas, the thief, instead."

Lukas nodded softly.

"What does this tell you about people?" the pastor asked him.

Lukas did not reply. He didn't want to get it wrong and end up under the water again. He could still feel the panic coursing through him.

"That people don't know what's good for them," the pastor continued. "People should not be allowed to decide for themselves. You understand that, don't you, Lukas?"

Lukas nodded. They had talked about this before. Most people were stupid. They didn't know what was good for them. For that reason God had chosen only a few who would go to heaven. Only the special ones. The initiated. Those who had realized this. Forty people from the church. And a few others. People from across the world whom they would meet in the course of time.

Pastor Simon looked straight at him and took his hand. "I am God," the pastor said.

At this Lukas felt the warmth instantly return to his body. He started tingling all over, more strongly than ever. From his toes up to his ankles, his thighs, his stomach up to his throat, his face was flushed and now also his ears.

"I am God," the pastor said. "And you are my Son."

Lukas sat with his mouth hanging open. The pastor was God. It was obvious now. This was how it was. It made perfect sense. When he talked to God in his office, he was talking to himself. The pastor was God. And he, Lukas, was the Son of God.

"Father," Lukas said in awe, and bowed

his head.

"My Son," the pastor said, placing his hand on Lukas's head.

Lukas felt the warmth from the hand of God spread across his scalp.

"You passed the test," the pastor said. "You put your life in my hands. And I hope that you trust me now. I could have killed you, but I didn't. Because you have greater tasks to accomplish before we go home."

"Home?" Lukas said cautiously.

"To heaven." The pastor smiled.

"Am . . . am I really the new Jesus?" Lukas stammered.

The pastor nodded. "Twenty-seven years ago, I sent you to earth."

Lukas could barely believe his ears. Of course. It all fit! And it explained why he had no parents.

"And I found you again." Lukas nodded reverently.

"You found me again," the pastor agreed.

"But the first Jesus accomplished great things. What have *I* done?" Lukas said.

"It will happen." The pastor smiled. "Today."

"Today?" Lukas said with anticipation in his voice.

The pastor walked back to the car. He returned holding a small bundle, which he placed carefully on the bench.

"For me?"

"Open it," the pastor told him.

Lukas unwrapped the bundle with trembling fingers. His eyes widened when he saw the contents. "A gun?"

The pastor nodded.

"What do you want me to do?"

The pastor leaned toward him and took his hand. "Last week an intruder came into the House of Light."

"Who?"

"A boy, sent by the devil."

Lukas could feel the rage explode inside him. The devil had sent a boy to stop them from traveling. He knew it. The pastor and Nils had been so quiet recently.

"But fortunately I am stronger than the devil." The pastor smiled. "I know him, but he does not know me."

Of course, Lukas thought.

Deo sic per diabolum.

The path to God is through the devil.

Understand the devil. *Get to know him.* This was what the pastor had meant.

"And where is the boy, now?"

"He's being held in the safe room."

"And what are we going to do with him?"

"You are going to kill him," the pastor said.

Lukas looked at the gun in front of him and nodded softly.

"There is just one small problem."

"What is that?"

"He has taken Rakel prisoner. My Rakel."

"Vile demon," Lukas sneered.

"So you must be careful. Kill the boy, but don't harm Rakel. I need my Rakel in heaven."

"I promise to do my best."

Lukas bowed and kissed the pastor's hand. The pastor rose. Lukas wrapped the pistol in the cloth again and carried it back to the car.

"When we get to heaven, you'll have your very own Rakel."

"Oh?" Lukas said.

"I promise," the pastor assured him. "You know the little angels who have been hanging from the trees?"

"The girls everyone is talking about?"

"Yes," the pastor replied. "They will meet us up there. You can choose one of them."

His very own girl? But he didn't want a girl. God was enough for him. What on earth would he do with a little girl? Lukas decided not to say anything; he didn't want to argue with the pastor. He put on his seat belt, started the car, drove calmly down the forest track to the farm.

69

Kim Kolsø sat at the back of the incident room listening to everything falling apart. Not for him, but for Munch and Mia. And not that either of them was there. Had they been, they might have been able to answer some of Mikkelson's questions. Mia had been unavailable all day, but Kim believed that Anette had spoken to her and learned that Mia had been to Åsgårdstrand and was now on her way back. No one had heard from Munch.

Kim Kolsø sighed and drummed his fingers on the table. He looked up at Mikkelson, who was pacing to and fro in front of the board like a teacher, his forehead furrowed above his glasses and his hands behind his back. They had been cast as his pupils who were about to receive a telling-off. Kim glanced at Curry, who mouthed *Bullshit* and rolled his eyes. Kim had to look away so as not to laugh, but he totally agreed. Their workload was insane. Not one member of the team was able to sit still. Not even Ludvig, who was coming up for retirement; he was squirming like a fidgety little kid on the edge of his chair. Gabriel Mørk seemed to have borne the brunt of it. He'd been dragged out of his office, where he'd been Skyping with a friend, who was cleaning up the sound on the Kiese movie. The young man was rocking back and forth in his chair and looked as if he were on the verge of a meltdown.

"Right," Mikkelson said, glaring across the room. "Is everyone here?"

No one said anything. If Mikkelson was the teacher, they were the naughty kids who'd been put in detention due to their lack of respect for authority. The room was a powder keg. The air was laden with tension.

"Can anyone update us?"

Mikkelson pushed his glasses up his nose and glared across the room again. No one said anything. The class rebellion against the teacher continued. It was childish, but the anger was real. Munch's and Mia's most loyal friends and colleagues sat in this room. No one had any interest in seeing them discredited.

"Where is Holger Munch?" Mikkelson

said. "Where is Mia Krüger?"

At length Anette rose to her feet. "We haven't heard from Holger," she said calmly. "I have spoken to Mia."

"Status?"

"She was on her way here the last time I talked to her."

"And Munch?"

"We haven't heard from him for a while, but Mia had a theory," Anette continued.

"I bet she had," Mikkelson said sarcastically, without getting much of a reaction from the team. "And what was that?"

"That Munch must have received a call from the killer," Anette said. "That the killer ordered him to meet up alone, and that's what he has gone to do."

"But all our phones are being monitored. Is there anything to suggest that this might be the case?" Mikkelson said.

"No," Gabriel Mørk said. "Nothing from his phone before he turned it off."

"Couldn't the killer have contacted him some other way?" Ludvig Grønlie ventured cautiously.

"What do you mean?" Mikkelson said.

"Well, I don't know, but there are private email accounts — I mean, on the Net, Gmail, and so on. We don't have access to those, or do we?"

Grønlie looked tentatively at Gabriel Mørk; he was well aware that he belonged to a different generation of police officers and hoped that he'd not been mistaken.

"Are you telling me that everything we do online is being monitored? I certainly hope not," Curry quipped.

A few of the others tittered.

"No, we don't have access to those," Gabriel Mørk said.

"So Munch could have gotten a message," Anette said. "Something that meant he had to turn up for a meeting alone?"

Mikkelson sighed. "And is that how we work?"

He looked across the gathering, still without getting the response he was seeking.

"And is that how we work?" he said again, a little louder this time. "No, it is not. We're a team. A team. We don't have room for maverick operations. Here we keep each other informed about what is happening and we work together. No wonder you haven't come up with anything."

"Actually, we've discovered quite a lot." Ludvig coughed and got up.

Kim really liked Ludvig Grønlie. He had exactly what it took to belong to the special unit. It was odd, really. Several people had joined the unit only to leave soon afterward because they just didn't fit in. No one could quite put a finger on what it was. It was more than ability, age, background, or specialization, it was also chemistry. A shared tacit understanding. This is what we do, and this is what we don't do. Kim had met several talented colleagues who'd joined them but never settled in. People who couldn't stand the sight of Munch. Who thought that Mia Krüger was the most over-rated investigator of her generation. Kim had worked with both Munch and Mia for a long time. And he couldn't imagine doing any other job in the whole world.

Ludvig Grønlie gave Mikkelson a brief account of what they had discovered so far. Malin Stoltz. The apartment filled with mirrors. The link between Høvikveien Nursing Home and a support group for childless women in Hønefoss. The Kiese movie, which, if Mikkelson hadn't insisted they all sat here like naughty children, would soon provide them with a location where Stoltz was holding Marion Munch.

"Right, right," Mikkelson said, pushing his glasses back in place. "And where do we stand?"

"Can I go now?"

It was Gabriel Mørk speaking. Kim Kolsø

smiled discreetly to himself. He liked this young man. He had appeared out of nowhere and in no time become an important member of the team. A Munch special. Munch had brought in Mia Krüger in the same way. Rumor had it that she wasn't even required to complete her training at the police academy.

"Why?" Mikkelson said with a frown.

"Munch has gone someplace to find the killer, so it might be a good idea for us to know where that place is," Gabriel Mørk said. "We're in the process of cleaning up the film — I have a pal who's brilliant at this. We'll have the GPS coordinates soon. Perhaps it would be a better use of my time than sitting here."

Kim laughed to himself. When he'd first met Gabriel Mørk in the street, the lad had looked afraid of his own shadow. Now it was as if he'd been with the team from the start.

"And who are you again?" Mikkelson said, taking off his glasses.

"Gabriel," Mørk replied.

"How much police experience did you say you had?"

"Two weeks," Mørk replied, deadpan.

"I have twenty years," Mikkelson said, putting on his glasses again. "Perhaps I should be the judge of what we should be spending our time on, don't you think?"

His attempt at sarcasm landed on stony ground. Kim could see Curry winking at Gabriel Mørk, who responded with a shrug.

"Anette?" Mikkelson said, seeking support.

"Gabriel is right," Anette said, getting up. "The Kiese film is important and should be our number-one priority. If Munch has chosen to shut us out because Stoltz gave him an ultimatum, it's understandable. He loves his granddaughter. I would have done exactly the same."

Kim could see the color change in Mikkelson's face. If he'd thought that Anette Goli was on his side, he'd been very much mistaken.

"I see," Mikkelson said, sounding wounded as he looked down and flicked through some papers. "So what do we do now?"

Kim Kolsø had turned off the alerts on his cell phone, but he'd forgotten to turn off vibration. His phone suddenly jumped on the table in front of him, displaying an unknown number.

"Yes?" Mikkelson said irritably, glaring at him.

"I have to take this one," Kim said, getting up.

"Really?" Mikkelson said.

"Yes," Kim insisted.

"Then . . ." Mikkelson said.

Kim left the room and never heard the rest. He went to the kitchen to make himself a cup of coffee as he took the call.

"Kim Kolsø speaking."

The caller was a woman.

"Yes, hi, my name is Emilie Isaksen."

"Right, hi. What can I do for you?"

Kim opened the fridge and found a carton of milk. If there was one thing he and Mia Krüger agreed about, it was that you risked your life drinking the stuff that came out of the coffee machine.

"I found your business card inside a mattress," the woman said. "And I don't know what to do. I'm hoping you might be able to help."

"I might well be. What do you need help with?" Kim said, adding some milk to his coffee.

70

Tobias passed the blanket to Rakel and turned off his flashlight. This made the safe room seem completely dark, but they had no other choice. They had to conserve the flashlight's batteries, and their eyes quickly adjusted. Tobias didn't know for how long they'd been held prisoner in the underground room, but he estimated four to five days. He had opened the hatch and peered inside. He had whispered the name Rakel, the name of the girl he'd just met, the Christian girl behind the fence, the girl in need of help, when someone had come up behind him and pushed him down inside. He had felt frightened and stupid, and he had hurt himself. He had fallen a long way, past a ladder, into a black hole where he'd ended up on a hard concrete floor. Fortunately, he'd landed not on his head or his arms but on his side, and he believed that this had cushioned his fall, because he wasn't in too much pain, only a bit in one hip and one leg.

"Should we try the hatch again?" Rakel said in a soft voice through the darkness; he could barely make her out, although she was not sitting far away from him.

"I don't think there's any point," Tobias said.

He didn't want to come across as defeatist, but they'd made several attempts, most recently a few hours ago. He had climbed up the ladder and pressed his shoulder against the wooden hatch, but it wouldn't budge; it had been locked from the outside again, and having the lock pick was no use with the lock on the other side.

Fortunately, they had food. And blankets. And a flashlight. They had decided to conserve the batteries because they hadn't found any spares. They were in a safe room. Rakel had explained it all to him. She'd been down here several times. This was where they normally locked up naughty children. The ones who refused to do as they were told. Normally they didn't have to sit there very long, depending on the offense. As far as Tobias had gathered, there were lots of different punishments on this farm. Being banned from talking for one week was one of them. Hence the notes

Rakel had written and stuck through the fence. She was *able* to talk — she hadn't lost her voice, which was what he had first assumed — and then he wondered if she was being difficult on purpose like Chief Bromden in *One Flew Over the Cuckoo's Nest.* No, Rakel could talk, all right, and after someone pushed him down into the safe room where she was, she talked almost nonstop. Tobias liked hearing her voice. She was unlike any other girl he'd ever met and nothing like the ones at school, who mostly giggled or said silly things. Rakel spoke properly, almost like an adult. And she knew where everything in the safe room was. There was food in the boxes and large canisters of water and gasoline and clothes. Everything you might need, although they had yet to find more batteries, but they surely had to be there somewhere.

Tobias had been inside a safe room before; they had one at his school, and it had formed part of a drill. The Home Guard would sound the alarm, and everyone had to walk in single file and pretend that war had broken out. The safe room at his school contained nothing but old PE mats and hockey sticks — not like this one, which was fully equipped. He'd been scared for the first few days, but the feeling was subsiding. After all, nothing bad had happened so far, and they'd been there for a long time. *They will let you out again,* Rakel had said. *They let you out in the end. Sometimes it just takes time.* He was more worried about his brother. Torben would be upset when he came home and found Tobias missing. Tobias had written him a note, at least he'd done that, and hidden it inside the mattress on his bed, the one with the zipper, which was their secret hiding place. *"I'm going to spy on the Christian girls, I will be back soon,"* he had written. He hoped it would reassure Torben a bit.

"I don't think God exists anymore," Rakel said, fumbling for his hand.

Tobias had held a girl's hand before, but this was different. Rakel liked holding his hand, and he liked holding hers. Her fingers were soft and warm, and when she sat close to him, he could also sense the heat from her body. It was almost cozy; he wouldn't have minded the two of them sitting like this for a long time. That is, if they weren't trapped underground.

"I don't believe in God either," Tobias said, and not for the first time.

They had discussed this at length. It seemed important to Rakel. Talking about God. Sometimes he felt that she spoke mostly to herself, but he tried to reply to the best of his ability.

"If there really is a God, he wouldn't let people do horrible, disgusting things, don't you agree?"

Rakel moved a little closer and squeezed his hand. He squeezed back. They would do this from time to time.

Everything will be fine. We're together.

"When do you think they'll let us out? What's the longest anyone has ever sat here?"

"I'm not sure," Rakel said. "There was a girl named Sara, and she was here for two weeks, I believe, but she wasn't here when I arrived."

"What did she do?"

"They said she tried to run away."

"Like you?"

"Yes."

The room was colder now. Perhaps it was evening outside, maybe that would account for it. Tobias took a corner of the blanket and draped it around his shoulder. Rakel moved even closer and put the blanket all around him. They sat quietly for a while, close to each other under the blanket, holding hands tightly. Rakel rested her head on his shoulder, and after a while he could hear her breathing deepen. She was dozing now.

Tobias sat very still, so as not to wake her, and closed his eyes. Soon he, too, was asleep. Not soundly, like at home in his bed, just napping. He didn't realize that he'd been sound asleep until he heard a loud noise. He woke with a start and saw that the hatch above them was in the process of being opened.

At last, he thought as the beam from a flashlight shone down the ladder.

Tobias Iversen roused the girl with the fine freckles and got up from the floor.

The rain had eased off when Mia pulled up outside Høvikveien Nursing Home. She could see the dark clouds drift toward the center of Oslo as she got out of the car and went up the steps.

Karen was behind the reception desk when she arrived. The same place Malin Stoltz had been standing the time Mia discovered Veronica Bache's canasta certificate on the wall. What a dimwit she'd been. She hadn't made the connection. She was no longer functioning fully; maybe that was why. Nor had she realized that Stoltz was coming after her. Munch yes, but the wrong Munch. Edvard Munch, not Holger. That would explain why the bodies had been displayed at Isegran Fort. The planned statues of Munch's mothers. Mia Krüger had worked on the Hønefoss case. Was that the killer's thinking? Mia was a woman. A police officer and a woman. She should have known better. She should have found the baby because she was a woman? Mia could no longer think straight. Her trip to the cemetery had drained her of her last strength. Her grandmother was dead. Her father was dead. Her mother was dead. Sigrid was dead. She was all alone. She looked forward to all of it being over. There'd been times at Hitra when she'd started having doubts as to whether she'd made the right choice. Kill herself. Leave this world. What if she were wrong? But not anymore. She was certain now. She had made the right choice. She should never have left the island. In her mind she saw the pills waiting for her on the table. She realized she was looking forward to it.

Come to me, Mia, come.

But first she must find Marion. Gather the last of her strength and find the smiling little girl, the apple of Holger Munch's eye. Track down Malin Stoltz. She thought briefly about Munch, who had received a telephone call and then disappeared. She hoped he was okay. Perhaps he might even have caught Malin by now. Found his granddaughter. Mia mustered a small smile. She didn't want the world to see how bad she really felt.

"Hi, Karen."

"Hi, Mia."

"Thanks for calling, it was good of you. I'm sorry if I sounded a bit off. It's just we're quite busy at work."

"Has something happened?" Karen asked with an anxious expression on her face.

She cares about Holger, Mia thought. It was obvious now.

"Oh, no, just the usual pressure," Mia lied. "Did you find that key?"

"Yes, I have it here," Karen said. "Let me just put on my jacket."

"Has the car been there for a long time?"

"I don't know," Karen said, ushering her out the door and down the stairs to the underground parking garage. "I took the rubbish down this morning — it's not really my job, you understand, but . . . well, we all have to pitch in when we're busy — and that's when I spotted it. I don't know how long it's been here."

"Why didn't she use it to drive herself home?" Mia wondered out loud.

"I've no idea," Karen said as she led the way into the garage.

Ladybird, ladybird, fly away home.

Her grandmother's words on her death-bed. Mia no longer felt like she could fly. Karen was about her age, a little older perhaps, but she looked in much better shape. Younger. Softer. Not a single wrinkle. She didn't carry the weight of the world on her shoulders. She worked in a nursing home. A world *away* from that of a worn-out investigator with thin skin.

"Here it is," Karen said with a smile, indicating the white Citroën parked in a corner. "And here's the key." She smiled again.

Mia unlocked the car and peered inside. At first glance there was nothing to suggest that she was looking at a serial killer's car. Everything seemed normal. A cup from McDonald's. A newspaper. Mia walked around the car and unlocked the trunk. Nothing except what you would expect to find. A warning triangle. A pair of boots. Damn it, what had she expected? That Stoltz would have left some of the girls' belongings there? She was much too clever for that. Cynical. Callous. Years of planning. She wouldn't have left behind evidence in her car. She had even visited Sigrid's grave. The very thought enraged Mia. She felt her cell phone vibrate in her pocket. The photograph from Ludvig. So at least parts of her brain were working. She was pleased that she'd been right. A support group for childless women. It felt good to know that she had contributed something. She took out the phone and opened Ludvig's message. A photograph. The support group in Høne-foss. *"Christmas get-together 2005."* There were six women in total. Smiling in front of a Christmas tree. Mia recognized her immediately. Malin Stoltz. Not with different-colored eyes. Two blue eyes. Lenses. Mia enlarged the picture slightly. Malin Stoltz. How strange. She looked so normal. An ordinary woman who longed for a child but couldn't have one. Smiling, with her arm around the woman standing next to her. The woman standing next to her. Mia enlarged the photograph to get a better look at her.

But what the hell?

She spun around, but she was too late. The woman in the photograph. The woman behind her. She felt the needle penetrate her neck, the back of her head hitting the metal of the open trunk.

"Count backward from ten." Karen smiled. "That's what they usually say. Count backward from ten, and then you'll be asleep. Isn't that funny? Ten, nine, eight . . ."

Mia Krüger was gone before she heard six.

VI

72

Anette Goli did not like the mood in the incident room. Mikkelson had taken over the case; he wanted to be in charge, but he didn't have enough insight into the case to inspire the team, to get things done. She was starting to feel quite frustrated. They needed a break in this case now, quickly, as soon as possible. They did not have time to bring Mikkelson up to speed. And where on earth was Mia? Anette had only just spoken to her. And why had Munch turned off his cell phone? Because he was on his way to meet the killer possibly, but then why not leave his phone on so that they could trace him? Because he didn't *want* them to trace him? She debated this with herself and so missed what Kim had just said.

"Do you have to do that now?" Mikkelson said. "Don't we have more important things to do?"

Kim sighed. "Yes, but it strikes me there

might be a link."

"And what is the link?" Mikkelson asked.

Anette Goli had to bite her tongue and remind herself that Mikkelson had yet to catch up with the rest of them.

"Tobias Iversen is the boy who discovered Johanne's body," Kim said. "And now he's gone missing. I've just spoken to his teacher — no one has seen him for a week. And he left behind a note for his brother telling him he was going to visit some religious sect in a forest."

"It could be a coincidence," Mikkelson said.

Anette could no longer stay silent.

"Or it might be important," she spoke up. "If we're talking about a sect in the forest close to where Johanne was found, it's definitely worth checking out. After all, there's a church heavily mixed up in this. We don't know how, but there's something suspect about them."

Mikkelson looked at her, weighing the situation.

"Okay," he said at length. "But don't spend too much time on it, Kim. And keep your phone on in case we need you."

"Okay." Kim nodded.

He saluted Mikkelson and left the room. He winked to Anette as he closed the door behind him. She smiled and winked back at him. She liked Kim Kolsø. In fact, she liked everyone on the team. Munch had his weaknesses, definitely, but he knew how to pick the right people. Never before had she worked with such a close-knit and motivated group. Not that they were very motivated right now. Mikkelson suited the managerial chair down at Grønland to a tee, but he was not a natural investigator or a team leader. His social skills were poor, his antennae not sensitive enough. The normally inspired team looked like they would rather be anywhere but the incident room. No wonder. They had a million things to do, and the clock was ticking. No one had seen anything suspicious near the apartment where Miriam and Marion had been staying. Marion was missing without a trace. Anette thought about Munch. Perhaps he was with Marion now. Alone and without backup, in mortal danger, but at least he was with her. If that was where he was, surely he had to be in danger? Anette couldn't imagine anything else.

"So where are we as concerns Marion Munch?" Mikkelson asked just as Anette's phone rang. He looked daggers at her.

"The duty officer at Grønland," Anette said. "I have to take it."

She left the room.

"Yes? Anette speaking."

"Hi. Heide Myhr. Listen, I have someone here who wants to meet with you."

"With me personally?"

"No, just one of you. I've tried Munch and Mia, but there was no reply."

No reply from Mia? Where could she be?

"I'm really busy now. It had better be important."

"Oh, it's important all right."

"Who is it?"

"Malin Stoltz."

Anette nearly dropped her phone. "What did you just say?"

"I have Malin Stoltz here."

Anette was so flustered that she completely forgot to say anything. She hung up and ran back into the incident room.

"We have Stoltz!" she called out.

"What?" Mikkelson said. "But how?"

"She's down at Grønland. Curry, you're coming with me."

"Sure," Curry said, grabbing his jacket.

73

Holger Munch sat up in bed. He had a pounding headache, and his mouth felt parched. Dazed, he looked around. The room was clinical. Institutional. The nursing home. He was still at Høvikveien Nursing Home.

What the hell?

He quickly got up but had to sit down again. He felt that the room was spinning. The window. It was dark outside. Evening. He had slept the whole day. In a bed at Høvikveien Nursing Home, fully dressed. He rummaged around in his pockets but couldn't find his cell phone anywhere. What on earth was going on? Where was Karen? Wasn't she supposed to wake him? He attempted to stand up once more, and this time he managed it. He stumbled to the door and tried opening it, but it wouldn't budge. It was locked from the outside. He fumbled for the lock on the inside, but there was nothing there. Someone had locked him in. This was insane. Holger Munch could feel his panic rising when he realized what had happened.

Shit.

He banged his fists against the door, screaming frantically.

"Hello?"

His banging became more desperate while he tried to clear his head.

"Is anyone there?"

He rummaged through his pockets again. Searched his duffel coat and his trousers. Staggered back to the bed and started pulling off the bedlinen. There was no sign of his phone anywhere.

The door behind him opened, and a caregiver he'd never met before popped her head in.

She looked at him, startled. "Who are you? What are you doing here?"

"Munch, Oslo Police, Violent Crimes Section," Munch said as he forced his way past her. "Have you seen Karen?"

"Karen?" the terrified woman said. "Her shift has finished. Why?"

"I need to borrow your phone," Munch said as he stumbled toward reception.

"No, wait, you can't just —"

"Munch, police, my mother is a resident

here," he mumbled, and picked up the handset.

He held it in his hand, still feeling groggy. Damn modern technology, he didn't know any telephone numbers by heart these days. He called information and asked to be put through to police headquarters in Grønland. Finally his call was answered, and he asked to be put through to the special unit. Ludvig picked up the phone.

"Grønlie speaking."

"It's Munch."

"Holger, where on earth have you been?"

"I haven't got time to explain, Ludvig. Is Mia there?"

"No, she's gone."

"What do you mean, gone? Where is she?"

"She's not here," Ludvig said.

"But what the hell?" Munch said. "Is Gabriel there?"

"Munch —" Ludvig began.

"Put me through to Gabriel. He must be able to trace her cell phone. Get me Gabriel."

"Munch!" Ludvig said again.

"For Christ's sake, Ludvig, just put me through to Gabriel!"

"Your granddaughter has gone missing," Ludvig said on the other end.

Munch fell completely silent.

"Marion is gone," Ludvig repeated. "Someone took her from the apartment. But it's going to be all right, Munch. We have Stoltz. She turned herself in. Did you hear me? We have Malin Stoltz. Anette and Curry are interviewing her as we speak. Everything will be all right."

Munch slowly woke up. Like a bear from hibernation. "It's not her," he growled.

"What do you mean?"

The whole world was spinning for Munch now. "Send a car."

"But, Munch . . . ?"

"Send me a bloody car!" he screamed through the phone.

"But I don't know where you are!" Ludvig screamed back at him.

"Sorry," Munch said, realizing he was shaking all over. "Høvikveien Nursing Home. Send a car, Ludvig. I'm not fit to drive. Send a car."

He put down the handset and staggered out into the evening twilight.

74

There was an atmosphere of both tension and relief in the modern interview room in the basement of police headquarters in Grønland. They'd been looking for her for so long. First as an invisible face, a serial killer whose identity they did not know, then for every woman with different-colored eyes living in an apartment covered with mirrors. And now she was here. Just a few feet away. Anette watched her furtively while Curry poured yet another glass of water. Malin Stoltz. Anette didn't know quite what she'd expected, but probably not this. Stoltz was so delicate and frail. Long black hair covering a pale face. Thin fingers that could barely manage to raise the water glass to her dry lips.

"Thank you," Malin Stoltz said timidly, bowing her head again.

Anette almost felt sorry for her.

"You have the right to have a lawyer pres-

597

ent. Do you understand that?" Curry said, sitting down.

Malin Stoltz nodded faintly. "I don't need one," she whispered.

"It might be a good idea," Anette suggested.

Malin Stoltz glanced up at her. One brown and one blue eye looking as if they had lost the will to live.

"I don't need one," Malin Stoltz repeated, then raked a thin hand through her black hair. "I'll tell you everything I know."

"The suspect has declined her right to legal counsel," Curry said into the small microphone on the table.

"Are you sure?" Anette said.

Malin Stoltz nodded once more, still very carefully. She was so fragile. Anette feared that she would break if she spoke too loudly or even just snapped her fingers.

"I will tell you everything I know," Stoltz continued. "But I want you to call someone."

"And who would that be?" Curry said brusquely.

Anette signaled for him to back off. There was no cause for aggression. Malin Stoltz was already broken.

"I'm ill," Malin said. "I have a disease. I want you to call my doctor, please?" Malin looked at her again, this time with a pleading expression.

"Of course," Anette agreed. "What is the number?"

"I know it by heart," Malin said.

Curry pushed a notepad and pen across the table. His cell phone beeped. He checked the message while Malin wrote down the number. He raised his eyebrows and slid his phone across to Anette. It was from Ludvig.

Munch is on his way.

Anette smiled and returned his phone. Munch was back. At last. Anette took the notepad from Malin Stoltz and passed it to Curry.

"Please, would you make the call?"

Curry nodded and left the room.

"Would you like some more water?" Anette asked her when they were alone.

"No, thank you," Stoltz whispered, hanging her head again.

"What is wrong with you?"

"The doctors can't figure it out," Malin said. "But it's in my head. My mind is not sound. Sometimes I don't know who I am. But they can't figure out what it is."

"Where is Marion Munch?" Anette asked her.

"Who?" Malin Stoltz looked perplexed.

"Marion Munch. You took her from the apartment, didn't you? Where are you keeping her?"

"Who?" Stoltz said again. She seemed genuinely mystified now.

"You know why you're here, don't you?"

"Yes." Malin nodded.

"And why are you here?"

"We conned the old people," Malin said in a weak voice.

This time it was Anette's turn to look astounded. "What do you mean?"

Malin looked up at her.

"We conned the old people. We didn't mean to. That was just how it ended up. Karen and I. We needed the money. I was going to adopt a child. It's difficult when you're single and you're not in good health. Do you know how difficult and expensive it is to adopt a child?"

Anette had absolutely no idea what she was talking about. "Are you ill at this moment, Malin?"

"What? Am I?" Malin Stoltz sat up with a jolt and looked around.

"Right now are you Malin or someone else?"

600

"My name is not Malin," Stoltz said.

"Then what is your name?"

"My name is Maiken Storberget," Malin Stoltz said.

"So why do you call yourself Malin?"

"It was Karen's idea," the skinny woman said.

Maiken Storberget. Anette was really confused now, but she didn't let the other woman see.

Curry returned to the interview room. "Right, I have had a chat with your doctor. He asked me to give you his best and tell you that he's on the way."

He had completely turned off his aggression. And there was no need for it anyway. As she sat in front of them, Anette began to wonder if Malin Stoltz really was the woman they were looking for. She would have to be a very good liar. Which was a possibility. She'd told them she had a mental illness. That she was not always herself. But Anette had met her fair share of liars throughout the years, and if Malin Stoltz was one of them, she was extremely good. Anette switched off the recorder and excused herself. She pulled Curry out into the corridor, leaving Malin Stoltz alone in the interview room.

"What did the doctor say?"

"Malin is telling the truth," Curry replied. "She's been in and out of institutions since she was a kid. If the man I spoke to really was a doctor, then this case is so strange that I don't know what to believe anymore."

"Did he tell you what she suffers from?"

"No, doctor-patient confidentiality and all that, but he was happy to confirm that she's off her rocker."

"Curry . . ."

"Mentally ill. Damn it, Anette, that woman has killed four children, and I have to watch my tongue?"

"Make sure he is a real doctor, and get someone to run a check on Maiken Storberget."

"Who is she?"

Anette nodded in the direction of the room.

"Stoltz?"

"So she says. Please?"

"Sure," Curry said.

Anette returned to the interview room and restarted the recorder.

"Friday, May fourth, 2012, the time is 2240, present is Police Prosecutor Anette Goli, who is interviewing Malin Stoltz."

"Maiken Storberget," Stoltz said, but suddenly she didn't seem quite so sure.

"What would you like me to call you?"

Anette asked her kindly.

"Maiken, I think," Stoltz said.

"Right, Maiken it is. Would you like some more water, Maiken?"

"No, thank you, this is fine."

"Do you know why you're here, Maiken?"

"Yes, because Karen and I tricked the old people. I'm so sorry."

"That's not why you're here, Maiken."

"Isn't it?" Maiken Storberget gave Anette an odd look.

"Are you quite sure that you don't want a lawyer present?"

"Yes, I'm sure. So why *am* I here?"

"You're suspected of the murder of four girls aged six and the abduction of six-year-old Marion Munch."

"Oh . . . no, no, no, no."

"You need to sit down, Maiken."

"Oh, no, no . . . no, no, I'm telling you no, I don't have anything to do with that. Oh, no. No, no, no."

Anette already regretted agreeing to take off her handcuffs. Maiken Storberget looked as if she were about to harm herself.

"Please sit down, Maiken."

"I've got nothing to do with that."

"Please sit down, Maiken."

"That business, oh, no, no, no. I didn't do it, I'm telling you."

603

"If you promise me that you'll sit down, then I will listen to you, how about that?" Anette said in her nicest voice as her finger edged nearer the button under the table. She was reluctant to summon uniformed officers, which would be strictly a last resort.

Maiken Storberget looked at her momentarily before she decided to sit down.

"Maiken?"

"Yes?"

"Let's forget what I said, shall we?"

"Okay," Maiken said quizzically, and wiped away a tear.

"What were you just telling me about?"

"The old people?" Maiken nodded, sitting up in the chair.

"Which old people?"

"Old people in the nursing home," Maiken said quietly. "I met Karen in Hønefoss. At a group for people who can't have children. We became friends. It was her idea, she said she knew someone."

"Who?"

"A priest. Well, he wasn't a priest to begin with — I think he sold cars — but he became a priest and took money from people who were going to die."

"Their inheritance?"

Mia had briefed the team about the church that had been trying to con Munch's mother out of her money.

Maiken Storberget nodded. "We got paid for every name we supplied them with, people who were . . ."

"People who were?"

Maiken hesitated. "Well, you know, old, whom we might persuade to believe in God."

She was clearly ashamed now. She wrung her thin hands in her lap.

"And for how long did this continue?"

"Oh, a long time. A long time. We conned a lot of people."

The door opened, and Curry entered the room. Anette spoke into the microphone.

"The time is 2247. Investigator Jon Larsen has just entered the room. The interview with Malin Stoltz, Maiken Storberget continues." She looked up at Curry, who nodded.

"It's all true," he said.

"So who is Karen?" Anette said.

"Don't you know Karen?" Maiken said.

"Who is Karen?" Curry said.

"No, we don't know Karen," Anette said.

"I know Karen," said Munch, who had suddenly appeared in the room.

Anette hadn't even heard the door open.

"The time is 2249. The head of the special unit, Holger Munch, has just entered the interview room," Anette said into the micro-phone.

"Where is Karen?" Munch said, taking a seat at the head of the table.

Maiken Storberget looked embarrassed at Munch's arrival. They recognized each other. And Maiken had been part of the attempt to trick the Munch family out of their inheritance.

"I'm sorry, Holger," Maiken mumbled, looking at her lap. "I just wanted a baby. Why can't I have a baby when everybody else can?"

"It's quite all right, Malin," Munch said calmly, placing his hand on her shoulder. "I just want to know where Karen is."

"Maiken," Anette corrected him.

"Eh?" Munch said, turning to her.

Anette had seen her boss exhausted before, but never like this. He could barely lift his head. If she hadn't known that he never touched alcohol, she would have sworn that he'd been drinking.

"Maiken Storberget," Curry said, nodding to Munch to reassure him.

"Maiken? Okay, Maiken," Munch said. "Where is Karen?"

"Oh, no, no," Maiken said, rocking back and forth in her chair.

"Munch?" Anette said, but he took no

notice of her.

"I need to know where Karen is, do you understand? I have to know where she is, now!"

Munch leaned forward and grabbed the skinny woman's shoulders. Maiken Storberget reacted intuitively and covered her face with her hands.

"No, no, no!"

"Munch," Anette warned him.

"Where is Karen?" Munch shouted, shaking the frail woman.

"Munch!" Anette screamed.

"Where is Karen!?"

Munch was throttling her violently now. Anette was about to get up, but Curry beat her to it. The stocky police officer put his strong arms around Munch and guided him out of the interview room.

"Are you all right, Maiken?" Anette said when they were alone once more.

The emaciated woman looked up at her with terrified eyes and nodded softly.

"I just need a word with the other two, and then I'll be back, okay?"

Maiken Storberget nodded again.

"And listen?"

Maiken looked up at her. "Yes?"

"It will be all right. I believe you."

Maiken wiped away a tear. "Thank you so much."

Anette smiled, placed her hand on Maiken's shoulder, and left the room.

"What do you think you're doing, Munch?"

Outside in the corridor, Curry still had Munch in a tight hold.

"Sorry," Munch babbled. "She has Marion. Karen. She has my granddaughter. She has Marion."

"Calm down," Curry said.

"Find a cell for Maiken," Anette said calmly. "I'll deal with Holger."

Curry reluctantly released his hold of the light-brown duffel coat. He returned to the interview room and left the two of them alone in the corridor.

"Are you okay, Holger?" Anette said, putting her hand on her boss's shoulder.

"She has my granddaughter," Munch said again.

"Who is Karen?" Anette said, still calm.

"She works at the nursing home," Munch groaned. "She has my granddaughter, Anette. My granddaughter."

"We will find her," Anette said as her cell rang.

"Anette speaking."

"Get me Holger," said a breathless Gabriel Mørk.

She handed the phone to Munch.

"Yes?"

Munch listened briefly to Gabriel and ended the call almost immediately.

"The Kiese film. We have the GPS co-ordinates. Take Curry with you, okay?"

Munch ran down the corridor without waiting for an answer.

75

Mia Krüger awoke to the sound of what she presumed must be seagulls. She was back on her island. In the house she'd bought to be alone. To get away from people. To get away from herself. She had self-medicated almost to death. The sea. The air. The birds. The calm. She was going to join Sigrid. It was too hard to be alone. When your whole family is gone. Dead. It was too hard not to have someone who understands. Sigrid had always understood. Lovely, beautiful, adorable Sigrid. Mia had never needed to say anything. *I understand, Mia.* Without even opening her mouth. Her lovely warm eyes behind the blond hair.

Now Mia was alone. No comfort. No peace. Just this house and the seagulls. Tough, intelligent, one-in-a-million Mia Krüger, Mia Moonbeam, the Native American with the sparkling blue eyes, one of Norway's best murder detectives. Reduced to an exhausted eccentric on a remote island.

Mia's mouth felt dry. She tried to open her eyes, but it was heavy going. A slow-motion transition from dream to reality, with music in the background. A radio. Then the music stopped. She tried to open her eyes again, but her eyelids were stuck, and it wasn't just her eyelids, it was all of her. She couldn't move. Mia slipped quietly back into her dream — the coffee brewing, the sound of the kettle in her kitchen on Hitra.

"Hello, Mia?"

Mia Krüger opened her eyes to find Karen Nylund standing in front of her. The strawberry blonde smiled and held up a bottle of water.

"Would you like something to drink? I imagine you must be terribly thirsty."

Mia suddenly remembered what had happened, and her body jerked automatically, trying to free itself. Something was covering her mouth. Her hands were taped to a chair. Her legs. Her legs as well. Taped down. The movements were instinctive — they came from her body, not from her brain, muscular panic — but it was futile. All she could move was her head.

"You're very sweet, you really are." Karen

laughed, waving the water bottle in front of her. "Do you intend to go on like that? It's fun to watch, so don't let me stop you."

Mia could feel that she was panicking but managed to calm herself down, push the panic aside. She breathed deeply into her diaphragm and looked around. Her police gaze. She was in a small house. A cabin. No, a house. The windowsills were white. The countryside. She was in the country. There was a film of some kind on the windowpanes. You could look out, but no one could look in. Warmth and crackling behind her. An oven, no, an open fireplace. A sofa. A chair, 1960s. A rug on the floor. Multicolored. A door to the left. An old fridge. The kitchen. Another door, ajar. A passage. A pair of muddy boots. A sweater. A raincoat.

"Yes, it's nice here, isn't it?" Karen said, setting the bottle on the floor. "Would you like me to show and tell?"

Mia tried to say something but managed only a gurgling sound in her throat. The tape was covering her mouth. She stuck out her tongue, pressed it between her lips, and felt the taste of adhesive.

"If you want something to drink, then you mustn't shout," Karen said. "We're a long way from other people, so they can't help

612

you, but I don't want you waking the child."

There was a television screen in front of her. No, it wasn't a television, it was a monitor connected to a computer. A keyboard. A mouse.

Karen turned on the screen.

"She's asleep. We must be quiet. Shhh."

Karen Nylund smiled and pressed her finger against her lips. The screen slowly came to life, displaying the image of a sleeping girl. Marion. In a white room somewhere. The angle was a bird's-eye perspective, a webcam mounted in a corner.

"Gorgeous, isn't she?" Karen smiled. She sat down by the table, softly caressing the screen. "We mustn't wake the sleeping child."

Karen took a step forward and swiftly tore the tape off Mia's face. Mia gasped for breath and coughed. She felt nauseous. The injection to her neck. She thought she was going to throw up.

"There, have some water," Karen said, putting the bottle to her lips.

Mia gulped as much water as she could manage, the rest trickling down her chin and onto her sweater, into her lap, wetting her thighs.

"Good girl," Karen said, wiping her chin and the corners of her mouth with the back of her hand.

"Have you hurt her?" Mia spluttered. Her voice sounded strange and rusty.

"Is that what you think?" Karen smiled. "Of course I haven't hurt her. I'm going to kill her, that's true, but how can that hurt her?"

"You bitch," Mia hissed, and spit at her.

Karen jumped aside and just avoided being hit.

"Tsk-tsk, Mia. Do you want me to put the tape back, or will we try to behave?"

Mia could feel the rage surge violently inside her, but at the last second she managed to control herself.

"I'll be good," she said quietly. "Sorry."

"There, there, that's better." Karen sat down again.

"Why me?" Mia said.

"Wow, straight to the point, is that how we're doing it? Isn't that a bit dull?" Karen laughed. "Why don't we play a little game first? I like games. Games are fun, don't you think? Don't you like playing games, Mia? Mia Moonbeam, what a lovely name. A little Native American girl who's been captured? How appropriate, wouldn't you say?"

Mia said nothing. She closed her eyes and let her head slump toward her chest. Karen rose and came over to her.

"Mia? Mia? Now, don't you fall asleep, Mia, we're going to play a game."

Mia opened her eyes and spit again, this time right into Karen's face.

The strawberry blonde was unprepared, and her personality changed in a fraction of a second. Her smile was gone. Her eyes were flashing.

"You fucking cunt."

Karen Nylund raised her hand and slapped Mia across the face. The blow was hard. Mia's head was flung backward. She blacked out for a second, and her eyes closed.

When she opened them again, the grotesque smile was back in place.

"Would you like some cake?" Karen tilted her head winsomely to one side. "I baked it especially for you."

"Who the hell are you really?"

"Now, no swearing," Karen said. "It's not necessary. That's a rule. Agreed? That's the rule of the game."

Mia regained her composure and nodded. She glanced around a second time. The police gaze. She was trapped here. She was far away from other people. She was restrained. She would have to talk her way out. It was her only hope. Play along.

"That's a good rule," she said quietly, attempting a smile of her own.

"Excellent," Karen said, clapping her hands. "Who will begin? Why don't I start?"

Mia nodded.

"I grew up in this house," Karen said. "There was me, my mother, my sister, and he who must not be mentioned."

"Your father?" Mia said.

"We don't say his name." Karen smiled, sitting down by the table again. "Your turn?"

"I grew up in Åsgårdstrand," Mia said. "With my sister and my parents. We lived in a white house, not far from Edvard Munch's house. My grandmother lived close by."

"Boring," Karen said. "Party pooper. We already know that. Tell us something new, something we don't know. Why don't I say something?"

Mia nodded again.

"My mother worked at Hamar Hospital. I came with her to work. She showed me everything. She had the softest hair in the world. I got to brush it. My sister was far too young, so she only got to watch. One day my mother didn't come home from work. Everyone knew what had happened, but the police did nothing. Isn't that strange? That we live in a country where the police don't care?"

Karen smiled and tucked her hair behind

her ear. She glanced up at the ceiling, and she seemed to be contemplating something.

Hamar Hospital. Mia guessed they must be near Hamar. Karen Nylund's father had murdered her mother. The police had done nothing. That explained her hatred of the police.

"Am I allowed to ask questions?" Mia said.

"Everything is allowed." Karen laughed. "Everything is allowed in this game!"

"Except swearing," Mia said, forcing out another smile; she hoped it looked genuine.

"That's right." Karen giggled. "We don't like that."

"What did you call her?" Mia said.

"Who?"

"The baby from the maternity ward."

Karen had stopped smiling.

"Margrete," she said.

"Beautiful name," Mia said.

"Yes, it is, isn't it?"

"Yes, very beautiful. Was that her room?" She nodded in the direction of the monitor.

"Yes," Karen said forlornly. "Or no, it wasn't as nice as that. That was where it was, but I had a new one built. The old one became so sad."

"What happened to her?"

"Oh, no, my turn, my turn."

Mia took her eyes off the screen. She could not bear to watch it. Marion was lying on the bed, wearing a white doll's dress trimmed with lace.

"He bled to death inside." Karen smiled.

"Who?"

"The one we never mention. I put rat poison in his food. After the police said that my mom had run away, I had to cook for all three of us. It was fun watching him die. We watched him, my sister and I. He bled from his mouth, from everywhere. It was really good to watch. A red-letter day, you could say. Almost like Christmas."

"Where did you bury him?" Mia said, trying her hardest not to look at the screen.

Focus now, Mia, focus.

"Right behind the outhouse." Karen smiled. "Stinky, stinky, filthy, filthy, filthy. Very apt. Are you sure you don't want some cake?"

"Maybe later." Mia smiled.

"It's very good." Karen nodded and disappeared inside her own head for a moment.

"Malin Stoltz."

"Oh, you mean Maiken?"

"Two different-colored eyes? Malin?"

"Maiken." Karen nodded again. "Poor Maiken. She's as mad as a hatter, did you know? But together we made loads of money."

Slowly it began to dawn on Mia how everything was connected.

"Through the church?"

Karen Nylund gleefully clapped her hands again.

"Well done, Mia. Clever girl. You've no idea how easy it is to make old ladies give all their money to Jesus when they think they're about to die."

She laughed briefly.

"The church got sixty percent, we got forty. A fair deal in my opinion. That's a lot of money, Mia. Do you know how much money that is?"

"No," Mia said.

"It's a lot." Karen winked at her. "Let's put it this way, this is not my real home."

"But she didn't know anything about Margrete or the other girls?"

"Oh, no!" Karen laughed. "Maiken is downright crazy, no doubt about it, but much too soft for anything like that. That stupid friend of hers, Roger Bakken, at least I could use him for something. He could never make up his mind whether he was a man or a woman — a bit bizarre, really. People like that are always weak, easy to manipulate."

"Wow, that's quite a scam," Mia said. "Working with the church. Clever for sure. Everyone's a winner."

"Yes, they are, aren't they?" Karen said proudly.

"So what happened to her?" Mia continued.

"Who?"

"Margrete. The baby?"

Karen fell silent for a moment before she replied. "I was hit by a car. I broke my foot and both arms," she said, pressing her lips together. "I was admitted to the hospital."

"For a long time?"

Karen nodded. "I can't blame them either," she said, putting on her smile again. "The old people, I mean. Giving away their money. They lie there all alone. Their bodies are packing up. They look back on their lives and have regrets. Oh, they have so many regrets, Mia. I have seen them. Heard them talk. About all the things they wish they'd done differently. Worried less about other people. Put themselves first. Traveled more, had more fun, explored the world. They're all terrified. They have fear in their eyes. It's extreme, Mia, you should have seen some of them. They realize that they've made mistakes. They panic. They hope for another go. They want to buy their way to a second chance. I can't blame them, really. How does it feel to be about to die, Mia?"

"Are you going to kill me?" Mia said.

Karen looked at her strangely. "Yes, of course I am. Why do you ask?"

"Why me?"

"Have you really not figured that out? And here I was thinking you were so clever!"

"No, I have not figured it out," Mia said quietly.

"No, you haven't, because I'm smarter than you."

Karen smiled triumphantly and clapped her hands again in a childish fashion.

"I killed a dog, did you know? So that the girls would have someone to play with, wasn't that nice?"

"I didn't know that," Mia mumbled.

"That's because you're stupid." Karen Nylund smiled even wider.

"Yes, you're smarter than me."

"That's right, I am."

"So why are you going to kill me?"

"Do you not know? Do you really not know?" said the woman with the strawberry-blond hair, laughing.

"No."

"Do you want me to tell you?"

"Yes."

"Because you killed my sister," Karen said, and she disappeared into the kitchen.

76

The first time Liv-Hege Nylund sniffed glue was in a back alley in Hamar when she was thirteen years old. She had dropped out of school ages before. She hadn't liked it there — studying was not for her — she hadn't liked the people either, and anyway, no one cared about where she was. Her sister, Karen, used to care; she was ten years older than Liv-Hege and had always looked after her while they were growing up in Tangen, in a small house far away from other people. Their father had been a bully. Physical and psychological abuse had characterized life for the two sisters and their mother, who had finally vanished from the surface of the earth. Young Liv-Hege had witnessed things her mind and her body could not process. The cloth filled with glue had offered her a much-needed break from reality. While Karen was around, life had been easier. Going to school. Looking after herself. Believing she was going to be all right. But once their parents were gone, Karen had grown so strange and her personality changed. She lost her temper at the slightest provocation. Without warning, she would laugh out loud at things that weren't funny. Liv-Hege remembered a bird that had crashed into the living-room window. She had picked up the bird, brought it inside, and tried to keep it alive in a small cardboard box lined with cotton wool. One day after the school bus had dropped her off, she came back to discover Karen in the kitchen; she had a saucepan of water on the stove and was watching the screaming, little bird being boiled alive. She had turned to Liv-Hege with a huge grin on her face. As if she enjoyed watching the bird die. Their mother had worked at Hamar Hospital, and Karen had been allowed to come with her to work. What their mother hadn't known was that Karen had stolen medication. She'd shown Liv-Hege a box in the attic once when they were home alone, full of syringes and vials and bottles of pills with all sorts of strange names. Liv-Hege didn't know what her sister intended to use it all for, but it was most likely to kill someone. Karen enjoyed killing.

Liv-Hege, however, only wanted to forget.

The glue-soaked cloth was merely the start of the journey that had only one destination. To begin with, Liv-Hege had hitchhiked from Tangen into Hamar, but that soon stopped, and she no longer went home. She and her friends would sniff glue at Domkirkeodden and sleep rough under the bushes. They took poppers, heart medication, and slept on benches and in stairwells. They stole food and spent most of their time trying to get high. The more often Liv-Hege got high, the harder it was for her to stay clean. She had boyfriends, but they weren't important. A guy who offered her a bed and some weed. Another one who let her shower and gave her alcohol.

But then she met Markus Skog. Liv-Hege had fallen asleep in someone's car and woken up in Oslo. Her friend was picking up a packet of something. Speed. Whatever. And there he was, in an apartment in Grønland. Liv-Hege fell head over heels in love, and they became an item. Markus Skog introduced her to heroin, so now she had two loves. Heroin was the perfect drug for her. Much better than glue, with all its waste products and impurities. Glue made her zone out, true, but also sick and nauseous most of the time. Heroin was completely different. Markus Skog injected her for the first time on a summer's day down by the river Aker, and Liv-Hege barely believed such bliss was possible. It was as if her body had been in tension her whole life, and finally it could relax. All the sharp barbs and her piercing misery turned into a huge smile. One big, beaming, lovely smile framed by pink clouds of eternal beauty. People were good. The world was fantastic. Forever. Since that day they were never apart. A perfect heavenly triangle. Markus and her and heroin. They had moved about, living here, there, and everywhere. Markus knew a lot of people. And when he started dealing, they got to know even more. Dealers were the celebrities of the underworld, always surrounded by an entourage of famous and obscure faces, and even though he was only a street dealer, they did well. One autumn they lived in a camper up at Tryvann. The party atmosphere was pretty good — a lot of cocaine and speed, but not enough heroin, and Liv-Hege missed it. It would be good to score some. Get properly high again. Fortunately, the party crew withdrew to the city center over time. And then there was just the three of them left in the camper van. Markus, her, and the lovely liquid gold that would soon be going into her veins.

"Please, can you hook me up?"

Liv-Hege looked beseechingly at Markus Skog, who was pacing back and forth inside the camper van.

He had just snorted two lines of speed and cocaine mixed together and was quite manic. He was talking to himself constantly, and his eyes were the size of saucers.

"Markus?" she pleaded with him again. "Hook me up, will you?"

Liv-Hege lifted the sleeve of her sweater and rested her arm on the small gray plastic table.

"Damn it, Liv-Hege, do it yourself. Why do I have to do everything for you?" Markus Skog grunted as he cut more lines on the table.

"But I like it when you do it," Live-Hege said. "Please?"

"You're a real nag, did you know that? I don't know why I put up with your bony ass. Tell me, Liv-Hege, why do I? It's not as if you contribute anything, is it?"

Liv-Hege stared shamefully at the floor and tightened the rubber tube around her arm herself. Markus bent down and snorted both lines, one in each nostril.

"Ah, here we go, that's it. That's right, now we're going places."

He laughed out loud to himself and

slammed his fist into the wall. Liv-Hege jolted, almost missing the vein with the needle, but she got it in at last. The warmth started flooding through her body. Finally. Pink clouds. Endless beaches.

She had just dropped the needle onto the floor when there was a knock on the door to the camper van.

"Hello?" A woman's voice.

"What the hell?" Markus said.

He tried looking through the curtain but had forgotten that they had cardboard for windows and that he couldn't see out.

"Police." A male voice this time.

"Shit," Markus said, starting to clear the table of drugs. "Liv-Hege? Help me, will you?!"

But Liv-Hege saw no reason to do anything. She had a big smile on her face and was heading for a place where all was well. Just exactly how it happened, Live-Hege could not remember, but suddenly a female police officer was inside the camper van.

"Mia Krüger, Violent Crimes Section. We're looking for this girl. Have you seen her?"

"Ah, that's Pia." Liv-Hege smiled when she saw the picture.

"Shut your mouth!" Markus yelled at her.

"But it is Pia, isn't it, Markus? Can't you see?"

"I said shut your mouth!" Markus Skog screamed again.

"Markus?" the policewoman said suddenly. "Markus Skog?"

"What's going on, Mia?" It was the male police officer outside.

"Mia Krüger, now, who would have thought it?" Markus grinned. "It's been a long time."

The police officer named Mia looked as if she'd seen a ghost.

"How's your sister?" Markus laughed. The two last lines had kicked in now, and his mouth was one big gaping hole of teeth and laughter.

"Oh, no, that's right, she croaked, yeah? Yes, she did, couldn't handle the pressure, ha, ha. I've seen it happen so many times, good girls from nice families. Can't take the heat 'cause they've had it too easy."

Liv-Hege had not seen the police officer pull out a gun, but it was there now, looking very large in the small, dirty camper van. Liv-Hege herself had mentally left the cramped quarters. She was sitting on a mountaintop, watching from a distance. It was nice and warm. The wind was blowing briskly through her hair.

In the room faraway, the one she had left, Markus had picked up a syringe from the table. He was frothing at the mouth now. He waved the syringe at the police officer and laughed maniacally.

"Want to try it, Mia? Eh, are you sure you don't want a taste? Your sister couldn't get enough of it. Spineless cunt, poor little Sigrid, ha, ha."

From the lovely mountaintop where she was sitting, Liv-Hege had a clear view of what happened next. It was almost like being at the movies. Markus hawked up a gob and spit at the policewoman while at the same time trying to stab her with the syringe. The policewoman jumped back, and a bang sounded. Liv-Hege's mountaintop turned into a volcano now — there was rumbling underneath her. The policewoman fired her weapon twice. Markus Skog was flung back across the room and lay bleeding on the floor.

Liv-Hege Nylund woke up two weeks later to find herself suffering serious withdrawal symptoms in a room she didn't recognize. Karen was sitting next to her and for a whole week never left her side. They had strapped Liv-Hege to the bed. She'd never experienced anything so horrendous. She was in hell. It was as if every cell in her body were wide awake and screaming. A billion hangovers at the same time; she howled as if the devil himself had taken residence in her. She lay strapped to the bed in the white room until the drugs left her system. All the time with Karen by her side. Her sister had watched her, fed her, held her hand, calmed her down. She'd been gone, but now she was back.

Finally she was allowed out of bed. She could to go to the bathroom on her own, eat her own food at the table. Karen never left her alone. Then she was allowed out into the garden. Sit on the grass. Gaze at the sun. Look at the trees. Karen was smiling now. Liv-Hege had not seen Karen smile during the whole of her detox, but now her sister was happy.

What Karen Nylund did not know was that Liv-Hege had no intention of staying alive. She had lost everything. Her two loves. Markus Skog and heroin. What could this world offer her? Nothing.

One week later, the first time she was allowed out for a walk on her own, she climbed a spruce in the forest as high as she could, tied a rope around her neck.

And jumped into freedom.

77

"I'm so sorry," Mia said.

"Oh, it's fine. You killed her. And now you're going to die. It all fits together rather neatly, don't you think?"

Karen patted Mia's hand. She went back to the kitchen and returned with a slice of chocolate cake.

"Would you like some cake, Mia?"

Mia shook her head.

"But you have to eat something. It's really good, I promise — it's my mother's recipe."

Mia glanced sideways at the screen on the table. Marion Munch was lying immobile on the bed in the basement room. Mia saw her stir. Thank God. The little girl was merely asleep. Karen Nylund smiled and ran two fingers across the screen.

"I look forward to getting her ready. It's important that children are clean, don't you think?"

Karen smiled at her. Mia started to feel

scared. She'd been relatively calm so far, but her terror was taking control of her now. She felt she was in the presence of evil. She had never seen eyes like that before. It was as if the woman in front of her was fully aware of what she was saying and doing and yet was completely devoid of empathy and normal human emotions.

"Do you want to know what happens next? Shall we play that game?" Karen got up.

"Can't we play another game?" Mia said.

She had to stall for time now. For her own sake, but mostly for Marion's. Her body was aching. She thought about Munch. How he would react if Marion were killed. She couldn't bear to think of it. It was too unreal.

"So what do you want to play, then?" Karen smiled.

"Anything," Mia said, attempting a smile as well. "Perhaps we could talk about Margrete?"

Karen grew more serious now. She frowned and folded her arms across her chest. Mia Krüger tried desperately to read what was going on inside her mind, how this woman was thinking, to find a weakness, but it was impossible to penetrate.

"Margrete is fine," Karen chirped, smiling

again now. "She goes to school in heaven and has four classmates. Soon she will have five and a teacher."

"Classmates?" Mia said, baffled.

"Oh, yes, they're about to start school. Haven't you figured that out?"

Finally the pieces came together in Mia's head. *I'm traveling alone.* The backpacks. The schoolbooks. The jump rope. Karen Nylund had some twisted notion of creating a class in heaven where she would be the teacher. That had to be the logic inside the mind of this psychopath. Mia felt a pang of guilt. Why had she not worked this out sooner? If she had, then Marion might not be lying prisoner in a small room in the basement in this isolated house of horrors.

"She also has a dog," Karen continued. "A lovely little German shepherd puppy. She loves playing with the puppy. Look how happy she is, Mia, look."

Karen pointed toward the ceiling and remained standing with a sheepish grin on her face.

"Mommy is coming soon, Margrete. Not long now."

Karen blew a kiss toward the sky.

"Why ten dresses and only five girls?" Mia tried.

"What?" Karen said.

634

"You ordered ten dresses, but you've only taken five girls."

"No girl should have just one dress, don't you think? Did you have just one dress, Mia? Back home in Åsgårdstrand? When you played with little Sigrid?"

Mia bit her lip when she heard Sigrid's name. She felt the rage tear at her body again, but she managed not to lose her temper.

"So you'll stop at five?" She smiled.

"Yes." Karen nodded pensively, as if considering whether she should have added more. "Best, really, small class sizes, so everyone gets a chance to be seen and heard. It's important, don't you think, that everyone is seen and heard? Perhaps I should have gone for ten — what do you think? Is five enough?"

"Oh, absolutely," Mia agreed. "You've done well. I think you've done very well."

"Do you really?" Karen frowned.

"Oh, yes, definitely," Mia continued. "It's a good idea and a fine plan. Margrete could not go to school alone. I mean, seriously?"

"Exactly," Karen said, sitting down at the table again. "It was the least I could do, really."

"It was well thought out," Mia went on. "And incredibly well executed. I mean, we were clueless. You completely tricked us. You're seriously clever."

"Yes, I am, aren't I?" Karen smiled and clapped her hands.

"You're the smartest person I've ever met." Mia nodded.

"I've been planning it for such a *long* time," Karen said. "Every detail. But in the end it turned out to be so easy, and that's the worst part — it was so easy, so easy, you were barking up the wrong tree. It's been a really fun game, don't you think?"

"Yes, really fun." Mia smiled.

"And now it's nearly over. That will be nice," Karen said with a sigh. "All that needs to happen is that we all die, and then we'll be done."

"Yes, that will be good." Mia's thoughts raced around inside her head. "Did you say now, Karen? Right now? Who is going to die now?"

"You first," Karen said. "Then Marion. No, wait. I haven't made up my mind yet."

"Oh?" Mia said. "I thought you said you had a plan. That's unlike you!"

"I know." Karen chuckled. "But I can't decide *everything*. Some things depend a little on chance."

"Do they? Please tell."

"I had a guy who helped me," Karen said,

sitting down again. "Men are idiots, but you know that, don't you?"

"Complete idiots," Mia concurred.

"Yes, they are, aren't they? Quite incredibly dense. But this one, he really took the cake. He was stupid, very stupid — do you know what I mean?" Karen laughed.

"And who was he?"

"Oh, just some guy, what was his name again? Oh, yes, William, that was it. He was married, but he wanted me — they do, you know, men are disgusting. He helped rebuild the room. I didn't want the old room. I wanted a new one."

"Because Margrete had lived there?"

"Yes, it wasn't nice anymore."

"I understand."

"So he helped rebuild it, and then I thought of something funny."

"What?"

Karen could barely contain herself now. She snorted and giggled like a little schoolgirl.

"We made a film," she tittered.

"A film?"

"Yes, with his cell phone. I laughed so hard afterward."

The Kiese film. It was a hoax.

Mia tried to keep a straight face.

"What kind of film was it?"

"He pretended to be really terrified." Karen laughed. "And he gave the wrong coordinates about his location. You know, GPS, the kind of thing they have in cars?"

"Yes?"

"He gave the wrong coordinates, isn't that funny?"

"Hilarious," Mia said, not quite managing to smile anymore. "And what coordinates did *you* give?" She cleared her throat.

"Well, that's the best part." Karen giggled. "The coordinates for a house farther down the road. Isn't that brilliant? You did get the film, didn't you?"

Karen moved very close to Mia. The unstable woman stroked her face with a cold hand.

"Don't think for a moment that you're pulling the wool over my eyes, Mia. Acting as if we're friends? Do you think I'm stupid, Mia?"

Mia felt the cold fingers on her eyes and lips.

"You did get the film, didn't you? From his wife?"

Mia nodded feebly.

"I'm not stupid, you know that, Mia. You won't outwit me. Telling me what you think I want to hear. Why did it take so long for that movie to reach you? To be honest, I thought you would have gotten it a long time ago."

Mia felt sick. Karen ran her icy fingers across her face as if she were a blind person trying to imagine what Mia looked like.

"What happened, Mia?"

Mia was really struggling to stay calm. She was sorely tempted to bite the sick woman's finger, but she refrained.

"The wife couldn't be bothered to hand in the film. She only showed up a couple of days ago," Mia said calmly.

"Aha." Karen smiled. "She didn't like him very much, did she?"

Mia made no reply.

"I can see her point." Karen laughed. "He was so thick. But you have it now?"

"Yes," Mia said softly.

"Good. Then all we need to do is wait for it to go bang." Karen smiled and sat down at the table again.

"So the house isn't far from where we are?" Mia said.

"Yes, isn't it brilliant? We'll hear it go bang, and perhaps we'll get to see something as well. If we have time."

Karen got up and disappeared from view. Mia could feel the chill from the evil woman behind her. She glanced at the monitor again. She had a shock when she realized that Marion was about to wake up.

No, no, Marion, lie still.

"Not you, by the way," a voice whispered in her ear. "You won't hear it go bang."

Karen stroked her cheek.

"You're going to die now. Won't that be nice?"

Mia made a last, desperate attempt to free herself, but she was still stuck. She couldn't control herself anymore. She felt the rage boil inside her, and it was unstoppable. Her body felt as if it were about to explode.

"You crazy bitch!" she screamed.

"Now, now, now, language, Mia," Karen warned her.

Mia felt the tape go over her mouth again. The taste of adhesive on her tongue. Breathing became difficult. Panic. *Don't panic. Breathe calmly through your nose. Don't wake up, Marion, don't let her see you — lie still. This is a trap, Holger. Don't send anyone into the house. She's going to take everybody with her. Don't let anyone enter, Holger. Don't go in. Don't send in Kim or Curry or Ludvig or Gabriel or Anette. Don't send anyone in. We can't afford to lose anyone, Holger.*

Mia felt a prick in her right hand. She looked down and saw that Karen had inserted an intravenous needle. Mia could hear the psychopath fumble with something behind her. She hung a bag on a stand, and Mia felt something seep into her. It stung, it made her veins cold and numb.

"There we are," Karen said, sitting down at the table again. "It's a shame that we couldn't play any longer, but it's best that you die now. I would like a little time alone with Marion. We need some time together before we go, just her and me. We can't have you around then."

She giggled.

"Won't it be funny when they find out that you died just a few houses away? If they survive, that is. Those who survive. Who do you think will live, Mia? Munch? Kim? That Larsen guy who thinks he's so tough? Won't that be fun to know?"

Mia mumbled behind the tape. The psychopath was not entirely lucid. She didn't realize that Mia could not reply. Karen drummed her fingers on the table. Made small clucking sounds with her tongue. Scratched her face. Got up. Disappeared outside of Mia's field of vision. Returned with a double-barreled shotgun. Broke the weapon open, checked that there were cartridges in both barrels. Snapped it shut and laid it on the table next to her.

"The one we never mention liked hunting," she said, scratching her face again.

641

"We had that in common. We both liked killing. Watching something die is funny, isn't it, Mia? It's fun when they stop breathing. When they finally depart."

Karen got up and went out into the hallway. Mia could hear a door open and close. A small gust of fresh air slipped into the room. Then it disappeared. Karen returned.

"I'm not going to shoot myself, if that's what you're thinking. I don't imagine that the girls will like having a teacher without a face, do you? No, it's just in case anyone should come in. You can never be too careful, isn't that right, Mia?"

Mia felt the back of her hand sting again. Something almost metallic was entering her bloodstream. She began having problems seeing clearly. She tried focusing on the monitor. Marion was no longer there. Marion was gone. Had Karen been down there? What had she done to the little girl?

Karen shook her head faintly and smiled to herself.

"I like watching people fall. That idiot who made the movie, he fell really well. For a moment I thought he might be able to fly. Just like Roger Bakken. Roger even had wings. It was wonderful to watch. Did you feel like that, Mia? When you killed?"

Mia disappeared for a moment, went away, almost leaving the disgusting room for good. She jerked as she came around again. And saw that Karen had packed a suitcase.

"And I was so sure that you knew," Karen said again. "That you knew why."

Mia could see Sigrid now. In her white dress. Running in slow motion through the field.

Come to me, Mia, come.

"Markus Skog," Karen said again. "She wasn't very bright, my sister, she wasn't, but she was kind. It wasn't her fault. He wasn't a good person. But what can you do? Men, eh? Not worth the hassle, are they? She killed herself after you shot him. Not with an overdose, no, she hanged herself. An overdose would have been better, don't you think, Mia? Like Sigrid? I bet she felt good when she died? She didn't have to jump from a tree with a rope around her neck."

Karen glanced at the door, scratched her face briefly again.

"Well, that's love for you. What would I know?"

Mia could no longer keep her eyes open. She had lost sensation in her arms and legs.

Karen got up from the table, came over to

her, and caressed her cheek. "Have a nice trip, Mia Moonbeam."

Across the field Sigrid came running toward Mia. She stopped in front of her with a teasing look. She waved to her sister.

Come to me, Mia, come!

I'm coming, Sigrid, wait.

I'll be Sleeping Beauty, and you'll be Snow White?

Yes, Sigrid, I'd like that.

Come to me, Mia, come!

I'm coming, Sigrid. I'm coming now!

Mia let go.

And she followed her sister's billowing white dress across a field of golden wheat.

78

"Delta One, come in. Over."

Munch released the TRANSMIT button on the walkie-talkie and waited for a reply.

"Nine, this is Delta One. Over."

"This is Nine. What's your position? Over."

Munch glanced at Kim, who sat with the Glock in his lap. He wore a bulletproof vest and a grim expression on his face. Curry was sitting in the back; he, too, was wearing a bulletproof vest and holding a pistol in his hand. They had driven down the forest track with the headlights switched off, and they could make out the house now. It was not far away.

"Nine, this is Delta One. Eyes on location in forty meters. No target in sight. Over."

"Delta One, this is Nine. Hold your position, and don't shoot until I give the order. Received? Over."

"Nine, this is Delta One. Received, over

and out."

"It's pitch-black," Curry whispered, leaning forward between the seats.

Munch took out his night-vision binoculars and aimed them at the dilapidated old building in front of them. There was nothing to suggest that the small cottage was inhabited. That was probably the intention. The GPS coordinates from the film had taken them to this place. He was grateful to Gabriel Mørk, who with the help of a friend had managed to identify the location in record time. The guy had really turned out to be a find. Munch pressed the walkie-talkie again.

"Delta Two, this is Nine, come in."

"Nine, this is Delta Two. Over."

"Position? Over."

"This is Delta Two. We have two men behind the house, east. Three in front of the entrance, northwest. In position fifteen zero meters. Over."

"Delta Two, this is Nine. Await further instructions. Over and out."

"Strange that there's not a single light, isn't it?" Kim Kolsø said as Munch handed him the night-vision binoculars.

"Perhaps she's not there?" Curry wondered out loud.

"Or they're in the basement," Munch said.

He took the binoculars back from Kim and aimed them at the small house. There were three units attending. Two from the armed-response unit, Delta, who had turned up with a group of marksmen and a SWAT team, in addition to Munch, Kim, and Curry. Munch returned the binoculars to Kim and almost had to smile as he remembered how Ludvig and Gabriel had both insisted on coming with them. Ludvig was one thing — after all, he'd been a police officer for a long time — but Gabriel? The boy had probably only ever let off fireworks. But he had guts. A real coup for the team, definitely. Munch had told them to man the office. He had enough of a force here.

"Are we sure that she also has Mia?" Kim said.

"We don't know, but at the same time we do, don't we?" Curry said.

"Her car was found outside the nursing home," Munch said. "And the last message from her cell phone was sent from somewhere on Drammensveien."

"Thrown out a window, probably," Curry snarled.

"Did you discover anything about the boy? Iversen?" Munch said.

Kim had worked on his own case and come back just in time to join the team heading to the house.

"I spoke to his teacher, Emilie Isaksen," Kim replied. "Very resourceful woman with a great social conscience. Wish there were more like her. The boy is gone. The parents are gone. She had just rescued the younger brother from the house — he was there without food for a week. I told her not to do anything on her own, but I doubt that she'll listen. She's probably on her way up to the forest to look for Tobias as we speak."

"Talk to Ludvig," Munch said. "Get Hønefoss Police to dispatch a unit."

"Already done," Kim told him.

Munch nodded affirmatively in response. If you could trust anyone, it would be Kim Kolsø. Curry, however, he had to keep an eye on. Kim sat motionless in the passenger seat, while Curry in the back could barely sit still.

"So what do we do?" Curry said, leaning forward between them again.

"We wait," Munch said.

"What are we waiting for? That crazy woman has Mia inside. Who knows what she's doing to her? Why don't we just kick the door in and take the bitch out?"

"Curry," Kim said to calm him down.

"I know what's at stake," Munch said in a

steady voice. "My granddaughter is in there."

He gave Curry a look that could not be misinterpreted. Curry grunted, somewhat apologetically, and sat back in his seat.

Marion was in there.

Munch pulled himself together. He could not assume that mantle now. The mantle of grandfather. Mikkelson had tried to insist that Munch stay home, letting others do the job, but not even a bulldozer could have held Munch back. He raised the binoculars to his eyes again and looked toward the dark house.

"How long do we wait?" Curry said impatiently from the rear seat.

"Curry," Kim said again.

"No, he's right," Munch said gruffly. "There's nothing to wait for."

He pressed the walkie-talkie again.

"Delta Two, this is Nine, come in."

"Nine, this is Delta Two. Over."

"Delta Two, this is Nine, stand by for entry. Over."

"Delta Two. Received, over and out."

Munch checked that the safety catch had been released on the Glock before looking to the other two. "Are we ready?"

Kim nodded.

"Oh, yes," Curry said.

Munch carefully opened the door and got out of the Audi as quietly as he could.

79

Marion Munch awoke with that strange taste in her mouth again. She'd had such a lovely dream. That she was at home, that her parents were there, and that everything was back to normal. She opened her eyes only to discover that she was still trapped in the small, chilly white room. Still wearing the same stupid, bulky dress. She curled up under the thin duvet and started to cry. She did not know how long she'd been there now; it was difficult to tell because the light never went off. She had looked for the switch, but there was no switch to be found, just cold walls and no windows or doors. Marion had cried so much that her eyes had almost run out of tears. She'd banged on the walls, screamed and shouted, but no one had come. At first she couldn't understand why. They always came when she cried. Her parents, they would always come. Like the time she'd had a temperature and dreamed that Pooh bear had turned into a giant monster that was trying to eat her. At that time both her parents had come immediately. But no one was coming now. Not to this room. No one took care of her. She was all alone.

Marion Munch stuck her thumb into her mouth and curled into a tiny ball on the bed. She had stopped sucking her thumb sometime ago, but now she'd started again. She pressed her tongue hard against her thumb — it felt safe and good. Licked her thumb. The nail felt rough. She took her thumb out of her mouth and stared at it in surprise. Someone had scratched something onto her fingernail. There was a dent there, almost like a letter. Like Vivian's initial at nursery school: *V*. She had a *V* on her thumb. Marion stuck her thumb into her mouth again and traced the sharp edges in the nail letter with her tongue.

At the start she had drawn pictures. Or tried to draw pictures — it hadn't been easy. There was no one she could show her drawings to; there was just her. She had drawn pictures of her parents and her grandfather. Then she drew a superhero. The superhero was a woman she could talk to and who would look after her, and since then being here had felt a little easier. There seemed to be no days in the white room. At home it would be morning or day or night — it was easy to know when things happened — but here it was impossible. It was light all the time, and there were no noises anywhere, except when her meals arrived from the hatch in the wall. The one with the noisy, windup monkey inside. The food was strange and not terribly good, but she ate it all up because she was incredibly hungry. Eating and drinking was a mistake, because then she would need the toilet. And there was no toilet in the room, just a wastebasket, and it really stank, it really did all the time. Marion had made a lid out of paper from her sketchpad, and that had reduced the stench a little. But even so, she dreaded every time she had to remove the lid and squat down, because it was getting quite full and it was disgusting.

Even though it was light all the time, she didn't find it difficult to sleep. Weird, really. The same thing would happen every time: after she ate, she would fall asleep. Even though she hadn't felt tired at all. It was almost as if the food made her sleepy. As if the food were magic. She remembered Alice in Wonderland, who had felt strange after eating something. First she turned big, then she grew small, so magic food probably existed. Was it possible for food to be magic even though it tasted bad? Marion ran her tongue across the dent in her nail just as she heard the wall starting to hum again. *Brr, vrr,* the magic food was coming, traveling down to her through the wall. She got up and went over to the hatch. Stood there waiting for the food to land. She recognized the sounds now. *Brr, vrr, brr, vrr* and a *clonk.* Then she could open the hatch to see what she'd gotten. It was mostly mashed potatoes and carrots and that stuff she didn't like. Cauliflower. No, broccoli. Never pizza or sausages or tomato soup, never her favorite things. Marion waited for the *clonk,* still with her thumb in her mouth. Come to think of it, she never heard the elevator go back up again. It only ever came down. She would take out the food, eat it, and then the elevator would come back down again. Because she'd been asleep, was that it? It probably was. The magic food made her sleep, and then the elevator would go up through the wall again while she was asleep — that had to be how it was.

There was a *clonk.* Marion Munch opened the hatch to see what she'd gotten. A bottle of soda this time, that was good. But the food looked revolting. There was something made from potatoes and that green stuff again. Broccoli.

What if she didn't eat the food? She had
no idea where that thought had come from,
but suddenly it just appeared in her mind.
What if she didn't eat the food — then
what? Would she stay awake? Would she hear
the elevator go back up again? She glanced
at the hatch in the wall. How did she get
that idea? Out of nothing and into her head.
Because it was a brilliant idea, wasn't it? If
she didn't eat the food, would the elevator
still go back up? She quickly got up and
went over to the hatch. She opened it and
peered inside. She could fit inside it,
couldn't she? She had hidden out in much
smaller places. Once they'd played hide-
and-seek and she hid in the kitchen cabinet
where they kept the pots and pans, and no
one had found her; in the end she had to
give herself up. And that cabinet was really
tight. No one had suspected a thing; they'd
all been terribly impressed. She was going
to trick the elevator, that was her plan. She
would pretend to eat the food but empty it
into the toilet wastebasket, then put the
plate in the corner with the others and lie
down on the bed. The elevator must go
when she slept. Perhaps it would still do so
if she pretended to be asleep. Marion
positioned herself with her back to the

elevator and picked up the plate from the table. It was important that the elevator not see what she was doing. Or it might change its mind. She carefully raised the paper lid from the waste-basket and tipped the food into it as swiftly as she could. She quickly sat down again and glanced at the hatch in the wall.

"Oh, my tummy is all full now," she said out loud, and patted her stomach a few times.

The elevator did nothing. It had clearly not noticed that anything was amiss.

"Oh, I feel so tired now," she said, letting out a fake yawn.

She put the plate in the pile with the others and went to bed. She lay facing the elevator and closed her eyes. She lay very still with her thumb in her mouth. She was good at lying still. That time she hid in the kitchen cabinet, she'd lain still for . . . well, for a long time. So long that her parents had started calling her name. Marion squeezed her eyes shut and lay still now, waiting for the elevator to move. There was no sound. She could feel herself getting a little impatient. This was not like lying in the kitchen cabinet, when she knew that there was someone outside. Knew that someone was looking for her. Who would be delighted to find her. Here there was no one. She felt the tears press against the insides of her eyelids again, but she managed to keep them at bay. If she was crying, then she couldn't be asleep. The elevator would probably know that. She stuck her thumb even deeper into her mouth and tried to think of something else. When she'd curled up in the kitchen cabinet, she made up a game in her head. A story. A story from Monster High, a story she hadn't seen on television, one she had invented all by herself. The time had flown by, and there'd been no problems at all. She pretended to be Draculaura, who had forgotten to do her homework. Marion was just about to decide why Draculaura had forgotten to do her homework when she suddenly heard the elevator starting to stir. *Brr, vrr.* On impulse she leaped out of bed and ran to the hatch. She quickly pulled it open and crept inside the hole in the wall. The elevator was very small, and at first she couldn't get her foot inside. She pulled it in with a jerk, and suddenly all of her was inside it. She was inside the elevator! And it was going up!

The elevator squeaked and creaked its way upward through the wall, and she couldn't see a thing. Marion curled into a tiny ball and tried not to be scared of the dark. Her heart pounded inside her small chest. She was almost afraid to breathe. *Brr, vrr.* It moved slowly, slowly upward, and then, suddenly, *clonk.* The elevator had stopped. It had stopped without noticing that she was inside it. She carefully nudged the hatch and discovered to her delight that it opened. Marion Munch climbed out of the hatch and stood on the floor and gawked.

She was in a living room. In a house she'd never seen before. There weren't any windows here either — no, there were, but the curtains were closed. There was a woman in a chair by a table in the middle of the room. Marion looked around and reluctantly walked up to her. She had her eyes closed, and gray tape covered her mouth. A tube with water or something from a bag was going into her hand.

Marion Munch stood in the middle of the room, not knowing what to do while she glanced around frantically. There was a hallway lined with shoes and boots, just like at home. And a door. A front door. Marion tiptoed to the door. The stupid dress made it difficult for her to walk, and it also made a lot of stupid noise. Did she dare open the door? How would she know what might lie behind it? In this house where everything was so strange?

"Stop!"

Marion Munch jumped when she heard the shrill woman's voice behind her.

"Stop! Stop!"

Marion Munch put her hand on the door handle, pushed open the door, and ran out into the darkness as quickly as her little legs could carry her.

80

Karianne Kolstad hated selling lottery
tickets. Selling lottery tickets was the worst
thing she knew. The fourteen-year-old had
considered quitting the Girl Guides simply
because of those stupid lottery tickets. She
didn't mind fund-raising activities — she
had picked strawberries and cleared rocks
from fields for farmers — it was just these
stupid lottery tickets that she couldn't
stand. Karianne Kolstad was shy. That was
why she hated selling lottery tickets. She
had to ring people's doorbells and talk to
them.

Karianne Kolstad tightened her jacket and
walked down the road to Tom Lauritz
Larsen's farm. She didn't mind knocking
on *his* door; she knew he would be all right.
The pig farmer was a bit eccentric, but he
was nice and she'd spoken to him before.
The last time she visited, he bought practically all her tickets. She hoped she might be

just as lucky today. Karianne Kolstad opened the gate and entered the farmyard.

Tom Lauritz Larsen had become something of a minor celebrity after someone had cut the head off one of his sows. Their local newspaper, *Hamar Arbeiderblad,* had written about it several times. First when the head went missing and then when it reappeared. LOCAL PIG FOUND ON STAKE IN "BABES IN THE WOODS" CASE had been the headline, and there were photographs of Larsen as well as his farmhand.

Karianne Kolstad knew everything about the dead girls, had read every word about the case in the newspapers. There'd been meetings as well, first at school, then with the Girl Guides, then in the village hall, where everyone had turned up, not just people with daughters about to start school but practically everyone in the village. They'd lit candles for the dead and missing girls, and she had helped start a Facebook group to show her respect to the girls. Starting a Facebook group was easy — all she had to do was sit in front of her laptop, not like now when she had to talk to real people. She went up to the farmhouse and knocked on the door. It was starting to get dark, but the light was on in the kitchen window. She could hear music, too, so he was probably at home. She knocked again, and the door opened. She breathed in and braced herself, trying to put on a smile.

"Hello?" Larsen said, looking at her kindly. "Are you out selling lottery tickets again?"

Phew, thank God, at least she wouldn't have to tell him that.

"Yes." She nodded, relieved.

"You had better come in," Larsen said, peering into the darkness behind her.

"Are you out this late all on your own?" he asked when she stepped inside the kitchen.

"Yes," Karianne said shyly.

"And what is it for this time?" Tom Lauritz Larsen had already produced his wallet and was holding it in his hand.

"Our group is going on a camping trip. To Sweden."

"Well, I imagine that will be nice."

"Yes, I hope so," Karianne agreed politely.

"I'm usually unlucky at gambling." Larsen chortled as he took out a hundred-kroner note from his wallet. "But you have to support the young, don't you think?"

"Thank you," Karianne said. "The tickets are twenty kroner each, and you can win a fruit basket and some coffee, plus some things that we made ourselves."

"Oh, I don't suppose I'll win anything, but I'll certainly buy some tickets." Larsen smiled at her. "Unfortunately, I only have one hundred kroner, that's all."

One hundred kroner. Five tickets. It meant she would have to keep going tonight. She had left it to the last minute. Unsold tickets had to be returned to the group tomorrow, and she still had many tickets left to sell.

"Well, at least it's a start," Larsen said, giving her the hundred-kroner note and taking the tickets she gave him.

"Now, be careful," he said, sounding a little anxious when she was back on his front steps again.

He stared out into the darkness behind her and wrinkled his nose. It was clear that something had happened to him after the pig-head incident. He hadn't seemed so nervous the last time she came by.

Karianne Kolstad walked across the yard and back out through the gate. She continued toward Vik Bridge and was sorely tempted to just go home and forget all about selling tickets when an unreal scene suddenly unfolded right in front of her.

At first she couldn't believe her own eyes. It seemed impossible. Here in Tangen. The most boring place on earth, where nothing ever happened. Right across the road, there was a small house. She didn't think anyone lived here — she'd always believed that it was empty, and no one had ever seen anyone come or go. Now the front door was wide open and a small girl was running out of it. The girl wore a strange dress and was screaming at the top of her lungs. Karianne Kolstad recognized her immediately. She'd seen her in the newspapers. There were pictures of her on Karianne's Facebook page. It was girl number five. It was Marion Munch.

Karianne froze with her mouth wide open. The little girl had jumped down the steps but tripped and fallen in the gravel. A woman came chasing after her. Marion got back on her feet, glanced over her shoulder, let out a scream, and ran on. The woman behind her was much faster. The woman snatched her, placed her hand over the little girl's mouth, carried her back inside the house, and closed the door.

Then everything fell quiet again.

For a moment Karianne Kolstad was in shock. She had dropped the lottery tickets and the money and her cell phone on the ground.

Then she bent down quickly, picked up

her phone, and pressed 112 with trembling
fingers.

81

Lukas put the gun on the ground and inserted the key into the padlock. It was chilly outside now; he could feel the cold evening air on his neck. He unlocked the padlock and lifted up the heavy wooden hatch. He shone his flashlight into the dark space. The light swept down a long ladder and hit the concrete floor some meters farther below. He stuck the gun into the lining of his trousers and descended the ladder. The boy and Rakel were standing with a blanket wrapped around them when he reached the bottom. He pointed the light at them but lowered it when he saw them shield their eyes against the strong beam.

"I'm Jesus," he said, making his voice as calm as he could. "Don't be scared, I'm not here to hurt you."

He shone the flashlight around the room and found what he was looking for. A jerry can in front of a shelf stacked with cardboard boxes. The boy and Rakel crossed the concrete floor and came toward him reluctantly.

"Can we go now?" the boy asked tentatively.

"Yes, you can go now," Lukas said. "Go with God. The gate is open."

He caught a glimpse of the boy's eyes as he passed him in the cold room.

"Thank you," Tobias said, placing his hand gently on Lukas's arm.

"I am Jesus." Lukas smiled again and showed them the way with the flashlight, so that the boy and Rakel could see the ladder.

He waited until they had both crawled out through the hatch before he aimed the flashlight at the shelves again and found the jerry can. It was heavy, but he managed to carry it up the ladder, dragging it with his flashlight tucked under one arm. He closed the hatch and stood watching the stars for a moment. He had rarely seen a more beautiful sight. Hope and joy twinkled across the sky. He smiled to himself as he crossed the yard.

The pastor was standing inside the church in front of the altar at the end wall, with his back to Lukas. He turned when he heard Lukas enter.

"How did it go?" The pastor smiled, walking toward him with open arms.

He stopped, shocked, in the middle of the church when he saw what Lukas had in his hand. Lukas had drawn the gun from the lining of his trousers and was holding it in his outstretched arm with the muzzle pointing straight at the pastor's chest.

"Lukas? What are you doing?"

"I'm saving you." Now Lukas smiled, walking softly toward the man with the white hair.

"What do you mean, my Son?" the pastor asked, gritting his teeth. "Come to me, my Son. Give me the gun. You don't know what you're doing."

He held out his arms toward the young man with the blond hair.

"Shhh," Lukas said, his eyes sparkling now. "Haven't you realized it yet?"

"W-what?" the pastor stammered.

"That the devil is inside you."

"You're talking nonsense, my Son," the white-haired man sputtered.

"No," Lukas said gravely. "The devil has taken residence in you, but it's not too late. I was put on this earth to save you. This is my mission."

"What the hell, Lukas . . . ?"

"Don't you see?" Lukas said calmly. "The devil has taken your heart. He's talking through your mouth. We don't treat children like that. We don't treat people like that. We help them, we don't hurt them. That's not the will of God. It's not your fault. You're innocent. The devil tricked you. He got you to invite him in. Took your soul. Made you want to hurt other people. Everything will be all right now, Father. We can travel right now. We don't need to wait. Let us go to heaven together."

"Give me that gun, you damned . . . !" the pastor screamed frantically, but it was too late.

Lukas pulled the trigger, shot the white-haired man twice in the chest, and dropped the gun on the church floor. The pastor was flung backward by the heavy blow and collapsed gasping in front of him. Lukas opened the jerry can and started pouring its contents along the walls. He took his time. They were in no hurry. The smell of gasoline started wafting through the small church. Pastor Simon was lying on his back on the floor, his mouth half open, watching Lukas with panicky eyes, clutching his chest with stiff, spasmodic hands. *How beautiful,* Lukas thought when he saw the fresh blood trickle in small streams across the newly polished floor. He tipped out the rest of the gasoline by the altar and returned to the pastor, who was grasping his throat now, trying to say something, but only gurgling noises emerged from his mouth.

"Don't be scared," Lukas said, stroking the pastor's white hair.

He stood up again and took a lighter from his pocket. Checked to see if it worked. Watched the little flame flicker in front of him. He started in one corner. The gas quickly caught fire. He went over to the other side, put the lighter to the floor, ignited the fuel, and continued until the whole of the white church was filled with burning light. He threw aside the lighter, went back to the pastor, knelt by his side, and held his hand. The church was ablaze now — curtains, walls, the floor, the altar. Lukas smiled to himself and started chanting. He carefully stroked the pastor's white mane.

"Can you see the devil? He's leaving you now. Isn't it wondrous?" The young man laughed.

The pastor stared at him, horrified. His body was shaking. The blood was pouring out of the holes in his chest.

The flames started licking the ceiling. The whole building was burning now.

"I'll see you at home, Father." Lukas smiled.

And closed his eyes.

82

Holger Munch crept quietly toward the old cottage, with a feeling that something was wrong. The windows were bolted shut. There was a gaping hole in the roof. There were no signs that anyone had lived there for years. The cottage looked as if it might collapse at any moment. Could this place really be Karen's hideout? This dilapidated hut? Strange. The closer they got to the house, the stronger was his feeling that something was amiss.

"All Delta units, this is Nine," he whispered into the walkie-talkie just as he felt his phone vibrate in his pocket. "Anyone see anything? Over."

"Negative. Over," came the reply into his ear.

He could see Curry shifting from foot to foot only a few meters in front of him, his pistol at the ready. Curry shrugged his shoulders as if to say, *What are we waiting for?*

This house really was uninhabitable. Had she built somewhere she could live underneath it? The small room they'd seen on the Kiese movie? From what he had seen of the short film, that room was far too small to live in. Of course, there might be several such rooms next to one another, but it seemed unlikely.

He tried frantically to make a decision. They had absolutely no time to lose. She had Marion. She had Mia. They had to do something. They might be too late already.

Too late already.

He did not even dare to think of the consequences if the latter were true. For Miriam. Marianne. For everyone. Everyone in the unit. Not least him.

"Nine, this is Delta One," he heard in his earpiece. "We're on standby and ready for entry. Clear signal for go? Over."

Curry shrugged again, almost overeager now. He seemed to be up for anything, and unless Munch gave the order soon, he would storm the house single-handed.

Munch had crouched down on one knee on the grass, not far from the cottage, trying to get a clearer view of the situation, when he felt his phone vibrate in his pocket for the second time.

No, this was not it. It did not feel right. Building a small, underground, sealed room was one thing, but a place you could actually live in? Why on earth would anyone do that? Surely it would be much simpler to make changes to the basement in a house that was *not* about to cave in?

"Nine?" He could hear the question in his walkie-talkie again.

It was not only Curry who was getting twitchy now. The whole entry team was on edge.

Munch's phone buzzed again like an angry wasp against his trouser leg. *What the hell?*

He eased it out of his pocket and glanced at it while he tried to screen the light from the display with his hand so he would not be seen.

He had two missed calls from Ludvig Grønlie and a text message that was now glowing at him.

Wrong place!!! Witness reports eye contact with Marion. Call me!!!!

"Delta all, Delta all, this is Nine," he said quickly and firmly into his walkie-talkie. "We have a new location. Regroup and

674

await new orders. I repeat, no entry, we have a new location, regroup and await new orders. Over."

He got up, walked quickly back to the car, and phoned Ludvig Grønlie.

83

Emilie Isaksen sat behind the wheel of her car as she drove up the narrow gravel track leading into the forest. She had spent a long time weighing the pros and cons. After all, she *had* promised Torben a pizza, but the boy seemed happy with some chocolate and a banana she had in her bag. She didn't know why, but she had a hunch that time was of the essence. Tobias had been missing for a week. On his way to a kind of cult in the forest, to the Christian girls, as Torben had called them. The thought that he might be there and in need of help was unbearable — she had to do something now, even if it was a futile gesture. Realistically, she didn't even know exactly where this place was. But she'd been provoked by the slow response from the police and decided to take matters into her own hands. Torben, sitting next to her with a small smile and chocolate around the corners of his mouth, seemed quite content.

She had never known a case like this. These kids needed a new home. No doubt about it. You should not be allowed to treat children this way. Emilie Isaksen was so angry that she wanted to bang her fist against the steering wheel, but she controlled herself for the sake of the little boy. Even so, she had some doubts as to whether she'd made the right choice. It was dark outside now. The only light came from her headlights; the track was winding and they were surrounded by forest. If an elk suddenly ran out from between the trees, she wouldn't be able to stop in time. So she drove slowly. The car crept across the gravel track, and as if visibility were bad enough to begin with, small drops of rain started falling on her windshield. Social workers. She didn't know much about how they worked; they probably had to follow procedures, write letters, summon the parents, give them an opportunity to explain themselves — endless bureaucracy, possibly legal proceedings. You couldn't just take children from their parents, and that was probably a good thing, but in this case, when they couldn't even contact the parents . . . ?

She had a friend who worked for Social Services, Agnete. They'd met at an aerobics class and had coffee together a couple of times. Emilie made up her mind there and then to call her once they got off this horrible gravel track. Agnete would probably know what to do.

It was raining more heavily now and near impossible to see anything out of the windshield. She didn't even know how far away the farm was. It seemed irresponsible to go on. After all, she had a small boy in the car. Better to turn around and drive back. Let the police look for Tobias while she looked after Torben. Give the boy some more food and a warm bed. Contact Social Services. Start the process that would provide these boys with a good foster home, with trusted, responsible adults who would care for them, love them, as children should be loved.

She was just about to look for a place to turn around when two figures suddenly appeared in the middle of the road, hand in hand, blinded by her headlights.

Tobias.

Emilie Isaksen's heart almost jumped out of her throat when she saw the two terrified teenagers abandon the road after spotting the unfamiliar car and run into the forest.

She hit the brakes hard and stepped out into the rain with the engine running and the emergency brake on.

"Tobias!" she called out.

Not a sound from anywhere. Just heavy rain hitting the gravel and drumming ominously against the car's hood.

"Tobias!" she called out again with the water pouring over her face. "It's me, Emilie! Don't be afraid. You can come out now. Everything is all right. I'm here to get you to someplace safe. Tobias? Are you in there?"

The seconds passed and seemed to Emilie like an eternity, but then some branches stirred not far from her, and soon two quizzical faces appeared in between them.

"Emilie?" Tobias said tentatively as he walked slowly toward her.

"Yes." Emilie smiled. "Are you okay? Is everything all right with you?"

The handsome boy looked worn out and confused, but at least he was alive. She heaved a sigh of relief.

"This is Rakel," Tobias said cautiously, gesturing to the girl who was hiding behind him.

The girl, who was wearing a heavy, gray woolen dress and a white bonnet, as if she were from a different century, was standing trembling behind Tobias, not daring to quite show herself.

"She needs help," Tobias said, and it was not until now that Emilie realized how exhausted the boy was. His eyes threatened to roll into the back of his head, and he could barely manage to stay on his feet.

"Get in," Emilie said, opening the rear door.

"Tobias!" Torben cried out when he saw his shattered brother climb into the car.

The little boy undid his seat belt in a second and made his way into the back, where he gave his brother a big, long hug.

How could this be allowed to happen? What on earth have people done to these children?

Emilie got behind the wheel again and found a place to turn around.

"Are you all right in the back?" she said when they had driven some way down the road.

She caught Tobias's eye in the rearview mirror. The boy still looked dazed, but it seemed as if, regardless of the kind of cruelty he and Rakel — and his little brother — had been subjected to, he was slowly starting to believe that they were in safe hands.

"We're fine," he told her, his voice trembling. "Will you help us?" He held Emilie's gaze in the rearview mirror.

"Definitely." Emilie nodded. "Everything will be all right now, Tobias, I promise you."

Emilie Isaksen drove as quickly as she

dared down the narrow gravel track. And then she headed into town.

84

For the second time in less than an hour, Holger Munch was sitting in his car with the binoculars raised to his eyes, with a Delta team ready for entry, but this time outside the right location. Definitely the right one. A girl had seen Marion run out of this very house. Only to be brought back inside. By Karen Nylund. The girl was local, and she knew what she was talking about; there was no longer any doubt. And where everything about the ramshackle cottage they'd just left had felt wrong, everything here felt absolutely right. It was an old red house, a little shabby but clearly habitable. There was a faint light coming from behind the windows, as if someone had covered them with film to prevent anyone from looking in. A thin column of smoke rose from a brick chimney on the roof. An idyllic little cottage in the country. From the outside. But it was clear to them that the inside was another story. Karen Nylund was inside. She had murdered four six-year-old girls. She had ruined the lives of innocent parents, grandparents, siblings, friends, neighbors, inflicted pain on them so extreme that it would never go away. She had tricked him into thinking he might experience love again. He felt hatred well up in his chest, his forehead grow hot and his palms sweaty, but he tried to stay calm. Professional. No acting rashly. She had Marion. Marion was alive. Or at least she had been less than an hour ago. Holger Munch didn't dare to contemplate whether Mia was inside and what might have happened to *her*.

It was a matter of acting quickly but not too quickly. They had to get an overview of the situation. Get every team member into place. Munch glanced farther down the road, where three ambulances had pulled up a short while ago, all with their lights turned off so as not to draw attention to themselves. Curry sat impatiently in the back, tapping his pistol against his thigh. As usual, Kim Kolsø sat like a stone pillar in the seat next to Holger Munch, with his gaze fixed on the door they would soon break down.

"Delta One, this is Nine, come in."

683

"Nine, this is Delta One, we're in position. Over."

"Delta Two, this is Nine, come in."

"Nine, this is Delta Two. We need a few minutes. Over."

"Delta Two, this is Nine, received, we'll wait. Over."

"What the hell is going on?" Curry said impatiently from the back.

"We're waiting," Munch said briefly.

"What are we waiting for? Mia is in there, for God's sake."

The bald police officer could barely keep still any longer, his fingers going like drumsticks against his thigh and his eyes narrow and filled with rage.

"We're waiting for Delta Two to get into position," Munch said as evenly as he could manage.

"Calm down, Curry," Kim said, still sitting motionless in the front.

"Fuck this," they suddenly heard from the back.

It all happened so quickly that Munch had no time to react. Curry had already opened the rear door and was heading for the house.

Munch flung open his door and was followed by Kim leaping out of the car. He wanted to shout, but he didn't want to alert Karen.

Damn.

Munch increased his speed as much as his heavy body could manage, running down the gravel track, through the gate, across the flagstones, and reaching the steps just as Curry pushed on the door handle and stormed inside the house.

From then on, everything happened in slow motion. Munch caught a glimpse of Karen's startled reaction to the noise. She'd been caught off guard. It was clear that she hadn't been expecting this, but she still had time to swing the barrel of the shotgun toward Curry, who threw himself to one side as the shot was fired.

Did she hit him?

Curry, you bloody idiot!

Still in slow motion, she turned and faced Munch. Her hands gripped the weapon so hard that her knuckles were white. It looked as if she were opening her mouth to say something as her finger curled around the trigger, but by now Holger Munch had had enough of slow-motion movies.

He raised his gun and fired twice. Once to the neck. Once right through her heart. Karen Nylund twitched, fell backward, and lay lifeless on the floor as the blood ran slowly down her chest and along her arms.

And that was when he spotted Mia. She

was tied to a chair near a wall. Tape covering her mouth. A needle in her hand connected to a tube from some kind of stand.

Oh, no.

Oh, please, no, no, no.

Holger Munch froze right in front of his lifeless colleague, unaware of all the people who had come rushing in behind him. Kim. The Delta teams. The doctor. The paramedics. He stayed where he was, unable to utter a single word, watching people who seemed miles away free Mia from the chair and carry her out into the waiting ambulance. He didn't see Curry get up from the floor, clutching his arm and being supported down the steps. Holger Munch didn't snap out of his trance until Kim appeared with a small, trembling figure in his arms.

Marion.

She was alive.

In poor shape, but she was breathing.

"Ambulance!" Holger Munch shouted, and helped his colleague carry the little girl down the steps.

"Doctor! We need a doctor here!"

And this time the ambulances did not move discreetly. A noisy motorcade of flashing blue lights and sirens left the house and

sped through the evening darkness toward
the E6.

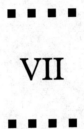

VII

85

The waiting area outside Ullevål Hospital's intensive-care unit was packed to the rafters. One of the nurses had come over several times to ask them if they could possibly wait elsewhere, but every time Munch had just dismissed her with a wave of his hand.

The mood in the room was strained. Gabriel Mørk sat in a chair with his hands in his lap, for once not in front of a computer monitor, staring into space. Anette and Ludvig sat on the sofa and made room for Kim and Kyrre. The whole team was gathered in the small room; they looked glum, and nobody said very much.

Anette had just stepped outside to call Mikkelson. She gave Munch a little wave when she came back in again, and Munch nodded and gave her a small smile in return before the tension resumed.

Curry was pacing up and down, refusing to sit, unable to make his small, compact body relax.

"For God's sake," he said, flinging out his uninjured hand. "Surely we're entitled to know what's going on?"

"Sit down," Anette said. "We won't be told anything before they're sure, that's how it works."

"Damn," Curry swore, and he continued to wander to and fro on the blue linoleum.

"Coffee, anyone?" Ludvig offered, getting up.

The experienced police officer had a dark expression on his face and looked just as oppressed by the situation as the rest of the team. A couple of hands shot up. Ludvig nodded and disappeared up the corridor.

Miriam arrived. Munch went to meet her and gave her a hug.

"Is everything all right with you?"

His daughter nodded and squeezed his hand. "I'm fine, I'm all right now."

She spotted Kim on the sofa and ran up to him.

"Thank you," she said, wiping away a tear.

"It's nothing," Kim said. "I was just doing my job."

"No, thank you, I mean it. Thank you," Miriam said, putting her arms around his neck before running over to Curry and repeating the gesture.

Curry seemed almost embarrassed at the attention. He nodded to Miriam and gave her a long hug in return.

"Is she all right?" Munch said, going up to his daughter.

"Marion is fine." Miriam nodded, wiping another tear from her cheek. "She's with Johannes. She was exhausted but in surprisingly good shape, and she asked after her granddad."

Munch smiled.

"Any news about Mia?" Miriam asked anxiously.

"No," Munch said, and his eyes turned dark again.

A doctor came down the corridor with some papers in her hands. "Jon Larsen?" she inquired, looking across the gathering.

"Curry," Anette said, pointing him out to the doctor.

"Eh?" Curry grunted.

"She's asking for you."

Curry turned around.

"Jon Larsen?" the doctor said again as she looked down at her papers.

"Yes, that's me," Curry said, raising his good hand. He kept the other one pressed to his chest.

"Want me to take a look at you?"

"No, no, I'm all right," Curry said, dismissing her with his undamaged hand.

Munch looked sternly at his colleague, who was still evading his gaze. Curry had almost wrecked the whole operation, risked all their lives with his impulsive behavior, but they would have to deal with that later. The time for disciplining was not now.

Munch glanced at the door to the ward, but there was still no sign of movement.

"I think we should take a look at you all the same," the doctor said, smiling at Curry.

Curry sighed and reluctantly followed the doctor down the corridor. "Keep me in the loop!" he called out, jabbing a finger on his one good hand sternly at them.

"Debrief tonight?" Anette asked, looking at Munch.

"No, no, we'll wait," Munch said, combing his fingers through his beard as the door opened and another doctor appeared.

"Mia Krüger's next of kin?"

A sea of hands went up immediately.

"How is she?" Munch said, walking up to the doctor.

"It was touch and go. But she'll be fine."

The relief was palpable in the small room. Gabriel got up and hugged Anette. Kim was grinning from ear to ear.

"Can we see her?" Munch asked.

"She's exhausted," the doctor said. "But

we will allow one visit. Provided it's short."

"Me," Munch said.

He took off his duffel coat, gave it to Miriam, and followed the doctor through the door.

Mia was lying in a bed with her eyes closed when they entered the private room.

"A short visit," the doctor said firmly, and disappeared.

Munch went over to the bed and took her hand in his. Mia slowly opened her eyes and smiled when she saw him.

"Have you been smoking?" she whispered.

"Not for a while." Munch smiled back at her.

"Good for you," Mia said, closing her eyes again.

Munch gently squeezed her hand.

"Did we get her?" Mia said weakly.

"We got her," Munch said.

"And Marion?"

"Marion is fine," Munch said.

Mia opened her eyes again and gave him a tentative smile.

"Yes?"

"Yes." Munch nodded.

He watched as her body suddenly relaxed. Her hand in his grew limp, and her head sank deeper into the pillow.

"Will you come visit me?" she asked.

"On Hitra?"

Mia nodded.

"Maybe on holiday," Munch said. "But I think you should stay here. I need someone to keep me company."

"Okay," Mia mumbled, and closed her eyes.

The doctor popped his head around the door and tapped his wrist. Munch acknowledged the signal to leave.

When he turned to look at Mia, she was already fast asleep.

ABOUT THE AUTHOR

Samuel Bjørk is the pen name of Norwegian novelist, playwright and singer/songwriter Frode Sander Øien. Øien wrote his first stageplay at the age of twenty-one and has since written two highly acclaimed novels, released six albums, written five plays, and translated Shakespeare, all in his native Norway. Øien currently lives and works in Oslo. *I'm Traveling Alone* is his American debut.